CHICAGO STRIKERS SERIES
BOOK ONE

False play

YINN QUIRÓS

Cover Art: Bruna Garret @brunagarretart

Cover Designer: Layla @designwithlaylaanddaniel

Editor: Andrea Halland, Editing by Andrea

Proofread Editor: Ramona Mihai @proofreadereditor

Formating: Yinn Quirós

CONTENT WARNING

Trigger warnings include, but are not limited to: Sexual explicit content, talks about anxiety, anger management issues and domestic violence (not between main characters).

Your mental health matters. Please stay safe.

"To be loved is to be seen." -Anonymous

*For those who think emotional intimacy is hot, but so is a 6'7"
hockey player who begs. Today's your lucky day.*

ONE

HENRY

CALL ME THE RINGMASTER.

I'D DONE a lot of stupid shit over the years.

Underage drinking in college? *Check.*

Ironwood University may have had one of the best collegiate hockey teams, but that was all they had going for themselves. College life was practically nonexistent in that town, so we had to make do with what we had.

Taking my pranks a little too far? *Also check.*

Once, I sent two puck bunnies to Coach Sloane's room and blamed it on Wesley Hayes, left winger of the Chicago Strikers and my childhood best friend. I was fairly certain Hayes hadn't forgiven me for that, either.

Fighting on the ice? *Check. Check. Triple check.*

And the reason I sat in the locker room, icing my hand, when I should have been out there playing with the boys.

The fans loved a good show, and baby, call me the ringmaster, because everyone knew I ran that circus.

It was a role I took to heart, because I wasn't in the business of disappointing my fans. All the shit I pulled during my rookie years stuck with me, and it was the reality I lived in. If a cocky, self-centered hockey player was what people wanted, that's exactly who they got.

I flexed my fist and hissed at the pull of raw knuckles stretching. Thankfully, I wasn't bleeding anymore, but *damn*, it hurt like a bitch. I'd forgotten how much the pain settled once the adrenaline started to wear off. Still, the rough feel of my skin splitting was a welcome reprieve. It beat having to drown in my thoughts.

Deflecting was practically my middle name.

As soon as I got *not-so-gracefully* ejected from the game, Coach Sloane told me to wait in the locker room. Uhm, well... to *directly* quote him, he said—more like *yelled*—"Get your fucking ass to the locker room and see if you can come up with reasons as to why you decided to start acting like a *petulant child*."

He could be a real pain in the ass sometimes, but there was no denying I deserved it.

It wasn't a secret how I ran things on the ice. I was heavily criticized as much as I was adored for it. Sports commentators loved to argue that, as a starting center, my focus should always be on staying on the ice as much as possible.

"*A waste of natural talent*," some loved to argue.

"*A waste of payroll, if you ask me*," many haters commented.

But I'd gotten pretty good at shutting them up with my performance. I may have spent a lot of time in the sin bin, but I made up for it tenfold when it mattered. That had always been the deal between me and Coach. I did my damn best to keep my word, because the last thing I wanted to do was disappoint people.

Only that's *exactly* what I'd just done.

Guilt sneaked up on me and settled in the pit of my

stomach like a heavy rock. I should have been out there with my team, having fun and bagging an easy W.

The unrelenting anger tried to surface and sink its teeth into me, but I pushed back with what little mental strength I had left. I leaned forward in my seat, resting my elbows on my thighs as I threaded my fingers through my freshly washed hair, shutting my eyes tightly. Trying to center myself had been proven useless, but I was nothing if not determined, and I refused to go down without a fight.

At the sound of the door opening, I lifted my gaze. The temperature inside the stuffy locker room rose to dangerous heat levels, and my throat instantly dried up as my eyes settled on none other than Kennedy Jones.

Hell. You didn't often see women like her. That much I was painfully aware of.

With each purposeful step she took toward me, my heartbeat stumbled between exhilaration and fear. It was dangerous territory, but *man*, did it get my adrenaline going.

I took a big gulp, hoping to ease the dryness in my throat. "Hi, Jonesy."

Her eye twitched when I mentioned her nickname. She hated it, and I loved annoying her. It was a win-win.

I leaned back on my chair with a lopsided grin. Anxiety still tried to sink its claws into me, but it was time to put on my usual mask. "To what do I owe this pleasure?"

She crossed her arms with an impatient look. "Came here to clean up your mess, pretty boy."

Kennedy was tall, about five-foot-eleven, if I had to guess. She always wore these powerful and sexy-as-sin heels that made her even taller. Today, they were these white, glossy pumps that even the light seemed to follow. Even so, she was fairly short next to my six-foot-seven frame.

The only useful thing I got from my father was my ridiculous height. *Yay, me.*

"You think I'm pretty?" I smirked, raking a hand through my hair. "God, I mean...I'm flattered. But at least take me out to dinner first."

Her stare was unimpressed. Fair, really. I'd been trying to get under her skin for like three years now. She was used to my ways. "How do you always manage to have selective hearing?"

"It's easy," I teased with a pop of my shoulder and a playful grin. "All I know is you called me pretty, so it's a good fucking day over here in Henryland."

The biggest pair of beautiful light-brown eyes pinned me in place with a death glare. Any normal person would have cowered at the intensity of them, but me? It was painful to admit I liked it...*a lot.* Her eyes were—hands down—her best fucking trait. They were a beautiful contrast to her rich brown skin and the dust of freckles that danced around her face.

She had the face of an angel, but the attitude of a devil. And the contraposition of the two was *glorious.*

"God, help me," she muttered as she took a seat next to me, crossing one long leg over the other. "We need to talk about what happened today."

I shrugged, putting on an innocent act. "What happened?"

"I'd tell you not to act stupid, but I'm beginning to think it's not an act." She thinned her lips, letting a silent beat pass between us. "Look, Anderson..."

And that's all I heard before my eyes, those greedy little bastards, started raking over her.

The best part about Kennedy Jones working for the Strikers? She was a wonderful distraction.

She had these perfect cupid's bow lips that glistened with some kind of gloss, making them look fuller and irresistible. Her unruly chestnut curls were shiny and beautiful, resting just below her shoulders. But those *goddamn* orbs captured me once again. Her gaze was intense, the type that burned in the best way possible.

I had no problem noticing every single thing about Kennedy Jones. It was hard not to.

I didn't want to notice her. I just did.

"Are you done gawking, or do you want me to get up and model for you, too?" She spit the question with a sharp venom.

I pretended to ponder as I sunk my teeth into my bottom lip. "I mean, I wouldn't mind if you stood up and twirled a little."

Her looks weren't any different than usual, but picturing her spin in that hot-pink power suit, with a white tank top that perfectly snugged over her chest—giving her the perfect amount of cleavage—and those damn heels? Yeah, I wouldn't say no to that.

The woman was a *drop-to-your-knees-and-worship* type of hot. And God knew, I'd be a willing worshiper for one night if she'd let me.

"Yeah, I'll get right on that," she snapped.

I pressed my lips together to hold back my laughter. "Why are you here again?"

"Glad you asked," she retorted sarcastically. "I'm here to clean up the mess you got us into."

I frowned in confusion. "Wait. Where's Brad?"

She raised a perfectly shaped brow. "Why?"

"He always deals with shit like this." The PR director had always been a hands-on kind of manager. And the bigger the problem, the more he wanted to be involved.

Not that it had ever gotten this far. This was my first time getting ejected from a game, believe it or not. A fact I kept in the back of my mind to remind myself when I felt like having a particularly shitty fucking day.

What can I say? I was a sucker for punishment.

Her brows etched into a frown. "Do you not think I can do a good job?"

I raised my hands in defense. "Hey, *whoa.* I did *not* say that." On the contrary, I would rather deal with her than anyone else. The other PR specialist, Matt, and I had never gotten along. There was something off about that guy that I couldn't pinpoint. And Kennedy, well...she was *annoyingly* efficient. She would call you on your bullshit and lay it all out on the table.

Her eyes flashed with what I'd come to know was annoyance. I wasn't joking when I said I noticed *everything* about Kennedy. I had been observing her for a long time. I remembered the exact day she waltzed through the arena doors ready to conquer the world. She was as fiery as they'd come, and if you didn't get out of her way, she would incinerate you without a second thought.

And, man, did I like being burned by her.

It was a fucking shame she was engaged.

Though single or not, I knew it wouldn't have made much of a difference. The woman couldn't stand me. But a man could always dream.

"Brad is retiring at the end of the season, so he's trying to delegate a little more," she said. "Unlucky for you, this means you get to deal with me."

"I mean, if it lets us have these lovely interactions, how unlucky can I really be?" I pushed her shoulder with mine playfully.

I was a sucker for moments like these with her. They were rare, but when they happened? I was one happy motherfucker. And God only knew how desperate I was for a hit or two of good old dopamine.

"*Very.*" She gave me a smug look. Fuck, even her overconfidence was sexy. "Walk me through what happened tonight."

My stomach tightened.

I liked to think I was a decent guy. Granted, being the one who started the fight didn't exactly put me in the best light, but I still had my good traits. I may have been a cocky son of a bitch —I'd never deny it—but there was more underneath. I was a son, a brother, and a good friend. I was the kind of man who would put his life on the line for the people I cared about.

And that's exactly what I was doing.

I'd promised my twin sister, Olivia, that I wouldn't meddle in her business and told her she had nothing to worry about. I could be a little overprotective when it came to her. And if you ever met Olivia, you'd know she didn't need protecting, but I didn't give a fuck.

In my eyes, she'd always be my little sister. That's the curse she got for being born two minutes later.

Still, I had every intention of keeping my word. But then Holt had to open his big, fat, stupid mouth and say some pretty nasty shit about her—stuff I refused to even voice out loud.

He was needling me, and I fell for it, hook, line, *and* sinker.

So, I broke his nose. And his jaw, too, I think. The details were... somewhat hazy. All I knew was I saw red, and not even God himself could have pulled me off the prick. I still don't know how the refs and my teammates managed to push me back. It was all a blur.

Was I proud of what I had done? People who thought they knew me probably thought I was.

But deep down? No. I wasn't. Far from it.

"Holt said some pretty nasty shit, so I hit him."

"What did he exactly say?" she pressed.

I shrugged, opting for silence. Details were a whole other thing I didn't need—or want—to get into.

"*Anderson*," she groaned. "Players talk shit on the ice all the time. *Especially* Holt."

I scoffed. I knew that. Hell, every team in the league knew that. "So?"

"What do you mean *so?*" she asked, aggravated. "We're in this situation because you couldn't keep your head cool, so now you have to *fix it.*" She let out a long, tired sigh. "This is what we're going to do, when the reporters ask you what happened, you're going to say you were having an off night, and then you're going to apologize."

I threw my head back with a sharp laugh. "Good one."

"Does it *look* like I'm joking?"

"I'm not publicly apologizing to anyone. I have a reputation to maintain, need I remind you," I quipped.

"*Oh.*" She snorted a dry laugh as she settled her eyes on me with an exasperated look. "Trust me, *I know.* God forbid you taint the reputation you've worked *so* hard for."

She wasn't wrong. My early years were all about proving I belonged, with a cocky smirk plastered on my face and a fist-fight or two to seal the deal. Back then, they called me *the young, wild rookie.* Now? They had rebranded me as *the pretty-as-sin bad boy.* It was catchy, I'd give them that.

And just so we're clear, this wasn't me having some sort of god complex. Those were the *exact* words from *Sports Illustrated* when they crowned me as one of the hottest hockey players the previous year.

God, I sound like such an asshole right now, don't I? Let me just go ahead and shut the fuck up before I dig this hole any deeper.

This was all to say, I'd done a great job feeding people this bullshit persona, though I was growing tired of it for many reasons I didn't want to think about or admit to myself.

What was that famous saying? Oh, yes. *Ignorance is bliss.*

I found joy in not facing the ugly truths. *Sue me.*

I waved my hand dismissively. "I'll pay whatever fine they want to give me."

"This is more than that. Anthony is *livid* with you right now."

I grimaced. "*Fuck.*"

Having the general manager pissed at me was *dangerous* territory.

It didn't matter if I brought them millions of dollars in revenue every year, or if my stats kept getting better, I still took a big chunk of their payroll. I struggled a lot with the knowledge. I'd only been playing for this team for three years, but I strongly believed Anthony only put up with my shit because I was a big, shiny dollar sign for the organization.

It didn't matter how much of a well-rounded player I was. All I was good for was putting on a good show. That was the only value I had going for me.

"Yeah, *fuck* indeed," she retorted. "You created this mess, and now you have to clean it up, pretty boy. You know how this works."

"Calling me pretty twice in one day?" I fanned my face with an exhale. "God, Jonesy. You sure know how to make a man blush." I bit the inside of my cheek to hold back my grin.

She stood abruptly with a clasp of her hands. "Listen, Anderson," she snapped. *Oh, she was pissed alright.* "I know you love to be the clown of the team and give everyone this *I'm-cool-as-fuck* vibe or whatever." She accentuated the words with air quotes. "But the fact is this—*you fucked up*. I don't know if this is registering in that brain of yours or not, but..." She sighed then nipped her bottom lip for the briefest moment. The movement was so irrationally sensual, I had to urge my body to calm itself down and not do something stupid like reach for her and run my thumb across her lip, followed by my tongue.

Yikes. That thought escalated quickly.

"All I know is you have thirty minutes to figure out how to swallow your pride and change your tune. For the sake of this organization and *your* career." She fixed me with a stern stare. "So, what's it going to be?"

I rubbed the back of my neck in contemplation. How exactly was I supposed to do that? I didn't play nice with outsiders, especially with guys as shitty as fucking Holt. But the way Kennedy was looking at me, with a fierce determination and an *if-you-don't-cooperate-I-will-murder-you-in-your-sleep* look, had me painfully shoving my pride down my throat.

Swallowing a big, fat rock would have been an easier task, but I still tried, for the sake of the team. For me. Hell, because Kennedy asked me, too.

"Fine," I groaned. "I'll play nice."

"Great." Her smile was wide, but it didn't reach her eyes. "Don't fuck it up."

TWO

KENNEDY

THE DEVIL MAY WORK HARD,
BUT I WORKED HARDER.

POST-GAME INTERVIEWS WERE ABOUT to kick off, and the rush I got every time I stepped into the media room flowed through my veins like lightning, quick and crackling with anticipation.

In here, I wasn't Kenny, the borderline homeless thirty-two-year-old woman who broke off a three-year engagement. I was Kennedy Jones, Senior PR Specialist, who had—or, well... *pretended* to have—her shit together. The woman who was doing everything in her power to show her worth. Because my boss was retiring at the end of the season, and that meant the spot was up for grabs. Since Brad had been working for the organization for over thirty years, the owners had left it up to him to decide who would take over and be the new head of the department. I showed my interest in the position, of course, because it had been my dream ever since I could remember. And that's why, when the Anderson situation happened, Brad called me into his office and said, "Show me what you got."

I'd never been so excited in my life. This was *my* moment. Even if my personal life was pure chaos, I wasn't going to let it mess with my career. This was the one thing I could *actually* control.

Still, impostor syndrome tried its best to creep in, to paralyze me.

As a woman in sports, I often questioned whether I was doing good enough or working hard enough. After everything, would I get the credit I deserved when the time came? People were going to have strong opinions when they inevitably found out I was actively pursuing the PR director role. But I wasn't going to let the uncertainty of things and people's opinions bring me down.

The pressure society had placed on women wasn't going to go away overnight, but I'd fight every day of my life to make it easier for future generations to come. Change took time. I knew that. I also knew I needed to brace for what was to come. I wasn't going to let *anything* get in the way of this.

"Heard you're pursuing the director position," Matt Smith, the other Senior PR specialist for the Strikers, said as he stood next to me. "What are you going to do? *Flirt* your way right to the top?" His tone was condescending, with a hint of pride. He sure as hell was patting himself on the back for that one.

I wish I could say I was surprised by this reaction, but this was a regular day in the life of a woman working in a male-dominated field. Don't let people fool you into believing positions such as public relations and marketing in this industry were easier for women to work in. It never mattered what positions we held; the opinions were one in the same.

It didn't help that Matt and I didn't get along. He was the type of guy who tried to act all *buddy-like* with someone, only to turn around and stab them in the back with a smile etched on his face. If there was one thing I hated the most, it was hypocrisy. He knew I saw him for who he *really* was, and he did *not* like that one bit. He'd also been bitter when I got promoted to a senior position a year after I started working for the Strikers and has had it out for me ever since.

"Interesting comment. Do you offer this level of professional critique to the men, too, or am I just lucky?" My voice was high-pitched—sarcasm on full swing.

"Women like you don't belong in positions like that, and we both know it."

It took everything in me not to roll my eyes. "Keep the hits coming, Matty. I'm assembling a bingo card of outdated gender stereotypes. Is this the part where you tell me how heels affect women's leadership skills?" I asked, crossing my arms while tapping my four-inch heels against the tiles with a sardonic smile.

He ground his teeth and shot me a menacing glare that was supposed to intimidate me, but it only managed to make me laugh.

The devil may work hard, but I worked harder.

I'd been told many things throughout my life.

That I was too much of a bitch.

Too eager and desperate to climb the corporate ladder.

Too uptight for my own good.

You name it—I'd probably heard it.

Would I have preferred to be left alone and to my own devices? *Yes.*

But people like him helped me develop the thickest of skins in this messed-up, misogynistic world. While I knew being the bigger person and rising above the jabs was the proper—and better—approach, there was something so satisfying about staring a mediocre man dead in the eyes and matching his small-dick energy.

"Always a *treat* talking to you," I said with an exaggerated wink before turning around.

The room quieted as the coaches from both teams strode into the room with their star center forwards.

Anderson's left eye was beginning to shut, and the bruises on his knuckles were more visible, too. My eyes landed on Holt, and I instinctively cringed at the sight of him. The beating he got was something to be concerned about. Both of his eyes were swollen, as well as his nose, and it seemed they had to give him a few stitches on his bottom lip.

Both teams needed to do some serious damage control.

Unrelenting nerves flowed through me as Holt took a seat. He was the kind of player who was adored by the media. All he needed to do was flash his boyish smile and the crowd would eat it up. But Jack Holt was a loose cannon in the making, especially after provoking Anderson tonight. Not that I had a leg to stand on; it wasn't like Anderson was any better. One of his favorite things to do was be sassy with reporters every chance he got. To his credit, they deserved it most of the time. Reporters loved talking to these players like they weren't actual human beings.

To many, players were only stats. It was the way the business unfortunately functioned.

The cameras started rolling, and one of the reporters quickly directed the first question to Jack Holt. "Rough game tonight for the Jaguars, Holt. But we're wondering, as the newly appointed captain, how can people trust you'll be able to lead the team to a win after what transpired tonight?"

The menacing laugh Holt barked made my shoulders tense. "The team chose me for a reason. My ability to lead us to a win has nothing to do with petty fights." He shrugged as he leaned back on his chair. "And you forget I wasn't the one who started it. We all know *his* reputation."

Anderson grazed his teeth with his tongue, trying to keep his smirk in check.

I shot him a sharp look with a quick shake of my head. He needed to keep it together. It was obvious Holt was trying to get to him with any cheap shots he could think of.

The reporter aimed the next question at Anderson. "What happened tonight, man?"

He relaxed on his chair with a shrug. "This is hockey, fighting happens."

Okay. Not the worst answer. I could work with this.

The reporter nodded, but I didn't miss the evil glint in his eyes. "Yeah, but you've been doing good for these past three years. People thought you had finally settled with the Strikers, and now tonight, you lost it."

Holt snorted a mocking laugh. "What else is new? We all know his favorite pastime is ruining his father's amazing legacy."

Anderson's jaw ticked as his eyes flickered with emotion. Irritation, maybe?

Vulnerability.

That couldn't be it. The media had always talked about how different he was from his father. It was a *constant* topic in the sports world. Why would that have bothered him at a time like this? Still, the temperature in my body dropped as chills ran down my spine. There was a crucial puzzle piece I was missing, and I knew it had become my job to find out what it was.

The room fell into complete silence at Holt's comment. Anderson's nostrils flared, and I waved my hands as I tried to catch his attention. But it was no use. His eyes were unfocused, almost like he had lost himself inside his head.

"I mean, who's surprised? He has been causing issues since he started playing professionally. We all know he thinks he's the king of the ice." Holt kept sputtering bullshit, and I wished I could have grabbed a mic and hit him in the head with it *repeatedly.* He was such a fucking asshole and a professional shit-talker. Definitely missed his true life calling.

After a few beats of silence so charged you could cut the tension with a knife, the reporter prompted, "Anderson, any comments?"

His expression remained enigmatic, but his gaze was lost on another planet. He casually grabbed the mic and stood without a word. My heart stammered, and I unintentionally held my breath, bracing for impact.

Holt smirked knowingly and rose from his chair, too. "Aw, *shucks*, did I hit a nerve?"

Anderson was impossibly tall and easily towered over Holt's frame, and Holt wasn't a small guy by any means. But Anderson was over 240 pounds of pure, *raw* muscle. I had seen him without a shirt more times than I could count, so I knew what lay underneath all those layers.

He was wearing a black turtleneck sweater and a plaid gray suit that on any other man would have looked horrible, but he rocked it. It hugged his broad, strong shoulders and arms and his stone-muscled thighs perfectly. His black hair was soft and perfectly styled, a rare but beautiful contrast to his intense blue-gray eyes and pale skin. His nose was a bit crooked with the number of hits he'd received over the years, and his jaw was strong and chiseled. Countless freckles dusted his cheeks, nose, and forehead, giving him this boyish, innocent look.

That was until he opened his mouth and his cocky personality made an appearance.

His eyes found mine, and a flicker of regret passed through them. In that moment, right before he opened his mouth, I knew the organization was about to spiral into chaos because he couldn't keep his temper in check.

"If any of you are expecting me to apologize for what happened tonight, that will not be happening." His eyes zeroed in on Holt, and a smug grin spread across his lips as he stepped even closer. "And Holt?" He threw out a humorless laugh that made every muscle in my body tense. "Let's make one thing straight—I don't have to believe *anything*. I *know* I'm the king of the ice. When I step on it, it's mine—always has been, and always will be. And don't you *ever* forget it." His voice was rough, with an unmistakable angry edge.

Oh, for fuck's sake.

It was worse than I could have ever imagined. There was cocky, and then there was...*this*.

Holt let out a long, low whistle. "Damn, no wonder your sister—"

He couldn't finish his sentence, because Anderson threw a solid punch to his already swollen nose. Holt began to fall onto his back, but Anderson was quick to grab him by the collar to continue his assault. The room became a total zoo as both coaches tried to pull them apart. Their attempts were futile as both players fell over the tables. Every photographer started taking pictures as reporters fired off questions, because if there was one thing about them that was certain, they *loved* the drama.

The coaches were finally able to pull the men apart, and before they could all leave the room, Anderson shouted, "Watch your back on the ice next time, because I'm going to fucking *kill* you." His eyes were manic and a few darker shades of blue as he threw the words at Holt with venom. I'd never seen Anderson so distraught. Pure, raw, unrelenting anger practically flowed out of him in heat waves, suffocating the room.

"Looking forward to it, *dick*," Holt said as he flipped Anderson off, then his coach pushed him out the door and they were finally out of sight.

"*Enough!*" Coach Sloane shouted. "Let's go, *now*." He pushed Anderson to the backroom exit that led to our offices.

"Get everyone out of here," I said to one of our media interns through gritted teeth. She quickly nodded and got to work.

With the throbbing pain in my chest tightening and my breathing becoming choppier, I quickened my steps toward the same exit Coach Sloane and Anderson used to escape.

The room was still loud as reporters started to rapid-fire questions my way.

"What does the Strikers GM think about Anderson's attitude?"

"How can we be sure Anderson will keep his head straight during this season?"

I took a sharp turn to address the room. The onslaught of questions died down, and they all stared at me expectantly. I didn't know if my chest was going to be able to handle it, but it didn't matter. This was part of my job.

There's nothing else you can do except for damage control. Take a breather, Kennedy. You got this.

"There will be no comments at this time. Thank you."

Questions started firing at a rapid pace again, but I turned around and made a quick escape.

"What does this mean for the team?" Was the last question I heard as I shut the door with more force than necessary. I was desperate for the thick piece of wood to drown out the chaos on the other side of the room.

I shut my eyes and took a few deep inhales, but it was impossible to breathe.

The only thing grounding me in the moment was the quiet taps of my heels as I strode toward my office. I needed someplace quiet to *think*. To *plan*. To calm myself down before I had to face Anderson again.

And to deal with the inevitable.

I knew it was too late to stop the asthma attack that was

starting to form in the center of my chest, but I always tried my best. The inhaler made my mouth dry and caused bad breath, so I used it as a last resort.

In total honesty—and kind of a trauma-dumping moment—it also made me feel...weak. Like there was something fundamentally wrong with me. The thought itself was insane, because this was a condition I was born with and something I had no power over, but I hated things that were out of my control.

With slumped shoulders and a small, resigned sigh, I entered my office, found my purse, and grabbed my trusty inhaler. I brought it to my mouth and took one puff. The pressure in my chest started to ease slightly after a minute. So, I kept doing puffs every forty-five to sixty seconds until, by the fourth puff, my chest finally felt completely light.

I sat on my desk and shut my eyes as I tilted my head backward with a long, tired sigh.

If those questions were any indication of the narrative the media was about to push, I had my work cut out for me.

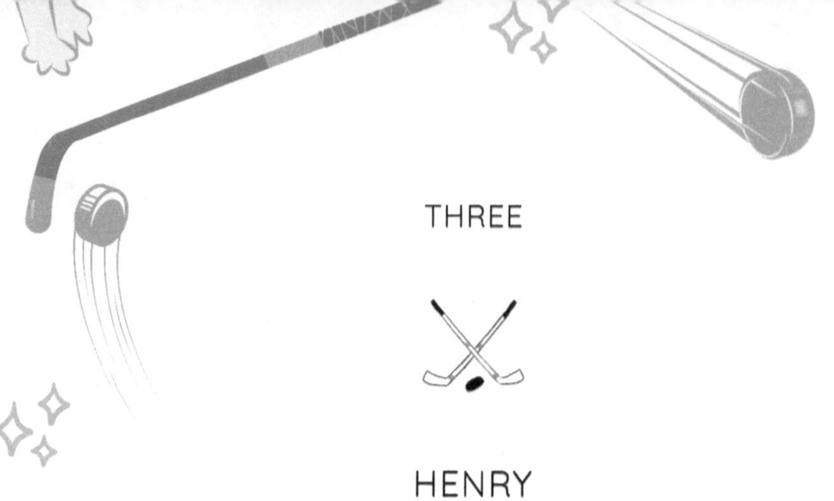

THREE

HENRY

BIG, DUMB JOCK WHO COULDN'T KEEP HIS COOL ONCE AGAIN.

THE AIR in Coach Sloane's office crackled with tension as anger pumped through my veins. I sat in one of the guest chairs as I inhaled and exhaled through my nose slowly. Calming myself down for the second time in the same night was my top priority.

"What the fuck was that!?" Coach Sloane barked as he slammed his fist against his desk with such force the pens rattled.

I knew how this looked. Big, dumb jock who couldn't keep his cool once again. But the reality was so different. Yet, I couldn't—*didn't*—tell a soul why I had such a drastic reaction.

One single text from my father was all it took for me to allow anger to push me over the cliff and lose myself. Holt certainly didn't help. But ultimately, I was the only one to blame.

The office door opened, and I looked over my shoulder as Anthony and Kennedy strode into the room quietly.

She took a seat next to me, with brows furrowed and lips thinned as she refused to even cast me a glance. I was utterly

and royally fucked. I could take an annoyed and mean Kennedy any day. But a quiet one? I knew I was in deep shit and it was going to be impossible for me to get off her bad side.

"In my twenty years of coaching, I have *never* had to deal with such an ill-tempered, manchild!" Coach Sloane roared, his voice echoing off the walls. The vein in his forehead—the one that only made an appearance when he was livid—pulsated visibly.

Most of the guys, myself included, were a bit terrified of Coach Sloane. He was awesome at his job, don't get me wrong. There was a reason we were all strong and well-rounded play-ers. He worked hard, so we worked twice as hard to prove we deserved a spot on the team. But when his temper made an appearance, the best thing to do was to get on our knees and pray to all the gods known to man for a quick, painless death.

But that quick death was unfortunately not coming to save me.

Anthony leaned against the desk and crossed his arms with a disapproving look plastered all over his face. I honestly couldn't give much of a fuck about Anthony's opinion of me at the moment.

Anger simmered beneath my skin at the reminder of Holt's words. *And that fucking text.*

My father was a sensitive topic for many reasons. The pedestal people put him on, even twenty years later, was annoying, to say the least. If they knew the truth about the *"great"* Vincent Anderson, I doubted the throne they put him on would have lasted much longer.

But it was my secret to bear. For the sake of me and my family. Though, if I were being honest, I cared very little about myself.

"What's the plan, Kennedy?" Anthony asked.

"I strongly advise not having Anderson make any sort of

statement for now. At this point, we need to show the world with actions rather than words that he's not a violent man. We can schedule a few photo ops with the charities he donates to. Having him be more involved with the community will help."

"The last thing I want people to think is that I'm playing nice with these charities for my image. I actually care about these organizations," I snapped with a cross of my arms.

"You're in no position to complain when I'm trying to fix the mess you created," she retorted as she mirrored my pose.

We gave each other a deadly glare. My chest heaved, and my pulse beat against my ear almost too painfully.

Fucking hell, Kennedy was frustrating. I knew she had a point. But I didn't want to fucking hear it. I wanted to lick my wounds. I wanted to be alone and soak in the consequences of my actions.

A glimmer of irritation crossed her brown eyes. Her stare was so intense, I decided to give in and look away. I was afraid my emotions were going to show more than I wanted to. I'd take any punishment the organization deemed acceptable. As long as I kept the real reasons close to my chest, everything was going to be fine.

She sighed and leaned back in her chair. "Maybe we can even have him assist with the learn-to-skate kids program at our training rinks some weekends. I think the media would love to see that, and it will help soften his image, too."

I scoffed. "How exactly do you suppose I do that? The weekends we don't have games, I have to train."

I knew I sounded like a grade-A asshole, but my career was the *only* lifeline I had. It was the *only* thing I had going for me. When I wasn't training, I was spending my time developing and caring for a non-profit I'd anonymously founded when I started playing and making real money. Not many knew this information, Kennedy included. I wasn't particularly eager to announce to the world what I did in my private time. It was hard as it was to keep the world out of my life. And this particular part? I cherished it with my whole fucking heart. It was too important to me. So I took the necessary measures to keep it a secret.

"Great idea, Kennedy." Coach nodded, and without missing a beat, he looked at me and said, "You can afford to miss a couple of training sessions, because you're benched until further notice."

I stood abruptly in disbelief and raised my arms in a *what the fuck?* gesture. "Coach, this is bullshit! You *need* me."

He shot me a withering glare. "What I *need* is for my star center to get his shit together. I understand you like to be the joker, to give the people what they want, and I've allowed it to happen, but tonight you went *too far*. If you don't fix this attitude of yours, your ass will keep warming the bench for the rest of the season for all I care." He scoffed then looked at Kennedy. "I want Henry to participate in any volunteer work you and the marketing department have planned as long as it doesn't interfere with our away games."

Kennedy shifted in her chair uncomfortably but gave him a court nod.

What the fuck? What was actually happening? I could feel my sanity slipping through my fingers as I desperately tried to hold on to it. If they took away from me the only thing that made me happy, the only thing that kept me sane...I honestly didn't know where I would end up.

"How are we supposed to have a chance at the Cup with me on the bench?" I asked, desperation taking hold of me. "You're seriously going to bench me for defending myself when Holt kept sputtering bullshit out of his goddamn mouth?" *Fuck, was I angry.* My hands were shaking, so I clenched them—*hard*. My nails bit into the flesh of my palms, but I couldn't bring myself to care. The physical pain numbed a much worse and deeper ache.

Coach smirked, though there was not a trace of humor behind his eyes. "You should have considered this before you decided to fight back, *king of the ice*," he replied mockingly.

Fuck. Fuck. *Fuck.*

I'd *never* been benched—not even during my rookie season. Benching me wasn't just a mistake; it was *reckless.*

I'd never been so terrified in my life until that moment. And I'd been through some pretty rough shit during my childhood. But nothing compared to the only thing that made my heart beat being ripped away from me.

My eyes found Anthony's. He knew damn well the revenue the Strikers were going to lose if they went through with this. There was no way he was going to allow such a rash decision. He was a smart businessman above anything else.

Anthony shook his head. "Don't look at me. I trust Sloane and what he thinks is best for this team."

"I'll do better. I promise." My voice cracked and my eyes burned, but I held back with the little strength I had left.

"You're lucky this isn't turning into something worse." Coach scrubbed his face with a resigned sigh. "We love having you here, Anderson. You know you're like a son to me, but, buddy, this has gone too fucking far. Enough is enough," he added softly, which, if you knew anything about Coach, you'd know he was anything *but* soft when it came to his players.

His comment made my back straighten real fucking quick. He didn't need to explicitly say what he meant. I heard him loud *and* clear.

You're lucky you're not being traded.

The thought squeezed my lungs with fear, making it impossible to breathe. This was the city I wanted to retire in. I was tired of packing up my shit and starting a new life every so often. The past three years had been...amazing. I was finally in a place where I belonged. My friends, the people I considered family, all lived here. Being traded *wasn't* an option.

He leveled me with a knowing look. "Prove to me you can keep a cool head, and I will put you back on the ice." He waved his hand at the door. "You're dismissed."

Rage still bubbled inside me. I was frustrated, tired, and I wanted to scream from the top of my lungs for someone to listen to me. I was drowning in the uncertainty of what was to come. But I shut my eyes and gave him a clipped nod before storming out of his office.

And, *fuck*, I hated this feeling that creeped up on me when I least expected it. The shame was hard to face, too. My mom was probably so disappointed in me. There was no way she hadn't heard what happened. I didn't even want to know what Olivia was thinking. She was probably livid. All I was managing to do at the ripe age of thirty was disappoint people I loved because I couldn't control my emotions.

I wondered if this was how *he* felt.

No. Don't go there. At least you have the decency to feel guilty about it. He never did. I reminded myself of the mantra I came up with years ago, hoping one day it would make me feel slightly better about myself.

Spoiler alert: *It didn't.*

The pain in my chest signaled the panic attack that was making its quick way to me, but when I looked up, I found Liam Donovan—right winger and captain of the team—jogging my way. So with a deep breath and a mental *keep-your-shit-together* pep talk, I shot him the smile I'd perfected over the years with a nod.

"What did Coach say?"

I shrugged, rubbing the back of my neck. "He benched me

until further notice, and I'm basically going to be babysat by Kennedy."

He pursed his lips as he gave me an exasperated look. The look alone managed to chip at my already fucked-up head. Having the captain of the team I played for disappointed in me stung. I was so sick and tired of upsetting people I cared about.

"What the hell were you thinking, man?"

I *wasn't* thinking. That was the root of the problem.

I shot him a glare but chose to stay silent. Despite my frustration, I had a lot of respect for Donovan—not just because he was our captain, but because he had this wisdom about him. He was only thirty-five years old, but he was the older brother of the group. Always steady and watching out for us. Which was very much needed, because most of us were a bunch of overgrown children.

"What the hell am I going to do, Donovan?" I groaned.

"At least you get to spend more time with your favorite girl." He grinned.

I frowned. "What the hell are you talking about?"

"*Please.* You're obsessed with Kennedy. Do you think I haven't noticed?"

"No, I'm not."

"Oh, yeah? Then why are you always tagging along to whatever photo op Kennedy is in charge of? To be a team player?" He snorted a disbelieving laugh.

Damn. Was I that fucking transparent?

"Whatever," I mumbled.

He shot me a knowing smirk. "Listen, I know this is probably the last thing you want to do, but we're going to Tim's for celebratory drinks. You should come."

Tim's was one of our go-to bars to eat and hang out. It was the only place where there was a lot of crowd control, and we could go in and relax without worrying about crazy fans or paparazzi. The owner—whose name was, *you guessed it*, Tim—always kicked them out in a heartbeat. He was a very *fuck-around-and-find-out* type of man. We loved the old, grumpy guy.

I knew it wasn't a good idea to go out. But damn it, we had won our first home game of the season and it deserved to be celebrated.

I was also in some serious need to blow off some steam.

So against my better judgment, I replied, "Fuck it. I'm in."

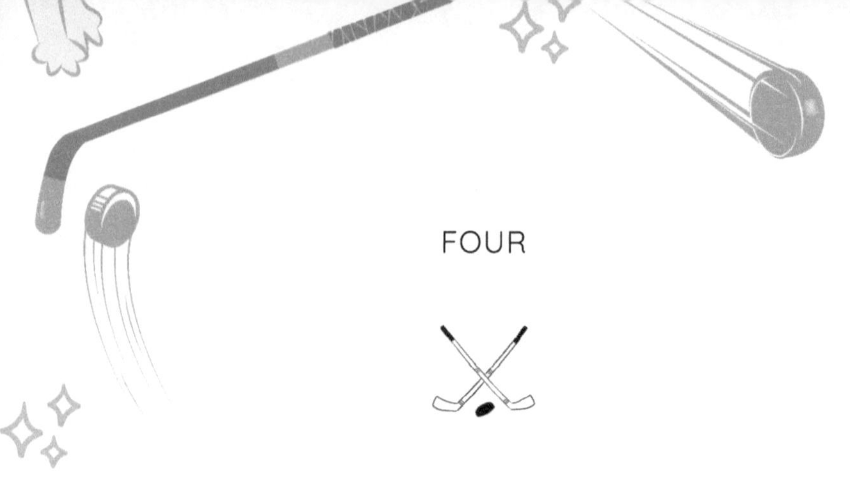

FOUR

HENRY

GANG-UP-ON-ANDERSON DAY.

AN HOUR LATER, I walked into Tim's with Donovan. The bar was busier than usual, but I recognized most faces since it was a normal hangout spot for the front office people as well. "Mr. Brightside" by The Killers played from the red jukebox, and all the tables were occupied with low chatter and laughs.

I loved this place. It had an '80s feel to it, with low lighting and a few fluorescent signs of beer brands and rock band posters. The floor was a dark wooden color, and it didn't matter how much they cleaned, the stickiness from all the beer that had fallen on these floors never went away. In the back of the room, there were a few green pool tables, and antique faux stained-glass lamps hung over them. The bar area was the typical wooden long table with red stools, and behind the bar, there were crystal shelves with all sorts of cheap alcohol.

I took a sharp inhale and let the smell of cheap beer and greasy food infiltrate my nostrils.

Oh, how I loved the smell of home, sweet home.

"Over here, guys," Hayes, our left winger, shouted as he waved to catch our attention.

We headed to the other side of the bar, where Hayes was sitting at a high-top table with our left defenseman, Levi Parker; our right defenseman, Elijah Morgan; and our goalie, Nicolas Owens.

The whole team was pretty close, but I considered these guys my brothers.

"I'm surprised you're here," Hayes quipped at me as he raised one of his dark-blond eyebrows.

Wesley Hayes and I had been friends since we were kids, and by some luck of the universe, the Detroit Panthers had traded him two years ago. Hayes, Donovan, and I played on the same line, and we'd always connected on the ice easily. It made me happy knowing we got to play the game we had loved since we were kids together. When I moved out of Canada with my mom and my sister to a little town in Oklahoma, I was happy we were finally away from *him*, but it hurt leaving all my friends behind. I was glad I had the opportunity to meet a man like Hayes, and better yet, I was also lucky enough to call him my best friend.

We patted each other on the back as I laughed. "Dude, I'm in desperate need of a beer." I turned around and lifted two of my fingers to catch the attention of Aly—Tim's daughter and one of the bartenders—and ask her for our usuals. She acknowledged me with a thumbs-up and quickly got back to work.

I wasn't kidding when I said we spent a ridiculous amount of time in this bar.

"What did Coach say?" Owens asked, taking a sip of his water.

The guy refused to drink during the season, and even when we were off, he still didn't drink much. I was surprised he made an appearance at all. Nicolas Owens was the typical quiet and grumpy goalie. We always tried to draw him out of his shell and force him to spend time with us. While he'd probably tell you he hated hanging out with us, I knew it was a lie. He loved us in his own, weird way.

"Bold for you to be here after that media shit storm," Morgan said with a shake of his head.

Elijah Morgan was the alternate captain and the ruler of the group. The man had a stick so far up his ass, it was impossible to remove. Still, we loved him with his faults and all.

I sat on one of the high stools. "I'm benched until further notice."

"Fuck, man," Hayes groaned.

"Tell me about it," I grumbled.

Aly dropped a few beers at our table with some plates of wings. Normally, I tried to stick to my meal plan during the season, but here and there, when I had a particularly hard day, I liked to eat my weight in delicious fried foods.

Owens grabbed his phone to read a text then lifted his gaze and looked over the crowd until his brown eyes lit up like a kid's on Christmas day as he waved to catch someone's attention. I looked over my shoulder, trying to figure out who he was waving at, and found Val smiling back at him.

Valentina García—also known as Val—was a senior marketing specialist for the Strikers and Owens's childhood best friend. They grew up in the same small town in Colorado or some shit like that. Those two were inseparable and had such a weird relationship.

A quick shift of chestnut curls entering the bar caught my attention, and my eyes followed the movement, finding Kennedy walking behind Valentina. I knew they were close friends, too, but it was rare to see Kennedy hanging out with anyone outside of work. My stomach dropped as I took her in. I couldn't remember the last time she stepped foot in here.

Okay, that was a blatant lie—I remembered perfectly.

It was after her first day of work. She had shorter hair then and a blinding smile that made her eyes sparkle. It was the kind that stamped itself on your brain and refused to leave. I was struck with the overwhelming urge to see if I could be the one to make her smile just so I could witness it again, but I knew better than to try.

My eyes raked over her body, because more than anything, I was a sucker for punishment. She had changed out of her power suit and into a pair of black jeans, a pink sweater, and pink Converse. It was borderline irritating how overwhelmingly beautiful I found Kennedy to be. She'd always be the most radiant woman in any room she stepped into.

It was starting to become a terrible problem.

"Your girl's here." Hayes elbowed my forearm.

I fixed him with an icy stare. "You think you're so fucking funny."

He shot me a smug smile. "It's not my fault you're obsessed with her."

"I am *not* obsessed with her," I said through gritted teeth. Seriously, what was up with my teammates all of a sudden? Since when did they love to get on my balls about her?

"Hey, guys!" Val waved at us excitedly then turned around to look for Kennedy and made a *come on* motion.

Owens stood and lifted Val into a tight hug. "Hey, Pecas.*"

She hugged him back just as tightly. "Hey, Nico. Freaking stop calling me that, dude."

"Never." He grinned then patted the seat he was using. "Sit. I'll go get you a drink."

My eyes found Kennedy, and she awkwardly stood next to Val. Her eyes roamed the bar, taking everything in. I couldn't blame her. The bar tended to become a crazy place to be after a game.

---

* Freckles.

I stood from my chair with a lazy grin. "Hey, Jonesy. Take my seat, and I'll grab you a drink."

She shot me a glare without a reply. Excitement spiked through me at her stare alone, and my grin widened.

Hayes draped an arm around her shoulders, and the movement caused my eye to twitch involuntarily. Fucking Hayes and his natural ability to flirt. I found it endearing, except when Kennedy was concerned. It was insane, I was aware. But I didn't give a single flying fuck.

"Kenny, how the hell are you?"

"I *was* having a good night, until now," she replied, side-eyeing me.

"Aw, I missed you too, *babe*." I threw her an exaggerated kiss with a wink.

"Did I miss something between you two?" he asked, amused.

"Oh, you know, I made her job harder today, so she's pissed at me," I replied casually with a half-shrug.

Before Hayes could reply, Parker called him to the other side of the table, where he was sitting with two very eager-looking women. One of them was practically eating Hayes alive with her eyes.

Levi Parker had been playing with us for a year after getting traded from the Detroit Panthers, too. Though he was in his early twenties, he was the laid-back guy of the group and, surprisingly, a ladies' man. You wouldn't expect it from his easygoing demeanor, but he could attract women like no one else—well, Hayes was another rigorous player. But with his outgoing personality, that was a given.

Hayes rubbed his palms together with a smirk. "It's wingman time."

I rolled my eyes at his comment as he walked away from us.

"For the record, today wasn't any different," Kennedy replied very matter-of-factly. "You're always a piece of work."

"*Ouch.*" I placed a hand over my chest dramatically. "You *wound* me."

"I'm sure I do," she muttered, settling into the chair I'd given her.

As she shifted to face me, her knee brushed against my thigh, and my pulse spiked at the fleeting touch. My God, I couldn't have been any more pathetic; it was humanly impossible.

"What are you doing here? You should stay home and away from the media. Or is it your lifelong goal to make my job more difficult?"

I was never the type of man who liked easy things. Kennedy was a woman who fought fire with fire and was unapologetic about it. *And I fucking reveled in that shit.*

"I thought you said today wasn't any different?" I mocked.

She crossed her arms as she pretended to ponder. Her eyes locked on mine for a moment, and I could practically feel the annoyance rolling off of her. I knew I was going to like whatever insult she was about to fire back with her pouty mouth. "Now that I think about it, it *was* sort of different. I've never seen you be so full of yourself before," she commented. "Fame getting to your head, pretty boy?"

I knew she used the term *pretty boy* as a derogatory remark. But, *fuck*, if it didn't make my pulse thrum like crazy every time she said it.

I shrugged as I took a sip of my beer to calm my nerves. Her big, brown eyes settled on my throat, where my Adam's apple bobbed as I swallowed the liquid. And call me crazy, but I could have sworn her eyes flared with some sort of...awareness. Dare I say...*interest?*

Another surge of exhilaration flooded through me with a

whoosh. Kennedy had never paid attention to me, like...*ever*. The moment had been fleeting, and I was already eager to figure out how to get her attention on me again.

"Keep calling me pretty, and it *might* just go to my head."

"Does it hurt to carry such a big, egocentric head around the ice?" A hint of mockery dripped from her sweet and raspy voice. *God, that voice.* I never tired of hearing it. It was pathetic —*I* was pathetic.

"I'm one of the fastest skaters in the league. Does that answer your question?" I replied innocently.

She gave me a blank, unamused expression without a word.

I placed my beer on the table and clasped my hands. "Now, how about that drink?"

"I can go get my own." She tried to stand, but I gripped her waist to keep her in place.

The touch was brief, barely a graze. And yet, electricity shot from my arm down my vertebrae, and a million little butterflies took residence in the inside of my stomach.

Butterflies, seriously? What the fuck was this? Fucking *high school?*

"Not happening, Jonesy. What do you want?"

Her eyes narrowed. "Stop trying to act nice to get in my good graces. It's not going to work."

"I don't need to get in your good graces. You already like me," I replied confidently. Knowing full-well it was complete and utter bullshit.

She swatted my hand away from her waist, and a pang of disappointment hit me at the lack of touch between us. "What gave you such an idiotic idea?"

I had about three beers by the time Kennedy showed up. I was a tall, broad dude, so it wasn't much alcohol. But I was fogged with...*her*. She clouded all of my senses.

I rested the palm of my hand on the table and tilted my

head closer to her ear. "You think I don't notice when you check me out every time I have to take my shirt off for a photo op?" I took a small step back and fixed her with a knowing look. "I almost think you choose these types of photo ops on purpose," I rasped. The low vibration of my voice settled in the center of my chest. All common sense had left the window once again tonight, and I only had a certain five-foot-eleven beautiful woman to blame.

"*Ha.*" She tilted her head back with a laugh. The movement exposed the length of her neck and hit me with her scent. *Fuck*, she smelled like goddamn heaven. Sweet and tropical, like coconut, with a hint of something woody...sandalwood, maybe. It was surprisingly delicate and a complete contrast to her strong personality. Strangely, it fit her.

"I don't force you to go to any photo ops." She patted my shoulder with another laugh. "But nice try."

A cheeky smile played at the corner of my lips. "I may not have any evidence yet, but I'll prove it one day."

She rolled her eyes and placed the palm of her hand on my chest as she pushed me slightly to create some distance between us.

"I swear to God, Jonesy, if you don't tell me what you want to drink in the next two seconds, I will purchase every drink and bring them over."

She scoffed. "If you—"

"She loves strawberry mojitos," Val chimed in with an innocent smile.

Kennedy snapped her gaze to her. "*Val.*"

I gave Val a grateful look. "One strawberry mojito coming right up."

Kennedy opened her purse, rummaging for her wallet. "Okay, fine. At least take my—"

"Not happening." I turned around before she could take

her card out and quickly walked to where Owens was standing, already ordering.

"Hey, Tim," I called out. "Can I get a strawberry mojito?" I stopped to think for a moment, trying to remember if there was anything Kennedy liked to eat. Then I remembered she had ordered a plate of nachos the one time she was here. "And an order of nachos, too. Add it to my tab."

He nodded. "It'll be ready in a few."

I turned around and leaned against the bar next to Owens.

"It's a shame about Kennedy, right?" he said, crossing his arms and moving his gaze to our table.

I frowned and followed his line of sight. Kennedy was animatedly talking with Val as she placed a few strands of curls behind her ear, nodding along to whatever her friend was telling her. "What the hell are you talking about?"

His puzzled gaze snapped to mine. "You haven't heard?"

"Clearly not, since I just asked you."

His eyes gleamed with amusement. And if there was one thing you needed to know about Owens, the guy was *rarely* amused. "Interesting."

"What?"

Before Owens could reply, Tim interrupted us and handed off our orders. When I turned back around to ask my teammate again what the hell he was talking about, he was already halfway to our table.

"Order up," I announced and placed both items in front of Kennedy.

She turned around to grab her drink, but her gaze dropped to the table with a frown. "I didn't order nachos."

"I know. But I remember you liking them." I shrugged and pushed the plate closer to her. "Eat." I didn't know if she had eaten or not, but Kennedy had patterns. And like the creep I was, I knew forgetting to eat when she was busy was one of them.

She met my eyes with a scrutinizing look as she pushed it back to me. "I've only been here once."

"I have many talents. Being observant is one of them." I pushed the plate back *again* with my knuckles.

I was a brave man, but I wasn't stupid enough to confess I only had an extremely good memory when it came to her, and *only* her. I swear to God I wasn't trying. *Or so I kept telling myself.*

"How much do I owe you?"

I snorted a dry laugh. "You're funny."

"Henry," she warned, exasperated.

My heart felt like it came to a full stop at the way my name rolled off her lips. Her tone was raspy, with a hint of command in it. My dick got a mind of its own and started to wonder what this woman could make me do if I were to get on my knees for her and follow her every command. I could *definitely* think of a thing or two.

I leaned in, our faces a few inches apart. Just because she was engaged, didn't mean I couldn't have a little fun. Harmless flirting never hurt anyone, *right?*

"You never call me by my first name. I kind of like it. Do it again, please." I grazed my tongue across my bottom lip then gave her a cheeky grin.

Honestly, I'd only been half-joking. But there was no mistaking the way my heart quickened in anticipation, anxiously waiting for her to repeat it. Fuck me if I wasn't going to keep insisting she called me by my first name now. I *needed* to hear it again.

She pushed me slightly and flicked her hair off her shoulder with a dry expression. A laugh got lodged in my throat as I followed the movement, and my eyes landed on her ring finger. Her *very naked, no-ring-in-sight* ring finger.

It *had* to be a mistake. She'd probably lost it. Or maybe they finally pulled the trigger and got hitched and her wedding band was being resized. I was grasping at any excuse I could think of, because the other possibility was much worse.

But I knew it was already too late. Hope sneaked up my spine like an adrenaline rush at the prospect of Kennedy fucking Jones being single.

I wanted to ask her. It was killing me not to. The question was on the tip of my tongue, but before I could even speak, Hayes interrupted us. "Val here is telling me you're looking for a new place to live, Kenny."

Her shoulders tensed, and she gave a quick nod. "Yeah. It's hard to find an affordable place so close to downtown."

Okay, that was odd. Didn't she live with her fiancé?

"What a coincidence. Anderson here is looking for a roommate." Hayes clasped my shoulders.

My thoughts screeched to a sudden stop like a vinyl record. "*Huh?*" I tilted my head and frowned at Hayes in confusion.

My best friend loved being a clown; we all knew that. The man had a natural talent for pushing the envelope too fucking far.

Owens gaped at Hayes in disbelief, while Parker, Morgan, and Donovan hid their shit-eating grins behind their drinks.

I looked at them and mouthed, *What the fuck?* but all they did was roll their lips and look at Hayes expectantly. "Wha—"

Hayes cut me off. "Yeah, the place is just too big for him. Plus, he needs someone to take care of Captain Sushi," he said with a *duh* tone.

Captain what?!

"Hayes, weren't you and Parker talking to some girls?" I blurted. This conversation had taken a turn I didn't understand, but I had the sneaking suspicion I needed to do everything in my power to stop it.

He waved dismissively, not missing a beat. "We already got their numbers. But that's not important right now. Your child, however, is."

Pardon my language, but what in the fuckity damn fuck is going on?!

"Who's Captain Sushi?" Val asked, tilting her head.

I blinked at Val, at a loss for words. What the hell was I supposed to say?

"His cat," Hayes replied before his green gaze met mine. The mirth in his eyes was so bright, I had the urge to punch him in the throat. By some miracle of God, I managed to hold back. "You haven't told anyone? Shame on you, Anderson."

What. The. Fuck.

"His cat," Kennedy repeated, her tone laced with suspicion as she squinted at Hayes.

It was deadly silent for a beat or two, until Hayes elbowed me in the ribs a little too hard, and I slightly bent over with a small cough. Breathing had become difficult, and finding my words? Practically impossible.

Think, Anderson. Think.

A light—not the brightest, if I was being honest—turned on over my head. *Okay.* This was easy. I could do this.

Why are you even entertaining this in the first place? my brain so gracefully pointed out.

"You remember that photo op you had me do last season at the animal shelter?" I chuckled nervously. "I signed up to receive emails of pets looking for a home, and when I saw the little guy with black fur—"

"And white paws," Hayes added.

I shot him a *seriously, dude?* expression. "Yeah," I squeaked and quickly cleared my throat to cover it up. Was I being cool?

Probably not. But this conversation had taken a bizarre turn. "I was a goner. So, I adopted him."

"But the idiot forgot he travels most of the time, and now needs someone to take care of him when he isn't home," Hayes said.

Your days are numbered, Wesley Hayes. Sleep with one eye open, I thought.

"There are automatic cat feeders," Kennedy replied dryly. "Cats are pretty self-sufficient." Her eyes ping-ponged between me and Hayes. She stared at us like we were two clueless idiots.

To be fair, she wasn't wrong.

"Didn't you say he had some pretty bad separation anxiety, Anderson?" Parker chimed in.

I shot Parker a disbelieving glare. I wasn't sure if this was a *gang-up-on-Anderson* day or if it was payback for getting ejected, but I was about done with these clowns. "Not sure what—"

Hayes cut me off *again.* "Right." He snapped his fingers with a firm nod. "He can't be alone for more than a day."

"Aw, poor little guy," Val said with a wistful sigh.

I couldn't believe what was happening. They *believed* him.

"Yeah, man. It's so sad," Hayes added solemnly.

Well, shit. My best friend was in the wrong field. I swear I didn't know how he managed to keep his shit together as he continued to dig a deeper hole for me. A-list actor. I wanted to give the man a damn Oscar.

Donovan added, "Sounds like you need some serious help, man."

I gave Donovan a look of pure shock and betrayal, and he simply shrugged with a cheeky grin. *Assholes.* Every single one of them.

"*Ha,*" I laughed weakly. The place started to feel ridiculously small and hot with every second that passed. Droplets of sweat traveled down my back as I tried to figure out how to get out of the situation. "I do," I blurted.

I could have sworn there was a spirit version of myself who was looking over me like I was the biggest idiot to ever exist. Just pointing and laughing at me like I was losing my mind.

"So, what do you say, Kenny?" Hayes asked as he dropped an arm around my shoulders. "Fancy a roommate?"

Oh, for the love of God.

I didn't want a roommate. She *would* kill me in my sleep. But I knew I was lying to myself, because I held my breath with eagerness as I waited for her answer.

"No, thank you," Kennedy replied as she shifted in her seat uncomfortably. "I travel with you guys sometimes, so I wouldn't be a good fit anyway."

A pang of unexpected disappointment hit me right in the chest at her answer. *Jeez.* What the hell was the matter with me? I was having a hard time making up my mind. But when it came to Kennedy, that seemed to be the norm.

"The cat can stay with Aurora the times you're traveling with us. Right, Donovan?" Hayes asked.

Donovan shot Hayes a withering glare.

I smirked. *Not so funny now that your wife is involved, is it?*

Aurora was the sweetest and the biggest animal lover you could ever meet, and she'd love nothing more than to hang out with pets all day, but that was besides the fucking point, because I *didn't* have a damn cat.

"So you don't need a roommate, then," Kennedy said.

My shoulders deflated slightly. The emotional whiplash my emotions were putting me through was exhausting. I couldn't make up my mind even if my life depended on it.

"My wife can't do it full time, unfortunately," Donovan said.

"It's a good idea," Val pointed out. "You love cats. You never got to have one because of Joe."

Kennedy's eyes settled on me, and my heart wanted to leap out of my chest at her intense stare. Call me crazy, but I could almost guarantee she could see through my fucking soul. I was ashamed—*ish*—to admit I was equally terrified *and* turned on.

You have a lot of problems, my brain pointed out so very matter-of-factly.

Yup. Well aware. But thanks for the reminder.

"You should do it," Parker commented.

Owen, Donovan, and Morgan nodded at Parker's comment, mumbling their agreement.

"Yeah," I croaked out. "My place is big. You'll barely notice I'm there," I added, trying to sound casual even though in the past two fucking minutes, I had taken an imaginary hit to the head and deluded myself into thinking this was a brilliant idea.

The way she stared at me after a few beats was sort of... different. With an edge of vulnerability I had never seen in her. In that moment, I knew I had made the right call. And I was determined to make her accept the hand I was willing to lend.

"How about this? We can talk another day. Just the two of us," I added softly.

She thinned her lips with a nod. "Fine. We'll talk."

I managed to give her a casual smile with a small nod, even though my heart wanted nothing more than to do a backflip at the thought of living with the woman I had a mild crush on.

I was so fucked.

FIVE

KENNEDY

I'M A GROWING BOY, I CAN HANDLE IT.

MY LIFE WAS A GIGANTIC JOKE.

At least since I lost everything.

You'd think shoving a three-year engagement down the drain would have been the hardest part, but *nope*. Moving out of the very spacious, three-bedroom condo because the place had been a gift to Joe by his parents was. I never felt comfortable with the fact we didn't own something together, and it was a constant conversation in our relationship, but ultimately, Joe convinced me to stay put until after our wedding. I couldn't argue with his logic, since the wedding expenses were quickly stacking up.

In the end, though, I was grateful we didn't own anything together. Considering how unhelpful Joe was with the aftermath of the wedding that never happened, I couldn't bring myself to imagine what a nightmare it would have been to divide any assets. I was already in enough debt as it was, and even though Joe should have been helping me pay-off everything we weren't able to cancel when we called the wedding off, I refused to lose the only thing I had going for me—pride.

I'd pay every goddamn cent to every single vendor by myself, even if it was the last thing I did.

Which is why I was considering moving in with a hockey player. And not any player, of course. Because life said, *"I know you've been having a few shitty months, but I'll raise you this one since you're so desperate. You're very welcome."*

Anderson didn't know this—no one did—but he was the only person throwing me a lifeline I so desperately needed. I didn't want to do this, but really, what other option did I have? I had toured every possible apartment building in the area, and nothing affordable was available. And crashing at Val's house wasn't ideal, because her boyfriend wasn't all too happy I was there, which made no sense, because he didn't even officially live with her anyway.

I hit my head against my desk and murmured, "God, Kennedy. You are pathetic."

Someone knocked on my office door, and when I looked up, Anderson's head popped in. "Hey, am I early?"

I waved him in with a shake of my head. "Right on time, come in."

He opened the door fully and walked in with a take-out bag in tow. My eyes involuntarily raked over him. I didn't know how he managed to do it, but his clothes were always so... perfectly tailored. His gray workout shirt hugged his biceps and pecs perfectly. And believe me, Anderson had a lot of muscle to show off.

My eyes shifted a little south, and oh God, the vein porn on his arms? Straight up diabolical. They made intricate patterns underneath his pale, freckled skin and disappeared underneath the sleeve of his shirt.

Stupid hockey players and their good looks. Or, well, this specific stupid hockey player.

I shifted in my seat and stared at my computer. I had countless emails sitting in my inbox that I suddenly became very interested in, because if he caught me staring, I would have never heard the end of it. That was the last type of ammunition I wanted to give him.

"Is this your lunch hour?" I asked. "You should have told me, we could have rescheduled or something."

"It is, but I'm leaving tomorrow night and won't return until Monday. This is the only time I have available. Plus, I figured you're probably hungry, too." He grabbed a Caesar salad, a small club sandwich, and a bottle of Diet Coke from the bag and placed the items in front of me.

My stomach grumbled at the sight of my favorite type of lunch. I'd been so slammed with work, eating was a forgotten task. Everything was a total nightmare, as expected. The media hadn't let up on the fight, even though it had been almost two weeks. Anthony made a statement that we took these types of situations seriously and were diligently working on it. There had been some rumors circulating that the organization was contemplating a trade, but we assured the loyal fans of Chicago that their favorite star center wasn't going anywhere.

My life had been centered on reaching out and scheduling photo ops for Anderson. I had also been planning the Family Skate we host closer to Christmas time with Val. And, to top it all off, Brad decided to assign Matt and me to organize *Strikers Unite*—the annual gala we hosted for our sponsors and season ticket holders toward the end of the season to raise money and awareness for our favorite nonprofit organizations. It was our biggest event every year, and even though it was months away, Matt was a total nightmare to work with.

How could I put this delicately? Matt was the type of man who liked to cut corners, and thought because he had a set of *balls*, the world owed him shit.

We butted heads a lot. It was also no secret he thought I

was "*too vocal*" and had even said I was "*too much of a woman*" behind my back.

Funny how it all worked, right? Because if I had been a man with the same personality traits, I'd have been considered "*strong*" and "*determined.*"

Double-standards sure were a bitch in the twenty-first century.

I loved my job. So what if I had to work with a misogynistic, stuck-up asshole? He knew damn well I'd fight him back every chance I got. He could call me everything he wanted—to my face or behind my back. I wasn't going to back down. Especially because I knew this was a test. I may have only been working here for three years, but I knew my boss well. Brad taught me many things, and he loved to challenge his employees to their maximum potential.

"This is my favorite type of lunch. How did you know?"

Anderson shrugged. "I ran into Val at the employees' cafeteria."

"Val isn't here today." I raised an eyebrow. "Why are you lying?"

He had the decency to look embarrassed as he relented, "Fine." Blush crept up his cheeks, making his ridiculously cute freckles pop. "You always get the same thing, so it was easy to remember. It was no big deal."

I reared back in my chair in shock. He sure was observant. It was the second time he had done something similar, and I had mixed feelings about it. Not even Joe remembered basic things like my favorite type of soda. He'd always been kind of clueless. It never bothered me, I guess. I understood that not every man was the detail-oriented type.

"Why are you being so nice? Still trying to get on my good side?"

He took a seat with a scoff. "It's just lunch, Kennedy. Not everyone's out to get you."

He wasn't wrong, but the comment still left a mark. I knew he didn't mean anything by it. He liked to mess with me, sure, but doing things for his benefit had never been his MO. I'd always questioned people's intentions because it was rare for people to be genuine around me, and over the years, it made me...cautious. Being guarded meant I came off as too rude, or a bitch. I couldn't help it.

I gave him a small smile. "Thanks, I guess," I mumbled. "I'll transfer you some money for it."

"Jonesy." He fixed me with a bored stare. "You do realize I make millions of dollars a year, right?"

I opened the bowl and grabbed the dressing packet and opened it with my teeth then squeezed it. I placed the lid back and shook it a few times to spread the dressing around. "Always so humble."

A knowing smirk tugged at the corner of his lips. "Why, thank you," he replied as he lifted the lid of his chicken, rice, and broccoli bowl. "So, what'd you wanna talk about?" he asked before taking a huge bite. He swallowed it so alarmingly fast, I was afraid he was going to choke in the middle of my office.

"You're going to choke eating that fast."

He lifted his shirt slightly, revealing his perfectly sculpted abs, and patted his chiseled stomach. "I'm a growing boy, I can handle it." He winked.

The movement alone was casual, but it still irritated the hell out of me. Yes, Anderson was the bane of my existence most of the time, but it was unfair how he managed to make every action sensual. I had been immune to it until recently. I didn't know how it happened, or when, but I started to notice these little things about him. It was annoying, to say the least.

"Is it true you're looking for a roommate?" I asked, not

wanting to dance around the topic anymore. "I don't want to be invading your space."

He nodded. "I do need someone to take care of"—he coughed and cringed—"Captain Sushi, at least part-time."

I laughed. "I thought the name was a joke."

"*Nope*. Unfortunately, not a joke," he muttered as his left leg began to bounce.

I nodded and took a bite of my salad as I stared at him. Maybe if I fixed him with my well-known intense stare, he would break. Or so I was hoping. Considering Hayes had been the one who brought it up, I was more than skeptical. Let's just say, though he was a nice guy and he meant well, he wasn't the most reliable of the bunch.

"He's the sweetest and won't cause any trouble," Anderson added.

"Is this like a temporary thing until the season is over?" I asked.

"You can stay for as long as you like." He shifted in his chair uncomfortably. "But can I ask you a question?"

My stomach dropped slightly. I had a feeling what he was about to ask, and against my will, I gave him a soft nod to continue.

"How come you need a place to live? Aren't you engaged?" I didn't miss the way his gaze flicked to my ring finger for a moment before meeting my eyes again.

I reached for my diet soda and twisted the cap open with a sigh before taking a sip. I wished it had some rum. Hell, I would have even settled for tequila.

It was a fair question. But I was a private person by nature. I guess working in PR had taught me to stay out of the way because when you shared too much, it'd inevitably bring consequences. But the guy was potentially going to be my roommate, so what was the point in hiding it?

I dropped my gaze to my desk. I had been avoiding people who wanted to talk about the topic. I hated the look on their faces. More than anything, I hated it when people pitied me. It irked me. I wasn't a damsel in distress. I could survive without a man. It wasn't the end of the world. And believe me when I say, I was better off alone. "I broke up with my fiancé recently and had to move out because the place was his, and finding an affordable place close to work has been impossible."

The reason I couldn't afford a place on my own was something I was going to keep under wraps. No one could ever find out. It was as embarrassing as it was stupid.

"I'm sorry to hear that," he said softly.

"I don't need your pity, Anderson." My words come out snappier than I intended.

He frowned. "I don't pity you."

I snorted a humorless laugh but left it at that. The last thing I needed was to piss off the man who was potentially opening his home to me.

He scrubbed his face as he leaned forward. "I was thinking you could move in on Wednesday. It's my day off, and that way I can be there to give you the tour and help you move."

"I still have most of my stuff at his place." Though it was barely anything. Clothes, mostly. The condo came fully furnished, and it wasn't much to my taste. It was more of a bachelor pad style. His parents had decorated it as if I were a mere afterthought. I didn't care, for the most part. We had agreed we would move and get a place in the suburbs after the wedding.

For a girl who didn't normally let people walk all over her, it annoyed me to no end knowing I let a lot of shit fly in our relationship. Now that we weren't together, the goggles had started to slowly lift. It was a reality I wasn't ready to face.

"Anderson, are you sure this is what you want?"

"It's what Captain Sushi needs. I want to make sure he's comfortable."

"Okay, but this will mean we will live together. I will be invading your privacy, surely—"

"Jonesy." He rolled his eyes, exasperated. "Are you moving in or not?"

Red flags waved in my head. But I wasn't in the position of turning down any sort of help. I needed to swallow my pride.

After a beat of silence, I straightened my back and nodded curtly. "Yeah. I am. *But*"—I pointed my index finger up—"I will be paying rent. We can come up with a fair agreement later."

He nodded as he closed the lid of his bowl and stood to his full height. "Sounds good to me, *roomie*."

I groaned. "I'm going to regret this, aren't I?"

He tilted his head back with a laugh. My eyes followed the movement of his Adam's apple bobbing with the rumble of laughter. Had throats always been attractive, or was this something only he managed to make sexy, too? I didn't want to know the answer. But boy, did the thought get stuck in my head.

"Probably, but I'll make it fun, I promise." The rasp of his voice sounded like an unspoken promise.

"Please don't," I retorted dryly, even though my stomach fluttered with an army of butterflies.

He gave me a knowing grin. "Whatever you say."

This...was going to be painful.

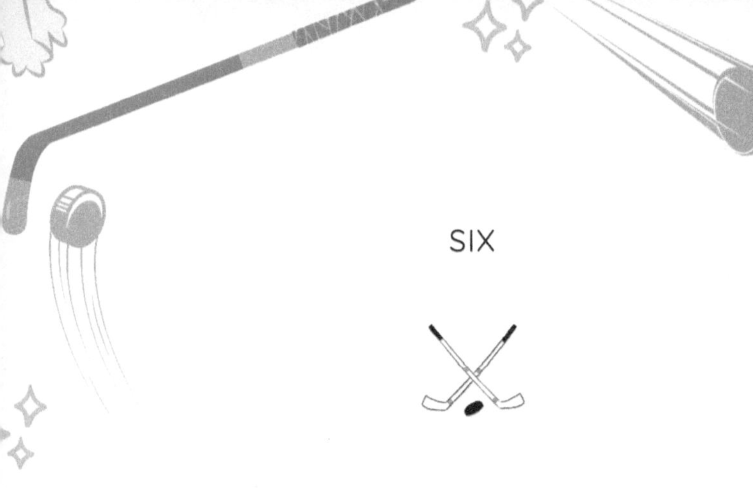

SIX

HENRY

YOU'RE A CAT DADDY.

"WHAT THE HELL are you doing here?" Hayes asked as he scratched his stomach with a yawn. "We got back super late last night. Do you ever sleep?"

After our away game in Toronto, where Coach Sloane kept his promise once again and had me warming the bench, and we lost 2-1, we caught a red-eye flight to make it back for a home game scheduled for tomorrow. Even though I didn't play, I was completely drained. The anxiety from the whole Kennedy situation hadn't let me sleep a wink. Thank God she didn't travel with us this time around, because I wasn't sure how I was going to face her and my bold lies.

I pushed him to the side, strode in, and shoved a cup of coffee in his hand. "We have to go adopt a fucking cat today, because thirty years ago you were born for the sole purpose of making my life hell. Get dressed. You have ten minutes."

Hayes and I lived in the same building, except I was one floor above. Something I was going to start reminding him of to annoy him, sponsored by the mess he got me in.

"I can't believe you're going through with this."

"It's your fault!"

"You could have said you had it covered," he pointed out before sipping his coffee.

"You put me on the spot," I shot back.

"*Please*. I did you a favor." The bastard dared to look smug while he said it.

"It sure doesn't feel like it right now," I retorted. "Go. Get. Dressed."

Honestly—and I would deny this until the day I died—I wasn't mad Hayes had cornered me into adopting a cat. I liked those cute little fuckers. I had been thinking of getting one for a few years now, but with how much I traveled, it didn't make sense. But my apartment was too big, and most of the time, I felt lonely. Having a little companion was a nice thought.

Well, two companions. I couldn't forget about my new roommate.

———

FOUR HOURS and eight animal shelters later, we were still empty-handed.

"You just had to say the cat had white paws, didn't you?" I scoffed.

"Seemed fitting," Hayes said as he opened the passenger door of my pickup truck and hopped in.

I opened the driver's door and followed suit. "Of course it did. Why did you do this? And don't you dare—"

"I saw an opportunity to get back at you for what you did with those puck bunnies and I took it." The asshole didn't even hesitate, like he had that response locked and loaded.

"This is so *not* the same," I groaned as I rested my head against the head restraint. "Your pranks are either too small or too big. You're quite literally the worst prankster ever. I might as well call you Winston from *New Girl*."

"That's not the insult you think it is. Winston *carried* that show. And he was a *great* prankster, thank you very much." He laughed to himself. "You remember when he got Jess and Nick evicted as a joke? Man, that was epic."

"God, help me," I murmured to myself as I hit my head against the steering wheel a few times.

I was defeated and ready to call it, but I still turned on the engine of my truck and drove to our last shelter of the day.

If we didn't find a cat to adopt, I didn't know how I was going to get myself out of the situation. If Kennedy ever found out we lied to her, she would probably kill me and make it look like an accident.

I shivered at the thought.

It was insane to say yes to this arrangement. But something shifted in me when I saw how uncomfortable she looked when Hayes and Val brought up her living situation. Kennedy was the type of woman who had her shit together and never showed any vulnerability. She was meticulous and a pain in the ass planner. Needless to say, seeing her so uncertain was unsettling.

After one long hour in traffic, we arrived at the last shelter. This one was in the suburbs, and the place looked run-down, with chipped paint and a sign that needed a serious upgrade. As my eyes took in the rundown shelter, the little confidence I had left flew out the window.

I pulled open the door, and the doorbell jingled. The inside, though still decades old, had a homey feel to it. There was soft rock music playing in the background, and there was an enclosed playground with beds, toys, and anything you could think of with some cute-looking pups. Some were playing, while others were chilling in their beds, not even aware of our arrival.

"Coming!" someone yelled from the back.

After a few minutes, an old, small lady came out of the back room. "What can I help you with, gentlemen?"

"Hi, ma'am." Hayes smiled at her. "We're looking to adopt a cat today!" he announced eagerly.

You may be wondering why I hadn't killed him yet. And honestly, your guess was as good as mine. He may have been my childhood best friend, but the dude was *annoying as fuck.*

"Anything in mind?"

"What do you have?" I asked.

She walked to the back door and beckoned us with her finger to follow her. The room was spacious and full of cages with dogs of all sizes, most of them barking and wagging their tails excitedly. The lady continued to the back, where there was a private room with three cats hanging around a fluffy tower.

"Dude!" Hayes slapped my chest with the back of his hand and nodded at the top of the tower, where a big, fluffy black cat was curled up sleeping. And what do you know? *It had white paws.*

"That one." I pointed at it. "Is he available?"

"He is, but..." She grimaced. "He has been returned a few times. He has a bit of a separation anxiety problem."

"Our prayers have been answered!" Hayes clasped his hands, looking up at the ceiling.

The woman stared at Hayes like he'd lost his mind. To her credit, she was probably not far from the truth.

My shoulders sagged in relief. "I'll take him."

———

"WELCOME HOME, CAPTAIN SUSHI." Hayes placed the cat crate in the foyer entrance and opened it.

The cat exited his crate, taking slow steps as he looked around, unsure of his surroundings. I left Hayes to deal with our new furry friend as I strode into the kitchen and dropped all the pet store shopping bags on the counters.

"You need anything else?" Hayes asked, striding into the kitchen with Captain Sushi in tow.

I cringed at the thought of the poor cat's name. I should have changed it. But it suited him. His eyes were this beautiful, strange orange color. I swear, it was like the cat dropped from heaven itself to do me a solid.

"A time machine to go back in time and never meet you," I grumbled as I took all the toys and food out of the bags.

"The way I see it, you're a cat daddy now." He leaned against the kitchen island and crossed one ankle over the other. "Cats are cute as hell, and you get to live with your crush."

"A cat I did not ask for!" I shouted as I pointed to the pet in question. "And can you stop spreading lies around? I *don't* have a crush on Kennedy."

Hayes gasped and picked Captain Sushi off the floor then blocked his ears. "He's your *baby*, and he can hear you." He brought the cat to his chest in a protective hug. "And please, if you want to live in denial, that's fine by me. But you *do* have a crush, and I *did* do you a favor," he replied with a shrug as he gave me an *I'm-right-and-you-know-it* look. "You can thank me when you read your vows at the wedding."

"What fucking wedding?"

He stared at me with a blank expression. "Yours and Kennedy's, of course."

I closed my eyes and rubbed my temples. I was over the ridiculous conversation. "Get the fuck out before I kill you, Hayes. You're giving me a pounding headache."

"That's no way to talk to the godfather of your child, you know."

I gaped at him in disbelief. "Godfather? *Ha.* You can barely take care of yourself, idiot."

He kissed Captain Sushi's head. "Don't listen to your daddy, he's just nervous because your future mommy is moving in here."

I took the cat from him and pushed him toward the exit. "Out. *Now.*"

I finally pushed him out the door and started to close it, but Hayes pushed it back, his head popping inside as he talked to the cat. "Don't worry, baby. Uncle Hayes will be back in no time with treats and toys."

"Get out, Hayes," I growled, frustrated.

"Good lu—" He didn't get to finish his sentence because I shut the door in his face. He pounded the door once as he shouted, "*Dick!*"

I rolled my eyes and looked at my new friend. "It's just you and me now, buddy."

How was my life even real? I still couldn't believe I was a pet owner.

The big, fluffy cat looked at me with his majestic, orange eyes and tilted his head like he was trying to decipher my words, or potentially plot my murder.

"Please don't kill me," I mumbled and bopped his nose softly. "You're kind of cute, and I don't want to die."

He simply meowed and jumped out of my arms.

"I hope that meow means you agree," I shouted once he was out of sight then rubbed my face and muttered, "*Fuck.*"

SEVEN

KENNEDY

MY EYES ARE UP HERE, PRETTY GIRL.

THE TOWERING skyscraper where Anderson resided sat in the heart of downtown Chicago, and it was only a ten-minute drive to our offices and training facilities. And by the looks of the *very* fancy building, there was no way I could afford whatever rent he would be asking for.

Why didn't I set the terms before agreeing? Since when was I this irresponsible?

You were desperate. That's all.

I parked my trusty old blue Honda Civic at one of the meters and put enough money in it to last until the next morning. Paying for a meter spot every day wasn't exactly ideal, plus there was the whole first-come-first-served basis, and I had too many late work nights to risk it. But judging by the exterior of where I was going to be living, I doubted I was going to be able to afford whatever they charged for a parking space.

With a tired sigh, I opened the trunk of my car and grabbed my suitcase. I glanced at the fancy-looking building one last time before striding into the lobby with my heart beating painfully against my ribcage.

The concierge made quick work of putting me in the system then they handed me a key that Anderson had requested to have waiting for me. So with keys in hand, I strode to the elevator, tapped the key fob on the elevator systems, and they automatically opened. Once I started ascending, my nerves settled in the pit of my stomach.

I tilted my head back, closed my eyes, and took a deliberate gulp, as if it could help alleviate the dread I was experiencing.

Is this really what my life had boiled down to? A mere few months ago, everything felt solid.

I had a plan. A good one—*or so I thought.*

It was straightforward. I was going to get married, move to the suburbs, and live a normal life. But all those plans unraveled so fast, it was like the rug got yanked out from under me, and I was still falling into the abyss.

"You're being dramatic," Joe said as he gripped the edges of the table we were sitting at. The restaurant was bustling with activity, and the last thing he wanted was to cause a scene. "I'll be making some serious money now, and you want to keep your silly job?" he asked in genuine disbelief.

At that point, I'd heard it all: that my job was simple and unimportant, that I should be focusing on other things—more ladylike things, as his mother loved to call them.

It started subtly at first, with little comments here and there. His parents had always had issues with me. His mom, more specifically, with her backhanded remarks about how much of a "working woman" I was and how I needed to shift my priorities. Code for: stay home and become a baby-making machine.

"This is not a silly fucking job, Joe. I work for one of the best hockey teams in the League, which has always been my dream. I made it to senior PR specialist in a year. Do you have any idea how hard I worked for it?" I replied, keeping my voice controlled. I couldn't show any signs of emotions in front of Joe.

He would try to use them against me. He'd point out how "emotional" I was being, which inevitably led to him gaslighting me into apologizing for having feelings in the first place.

It was fucked up and frustrating, but he always managed to get an apology out of me, even if it wasn't a genuine one.

"Why does it matter? You can stay home now and, I don't know, join a book club or something." He waved his hand dismissively.

I gripped my glass of wine, forcing myself to take a measured sip of the fruity liquid to calm my nerves. In reality, all I wanted to do was grab the bottle in front of me and down it in one go. I was just so sick of his constant condescending tone and treatment.

"What are you saying? That it's either you or my job?" There was no way he was being serious. I knew he'd been having issues with my job lately—the late nights and all—but this was too far.

When he'd come home earlier and said, "Get dressed. I have important news to share," I knew he was talking about his promotion. It was all he'd cared about for the past year and a half, and I was happy for him. I was his number-one supporter, because I thought that's what we were supposed to be for each other. Even though it had started to feel very one-sided lately, I'd looked the other way and ignored all the signs, convincing myself it was all in my head.

But then, after confirming he got the promotion, he'd dared to say, "Now you can quit your job and stay home." He knew full-well this was never part of my plan. I'd always been open about the fact that I wanted to focus on my career. It was no goddamn secret.

"Yes," he replied gruffly. "I want a wife who can stay home and focus on the kids and take care of the house."

The laugh that bubbled out of me was...strange. I couldn't

recognize it. It was like I'd entered another dimension. My life was bursting into flames, and I couldn't do anything to stop it.

"That's not who I am. You've always known that," I retorted.

He shrugged casually, as if we were discussing the weather and not my future and the years of hard work I had put in. "Things have changed. We'll have money now."

I scoffed. We both knew it was bullshit. He'd said many times that worst-case scenario, he'd go back to his dad's firm and become his right-hand man. Joe was anything but out of options —nepo baby and all.

"I'm not quitting," I croaked. "It's never been about the money for me, and you know it."

"K," he muttered, impatience lacing his tone. I hated when he called me that, and he knew it. But he loved to take any opportunity to get under my skin. "Why are you so obsessed with your job? Wouldn't you rather stay home?" he pressed.

"No, Joe," I replied, my tone icy. "I wouldn't rather stay home, that's not me. How many times do I have to say it? Have I not been clear for four fucking years?"

"So you want to, what, work your whole life?" He shook his head like the thought was insane. "I'm offering you something any other woman would say yes to without batting an eye," he added condescendingly.

I wish I could have sat there and pretended to be shocked, but I was used to our dynamic by then.

For most of our relationship, it was like we were competitors more than anything else. I used to think it was a fun way to push each other to be better. But then Joe became like a madman with wanting to have more than me, or always have the upper hand. It became toxic.

My eye twitched at his comment. Yeah, right. Because that's

what all women are supposed to want—a white-picket-fence house with kids and a book club, filling their time with hobbies and waiting for their husbands at home like a 1950s rom-com.

I understood some women wanted that life. Enjoyed it, even. That's why women like Susan B. Anthony and Alice Paul fought for the right to choose. Women deserved options.

And I respected homemakers. Hell, my mom was one and loved every second of it. But that was not the life I wanted for myself. Period.

"It's not what I want, Joe," I said, defeated.

He sighed, scrubbing his face. "K, come on. You know this is what's best for our future, our marriage. Don't you want to make this work? Isn't that what relationships are about? Sacrifices?"

It was in that moment I knew we were over. It was clear I didn't matter. My happiness and what I wanted to do with my life were an afterthought in his grand plan.

Without giving it a second thought and not wanting my resolve to crumble, I rose from my seat and slid off my engagement ring, placing it in front of him. The finality of it all felt like I was able to breathe properly. Like I hadn't taken a full inhale in the four years we were together.

Ending an engagement may have seemed drastic for some people. But what they didn't know was how long I had suffered in silence.

My heart and despair had found companionship in each other. They intertwined and rooted themselves inside me. No one could understand this emptiness I had, even though I was sharing my life with someone.

I was utterly and completely alone in a monogamous relationship.

Do you know how horrible that is? It was like standing in a house made out of glass as I watched how life passed me by.

Everyone around me was thriving and falling in love, and I was just...standing still. All alone.

I was sick of feeling like I had to beg to be loved. Like I had to shape myself to be what people expected from me. As though there was something so fundamentally wrong with me, and I was the only one to blame.

I was just...done. Once and for all.

The ding of the elevator doors opening snapped me out of the bitter memory.

That was a long night. Joe had a lot to say after he followed me home, and I found it hard to believe he was the same person I had spent so much time with. The most shocking part of it all? I wasn't heartbroken. I didn't know what I was, but I knew I didn't need to mourn our relationship.

I stepped out of the elevator and looked around until I spotted Anderson's apartment number. The team had an early practice, so I wasn't sure if he was back already or not. Still, it didn't feel right to use my new key, so I took a deep breath and knocked on the door instead.

"One sec," Anderson shouted from the other side of the door.

I heard his steps approaching, and the closer he got, the more queasy my stomach became. I swallowed hard, desperately trying to get rid of the dry, gritty sensation in my mouth.

This was a terrible idea. What the hell was I thinking?

Before I could dwell on it any longer and run back downstairs to get away from this place, he opened the door.

"Jonesy." He grinned, and while the nickname irritated the hell out of me, the lopsided smile he flashed—complete with those *stupid* dimples—made my stomach do an embarrassing flip. I shut down the nonsense feeling as fast as it showed up.

He opened the door wider, lifting his arm and leaning it against it. "Come in."

Without a word, I death-gripped the handle of my suitcase and hesitated for a moment before strolling in. My eyes roamed the area, taking everything in. The foyer was wide, with shiny white marble floors and a black matte table with shoe storage, not a trace of dust in sight. The walls were a cool light gray, adorned with minimalistic, mute paintings.

He shut the door, and when he stood closer to me, my nostrils were assaulted with his spicy, masculine scent. He smelled of bergamot with a hint of something earthy and smoky...like vetiver. It was a bold scent, which, oddly enough, suited him.

"Do you have any boxes in your car we need to bring up?"

"Not many. But I can take care of those later."

He reached for my suitcase handle, his knuckles grazing my hand. The touch was unexpectedly charged, so I retracted my hand quickly, desperately trying to tame the buzzing sensation rippling through my body.

"I'll give you the tour, and then I'll go get them while you get settled." He walked down the foyer, and I aimlessly followed after him.

I wasn't a stranger to fancy things. Joe's parents came from old money and loved to flaunt it every chance they got. But as I took in the apartment, I was at a loss for words.

The place was an open concept with floor-to-ceiling windows wrapped around the living room and the side of the kitchen, offering a perfect view of Navy Pier and the bustling city. The view alone took my breath away. It had to be beautiful at night, especially with the fireworks happening almost every evening at the Pier during the summer.

Something purred and rubbed against my legs, and when I looked down, I found a fluffy black cat with the cutest white paws. When he peered up at me, his majestic orange eyes locked on mine as he let out a soft meow.

I crouched down and started petting his head softly. "You must be Captain Sushi," I whispered. He meowed again like he was agreeing. "Hi, sweet boy."

"He likes you. He doesn't even rub against me like that."

"I thought Hayes said he had separation anxiety?" I looked up at him, squinting.

He cleared his throat with a quick nod. "He does, but that doesn't mean he's not an asshole sometimes."

The cat stared at him when he said that, and it was too late to stop the laugh that bubbled out of me. "I can't believe you have a cat."

He frowned. "Why not?"

I rose to my full height and pinned him with a glare. "Honestly? I thought you guys were full of shit."

"Why would you think that?"

"We both know you love fucking with me," I replied in a dry tone.

"No, I don't," he said, but I didn't miss the way he suppressed a smile.

"Oh, so we're going to pretend you don't love to get under my skin every chance you get?" I tilted my head.

He raised his hands in mock defeat. "To be fair, it's not my fault you get so easily riled up."

"I'm not easily riled up. You just so happen to have a natural talent for annoying everyone around you," I retorted.

He thinned his lips to contain his laughter, his eyes flashing with a *see? So easy* look. "Let me give you the tour." He waved his hand around and strode into the open-concept kitchen. "I have a chef who cooks my meals and stocks them in the fridge weekly. I try to follow a strict diet during the season, but he can make you whatever you want. Let me know if you're allergic to anything."

The kitchen was centered around a white granite island flanked by light-gray barstools. The gray cabinets had soft underlighting, adding a sense of warmth to the kitchen. Double ovens gleamed against the backdrop, alongside a fridge seamlessly integrated into the cabinetry, and a door I assumed led to the pantry.

I shook my head. "That's not necessary. I can cook for myself."

He shrugged. "I don't mind. Consider it a thank you, since I know your schedule has to be crazy because of me."

I gave him an awkward smile, opting to stay silent because he was mostly right. Working to fix his image on top of everything else I had going on kept me extremely busy. Most of the time, I was so tired I either ate a packet of ramen or skipped dinner altogether and went straight to bed.

He pointed at the living room. "The couch is stupidly comfortable. I've been victimized by it and fallen asleep there too many times to count. I have every streaming service, which you're welcome to use. I even created a profile for you. But there's also a TV in your room in case you prefer that."

The living room had a black L-shaped couch, paired with a cool-gray rug and a minimalistic white coffee table. The couch faced a massive TV seamlessly built into the wall, giving the area a modern, polished feel.

The image of him sprawled out on the couch in nothing but his boxers suddenly invaded my mind—his chiseled muscles, the sharp lines of his V-cut I'd seen many times during photo ops, and that trail of dark hair leading from his navel downward. The thought alone made my spine tingle.

Pull yourself together, Kennedy. This is not the time for inappropriate thoughts about your coworker and roommate.

He strode to the hallway where the rooms were located.

"Here's your room." He opened the door, letting me walk in first. "It's right next to mine. The other one across the hall is my office that I most definitely don't use, so you're welcome to use it. Every room has its own bathroom, so you have everything accessible."

The room was spacious. It almost looked like a master bedroom. Floor-to-ceiling windows lined the wall, offering another breathtaking view of the bustling city. A vanity desk with a cute pink velvet chair sat near the wall, and the bed was propped right in the center, adorned with fluffy white pillows and a heavenly-looking comforter.

Never in a million years would I expect Anderson's place to look like this. I thought it would resemble a typical bachelor pad. Don't get me wrong, this still screamed bachelor in so many languages—but in a much fancier way. It was almost as if he had bought an entire Ikea catalog—or whatever the fancy furniture store was for rich people like him—to decorate his apartment.

"This is great, seriously. Thank you." I took a big gulp, trying to push down whatever emotions threatened to boil over.

In a world where kindness and help had been in short supply—partly because I was stubborn as hell—he still offered, not even knowing the full story. And damn, if that didn't mess with my head a little. Who knew he was capable of being this nice?

I turned around, finding his gaze already settled on me. My stomach tightened at the look alone. "We never talked about how much rent I will be paying."

He leaned against the door frame, crossing his arms. His biceps bulged against the soft fabric of his shirt and hugged every ripped muscle of his upper arms. "Honestly, Kennedy, I don't need your money."

"No," I replied sharply. "We're not going to do this. The last thing I want is to be your charity case."

"You're not a charity case. You will be taking care of my cat. It's a fair trade."

I folded my arms across my chest with a frustrated groan. "*Henry.*"

"I love it when you call me by my name with that voice of yours. Do it again, please." His voice was so low and gravelly, involuntary goosebumps sparked all across my body.

I gave him an unimpressed glare and tried my best to mask the unexpected excitement spiking through me at his flirty comment. My body was betraying me, and I couldn't have that... But I also didn't know how to control it. "We don't have to say every thought we have inside our heads. You should try it sometime."

"No point in lying." He gave me a casual shrug then stretched his arms. The move caused his shirt to rise, giving me a peek at his chiseled abs.

Was it possible for someone to have such a deep V? And why did he have to wear his shorts so low? *Je-sus.*

Why are you suddenly so interested? You've seen this countless times. Snap out of it!

"My eyes are up here, pretty girl," he said with a knowing grin as he pointed to his eyes with his index and middle finger.

Shit. *Busted.*

Heat crept up my cheeks, but I lifted my chin slightly in defiance. "Oh, shut up."

"I mean..." He did a bigger stretch this time, making his shirt intentionally rise. He flexed, and somehow his abdomen became even more defined. *Oh, sweet mother.* I was ashamed to admit I had the smallest urge to lick him like an ice cream cone after a hot summer day. "You can take a picture if you want, it'll last longer." The asshole dared to sound smug while he said it.

"Get over yourself," I muttered as I placed the suitcase on the bed and unzipped it, wanting to keep myself busy.

I didn't know why I thought living with the most annoying guy on the team, who happened to be stupidly handsome despite how much I tried to ignore it, was a good idea.

This was my personal version of hell.

EIGHT

HENRY

CAN YOU PLEASE CALL ME DADDY AGAIN?

HAVING Kennedy at my apartment was strange, but somehow still a perfect fit. Though I was pretty sure I had already put my foot in my mouth, and she hadn't even had a chance to settle in yet.

I couldn't help it. Flirting with her came naturally to me. But now we were roommates, so it probably wasn't the greatest idea. The keyword was *probably*—because it was too fun, and I didn't want to stop.

Kennedy sat on the bed and crossed one leg over the other. The fabric of her leggings hugged every bit of her toned legs perfectly. I had never looked at a piece of fabric with so much hatred, wishing it would somehow disappear like a magic trick so I could admire the smoothness of her skin.

"How much rent am I paying?" she asked again.

"You're not paying rent, Jonesy."

Her steady gaze met mine in a challenge, and by the look she had on her face, I suspected she'd love nothing more than to wrap her delicate hands around my neck and choke me if she had the opportunity to get away with it.

Was it crazy to think I would have gladly let her under *"fun"* circumstances? Probably. Didn't mean I was thinking about it any less.

"I'm paying rent one way or another, Anderson."

I raised an eyebrow at her with a cheeky grin.

It took a moment for her words to register, but when they did, she grabbed one of the pillows and threw it at me. "Get your head out of your ass."

I caught it with ease. "Too slow."

"Stupid athletic reflexes," she muttered.

"Already getting sick of me? That must be some sort of record," I taunted as I tossed the pillow on the bed. "What a shame."

Her nostrils flared as she took a deep breath. "I know this must be very amusing to you, knowing I'm in your debt and all, but know this—I hate when people try to have something over me. I will be paying rent, end of discussion." Her eyes bored into me, and while most people would have said this was her menacing side coming out, there was a certain vulnerability underneath that shocked me to my core.

"Kennedy." Her eyes sparkled with surprise. It was rare when I used her full name. But I wanted to drive the point home and make sure she understood how serious I was being. "I'm not trying to play any tricks here. I genuinely want to help," I said softly.

I knew Kennedy didn't like me very much. And what happened with Holt certainly hadn't won me any points with her, either. But there was this need in me that wanted nothing more than to help.

When she avoided my gaze as her bottom lip quivered, my resolve started to crumble quicker than sand.

"I don't mean to offend you, but I need to do this. For myself," she managed to say.

I pulled on the back of my neck with a reluctant nod. I could hold out against a stubborn and confident Kennedy, but this was new territory. "Fine. How does five hundred a month sound?"

She tilted her head with furrowed brows. "Does that even cover any of your bills?"

Nope. But I wasn't about to admit it.

"Don't push it, Jonesy. I'm already charging you rent against my will. I'm willing to lend a hand, so take it." I gulped, my eyes meeting hers. *"Use me."*

Could you have sounded any more desperate? my brain mocked.

I'm sure I could have if I tried.

A beat of silence stretched between us as she kept staring at me. All she had to do was *orbit* around me for my heart to want to skip a whole fucking beat.

Kennedy was *breathtakingly* beautiful. She had no makeup on, and freckles danced across her brown skin like hundreds of tiny stars kissing her face. I loved how chestnut curls framed her soft jawline, and how the light brown of her eyes looked almost like honey melting in sunlight, warm and golden.

I wondered if she knew how beautiful she was.

What was I thinking? Of course, she did. Kennedy was the kind of woman who walked into a room and grabbed everyone's attention like it was her natural calling.

"Thank you," she replied, her voice taking a surprisingly soft edge.

With a triumphant smile, I nodded. "Give me your car keys and I'll get your stuff while you get settled."

"I can go with you. I parked at a meter."

I shook my head and made a grabbing motion with my hands. "The keys, Jonesy."

She sighed while she reached for her purse and grabbed the keys. "I need you to stop calling me that."

"Call me by my first name a few more times and maybe I'll stop," I quipped, grabbed her keys, and turned around.

"I have a—"

"A blue Honda Civic. I know," I replied without glancing back.

When was she going to figure out I knew everything about her?

———

TRUE TO HER WORD, Kennedy only had two small boxes. I struggled for a good thirty minutes to get in her tiny car and move it to the parking spot I rented for her. Her parking at a meter didn't sit right with me. The deeper we got into the season, the more I was going to travel, and I needed to make sure she was safe for my peace of mind.

Kennedy spent the rest of the day in her room, so I took up the living room to watch some game tapes. We were going up against some pretty strong teams, and I was ready to combust after two and a half weeks without playing. But bench or no bench, I always studied my opponents. It was fun for me to try to find their weak spots.

This season was too important to us, and I was desperate to get back on the ice as soon as possible to help us get another chance at The Cup. I trusted my teammates, and I knew they would fight tooth and nail, but I also knew they needed me. We all complemented each other on the ice, like a puzzle. And every time a piece was missing, it inevitably messed with the flow of the team.

I wanted, more than anything, to find a way to control my anger. But there was a part of me that believed it was easier to fall into these bad habits people expected from me. This bull-shit media persona I had perfected was an armor to protect the true scars I carried.

I knew better than anyone that no one ever expected me to make it this far. Most people thought I only made it because of my father's legacy.

It was a big, disgusting lie.

I fought for a chance with everything I had. I poured blood, sweat, and tears to get to where I was. But that didn't stop people from discrediting my work. The pressure of it all got to me at the worst of times.

Sometimes I wished I had changed my last name. Maybe even erased part of my DNA. Anything to forget the fact I came from...*him*. But God forbid people let me forget I was Vincent Anderson's son, the legendary hockey star from the '90s who was still *loved* by many. It was as shitty as it was frus-trating. If they knew what their favorite former center from Vancouver was really like, I was sure they would have been singing a different tune real fucking quick.

The words from one of my former therapists rang loudly in the back of my head. *You're responsible to love and believe in yourself. You can't blame people when they don't know the full truth. You can't blame yourself for things that are out of your control.*

I'd repeated those words more times than I could count, and it worked, for the most part. But little by little, they started to lose their strength. It pissed me off knowing people didn't know the truth. It was unfair.

But out of your control. Always remember that.

As if thinking of him summoned the man himself from the depths of hell, my phone pinged with a few texts.

DEADBEAT (DO NOT ANSWER)

When are you getting back on the ice?
Seriously, son, what the fuck was that? I
taught you better than that.

I snorted a disbelieving laugh at the text. The delusion of this man held no bounds. *Taught me better, my ass.* And the audacity to call me son when I couldn't remember the last time he'd acted like an actual father.

DEADBEAT (DO NOT ANSWER)

Staining our name? What are you even
thinking? And for your sister, no less. Don't
think I don't know Olivia was dating Jack
Holt.

DEADBEAT (DO NOT ANSWER)

Are you ever going to answer me?

"*Nope,*" I murmured to myself and placed the phone upside down on the coffee table with a little more force than necessary.

My father had always been the type of man who wanted to have the last word. He'd do just about anything to have it. But my mind wasn't in the right place, and I didn't have the energy to talk to him.

Captain Sushi purred as he got comfortable against one of my thighs and closed his eyes to take his late afternoon nap. He was settling fairly well. The cat, strangely, acted too much like a dog sometimes. He was weird, but the companionship was surprisingly nice.

I heard keys rattle on my front door, and a second later, Hayes shouted, "Anderson, you in here?"

"Of course, I'm in here. It's my fucking house." I stood from the couch, and Captain Sushi let out an irritated meow because I took his made-up pillow away. "Do you ever knock?"

He rolled his eyes. "Since when do I gotta knock?"

I lowered my voice. "Thanks to you, I have a roommate now. So, you know what?" Before he could react to my question, I grabbed my apartment key from his hands. "You've lost your key privileges."

He gave me a cheeky, knowing grin. "You love having her here, don't lie to yourself."

Before I could give Hayes a retort, the door to Kennedy's room cracked open, and she slowly came out.

"Hey, Kenny," Hayes said as he strode over to her to give her a side hug.

The move, unsurprisingly, instantly pissed me the fuck off.

Though I knew he didn't mean anything by it. My best friend was a natural flirt when it came to women, and the guy couldn't take anything seriously, even if his life depended on it. As hockey players, we weren't strangers to random hookups, but Hayes was on another level. The guy adored being on the road and enjoyed that life too much to ever be the relationship type.

Kennedy hugged him back awkwardly. Knowing she didn't pay any of the guys any attention gave me a sick sense of satisfaction. If *only* I could successfully find a way for her to give me attention, it would have been even better. But beggars couldn't be choosers.

"How are you settling in?" he asked.

"Good. I fell asleep longer than I planned. The bed is so comfortable." She laughed.

It better be, I thought.

When I knew Kennedy was *possibly* moving in, I bought everything I could think of. I hadn't set up a guest bedroom because when my family visited, which was rare, they always stayed at hotels. I wanted Kennedy to feel welcomed and comfortable. The room was minimalistic enough; I didn't want to decorate it in case she wanted to give it her own touch.

Hayes frowned. "Bed? But I thought the room was—"

I interrupted him, not wanting to be thrown under the bus. "What are you doing here?"

He dropped onto the couch. "I'm bored," he whined. "Wanna go work out?"

"We literally worked out this morning," I deadpanned. "Will you ever learn how to sit still?"

I didn't know why I asked. I knew the answer already. Wesley Hayes was the epitome of a high-energy dog. The man couldn't sit still, even if his life depended on it.

He grabbed Captain Sushi and hugged him. "*Fine.* Then I'll stay here and hang out with my favorite nephew. Isn't he the cutest, Kenny?"

She nodded with a soft smile. "He is."

"Too bad he has this one"—Hayes pointed at me with his thumb—"as a cat daddy."

Her eyes bulged. "Did you just say *cat daddy?*"

Hayes laughed. "Has a nice ring to it, doesn't it?"

"What do you think, Henry? Do you think you're a *cat daddy?*" Kennedy asked with that raspy and sweet voice of hers.

The word *daddy* rolling off her lips went straight to my dick, and I had to bite the inside of my cheek before I asked, "*Can you please call me daddy again?*" or something else completely inappropriate.

"Do you guys think cats are a babe magnet? Should I get one?" Hayes scrubbed his jaw, pondering.

"Why do you need a babe magnet?" Kennedy asked as she dropped herself on the couch. Captain Sushi was quick to get off Hayes's lap to get on hers. "You're a hockey player. I think that's enough."

"Into hockey players, are you, Jonesy?" I raised an eyebrow.

I wanted her to say yes. Moreover, I wanted it to be me. *Calling pathetic, party of one.*

Yup...that's me.

She scratched her nose with her middle finger to flip me off. "In your dreams, pretty boy."

"With the way you keep calling me pretty, I'm inclined to believe you only like *one* hockey player." I smirked.

"How does it feel to be so full of yourself?" she asked with a tilt of her head.

"Pretty good, thanks for asking." I smirked.

"Can we get back to me, please?" Hayes asked, looking at her. "Where did we land on the cat? Should I get one? Maybe I can also get a hot roommate like you."

"Hayes," I warned. "*Watch. It.*"

Kennedy glared at me. "Relax, *macho man*. I can handle myself."

I couldn't help but grin at her reaction. *Hell,* there was no explaining how much I liked her feisty personality.

"And please don't get a cat, Hayes," Kennedy said dryly.

"*Fine.* I'll just have to cuddle with this guy instead," he said, bopping Captain Sushi's nose. The cat lifted his head and shot him a glare with a low hiss. "*Whoa.* Since when is he a feisty little thing?" Hayes asked, frowning. "What happened to you, Sush? I thought you liked me."

"*Sush?*" I asked with a frown.

"His name is too fucking long, so I gave him a nickname."

I almost gave him a retort to remind him he had named the fucking cat in the first place, but I caught myself. At this point, if Kennedy were to find out the real reason Captain Sushi was in my apartment, she wouldn't have believed it. Because let's face it—the idea was certifiably insane.

I gave him an unimpressed look as I pointed to the door. "Get out."

"So now that you have a roommate, I'm not welcome?" He gave me a mischievous smile before looking over his shoulder to where Kennedy was sitting. "Do you see this? You should move in with me. I'm way more fun than this guy." He grinned. "I mean, my apartment is way more fun. And you do know about naked Thursdays, right?"

Kennedy raised an unimpressed eyebrow at him. "Let's calm down now, Joey Tribbiani."

"So, that's a no?" Hayes asked.

"You'd be correct," Kennedy replied.

"Get out, Hayes," I repeated through gritted teeth.

He raised his hands in defeat as he stood and walked backward to the exit. "Fine, *jeez*. You're no fun anymore."

"And you're a pain in my ass," I said.

"As if you'd have me any other way," Hayes shouted before striding out of my apartment. Once I heard the entrance door close, I relaxed my shoulders.

Who knew having a female roommate was going to be so damn stressful?

It's not the fact that she's a female. It's the fact that you have a big fat crush on the woman, my brain practically shouted at me.

"Is he always like this?"

I dropped onto the couch with a sigh. "Pretty much."

"You guys have been friends since you were teenagers, right?"

My eyes found hers, and a playful smirk tugged at the corner of my lips. "You've been stalking me?"

"I work in public relations, it's my job to know everything about *all* of you." She rolled her eyes. "Hey, I need my car keys. I gotta go to the store."

"I'll go with you," I said before I could stop myself.

She scrunched her nose. "Why?"

Yeah, Anderson. What could you possibly need from the store?

"Socks," I blurted.

"Socks..." Kennedy repeated, unconvinced.

"I ran out of socks. You know, athlete feet and all." I laughed weakly.

Nice going, idiot. Now she thinks your feet stink.

She tilted her head as her eyes studied me like I was some sort of puzzle. "You're weird."

"Thank you?" I replied more as a question.

"What about the cat, though? Won't he get stressed?"

"He's usually fine for a few hours." I shrugged. "We'll take my truck, come on."

She rose from the couch and shrugged. "Okay. Let me go get my shoes."

My eyes narrowed in her direction. "It was way too easy to convince you."

She laughed. "Honestly? I hate driving, and my favorite store is not within walking distance from here."

"Ah, so you're *using* me."

She grinned. "You told me to use you. I'm just taking you up on your offer."

It took everything in me not to reply with, *"Oh, you can use me, alright. For everything and anything you'd like."*

Instead, I laughed without a word.

This was fine. No reason to be nervous. We were going grocery shopping. Total normal roommate behavior.

And, come on, it was only a store. What could *possibly* go wrong?

NINE

KENNEDY

I CONSIDERED IT WELL-DESERVED KARMA.

IF YOU HAD TOLD me I was going to my favorite store with my brand-new roommate—who was Henry Anderson, of all people—I would have laughed in your face.

Oh, how life took strange turns.

The car ride was, unsurprisingly, plain awkward.

I'd kept my distance from the guys. Never went to Tim's or celebrated any big wins with them. Not because I didn't want to. I was sure most people thought I was a stuck-up bitch. But the reality was, I wanted the Strikers organization to recognize my worth for my work, not for being pals with their players. It opened a risk I wasn't willing to take.

Though Anderson had taken every opportunity over the years to get under my skin, and I couldn't lie—he succeeded a few times. He loved being a shameless flirt and a jokester. I'd always found his personality annoying, and...a lot. But now we were roommates, and I needed to work on being nicer to him and to the rest of the team, too.

When I broke up with Joe, I realized how secluded I'd become. It was why I went to Tim's after the home opener

game, despite the clusterfuck that day had been. I needed to go out and socialize more.

I was in the midst of a mid-life crisis, trying to figure out who I was, single. On top of that, I needed to learn how to let go of the reins a little. It felt like high school all over again—when you're trying to figure out who you are and where you belong. It was draining as hell.

Henry parked then put on a black cap and pulled up the hood of his gray hoodie, successfully hiding his face enough so he wouldn't get recognized.

He hopped out of the truck. "Stay right there."

Before I could question him, he shut his door, walked around to the passenger side, and opened the door for me.

I shot him an unimpressed glare. "You're such a cliché, Anderson."

"You say cliché, I say gentleman. My mother taught me how to treat women," he quipped very matter-of-factly.

"And what about that attitude of yours? Did she teach you that, too?" I asked as I hopped out of the truck.

He shut the door with a hearty laugh, sending unexpected shivers down my spine. "Fuck, I forget how feisty you tend to be."

A smug smile stretched across my face as I grabbed a shopping cart. "I'll take that as a compliment, so thanks."

He took the cart from me with as he shot me one of his killer smiles, the one that made his dimples deepen. "Good, because I meant it as one."

His words made their way to my stomach, making it flutter, so I cleared my throat to tame the feeling as I nodded at his outfit. "Do you ever get tired of doing this every time you go out?"

He shrugged halfheartedly. "I'm used to it."

"Still, it must suck."

"A little," he murmured.

I hummed in understanding. Most of these guys played because it was their passion, not because of the fame it came with. Honestly, if it were up to some of them, they'd preferred to stay out of the public eye. But that wasn't how the business worked.

"I have to get a few things, so we can meet outside in an hour."

His blue-gray eyes locked with mine, and he frowned. "Nonsense. I'll go with you."

A nervous laugh escaped me. I was looking forward to grabbing my favorite coffee and strolling down the aisles. Sure, I needed some things for my new room, but mostly, I enjoyed coming here to wander, as any normal person would.

Joe always hated coming with me. He'd complain the entire time—until he got tired enough to wait in the car. Then he'd bitch about it on the way home. Which was ironic, considering I never invited him in the first place. He always insisted on tagging along. I rarely went out by myself when we were together. If I did, he would be texting and calling constantly, and if I missed one call, forget about it. I'd never heard the end of it. So, I stopped taking time for myself, because it wasn't worth the hassle.

"I'll be quick."

He grabbed a packet of strawberries and placed them in the cart with a shrug. "I don't have anything to do, take your time." He threw me one of his lopsided smiles, and for the briefest moment, I brought my walls down low enough to take him at his word.

"I'm going to grab a coffee, then we'll go." Before I could take a step toward the coffee shop, his hand gripped my waist, squeezing it gently. The touch was completely unexpected and sent a jolt of electricity through me.

"I'll go grab it while you wander around."

Even though I was tall, I still had to crane my neck to meet his gaze. He was standing too close for comfort, and I could feel the heat radiating off his body. Yet, the warmth felt...unexpectedly nice.

I took an abrupt step back to get out of his hold. The burning sensation where he had touched me still lingered, but I ignored it the best I could. "I can go get my own coffee."

"I know you can, but I want to do it. If it makes you feel better, I'll even use your card." He shot me a knowing look.

"Promise me you'll use it," I said sternly while pulling my wallet out and retrieving my credit card.

He extended his hand and rolled his eyes. "Yes, I promise, Jonesy."

"Stupid-ass nickname," I muttered as I handed it to him.

He smirked but didn't say anything, only turned to walk away.

"Wait! I didn't tell you what I want."

He glanced over his shoulder. "Iced macchiato with oat milk, right?"

I frowned. "How the hell do you know that?"

"Told you, it's one of my talents," he called back a bit louder since he was already far ahead.

I stood there, dumbfounded. This weird warmth settled in the center of my chest and spread across my body like liquid fire. But it was a good kind of feeling, one I didn't want to let go of, but I still did. I had no business liking the fact that Anderson knew my coffee order by heart. We worked around each other a lot, and I was a creature of habit. It was an easy order to remember.

This particular store had a good home section, so I gripped the cart and strode through the aisles. The room had plenty of windows, and I was looking for the perfect small plant to keep at my bedside table.

A familiar laugh echoed from the next aisle, sending a chill down my spine. But I shook my head as I grabbed a small, pink blooming plant and placed it on my cart. Two sets of footsteps approached the aisle I was in, but I didn't bother looking up. As I was taking another step, my cart collided with someone else's and jerked me to a halt.

"I'm so sorry—" The rest of my sentence got lodged in my throat when two people came into focus.

"Kennedy?" The way my name rolled off his lips made my insides recoil.

I froze, and the grip on the cart handle tightened until my knuckles turned white. The pressure started to numb the palms of my hands, but I couldn't bring myself to care.

Why the hell was *he* here? This store wasn't close to our—I mean—*his* condo.

"Joe," I croaked but cleared my throat and straightened my back. Tension slowly crept up my spine and made every joint of my body tighten.

The air crackled with uncomfortable silence until a high-pitched voice said, "Hi, Kennedy."

It took me a minute to register the other voice. I did a double-take when I realized where it was coming from. The woman standing next to Joe looked somewhat familiar, though I couldn't quite place her.

"I'm Meghan. Scott's daughter, remember?" She smiled at me, though it was forced and didn't reach her eyes.

Ah. Scott was Joe's boss, if I remembered correctly.

"Right." I nodded quickly. "Nice to see you again."

Meghan was young and pretty in an obvious sort of way. She was petite and skinny, with perfectly styled blonde hair and green eyes. The type of girl I used to envy when I was a teenager. But the older I got, the more I learned to accept myself. Yes, I was different; there was no denying it. But I was still beautiful. I learned to love the complexity of my skin and my curls, and the normal brown color of my eyes. Though insecurity still crept in sometimes, because I was still human, I never stopped loving myself.

I could see Joe settling with her. She was the sort of woman Joe's parents expected him to be with. Dainty. Sweet. Someone who came from money and connections.

A pang of annoyance flickered through me as another uncomfortable silence passed between us. Chicago was a big city, but I still managed to run into him. *Un-fucking-believable.*

"Babe, go grab the ingredients for tonight's dinner, and I'll meet you in a few, yeah? I gotta talk to Kennedy."

Oh, goodie. I think getting my teeth pulled would have been more enjoyable than enduring a conversation with him.

She smiled at Joe then looked back at me and awkwardly waved before walking away with their shopping cart.

"I've been meaning to call you," Joe said.

"Well, here I am."

I was at a point in my life where I wasn't going to be pleasant if I didn't want to. I also didn't have the energy to pretend for the sake of a man's ego. Joe had made sure of that. Still, I knew it was mostly my fault. He didn't *force* me to be in a relationship with him. He didn't *force* me to waste my time. But the memory of how much I had settled stung. It was a normal way of feeling, I supposed. Though I hated every single second of it.

"You haven't picked up the rest of your stuff."

I crossed my arms and fisted my hands as I stabbed my palms with my perfectly manicured nails, not wanting to seem fidgety in front of him. "I've been busy."

His gaze shifted to my shopping cart, unimpressed. "Clearly," he scoffed.

"I'll try to go as soon as possible. Is that all?"

His eyes darted upward, refusing to meet my gaze. A nervous tick of his that always got on my nerves. "The sooner the better, because I'm in the process of selling the place." His comment took me by surprise, and it must have shown on my face, because he so gracefully—and for literally no reason—added, "I'm moving in with Meghan."

The words shocked me at first. I half-expected them to hurt like alcohol being rubbed into a freshly made wound. But when the pain didn't come, and what surged was bitterness instead, I drew a sharp breath as a dark chuckle slipped past my lips. "*Funny*. I thought you were incapable of letting that place go." The knot in my throat tightened with every word.

I didn't expect him to have a hard time moving on. When we broke up, we made our feelings pretty clear. The bitterness I felt wasn't because I was hurting or mourning the relationship we once had. There wasn't *anything* left to mourn.

But the dark thought crept out of the shadows and took hold of me.

It hurt knowing he *was* capable of change, *just not with me.* Part of me always knew I had never been Joe's first choice. Now that we were broken up and I could see it from a different perspective, the signs were there. I was just blind to it. But seeing it in real time was a much different dose of reality, one I wasn't ready to swallow.

The realization that I longed to be someone's priority hit me like an arrow straight in the chest, and my heart sank into the pit of my stomach. But as quickly as the pain spread from my chest to the rest of my body, I pushed it back, because if there was one thing I hated more than anything, it was showing any signs of weakness.

It was gut-wrenching to admit I was a simple girl who wanted *more*. Someone who wanted to be loved. Wanted. *Cherished*. Because I wasn't supposed to *want* those things. I had the career, the independence.

What could love possibly provide for me?

Hurt? Bitterness? Emptiness?

I tried it for four years, and it was...not something I wanted to go through again.

And yet, I couldn't shake this feeling off. My heart latched on to a hope for something that *didn't* exist. The knowledge of it was frustrating. Letting someone in meant I had to put myself in a box, because I knew I was too much, and I was far from perfect. I wholeheartedly believed no one could ever love all parts of me, and I wasn't willing to sacrifice myself for the sake of someone else. *Not again.*

"Can we not do this right now?" he snapped. "And I guess it's a good time as any to tell you I will be bringing Meghan to Evelyn's and David's anniversary dinner."

Fuck. *The anniversary.* I couldn't believe I had forgotten. Facing all of those people... I didn't even know if I was ready—scratch that—I *knew* I wasn't.

"I don't know if I'll be able to attend."

He scoffed. "Evelyn's your best friend."

I wanted to laugh at that. Because was she really?

We met Evelyn and David when we went on vacation a few years ago. When we realized we lived in the same city, we became friends quickly. I considered Evelyn one of my closest friends, but after the breakup, she sort of disappeared.

"I have to go," I muttered as I reached for my cart to get away from him.

He stepped into my line of sight, gripping the edge of my cart. "So, are you going to go or not?"

"Why do you even care? She hasn't even talked to me since you and I broke up."

I let out a shaky sigh. *Shit.* I hadn't meant to say that out loud. I needed to get out of there—*fast.*

The sharpness of every breath I took was eating me, and I was one second away from breaking down. My chest started to tighten, warning me of a possible asthma attack, and I was desperate to walk away. The last thing I wanted to add to my endless list of bizarre things that had happened to me in the past few months was *had a breakdown and asthma attack in front of my shitty ex.*

The struggle to get out of my head was proving to be difficult. The place felt small and hot as my anxious thoughts took over the driver's seat of my mind.

You aren't good enough.

You aren't worth the hassle.

"Too much of a woman" is sounding more realistic now, isn't it?

It's true. You're too much. Not even your ex-fiancé managed to handle you. Who in their right mind would?

That's why your supposed best friend hasn't even reached out to you. They all know you're a goddamn mess.

Like an angel sent from above, a raspy voice caught my attention and pulled me out of my thoughts. "Baby, there you are."

I lifted my gaze with a confused frown and found Anderson walking toward me.

His strides were strong and purposeful. His eyes were focused on me and only me. It was an exhilarating feeling to have Anderson's complete attention. But it was also...*terrifying,* because the look he had on his face conveyed understanding, and it made me feel exposed and vulnerable.

He pulled down his hood and shook his head slightly,

giving me a pointed *act cool* look as he handed me my coffee and slipped his arm around my waist as he gracefully moved to stand behind me.

The touch was soft and simple, but I stiffened at the charged electricity surging through my body. I took a few small breaths, hoping it would help me not look as stiff as a board. Anderson surprised me by leaning in and pressing a kiss on my cheek. The touch of his lips against my skin was like being seared by sun-warmed metal. I wanted to simultaneously get away from him and ask him to do it again.

He lifted my head slightly so I could meet his eyes. "Sorry it took so long. The line was ridiculous," he said casually, as if this was something we did every day.

"Henry Anderson?" Joe asked, confusion lacing his tone.

Anderson didn't even bother to cast Joe a glance. His intense blue-gray eyes remained focused on me and somehow managed to ground me. The knot in my throat started to lessen, and I hoped with all my heart that my eyes were conveying the sentiment.

"No autographs. I'm with my girlfriend right now." His voice was tight and to the point, one I recognized because it was the same way he talked to reporters every time we were in the media room.

Wait a damn minute. Girlfriend? What the hell was happening?

Joe reared back as he squared his shoulders. "We've met. I'm Kennedy's fiancé." His tone held some bite, but then he shook his head quickly. "I mean, *ex*-fiancé."

Anderson shifted his gaze from me to Joe, his expression unreadable. "Sorry, can't say I remember," he said flatly. "Guess you've got one of those forgettable faces." The bored lilt in his voice made my body tingle. This attitude of his was what usually annoyed me, but knowing Joe was on the receiving end brought a sense of glee. And to be quite honest? I found it hot. And *that* was a serious problem.

Joe's eyes narrowed as he shot me a pointed glance, irritation practically rolling off him in waves. It was a rare and satisfying sight. If there was one thing Joe despised, it was being dismissed like he didn't matter. "So, you and Anderson?"

I froze as I tried to form a coherent response, and I probably looked like a gaping fish. Anderson's hand tightened around my waist in a silent warning. This was a terrible idea. Not the kind of ammo I wanted to give to Joe. But what other option did I have?

All I managed to say was a casual, "Yup."

Joe snorted a bitter laugh. "No wonder you loved your job so much," he muttered, his voice dripping with sarcasm.

The comment was like a cold slap to my face.

I stared at him, stunned. How dare he insinuate something so *awful?* I was nothing but faithful during our relationship, even considering the lack thereof.

Another flare of annoyance gripped me and I was ready to snap a response, but Anderson stepped to the side, set his coffee in the cart holder, and squared his shoulders as he folded his arms across his broad, muscled chest. "What exactly are you implying?" He bit out the question through gritted teeth.

Joe stumbled back a step, his hands lifting in defense. "Whoa, hey. Why don't we all calm down?" It almost made me laugh to see him folding so quickly. Joe had always been all words, no bite. Some things truly never changed.

Anderson took a menacing step forward. He closed the distance between him and Joe and easily towered over Joe's five-foot-nine height. "I'm perfectly calm. You're the one sputtering bullshit out of your mouth right now."

Joe shifted his eyes between us and then settled his gaze on me. "You're going to let him talk to me like this? After everything?"

A smirk played on my lips, and I gave a lazy shrug. "Works for me."

Was this petty? *Absolutely.* But the number of times Joe's family and friends made jokes and inappropriate comments at my expense, and not once did he care enough to defend me, was too many to count. So, forgive me if I wasn't eager to stop Anderson from putting him in his place.

I considered it well-deserved karma.

Joe stared at me in disbelief. "Real classy getting with a jock, K."

"Do *not* fucking call her K. She doesn't like it," Anderson snapped.

I stared at him, stunned. *How did he even know that?*

Joe darted his tongue against his cheek with a clipped nod. "If this is how you wanna play it, fine. You've got until the end of next month to pick up your shit. After that, it's all going in the trash."

"How kind of you," I fired back.

Anderson took a step back and draped an arm around my shoulder protectively. "Don't worry, baby. We'll go on one of our days off and pick up your stuff, okay?"

"*Perfect.*" Joe's nostrils flared as his gaze bounced between Anderson and me. "Guess you've got it all figured out."

Anderson's lips twitched into a smirk. "You bet."

A charged silence fell between us, and Joe's jaw tightened as he met my stare. "You've changed, you know that?"

I tilted my head, forcing a cool smile even though my heart wanted to sputter out of my chest. "Yeah, I have. And trust me, it's been long overdue." The lie easily slipped out of my lips.

He didn't deserve the truth. He didn't deserve to know I was stuck in time, not knowing where to go or who I was. But if he thought I was changing, *great*. It meant I was doing an excellent job at faking it.

Without a word and a clipped nod, he finally stormed off.

Once he was out of sight, I inhaled a deep breath. My lungs were eager for air, but the tightness in my chest made it difficult. I didn't think it was going to push me over the asthma attack territory, but to be safe, I opened my purse and grabbed my inhaler. Anderson followed my movements with curious eyes, his brows furrowing when he saw me take two quick puffs.

My heart sank. *Damn.* I had done a great job of not letting anyone know this part of me. The last thing I wanted was to see Anderson's pity, so I instantly dropped my gaze, and once my chest started to lighten, I dropped the inhaler back into my purse without a word.

The delicious-looking iced caramel macchiato with oat milk stared back at me, and I let out a wistful sigh. I was looking forward to it, but drinking caffeine after a huge spike of anxiety was out of the question.

Anderson stood in front of me, his facial expression softening as he placed one of his calloused hands on my cheek. "You okay?" His tone was gentle, with a low gruffness.

I nodded. "I'm going to pick up a few more things, and then we can head out."

His mouth twitched in doubt. "You don't look too good. We can do an online order, and I'll come pick it up later."

"*I'm fine*," I replied through gritted teeth.

I was grateful he was there to be a buffer, but having him witness a moment when I was barely holding on was far from okay. It ate me alive.

He nodded as his hand moved from my cheek, reaching for a piece of my hair and placing it behind my ear. "Your ex-fiancé is kind of a dick."

My laugh was humorless. "Understatement of the century."

I shifted my gaze to meet his. The world around me grew dim for the briefest moment. The gray around his irises stood out more than usual and created a deeper and darker contrast against his usual blue hues. A light stubble dusted his face, somehow adding more charm to his features.

The realization of everything crashed against me like a car slamming on the brakes just in time, bringing me back to a halting reality.

"What the *hell* was that back there?"

"What?" He knitted his brows.

"*Baby, there you are,*" I said gruffly as I tried to imitate the depth of his voice, but miserably failed.

He rubbed the palm of his hand across his mouth as he tried his damn hardest to erase the smile that was threatening to escape him. "Are you imitating me?"

I hit him in the shoulder. "Stop evading my question."

"I saw the whole encounter. I knew he was your ex-fiancé, and you looked like you needed help."

"And now he's going to think I dumped him for a hockey player," I snapped.

He crossed his arms and tilted his head, staring at me with curious eyes. "I know it's none of my business, but why exactly do you care what he thinks?"

"We were engaged for three years, Anderson. It's not simple to erase all that history."

"He seems to be erasing it just fine with plastic Barbie over there," he remarked sarcastically.

And just like that, I was slapped for a second time that day. Frustration took hold of me at the condescending tone in his voice. He had a good point, but what the hell did a girl have to do around here to be left alone?

"Why are you being an asshole?"

"Maybe I'm just being honest?" he countered.

I gaped at him in disbelief. "Honestly, Anderson, you're being a complete dick when I didn't even ask for your opinion in the first place," I blurted, not able to hold back my anger any longer.

I shook my head and left him there standing without so much as a glance back. The last thing I wanted to do was stay there, and the less I had to look at the asshole, the better.

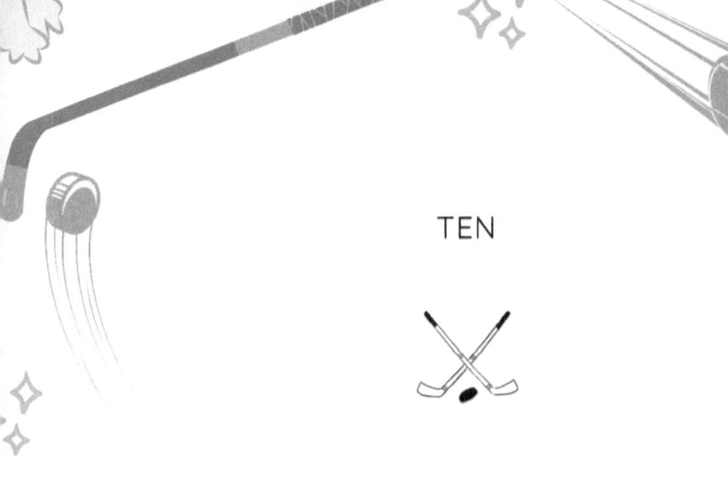

TEN

HENRY

DUMBEST JOCK IN THE WORLD.

KENNEDY HADN'T BEEN LIVING with me for a full twenty-four hours, and I had already managed to get on her bad side.

Great job, idiot. Fucking A.

I could practically imagine Michael Scott handing me a fucking Dundie Award for *Dumbest Jock in the World.*

I was one stupid motherfucker.

After we arrived home from the store last night, she went straight to her room and didn't even come out for dinner.

Should I have held my tongue? Probably—okay, *yes*—but the way she acted around him was a completely different Kennedy from what I was used to. I was aware I had only seen her in a professional setting, but I had been observing her from afar for *three* years. I knew how she acted. I knew the fire that resided inside her. Seeing the way her light dimmed around him pissed me the fuck off. If I had gotten my way, I would have punched his smug face. It would have been a fucking honor to do so.

"Morning," I said as I strode into the kitchen.

Kennedy leaned against the kitchen counter, waiting for the coffee to finish brewing. She was wearing one of her usual power suits, this one was light blue and complemented her brown skin beautifully, with some white shiny heels that added those few extra inches of height I liked so much.

I'd never been the kind of guy who liked short women. I was a sucker for long legs, and *fuck*, were Kennedy's legs long. Dare I say, it was my second favorite trait about her.

She had her hair styled in an updo, her curls adding a natural bounce to her look. Her face was fully glammed, and though that meant her freckles were nowhere in sight, she still looked insanely irresistible.

Fucking hell. This woman was stunning. And very pissed at me, too.

Kennedy nodded in acknowledgment without a word.

"Hey," I whispered and closed the distance between us. Her tropical, sweet scent hit me right in the face, and I took a hard gulp, because *fuck*, it was annoying how good she smelled all the time. "I'm sorry about yesterday. I realized I may have come off—"

"Like a presumptuous asshole?" she prompted.

I nodded sheepishly. "Yeah. I didn't mean to. It just sort of...happened."

She grabbed one of the mugs from the cabinet and served herself a hefty cup of coffee with a scoff. "Yeah, that's sort of your problem, Anderson. You do things without thinking of the consequences."

"It's part of my charm." I shrugged lazily as I grabbed a mug for myself.

"Right," she retorted dryly. "The same charm that got you benched until further notice?" she asked condescendingly. "Let's see how your *charm* can get you out of this situation."

"It'll be fine," I muttered. Even though she had a point, the truth still stung like a paper cut.

"Of course, it'll be fine." She shook her head with a mocking laugh. "The fans adore you. Big bad boy Anderson, the man who gets away with everything."

"What is that—"

A knock on the door interrupted us, followed by Hayes's voice, "Can someone please open the door?"

I stared at the ceiling with a tired sigh as Kennedy went to open it.

"Hello to you, too, Hayes." Her tone was lighter, almost playful, and it pissed me off knowing my best friend got that treatment while I was getting a completely different side of her.

Don't get me wrong, I liked her mean. But I didn't like her mad at me.

"Have you guys checked your phones?" Hayes asked as he perched himself on the kitchen island. Captain Sushi, who was resting on the couch, strode into the kitchen and jumped on the island—the damn cat could jump so fucking high, it was actually sort of terrifying—and sat next to Hayes.

Without a word, I grabbed the phone from my pocket. I had hundreds of social media notifications and texts, but one message in particular caught my attention.

COACH SLOANE

We need to talk.

COACH SLOANE

sent link attachment

I pressed on the link, and an article from *Vogue Elite*—one of the biggest web medias in the country—popped up. I could practically feel the way my face paled as I read the headline.

HAS THE NOTORIOUS BAD BOY FORWARD

HENRY ANDERSON RESORTED TO DESPERATE MEASURES?

There was a picture right in the center of the article that showed me and Kennedy at the store. Our bodies were pressed close as I tucked a piece of her hair behind her ear. I kept scrolling and found another photo—one of me standing in front of Joe when he was talking shit. My body looked visibly tense in the picture.

Fuck. Is that how I looked when I was pissed? *Yikes.*

"What the fuck?" I growled and snapped my head up to look at Hayes.

"It's all over social media and the only thing people have been talking about this morning," Hayes commented.

Kennedy strode over to me in a few quick steps and snatched the phone from my hands. She scrolled down quickly then started to read aloud. "Notorious bad boy, Henry Anderson, was seen in public looking a bit too cozy with one of the senior PR specialists of the Strikers, Kennedy Jones. Considering what has recently transpired between the star center forward of the Strikers and the NY Jaguars' newly appointed captain and star center forward Jack Holt, many fans are wondering if this is a desperate PR move from the Strikers organization. A way to possibly soften the player's image after getting ejected at their season opener game." Kennedy gripped my phone tightly as she shook her head in disbelief. "The source who took this photo stated they had been acting quite cozy since they arrived at the store, and they were then seen leaving together in his car."

"Oh, fuck," I whispered. My eyes widened as I tried to process the words.

Kennedy's phone pinged with a new text, and she swiftly

grabbed it from her pocket. "It's Anthony." She sighed. "He wants to see us."

"I'll drive," I said quickly and grabbed my car keys. The apartment keys I had taken from Hayes the day before were right next to them, so I grabbed and threw them at him. "Give Sush some food and then lock up."

———

WHAT NORMALLY WAS a ten-minute drive to the arena took me less than five minutes after breaking my fair share of traffic laws.

I quickly found a spot in the players' parking lot, but before I could get out of the truck, I muttered, "Stay right there." I unbuckled my seatbelt, got out, and walked around to open Kennedy's door, but she beat me to it.

"Are you *crazy?*" she snapped. "The last thing I need is you opening the door for me and giving people the wrong impression. I don't even know why I came here with you. I should have driven my own car!"

I groaned with exasperation. "Kennedy, it's just a door. What's the big deal?"

She shut the door as her finger pointed back and forth between us. "People already think we're together. We're going to get in so much shit because of this."

"The organization doesn't have any rules against relationships," I countered in an attempt to ease the tension radiating off her.

She tilted her head back with a disbelieving laugh. "You don't think I know that?"

"Kennedy, this is not a big deal." I frowned. "Believe me, I've been through worse. We'll explain what really happened, and they'll understand."

"How do you think it will look for me when we go in there and tell them we aren't dating?" She started pacing back and forth. "I'm doing everything I can to show Brad and the organization I'm worthy of the director position, and here I am, causing them a scandal instead, which is quite *literally* the opposite of my job description. I'm supposed to maintain a positive image for the organization, but instead, I'm part of the problem. You'll be fine, because you're Henry fucking Anderson and you're untouchable. But me?" She jabbed a finger into her chest with a clipped shake of her head. "This isn't good. Not for me." Her voice was shaky, and tears threatened to escape her brown eyes that carried so much fear and uncertainty.

The raw vulnerability was something I hadn't witnessed firsthand before, and without thinking, I gripped her arms and brought her in for a hug. When I wrapped my arms around her, she tensed beneath my touch, but I didn't let go. I rested my chin on top of her head and hugged her a bit tighter. We remained silent, and after a few minutes, she relaxed in my hold and rested her head against my chest. It took everything in me not to inhale a sharp breath, not wanting to scare her off. I wasn't expecting her to return my hug. I'd only done it because something told me she needed this for more than one reason.

I opened my mouth to speak, but I couldn't think of anything to say that would make the situation better.

The truth was, I didn't even think about the ramifications this article could cause. But she *was* right. If they found out we weren't dating, how were we going to explain those pictures? We were standing pretty close. The only reason we were in this situation was because when I saw how distraught she was after he left, something called to me, just like it had now, and I couldn't help myself. I wanted to touch her. Be near her in case she needed me. I exposed her to this stupid risk because I couldn't keep my hands to myself.

Me? I could take the hit from the media. It was what I'd been doing for most of my career. I wouldn't necessarily say my problems went away easily, but my name *did* carry some weight.

And *fuck*. This could affect her career. The way the media would drag her if they found out the truth? It wasn't right. Bringing a scandal to the organization, especially after what I did, is the last thing they needed. How could they trust her to do her job if they found out?

"What if it's not an issue?" The words blurted out of my mouth before I could stop and think what the hell I was doing.

She reared back, meeting my gaze. "How would it not be an issue?"

"We tell them we're dating."

She took a few steps back, getting out of my hold. My fingers itched to bring her in for another hug, because it hadn't been long enough. "*Excuse me?*"

"Think about it. The media thinks it's a PR relationship, so let's take advantage of it. We'll make everyone believe this is the real deal. That way the media won't drag you—"

"And we can clean your image in the process," she whispered to herself.

My brows etched together, and I frowned. I was about to protest, but I stopped myself. Instead, I quickly recovered and blurted, "Exactly." I wasn't even thinking about me, but if this was where her mind was at, I was willing to go with the flow. "I need to soften my image. What better way than being in a serious relationship?" Eagerness took over me as the puzzle pieces continued to connect inside my head.

She remained quiet for a full minute, like she was contemplating it, but then she shook her head. "How are they supposed to believe we're in a relationship? Everyone in the organization knew I was engaged. Add the fact that I don't exactly like you."

"Damn." I took a step back with a scoff. "I mean, I kind of knew already, but could you soften the truth next time?"

"The same way you softened the truth for me yesterday?" She gave me a hollow laugh. "Your ego doesn't need to be protected."

I winced. "Okay, fair. I deserved that. But this *is* a good idea..." I let the words hang between us as my eyes connected with hers in a silent plea.

I could confidently say with my full chest I didn't give one single fuck about my reputation. But I knew Kennedy well. If she found out I was only doing this for her, she would have shut it down quicker than I could have gotten on my knees and said the word *please*. She needed to believe I wanted this because it benefited me too.

After all, I was a dick, right? She could keep thinking that. I had no issues playing a role I knew like the back of my hand, even if a pang of disappointment hit me out of nowhere at the idea of lying to Kennedy.

"The only way I'd consider this crazy idea is if you take it seriously. It *could* soften your image and not put me in such a bad light. As much as it pains me to say this," she tightened her shoulders and cringed as she continued to say, "it isn't the worst idea you've had."

I smiled triumphantly as I leaned in closer. "Are you calling me smart?"

Her eyes practically rolled to the back of her head. "Stop putting words in my mouth, Anderson."

"You should probably start calling me Henry if I'm going to be your boyfriend, baby," I joked with a smirk.

She immediately feigned a gag and made a disgusted face. "I'd rather you call me Jonesy than baby."

I softly grazed her cheek with my knuckles with a playful tsk. "You and I both know that's a lie, but I'll let it slide, *baby*."

She swatted my hand away with a scowl etched on her face. Fuck me, she looked cute when she was pissed. She always scrunched her nose, like she couldn't decide if she was annoyed or secretly amused, making little creased lines appear on top of her nose.

It was safe to say I had a masochist kink when it came to Kennedy Jones and *only* Kennedy Jones.

I chuckled and leaned against my truck, my eyes never leaving hers. "What do you say?"

She bit her bottom lip momentarily. It took every ounce of self-control I had to not reach for it and nip it myself. *Fuck.* With those perfectly cupid-shaped lips, I wanted nothing more than to get a small taste and intoxicate myself with her.

But this was fake. A beneficiary contract. I was fairly certain she'd kick me in the balls with her pointy heels and a sardonic smile etched on her face if I ever attempted to get near her mouth.

I wasn't brave enough to find out. But boy, was I also eager. The internal battle was never-ending.

She sighed. "I hope this works."

"It will," I assured her, trying to sound confident.

There was too much riding on this for us to fuck it up, and this *was* a crazy idea. I was honestly a little shocked she'd agreed so quickly. But I wasn't in the business of betting against myself. I had to take my wins where I could get them.

We strode through the arena toward the GM's office, and the closer we got, the more I could feel my heart wanting to jolt out of my chest.

I had never dated anyone seriously. How was the media

supposed to buy this whole thing? We needed to come up with a solid plan. But it was too late to back out. More than that—*I didn't want to.* Deep down, I was kind of excited.

I knocked on Anthony's office door, and after a beat, he said, "Come in."

I opened the door and found Anthony sitting in his chair with Coach Sloane to his right, the director of human resources, Mac, and the director of public relations and Kennedy's boss, Brad, to his left.

"Please, take a seat, guys," Anthony said, his tone eerily calm.

The office was charged with something heavy, like a storm was going to hit at any moment. Coach's shoulders were practically up to his ears, while Mac's face gave nothing away. Brad was the only normal-looking man in this room, but he'd always been like that. You could never tell what the guy was thinking.

I swallowed hard as Kennedy and I took our seats.

Anthony leaned forward, elbows on the desk, fingers interlaced. He watched us with a level of scrutiny that made every muscle in my body tighten. The only sound in the room was the steady ticking of the clock with the Striker's logo on the back wall. Each second hung with a silence so thick, it was suffocating me.

"How bad is it?" Kennedy asked.

"Not gonna lie to you. It's not looking good," Anthony said.

"Reporters have a lot of questions," Brad commented.

"I'll fix it," Kennedy jumped in. "I promise."

"How long has this been happening?" Coach Sloane asked, face impassive.

I shot Kennedy a look. Her shoulders were tense, and she bit her lip in contemplation. I wanted her to answer, because more than anything, I needed her to know she held all the cards. Whatever she decided, I was going to follow her lead.

Without thinking too much—because, let's face it, I had never been someone to question things, and I wasn't about to start—I interlaced Kennedy's hand with mine. I couldn't say much with words, but I wanted her to know I was in her corner. No questions asked.

Her eyes moved to where our hands were connected. The way she was death-gripping my hand, I instantly knew how unsure she felt. That look of vulnerability settled on her once again, and something primal and possessive roared in my chest. I was ready to take charge. Not because I wanted to be controlling, but because she needed it.

I cleared my throat in a failed attempt to calm my nerves. "It's...recent. We've been dating for about a month, but we made it official as of yesterday."

"Those pictures were taken yesterday." Anthony narrowed his eyes at me. "Kind of weird timing, don't you think?"

My mind went blank, but we were too deep in this. I had to keep going. "Well—"

Kennedy cut in. "Since we decided to make it official, we didn't think going to the store together would matter much. We certainly didn't expect people to notice us. If you look at Henry's attire, he was wearing a cap and a hoodie. It was a complete accident."

Anthony leaned back on his chair. "As you guys know, the organization doesn't have any issues with employees dating, but they do have to disclose it," he said carefully. "Were you planning on disclosing this relationship?"

"Of course," I said. "We were planning on meeting with you today."

Everyone in the room looked at us expectantly, like they were waiting for us to break. I squeezed Kennedy's hand in reassurance. It was...*nice* to feel her palm against mine. Natural. Like they belonged.

Anthony nodded. "Okay, then. This is good. Now we can release an official statement and kill the rumors that this is a PR relationship."

"Because it isn't, right?" Brad interjected, raising an eyebrow.

I shook my head. "I'm crazy about her." My eyes found Kennedy, and I gave her a smitten smile. It was scary how good of an actor I was.

Oh, so this is what we're calling your little crush now? Acting? my brain mocked.

Kennedy smiled, too, though it was awkward as hell. "Right," she forced out.

We were going to have to come up with a plan and practice, because the tension rolling off her body was apparent.

"Okay, then. I will email both of you some paperwork. Please sign it as soon as possible," Mac said. "I'll go get it done right now." With that, he strolled out of the office.

"I'll draft the statement and give you the final version in an hour or so, Anthony. I'll schedule something for later today so we can address this with the press," Brad said.

Anthony clasped his hands. "Perfect. Kennedy and Brad, you're dismissed. Anderson, you stay here for a minute."

I tensed. *Shit.*

Kennedy nodded, and before she almost got out of my grip, I brought her hand to my lips and gave her a soft kiss. "I'll see you tonight?"

The move startled her. Her eyes became as big as saucers as she squeaked, "Sure," and quickly stood and walked out of the office.

We were most definitely not selling this. The woman was smart, beautiful, and strong as hell...but a *terrible* actor.

"What's up?" I asked once the office door was shut.

Anthony and Coach glanced at each other for a moment then stared at me with blank expressions.

"What's really going on?" Coach asked gruffly.

Anthony raised his hand to stop him. "What Sloane is trying to say is, if you are doing this for PR purposes, you don't have to. Yes, you fucked up, but you're not resorting to..."—he cringed—"desperate measures, right?"

I scoffed at them in disbelief. "What's that supposed to mean?"

Even if this was fake, I didn't like their tones one fucking bit.

Coach scrubbed his black beard with flecks of gray. "You have to understand I know my players well and I can tell when something's off."

"It's not a publicity stunt," I gritted out. Annoyance slowly crept in. I was getting tired of their questionnaire. "I respect the hell out of you both, but I suggest you choose your next words carefully, because when it comes to Kennedy, I'm not in the mood to play games."

An overwhelming instinct stirred inside me. One that made me want to shield Kennedy from everything and everyone. It didn't make a damn lick of sense. A strong woman like her didn't need a protector. But damn it all, I was still going to do it even if it was the last thing I did.

Coach Sloane was stunned. He looked almost...proud? But he schooled his face quickly.

Anthony thinned his lips, and something like amusement passed over his eyes. But he concealed it just as quickly. "I believe you. And I'm happy for you. You need a woman like Kennedy in your life."

"A woman who can put you in your place," Coach commented, amusement dripping from his tone. "And we all know how much she loves to do that."

I stifled a laugh, because yeah, they weren't wrong.

"You're dismissed," Anthony said.

I quickly nodded and mumbled, "Thanks."

As soon as I stepped out of the office, I exhaled the biggest sigh of relief known to man.

───────

LATER THAT DAY, I was at the players' gym with Hayes getting some weightlifting done. Just because I was going to start missing training some weekends, didn't mean I couldn't fit in some workouts during our days off. Hayes was even more obsessed with the gym than I was, so it was easy to convince my best friend to tag along with me.

"Can you spot me?" I asked Hayes as I set up the bench press. "I'm trying to see if I can bench over 300 pounds today."

Hayes dragged his cropped workout shirt across his forehead to clean his sweat then nodded. "Fucking hell, dude. Are you trying to break a record or something?"

"I never stop training, not even during the off-season. You know that."

Laying off training during the off-season was difficult for me. Many praised my dedication, while others thought I was too self-centered and wanted to stay on top of my physique for, hell...I didn't know. People would twist shit until it didn't make sense.

The reality, however, was much darker.

Overworking myself was engraved in my psyche the same way permanent ink made its way into one's skin when getting a tattoo. The way my father taught me discipline wasn't kind, to say the least. From the ages of four until fourteen, underneath my father's thumb, his voice seeped in and took residency inside my head. By the time my mother walked away, it was too late to shut his voice out. And believe me...I tried.

You have a name to live up to. You're an Anderson. Being a failure isn't in our vocabulary.

You're a disgrace. You'll never make it to the big leagues.

It was funny in a *ha-ha-here-go-my-daddy-issues-showing-up-once-again* type of way. I'd fought my whole life to become the opposite of what my father was, but there I was—nothing to show for it.

I couldn't lie to myself either. Training at the gym, doing drills until I couldn't feel my legs anymore, tamed the unwelcome beast that resided in me. When my blood pumped with anger, when anxiety flickered through me with unpleasant thoughts, my discipline was there to *center* me.

He laughed. "Right." He stood before me and darted his hands out while I started my warm-up reps. "What happened with Anthony today? Did he chew you up because of the pictures?"

"One sec." I gritted out and counted the last five reps then placed the barbell back where it belonged. I huffed a breath as I sat up, grabbed my water bottle, and took a sip. "They think we're dating."

His gaze snapped to mine in shock. "*What?*"

I leaned forward on the bench and rested my elbows above my knees with a weary sigh. There was no point in hiding the truth from Hayes. Or any of the guys, for that matter. They knew me too well.

I reluctantly began explaining everything, including the fact that this whole situation had been my idea. Once I was done, a silence so heavy you could hear a pin drop settled between us for a good fifteen seconds until Hayes started laughing hysterically. His face was red from his hearty laughs as his shoulders shook uncontrollably and he struggled to catch his breath.

"Why the *fuck* are you laughing?"

"God, you are *so* pathetic." He snorted another loud laugh. "You're so down bad for this woman, you somehow convinced her to *fake date you?*"

"Are you not listening to me?" I threw the bottle of water at him, but the fucker quickly snatched it with his quick reflexes. "I'm doing this for her. I don't want her to get in trouble."

The asshole fell onto the floor and held his belly as he kept laughing. "Who knew you were so fucking dense?"

I narrowed my eyes slightly. "Can you stop insulting me?"

He sat and crisscrossed his legs as he took a deep breath, finally calming himself down. "Anderson, Kennedy is a big girl. She would have been fine."

"I wasn't willing to take the risk, okay?" I groaned. "Forget I told you anything. Let it go."

"Accept you like her, and I'll *gladly* let it go."

"*I. Don't. Like. Her.*" I enunciated every word through clenched teeth. Sometimes I wanted to smack Hayes's head against the wall, because *fuck*, was he annoying.

He was right, but still annoying.

He scoffed and stared at me in disbelief. "I'm your best friend. You can admit it to me."

I closed my eyes and cracked my neck to let go of some of the tension that was creeping up my shoulders from this conversation. "*Okay*," I relented. "I have the tiniest crush on her. Always have," I mumbled.

"I mean, yeah, all of us know that already. You're not slick, you know?" Hayes raised an eyebrow. "But dude...fake dating? Seriously?"

"I came up with this idea to help her."

I didn't know what I could have said to make him believe

me, but it was the truth. I'd witnessed Kennedy work her ass off since she stepped foot into this place. If anyone deserved the promotion, it was her. She didn't deserve to lose a huge opportunity because of a picture that was taken out of context.

"Fair. I believe you. I know the world thinks you're a dick, but you're a decent man. You saw the love of your life—"

I cut him off. "I don't *love* her. I just can't get her out of my head, and I wouldn't mind if we, I don't know…" I shrugged. "Slept together once, so I can finally get her off my system."

He gave me a sly smile. "You wanna be her rebound?"

Her rebound, *of course*. How hadn't I thought about it before? It was the perfect solution to this little dilemma.

Except, she didn't like me. So, how exactly was I going to convince her to sleep with me?

"Yeah." I nodded. "I wouldn't mind being her boy toy until she gets over her shitty ex."

"Those are big shoes to fill. She was engaged, right?"

"For three years," I murmured. "I can't believe she was going to marry that asshole."

"Jealous much?" He mocked.

"Shut the fuck up," I said.

I had *no* reason to be jealous of him. He was the epitome of a finance bro. With his blond hair and perfect white teeth. The guy hadn't done a hard day of work—a total trust fund kid if I'd ever seen one. I pictured Kennedy with someone who could match her challenging energy, but also someone who could lift her and be her number one supporter. And let's just say *Joe-the-Ken-Doll* gave the most misogynistic vibes. I could tell by looking at him that he was a total piece of shit.

Hayes clasped his hands and stood to grab his phone from the sound system. His eyes sparkled, and knowing Wesley fucking Hayes, when those green eyes danced with mirth, I had to start coming up with different scenarios on how to dig myself out of whatever hole he was about to drag me into.

"What the hell are you doing?"

"Time to summon the Ka-Chow Kings," he exclaimed eagerly.

"No," I growled and stood from the bench, almost tripping onto the mat as I tried to reach for his phone. I was a second too late, because my phone pinged with a text.

With a defeated sigh, I brought my phone out of my pocket as text notifications started filtering in.

KA-CHOW KINGS
Wesley Hayes added Nicolas Owens to the KA-CHOW KINGS chat

HAYES

Gentlemen, we have been summoned.

OWENS

Nope.

Nicolas Owens left the KA-CHOW KINGS chat

HAYES

Donovan, do something. This is IMPORTANT!

Liam Donovan added Nicolas Owens to the KA-CHOW KINGS chat

DONOVAN

Owens, stay. Captain orders.

OWENS

Fine. But this better be worth it. I can't stand looking at this chat's name any longer.

ME

Guys, this is NOT important. Do not listen to Hayes.

DONOVAN

I'll be the judge.

HAYES

Okay, okay. Before I proceed, did everyone see the article about Anderson and Kenny this morning?

DONOVAN

Yes.

DONOVAN

Parker, stop lurking. You do know we can see who reads these messages, right?

PARKER

😒 Yes.

MORGAN

Yup.

OWENS

If I say no, can I leave this chat?

DONOVAN

Nope.

OWENS

Worth a fucking try.

HAYES

Welllllll, it turns out our boy here has decided to play the hero and FAKE date Kenny to "save" her job. Though if you ask me, it sounds like he's in love.

DONOVAN

Sounds like Anderson pulled a page right out of the romance books my wife loves to read.

OWENS

This is painful. Someone kill me now.

PARKER

Oh, Donovan, can you tell Aurora to send me a few recs?

DONOVAN

The fuck you need recs for?

PARKER

Those authors know what they're doing. I can always learn a thing or two.

MORGAN

You don't need any recs, Parker. You're enough of a liability as it is.

PARKER

Are you slut shaming me?

MORGAN

Yes. But we still love you, Parker. Slut and all.

HAYES

Can we get back to the topic?

ME

Actually, can we not?

HAYES

We need a plan to make Kennedy fall in love with Anderson.

ME

No, we don't. Hayes, this is ridiculous. I'm literally going to kill you. Like, kill you dead. Write your will and say your goodbyes. Maybe have one last good fuck, because you're done walking this Earth.

OWENS

Are there other ways of killing someone that don't end in…death? I'm confused.

DONOVAN

I have an idea. I'm going to ask Aurora for the best fake dating books and have Anderson read them.

HAYES

Oooooohh.

PARKER

Smart.

MORGAN

spitting drink and laughing GIF

ME

Not happening.

HAYES

Okay. We won't force you to read, I guess. So what can we do?

ME

How about, uhm…I don't know, STOP MEDDLING IN MY LIFE. HAS THAT THOUGHT EVER CROSSED YOUR MIND?

MORGAN

Donovan, you can ask Aurora what those fictional guys do in those fake dating books so Anderson can do them. Kind of like tips and tricks he can use.

OWENS

Morgan, I thought you were the sensible one in this group? That is a terrible idea.

MORGAN

Oh, I know it is, but sometimes I need some entertainment. You know?

MORGAN

evil laughter GIF

DONOVAN

One sec. Asking.

HAYES

OMG, why am I kind of nervous?

OWENS

Because you're an idiot.

ME

I'm done with this.

***Henry Anderson left the KA-CHOW KINGS chat
Liam Donovan added Henry Anderson to the KA-CHOW KINGS chat***

DONOVAN

Okay. I got the information. And you better fucking use it because she hit me in the head with her book for interrupting her. The enemies were about to become lovers, whatever the hell that means.

HAYES

I'm on the edge of my seat.

ME

You're literally standing up right now????

HAYES

Figure of speech! Ever heard of it?

DONOVAN

She said the things these books have in common are some sort of contract, or rules, or whatever. Also, fake dates. And during these dates, while she thinks they're fake, for you, it's an opportunity to show her your real self or something. She needs to see that you're a sensible guy. Bonus points if you are some troubled, broody guy with a dark past. Oh, and be overprotective, but don't be an alpha male asshole. Apparently, there is a fine line between the two.

DONOVAN

I don't understand half of the things she's saying, btw. I'm only the messenger.

HAYES

This is gold. Kiss Aurora and thank her for me. And tell her I miss her. She hasn't been to a game in a while.

DONOVAN

She said that if you miss her so much then you should give her your mom's potato salad recipe.

HAYES

Okay, I love your wife, but I don't love her that much. That's not happening.

DONOVAN

Worth a try, I guess.

DONOVAN

She's also forcing me to tell you all that fiction and the real world are completely different... and that we're all idiots.

OWENS

Are we done?

DONOVAN

Yup.

OWENS

Thank fuck.

Nicolas Owens left the KA-CHOW KINGS chat

"That went well." Hayes grinned.

I pinched the bridge of my nose. "God, give me strength," I murmured to myself. "Don't you think you're taking this prank a little too far?"

"I'm quite offended you think this is a prank. I'm doing this for you. You want to be her little boy toy, *right?*" He wiggled his eyebrows. "Well, call me your god fairy, because I'm going to make all of your dreams come true."

Convincing Hayes to let this go was going to be as futile as trying to get past a rock-solid defense on a 5-on-3 penalty kill. So I had no other option but to let it go and hope he got distracted with something else. As he normally would.

I rolled my eyes. "I'm done with this conversation. I have to finish training."

He gave me a knowing look but nodded, and we both got back to our training. But all I could think about was how risky this situation was already becoming. An idiotic part of me wondered, would it be a bad idea to listen to the guys?

What was the worst that could happen?

She would either kick me in the balls and say no, or...it could end up becoming something fun.

It was a dangerous thought. One I shouldn't have been entertaining.

But at this point, I knew I was going to make yet another drastic decision.

And hope with all my being it would pay off.

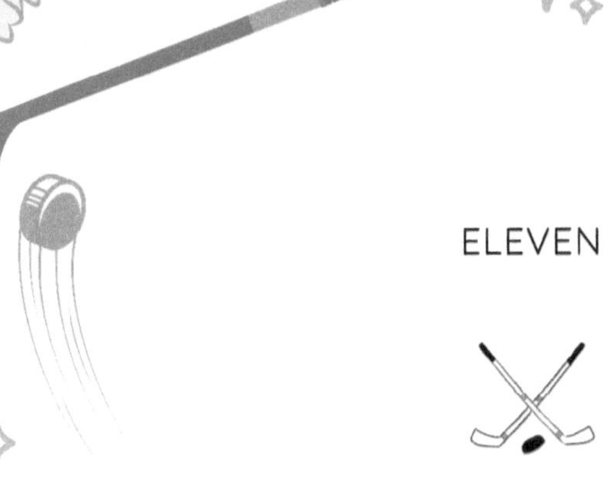

ELEVEN

KENNEDY

IN YOUR DREAMS, PRETTY BOY.

EVERY DEEP BREATH I took proved to be useless, but I kept doing them as I placed my sweaty hands against the flat surface of my white desk to center myself.

That meeting had *not* gone well.

Henry was, *shockingly*, a natural actor. Me, on the other hand? I was surprised I managed not to choke with my own saliva in the process.

Val opened the door of my office and shut it quickly. "Kennedy Jones, where the hell have you been?"

"Why, yes, Val. Please, do come in." I rubbed my temples with a sigh. "*Ugh.* Sorry. It's been a morning."

"Why did I just hear Mac say you're dating Henry Anderson?"

I left-clicked my mouse to bring my computer to life and looked over a few emails. "For being the HR director, he sure loves to gossip," I mumbled.

"So, it's true?"

"The truth is complicated." I winced. "And I don't want

you to become an accomplice, so the short answer is yes. Henry and I are dating."

She looked stunned. "Since when do you call him Henry?"

"Considering we're an item now, it would be weird to keep calling him by his last name." I laughed.

"Oh, God." Val gasped. "You're being serious." She took a seat on the edge of a chair. "You need to tell me *everything*."

"Not happening. I'm not dragging you into this."

Val's green eyes remained locked on me, but I typed out a quick email, choosing to ignore her.

I loved Val, and she was there for me when I needed a friend the most, but there was no way I was going to tell her why I was doing this. I still couldn't believe I succumbed to a new level of patheticness, and I didn't particularly want anyone catching wind of it.

"Do you know what's happening with the main rink schedule?" I asked. "I had the kids scheduled for Saturday, and it's not there anymore."

She tilted her head. "Did you check with Christopher?"

Christopher was the director of operations for the Strikers. And did a half-assed job most of the time, too. But the worst part of it all? He was best friends with Matt.

And this situation had Matt Smith painted all over it.

"He's not in today," I groaned as I quickly started typing an email to him.

"Can we get back to the very important topic of you and a certain hockey player?" Val asked.

Before I could reply, a knock on the door interrupted us as Matt's head popped in.

Great. Was IMing not a thing anymore? The last thing I wanted to do was to deal with him in person.

"Ah, lovely use of resources. Just two best friends gossiping," Matt quipped, a hint of sarcasm lacing his tone.

Val was still facing me, so she rolled her eyes, then stood and turned around, a fake smile plastered over her face. "Always so lovely to see you, Matty." Valentina was too nice for her own good. Sometimes, I wished I were as pragmatic as her. She turned to face me. "I'll talk to you later." With that, she quickly strode out of the office and mouthed, *Good luck.*

I interlaced my fingers and rested my hands on my desk. "What's up?"

He waltzed into my office like he owned it and shut the door then casually sat, even though I hadn't even invited him in. "I wanted to let you know I switched the main rink schedule. I need it for a photo op with the AHL team."

I reared back in my seat with a frown. "The rink is first-come-first-serve, and I had that scheduled for a while now. The press is going to be here. I *need* that rink. You know how this works. You can use the smaller one."

It had taken me almost a month and a half to plan this. And fuck him if he thought I was going to let him walk all over me.

He leaned back on the chair with a smug grin. "That does suck for you, but it's not my problem. The rink is mine now."

So this was how he wanted to play it? Fine by me.

"How you managed to switch the schedule without speaking to me, I don't know." I feigned innocence. I knew damn well he and Christopher were in cahoots. This was, unfortunately, not the first time this had happened. "But I'm going to need it back."

"Better luck next time. It's not going to happen," he said, casually.

"I'd hate to go to Brad and bring him up to speed on this unfortunate situation." A coy smile played on my lips. "I have screenshots and evidence that I scheduled the rink first. Next time, you can come to me and I'd be glad to be more accommodating." I stood from my chair, placed my hands on my desk, and leaned forward slightly. "That'd be all."

"You're going to run to Brad like a little girl and complain?" He scoffed. "Let's see how far that gets you."

"Fine. I won't go to Brad, but believe me when I say, I'll get that rink back one way or another." I strode to the office door and opened it. "Now, if you could please see yourself out, I have a lot of work to do."

"This attitude of yours won't get you very far in an industry that's already very difficult for you to work in."

I don't know how I managed to keep my face cool. There was no way he had said something so ridiculous to my face. *Again.* He was the one who waltzed into my office with a smug grin and a *sucks-to-suck* attitude, and somehow, I was catalogued as the rude one in this torture of a conversation. *Figures.*

"What exactly are you implying?" My voice was laced with amusement.

He stared over his shoulder with a knowing smile. "You're a smart girl, you can figure it out."

"I think it's time for you to go." I opened the door wider.

Matt stood from his chair, eating the distance between us in a few slow strides as he stared at me, trying to intimidate me.

He was going to have to try harder. *Two could play at this game.*

After a few moments, when he finally realized his staring contest was doing nothing to intimidate me, he stepped out of my office.

"Oh, and Matt?"

He stopped dead in his tracks and stared over his shoulder with a blank expression.

"Let this be the last time you reference me as a little girl. I have a name. *Use* it." My voice was tight and to the point.

"Have a great day!" I finished, a bit too chipper, then closed the door and muttered, "*Dick.*"

———

I HAD BEEN PUTTING out fires all day. What happened in Anthony's office that morning was a piece of cake compared to everything else.

My inbox was flooded with different sports media agencies wanting me to comment on the rumors of my relationship with Henry. We worked quickly, and Anthony finally made an official statement, confirming it wasn't a publicity stunt.

The biggest problem I had on my mind when I woke up was figuring out how I was going to survive Evelyn and David's anniversary party, and how I was going to face Joe and his new girlfriend without looking like a total idiot. Because knowing Joe, he'd love nothing more than to rub it in my face. It was immature, and I wanted no part of it.

Still, I had to put the situation at the back of my mind. My personal dilemma was child's play compared to the mess I got myself in at work.

I sent one last email for the day and turned off my computer with a tired sigh.

I loved my job, and working my ass off to get the promotion was the only thing holding my life together. Another part of me, though, ached for something, and I didn't know what it was.

Well, that's half a lie. I *knew*. I was fucking lonely, and the thought made no sense, because don't get me wrong, breaking up with my ex-fiancé was the best decision for me. I didn't regret it, not one bit. But I couldn't help but wonder, was this *it* for me?

What was I saying? Of course, it was. Who in their right

mind wanted to be with someone who, more than anything, loved being headstrong by nature? I wore my stubbornness like a shield, knowing full-well it was what was ultimately going to push anyone who tried to get close away.

What are you even saying, Kennedy? You should be happy. You have a good career, you're making shit happen. You got out of a—let's be honest here now— toxic relationship. Stop over-thinking shit.

When I opened my office door to leave for the day, I found Henry with his arm half-raised in a fist as if he was about to knock.

He startled. "Oh, hey."

"What are you doing here?"

He leaned against the door frame with a smirk, casually tucking a hand in one of his pockets. "I figured you needed a ride home since I drove you here today."

Home. Why did that word make me so *nervous?*

"Oh, right." I shook my head. "That's okay. Val could have taken me home."

He raised an eyebrow. "Afraid to be alone with me, Jonesy?"

The palm of my hand met his chest, and I pushed him out of the way so I could get out of my office and lock it. "You wish."

He scrubbed his jaw then licked his bottom lip. The move was so stupidly sexy, it instantly annoyed me. "Do I make you nervous?"

I locked my door with a scoff, and though my pulse spiked at his husky words, I still managed to say, "Shut up, Anderson."

He caged me against the door with a low laugh and leaned over until our faces were level. "You didn't answer my question."

I refused to meet his stare. I could still feel it, though, burning my cheek like a live wire just beneath my skin, causing a chill to run down my spine. "You're so damn cocky, it's repulsing."

He gripped my chin between his thumb and forefinger, lifting my face to meet his ocean-blue irises. The slight pressure of his fingers against my skin was unbearably hot, but I welcomed it. "I think you find my cockiness hot."

Oh. If he wanted to play, I was game. He was about to learn that backing down wasn't part of my vocabulary.

I stepped closer to him. My eyes flicked to his oval-shaped lips before I met his stare. I slowly licked my lips, my tongue savoring my strawberry-flavored lip gloss. His pupils dilated and darkened to a dangerous and delicious shade of blue-gray. His tongue darted out to wet his own lips in anticipation. My hand moved to his waist then slid upward. My fingertips grazed his abdomen and chest through the fabric before my palm settled against his sternum. His heartbeat quickened beneath my touch.

"In your dreams, pretty boy," I murmured through a genuine triumphant smile.

I shoved him lightly and added a deliberate sway to my hips as I walked away, a satisfied grin tugging at my lips.

He barked a soft laugh, following after me. "Fuck, you're trouble."

———

WHEN WE ARRIVED at his apartment—still felt strange to call the place mine—his chef was finishing preparing Henry's food for the week and offered to make us some dinner, but Henry shook his head and told him to go spend time with his newborn daughter and wife.

A complete 180 from the usual cocky jock, but hey, maybe he was in a good mood?

Or maybe he's nice, and you should open your eyes for once and stop being so dense.

"How does pizza sound?" He opened one of the kitchen drawers and grabbed a takeout menu.

My stomach grumbled at the thought of some carbs and cheesy goodness. "That sounds delicious. Can you order me a Caesar salad, too?"

"Way ahead of you," he called out since I was halfway to my room already.

After taking a shower and doing my nighttime skin care routine, I slipped into an oversize pink hoodie and a pair of white pajama pants with a sigh of relief. I loved wearing my power suits, but there was something so comfortable about wearing basic clothes.

I headed to the kitchen and started prepping dinner for my new furry best friend.

"You're surprisingly patient for a cat," I said to Captain Sushi as he sat on the kitchen island, his big cat eyes following my every movement like a hawk. He meowed and flicked his tail slowly. After I finished serving his food, I placed it in his eating area, and he jumped off the counter. His cute, little paws clicked against the sleek tiles until he arrived and started devouring his food at an alarmingly fast pace.

"You eat just like your father," I mumbled with a shake of my head.

"You didn't have to give him food. I don't expect you to take care of him when I'm here."

I jumped and turned around, finding Henry standing behind me. "*Jesus.* You're like a cat yourself. You don't make a single sound when you move. How do you manage to do that? You're practically *Hulk.*"

His laugh echoed through the apartment. "Wow, thanks for the compliment."

"I don't know why you're thanking me." I scrunched my nose in disgust. "It wasn't a compliment."

"Sure felt like one." He flexed his biceps with a smug grin. "I *am* pretty strong."

My eyes couldn't help but admire the way his muscles pulled the fabric of his shirt taut. *My God, was he strong.* Henry was all tall and manly. It was hard not to gawk at him.

My brain betrayed me by imagining how easily he could lift me and pin me against a wall without breaking a sweat. I had never been grabbed and treated like that. Joe was shorter than I was, something he loved making me feel bad about every time I tried wearing heels around him. But standing next to Henry, I felt almost petite. Don't get me wrong, I *loved* my height. It was one of my favorite things about myself. But still. It was nice. *Different.*

"I truly do wonder how your head hasn't exploded with all that inflated ego."

Before he could reply with what I was sure was going to be another cocky comment, Henry's phone rang. He picked it up and gave the concierge permission to send the delivery up then quickly hung up. "Food's on its way. I ordered a few options since I wasn't sure what you were in the mood for."

I shrugged. "I'm not picky. But thanks."

A few moments later, there was a knock on the door, and Henry went to grab the food while I looked for some plates and utensils.

"Hope you're hungry."

I looked over my shoulder and my eyes bulged in shock. "That's enough food for like five people! Are you crazy?"

He threw an exaggerated gasp. "Hey, I eat a lot. Are you body-shaming me, Jonesy? That's unbecoming."

I made a point to look at him from the top of his head down to his feet. "Body-shaming the guy with two hundred plus pounds of muscle? Yeah, right." I snorted a laugh. "Stop fishing for compliments, it's a pathetic look on you."

"It's working, though. So why would I stop?" he asked innocently, placing the pizza boxes and a plastic takeout bag on the counter.

"Where exactly did you hear a compliment?" I retorted as I opened the plastic bag and took out an order of wings and my salad, placing both items in front of our plates.

He leaned against the counter and crossed his arms. "You said I had two hundred plus pounds of muscle," he replied with a *duh* tone. "Sounds like a compliment to me."

"Facts aren't compliments."

"They are in my world."

"I have a genuine question." I mirrored his pose and craned my neck to be able to look him in the eyes. "Do you lay down on your bed every night and write all the cocky replies you can think of in a journal while giggling and kicking your feet?"

He tilted his head in mock contemplation, pushing his tongue against his cheek. "Not exactly." He let out an exaggerated sigh. "What I do, however, is stand in front of a mirror butt-ass naked and write down all the things I love about my body."

I snorted a dry laugh. "Obsessed much?"

"Can you blame me? I do have a fine-looking ass." He turned around and gave me a perfect view of his backside then looked over his shoulder with a knowing grin.

My eyes flicked to his ass, and *yup*. He wasn't wrong. Damn the world for giving Henry Anderson a fine body. The universe had created a menace to society because of it.

"You're salivating a little, Jonesy. Need a napkin?"

I met his stare with a squint, trying to mask my embarrassment. "Your delusion holds no bounds." I took a seat, and when I tried to reach for one of the pizza boxes, he stopped me.

"I got it." He swatted my hands away gently.

"You do know I can get my own food, right?" I wiggled my arms. "I have these, and they work perfectly fine."

"Not while you're dating me." He opened the pizza box, grabbed two slices, and dropped them on my plate.

"*Fake* dating," I corrected him in a weak attempt to calm down the unexpected excitement that surged through me. "And I only want one slice." I took one of them and dropped it back on the box.

"Nonsense." He picked up the same slice and dropped it on my plate again. "Knowing you, you probably didn't eat lunch today." He sat next to me, grabbed a pizza slice, and took more than half of it in a single bite. He quickly swallowed and nodded at my plate. "*Eat.*"

It annoyed me how well he knew me, because he *was* right. Putting all my energy and focus on work was the only thing helping me ignore the mess that was my life. Was it the healthiest way of coping? Probably not. But it beat crying, that's for sure.

I focused my eyes on my plate as I tried my best not to read too much into the small acts of service Henry did. Like knowing my coffee order, and ordering me a plate of nachos because he just *happened* to remember I liked them. They were simple actions that made my heart twist painfully in my chest. I never had anyone do little things like these for me. Someone making sure I was taken care of before focusing on themselves was a strange thought. Not even when I was with Joe did he do anything like this. I'd always prided myself on being self-sufficient and independent. Taking care of myself had always come easily for me, because depending on people was scary.

Henry was strange and not at all what I expected him to be

like. I couldn't deny I was utterly confused. My mind and heart were at a crossroads. Because...who *was* Henry Anderson? The two versions I now knew were complete opposites. It made no sense.

I shoved away my reeling thoughts and hit him in the arm. "Stop eating so fast! Your food isn't going anywhere."

He huffed a laugh. "Jonesy—"

I interrupted him with another hit on his arm. "And *stop* calling me that. Why do you keep doing it?"

He grabbed another slice and chewed thoroughly while he stared at me with a twinkle in his eyes. "You sure you want to know?"

"Yes." The gleefulness dancing between his eyes made me unsure if I really wanted to know.

He grabbed a napkin and cleaned his hands as he contemplated for a moment. "Honestly? Because I know you hate it, but it gets your attention, and that's ultimately what I most want."

I stared at him as my heart somersaulted in my chest at the sincerity of the moment. The timbre in his voice was low and gruff, making my thighs instinctively clench as a flicker of need rippled through me at his confession.

For once in my life...I was left utterly and completely stunned.

TWELVE

HENRY

CAT GOT YOUR TONGUE?

KENNEDY LOOKED SO FUCKING PRETTY when she was flustered.

The way she unthinkingly gnawed her bottom lip, her heaving chest betraying the cool demeanor she was trying so hard to maintain. She'd always been quick with her witty comebacks, which made needling her all the more fun, but the satisfaction that flowed through me at the stunned look on her face was pretty fucking epic, too.

"Cat got your tongue?" I tsked. "Interesting. *Very* interesting."

Did I lie? No. It was the honest-to-God truth. But did I have to go and say it out loud? *Jeez.* My filter around this woman was seriously lacking.

She snapped out of her hazy gaze and blurted, "We need some ground rules."

I frowned. "What?"

She nodded as she reached for her salad bowl and started eating. A painful silence stretched between us as I patiently waited for her to finish her thought.

She shifted in her seat and faced me. Her knee brushed my thigh slightly, and the movement alone had me like a dog panting for more attention. *Hell.* If I ever had the chance to see her bare legs, I knew I was going to combust. "Yeah, some ground rules for this fake dating thing."

"What we need are acting classes," I retorted with a laugh.

"You did just fine at the meeting. What the hell are you talking about?"

I rolled my lips to keep my grin in check. "I meant for you. You're a shit actress."

"Excuse me if not everyone can go through life lying through their teeth," she bit out.

While I knew she didn't mean anything by it, because she couldn't possibly know how true that statement was, the jab still left a mark.

I let people believe what they wanted because it was easier to let them form their own opinions than shine a light on the ugly truth. Giving attention to the core of the problem would only hurt people I cared about.

"What are these rules you're talking about?" I asked, trying to deter the conversation. I needed to get out of the gloomy, lingering thoughts that constantly haunted me.

She counted on her fingers as she rattled off the list without a pause. "No flirting, no kissing, no sex—"

"Whoa, hey." I raised my hands and gripped her forearms softly, interrupting her. "How do you expect we sell this, then?"

"What do you mean?"

"When we're in public, we're going to have to act like a couple. That includes flirting *and* kissing."

She grazed the top of her teeth with her tongue in contemplation. "I guess you have a point. *But*"—she pointed a finger at me—"none of that while we're behind doors. *Only* when the situation calls for it."

I quirked a brow. "Afraid you'll like it too much?"

"More like trying to avoid the way you'll *inevitably* fall in love with me, pretty boy." The way her eyes sparkled with amusement had my heart stammering wildly. My heart wanted to leap out of my chest and serve itself on a silver platter before her.

I liked mean and serious Kennedy a lot, but fun and playful Kennedy was someone I found myself being attracted to just as much.

"You sound so sure of yourself." I rested my elbows on the island and gave her a once-over. Even in basic, staying-in type clothes, she managed to be devastatingly beautiful.

She flipped her curls, and a whiff of her coconutty shampoo hit my nose. Of course, her shampoo also had to smell intoxicatingly good. The way my brain committed the smell to memory in excruciating detail should have been alarming.

"Confidence is practically my middle name, in case you've forgotten."

"Oh, trust me, I haven't forgotten. It's one of your best traits," I replied honestly.

"You're flirting again."

"Am I?" I asked innocently.

"Yes," she drawled.

I scrubbed my jaw. "*Hm.*"

"What?"

I shifted in my chair and twirled a piece of her beautiful chestnut curls around my index finger. "Let's get one thing clear," I rasped as my eyes met hers. It was hard not to get lost in them. I wondered how they would shine if she were on her knees for me, taking me in her mouth as deep as she could go. The thought alone made my cock stir with excitement. I'd bet all my money she would look like a goddamn perfect wet dream.

What was I saying to her again?

The flirting thing.

Oh. Right, okay.

"When I'm flirting, you'll know."

She let out a disbelieving laugh. "So, this isn't you flirting?"

"*Nope.*"

"Good to know, I guess."

"You sound disappointed." God, I hoped she was. I hoped that deep down, she wanted some of my attention. Because I was desperate for hers.

She scoffed. "You wish."

I let out a knowing chuckle. "Any more rules?"

She shook her head. "We should sign a contract."

I looked at her, dumbfounded. "What?"

"Write down the rules on a piece of paper and sign it," she said.

I could practically hear Donovan and Hayes laughing in the back of my head. This was turning out to be too similar to the books Donovan's wife read. We were a cliché rom-com in the making.

"Or we can be normal adults and follow the rules," I countered with a weak laugh.

She grabbed a piece of pepperoni and ate it while shooting me a knowing look. "I'd rather have a binding contract so you don't get any ideas."

"Ideas? Me?" I tilted my head, voice light. "I would *never.*"

Her laugh was sharp before she took a bite of her pizza and shook her head in disbelief.

"I'll sign whatever you want. But I have some stipulations of my own," I said then frowned slightly, not knowing where the fuck that came from.

Stipulations? What the fuck are you talking about right now?

Her eyes narrowed. "Why do I have the feeling I'm going to hate whatever you're about to propose?"

I smirked. "I want us to go on a date once a week, as long as my schedule allows it." She tried to speak, but I placed my forefinger on her lips and shushed her. "We need to sell this to the public, Kenny. You know how much scrutiny I'm under. If they catch wind of this being fake, we'll be fucked. We should also go to every work event together, of course."

I couldn't believe I was listening to my idiotic friends.

But it sounded fun and harmless. I'd never dated. I didn't have to when women practically jumped my bones anywhere I went. Buying them a drink or two was as far as I'd gone to hook up with someone. It made me sound like an asshole—believe me, I was aware—but that was the typical dating life of a professional hockey player.

"You called me Kenny," she whispered, stunned.

My finger still hovered over her lips, and the way her warm breath hit my digit had me taking a sharp inhale. I could practically feel the puff of air on my cock.

Damn. I needed to get laid. Since when did a trickle of breath turn me on?

A lazy smile pulled at my lips. "Don't get it twisted. I'll still be calling you Jonesy from time to time. Just because I love keeping you on your toes."

That comment won me a glare and a swat of my hand. "You're lucky I didn't pinch you. Don't ever shush me again."

I faked a shiver. "Don't threaten me with a good time."

"You have a masochist kink or something?" she asked, amusement lacing her tone.

Only for you, I almost blurted but held back the answer. Instead, I said, "I like to have fun in bed. Don't you?"

Her shrug was nonchalant. "Who doesn't?"

"*Oh?*" That piqued my interest. "Kennedy Jones, are you freaky in bed?"

She straightened her shoulders, and if I didn't know any better, I'd say she looked flustered. "Let's add not talking about our sex lives to our rules."

"All these rules." I sighed. "You sure know how to have fun." I grabbed a few wings and placed them on her plate then grabbed a few for myself.

She gave me a dry look but didn't say anything.

We ate in silence for a few minutes, then she broke the silence by stating, "We need to come up with a break-up date."

Before I could reply, she stood from her chair and went to her room. A few minutes later, she appeared in my line of vision, wiggling a piece of paper and a pen in the air. "For our trusty contract."

I laughed. *Goddamn.* I should have known she was talking about a literal contract. She was ridiculously endearing. My heart fluttered at the thought. Everything she made me feel was, *oh so dangerous*, but I never wanted it to go away.

"Does this mean you agree to my stipulation?" I asked.

She nodded.

The nod alone made my heart skip a beat with excitement. *Fuck, yeah.* Going out with her—even if it was fake—was exciting. And I was at a point where I would take whatever she was willing to give me.

"Okay, then," I pondered. "We could date until the end of the season?"

Her eyes met mine in surprise. "I was thinking more like until the New Year, but okay. Why until then?"

Because fake dating you sounds fun as hell.

Because I like spending time with you.

"I don't want it to seem suspicious. And I need Coach to

take me off the bench eventually. I'm hoping this will work," I replied, opting for half honesty.

While I threw this crazy plan together to save Kennedy's career, I did hope Coach saw the change in me and allowed me to get back on the ice before it was too late.

Playing for me was like breathing, and I was missing my source of air *badly*. I missed it all. The adrenaline when I stepped on the ice. The fans and their undying support. The feel of the blade gliding through ice at an unstoppable speed. How every anxious thought didn't exist when I put the uniform on and gave it my all.

She nodded in understanding as she started to write the rules down. She looked at me through her long, brown eyelashes. "I have one last stipulation." She cringed. "I have a party to attend in the spring. Can you be my date?"

I shrugged. "As long as I don't have an away game, I'm in. Is this the party Ken Doll was talking about the other day?"

Her brows knitted together. "Who's Ken Doll?"

"That's what I call your shitty ex."

She tilted her head back with a laugh. The sound sent a flutter to my chest and expanded with a million tiny butterflies throughout the rest of my body. I had to fight the shiver that wanted to break through. "Oh my God, you're right."

"I try to be a pretty open-minded guy, Jonesy, but I honestly don't understand what you ever saw in him."

The mood in the room suddenly dampened. Her shoulders deflated slightly.

I internally kicked myself for once *again* putting my foot in my mouth.

Before I could apologize, Kennedy straightened her back and gave me a forced laugh. The shift was so quick, it gave me whiplash. There was no mistaking the way her stunning brown irises were missing the usual spark I liked so much.

How did she manage to mask her feelings so well?

I had no right to wonder such a thing. After all, I did the same thing. But when it came to Kennedy, it was painful to know she forced herself to live in a world where she had to act to protect herself. I understood it well, and I wanted to tell her as such. But being the coward that I was, I didn't.

"Do you have any other rules or stipulations you want to add?" she asked. If this was the way she wanted to deter the conversation, I was going to let her.

I shook my head. "Can't think of anything else."

She signed the paper and pushed it toward me with the pen. "Pleasure doing business with you, then."

Amusement overtook me as I grabbed the pen and signed the ridiculous contract. "Famous last words."

"We'll see." She shrugged. The smile she gave me was cheeky as she grabbed the contract and placed it smack dab in the center of the fridge with a Strikers logo magnet. She turned around and crossed her arms. "I guess we're official, then."

I crossed my arms, too, and leaned back on my chair with a hum. "Try not to fall in love with me in the process, Kenny."

"I'll be just fine, pretty boy," she quipped as she dropped back onto the chair then grabbed a wing and continued eating.

This was a light and playful side I never expected Kennedy Jones to have.

But I'd be lying if I didn't admit I was absolutely and wholeheartedly obsessed with it.

THIRTEEN

HENRY

I VOLUNTEER AS TRIBUTE.

HAYES THREW his stick against his locker room stall with so much force, it broke in half. "*Fuck!*"

"Hayes, calm the fuck down," Donovan barked as he strode in behind him.

"I can't calm the fuck down when we got eaten alive out there!" Hayes shouted back.

I winced at Hayes's comment as I took my helmet off and ran my fingers through my hair.

The game against the Detroit Panthers went as I suspected —terribly. They had an ironclad defense, and while Zack Kendall—the rookie who was subbed in while I kept warming the fucking bench—was doing a great job, he wasn't me. The kid had a long way to get to my level. Getting past Detroit's blue line proved to be almost impossible. And when we did, their defensemen were quick on their feet to get control of the puck.

"I'm sorry, guys, I really tried," Kendall said sheepishly as he sat down.

Donovan sat next to Kendall and patted his back. "Hey, no. We're not gonna do that. We win as a team, and we lose as a team."

"Shit, what Donovan says it's true, Kendall. I just get extra pissy with Detroit, I hate those guys," Hayes muttered. "You're doing amazing work out there."

"The only animal who can usually get past those defenses is Anderson," Parker commented before throwing some water on his face.

"You just need to build more momentum. You need to glide at the speed of light to get past those guys. We can work on that," I said.

Kendall nodded, but before he could reply, Coach Sloane strode into the locker room. The rest of the team quieted down and sat, waiting for Coach to chew us a new one.

"It was a tough loss," Coach began, strangely calm. "There was nothing we could do."

"Does that mean we won't be doing drills tomorrow?" Kendall asked, his tone hopeful.

Parker and Hayes snorted a laugh at the same time. Coach pierced them with a withering glare, and they were quick to straighten in their seats. Parker coughed, looking anywhere but at Coach, and Hayes started whistling as he became extremely interested in his broken stick.

"Oh, there will be drills tomorrow. The transitions today were sloppy as hell. Clearly, we need more stop-and-start drills," he deadpanned. "You're all dismissed. Go grab a shower, and for the love of God, don't overdo it today at the bar. Practice is bright and early tomorrow."

We all mumbled, "Yes, sir," in unison.

The room started to filter out, some players eager as fuck to go home to their wives, others ready to go drink, despite our Coach's warning. I started to untie my laces, more than ready to get out of there, too. Not playing was the worst, and I needed a drink or two to get over it, even if it meant I had to hit the gym harder this week for breaking my diet.

"Anderson," Coach called out. He stepped onto my path with that no-nonsense stance that always made my stomach twist. "Where was Kennedy today?"

I frowned. "I don't know, sir."

He quirked an eyebrow with a knowing smirk. "I know she's typically busy with work, but I thought she would make an exception and watch your game now that she's your girl-friend and all."

Oh. Oh, Fuck. I hadn't thought about that.

"I'm not exactly playing, though," I said in an attempt to deflect.

"So? She's your girlfriend. She should be able to take a few minutes to support you."

"I'm sure she was around. You know her, always working." My laugh was weak, I hoped he didn't see through it.

He fixed me with a stare that made me take a hard gulp. "I hope you're not scheming anything, Anderson."

I could physically feel my face paling, but somehow, I managed to play it off. "We're not scheming anything, I promise." The lie tasted bitter in my mouth. Coach was the closest thing I had to a father figure these days, and lying to him felt like shit. But protecting Kennedy was more pressing to me.

"Okay, then." He gave me a skeptical nod.

I nodded quickly, grateful the conversation was over. Once he was out of the room, I grabbed my phone and shot Kennedy a text.

ME

Hey.

KENNY

Who's this?

ME

You don't have your boyfriend's number saved? Ouch. That hurts, Jonesy.

KENNY

Oh. You. What do you want?

ME

Are you at the arena?

KENNY

Obviously. Why?

ME

Coach was asking me why you weren't watching the game.

KENNY

You're not even playing, and I was busy. Did he forget I have a job to do?

ME

Don't shoot the messenger. I think he's onto us.

KENNY

How can he be onto us when we've only been seen in public once?

ME

Exactly. We need to go out more. Be seen together in public. The team is going to Tim's, let's go.

KENNY

Absolutely not. I'm tired.

ME

Come on, fake girlfriend, you gotta play your part tonight. Your handsome fake boyfriend is sad tonight because his team lost.

ME

I'll tell you what...this can count as the date of the week.

KENNY

Fine.

ME

Could you be any less excited?

KENNY

I am so excited to see you! I've missed you so much, my big teddy bear! <3

ME

I don't appreciate your sarcasm, but you're getting better at this girlfriend thing.

KENNY

FAKE girlfriend. Don't forget it, pretty boy.

ME

Gotta remind yourself this isn't real so you don't grow obsessed with me?

KENNY

I'll meet you there.

With a grin that made my cheeks hurt, I threw my phone into my stall and headed to the showers, feeling satisfied. This may have been fake, but I had every intention of making it fun.

———

IT TOOK me longer than I thought it would to arrive at Tim's, because my mother called me, and I had been avoiding her since the night I got ejected, so we had a lot to talk about. Talking to her lifted a weight off my shoulders, because a part of me thought she was going to be mad, but I should have known better. She was worried, and though it pained me to lie to her, I told her everything was fine.

The last thing I needed her to find out was that my father was actively still trying to contact me. She walked away for a reason, and she was happily married now, to a guy who adored the ground she walked on. Putting unnecessary stress on her was the last thing I was going to do. It was my responsibility to bear.

I parked in front of Tim's, and as soon as I stepped out of my truck, a few paparazzi came out of nowhere.

"Anderson, how long have you and Kennedy Jones been dating?" one shouted.

"What do you have to say about the rumors that this is a PR relationship?" another one shouted.

Fucking hell.

I tried my best to get through them, but they kept snapping pictures. Hundreds of dots danced around my eyes with every camera click, almost blinding me. Suddenly, I felt someone grab my hand. My heart quickened, immediately recognizing Kennedy's touch with the way electricity spread through my body.

The paparazzi went into an uproar when they saw Kennedy, taking more and more pictures by the second until she was finally able to push me inside as Tim held the door open.

"I better not see any of you out here again or I'll call the goddamn police," Tim shouted as he shook the bat he had in his other hand. "Or I'll hit you with my bat, either option works for me." He slammed the door shut and cursed under his breath. "Goddamn it, Anderson. You're a pain in my ass."

"It's not even my fault!"

He shook his head. "Yeah, but now that you've got a girlfriend, they're going crazy. They've been here almost every day, waiting for you to show up."

I looked around. The bar was pretty full tonight. "How about I buy everyone here a round of drinks for the trouble?"

"Now that's what I like to hear." He patted me on the shoulder then walked back to the bar.

"You're here!" Hayes shouted and threw his arms around me. "My best friend. I missed you."

"Jesus, Hayes, you reek like a distillery. I was only an hour late, how the fuck did you get drunk so fast?" I held a finger under my nose, trying to keep the smell out of my nostrils.

Kennedy tried to tame her laugh but failed. "Yeah, we tried to slow him down, but he took the loss pretty hard today."

I shook my head. "Fucking hell, dude. You're going to be a mess tomorrow during practice."

"I got this," he slurred.

Donovan appeared out of nowhere, grabbed Hayes by the shirt, and pulled him off me. "You're officially cut off."

"You're not the boss of me!"

"Not your boss, just a concerned captain. Let's go, buddy."

"*Nooooo*," Hayes whined. "I was totally going to score with a girl tonight. You should see her, Anderson. Her tits are fucking—"

I hit him in the back of the head. "Watch your mouth in front of my girlfriend, asshole."

Hayes hiccuped. "Oh, *what-fucking-ever*. Kenny knows how it is for us players."

I tensed at his comment.

Man, he was *such* a lousy drunk. It was no secret that women threw themselves at us when we were out. But fake or not, the last thing I wanted to do was give Kennedy the wrong impression.

Donovan pushed him. "That's enough, let's go get you some greasy food and water."

Once they were out of earshot, I turned around. "Sorry about that."

"Why would you apologize? I know how you players are."

I shrugged with a playful smile. "I don't know what you're talking about. I'm a taken man."

She leaned against the wall and crossed her arms with a laugh. "We're fake dating. I don't expect you to stop sleeping around or flirting with any woman that crosses your path."

I frowned and stood in front of her, a little closer than necessary.

Her bold, strong perfume clouded my senses, and my eyes fluttered shut for a millisecond. *God, she smelled good.* Tempting. Like she could bring me to her knees if she truly wanted to.

My eyes settled on her. The blue and red neon lights danced around her face and hair, but there was no mistaking the color of her chestnut curls that framed her angelical face.

"What's that supposed to mean?"

"You can sleep with whoever you want and do whatever you want," she said, then quickly added, "as long as they're discreet."

I placed my hand on the wall just above her head and leaned in, successfully caging her in. Her gaze followed the movement, and my body heat spiked to dangerous levels at the sight of it. A light sparkle danced between her eyes, and I never thought something so simple as eyes could be so dangerously sexy, but I guess there was a first time for everything.

"What are you doing?" she asked with a bored tone.

My hand reached for one of her beautiful, bouncy curls, and I twirled it once around my finger then looked at her. "What makes you think I want to sleep around?"

She gave me a deadpan look. "You're a hockey player. Being a playboy is practically embedded in your DNA."

"Nice burn," I quipped.

"Thanks. I've been holding that one in for a while." She smirked.

This woman was fucking *infuriating*, and I loved every goddamn second of it.

Thank God for contracts and their loopholes, because knowing I was allowed to flirt in public meant I was more than ready to play some dangerous games.

With that risky thought in mind, I leaned even closer. Our bodies pressed against each other. My lips were just a few short inches from hers, and my heart thrashed against my chest. My eyes flicked to her throat and the way she visibly gulped. I wanted to wrap my hand around her pretty neck and feel the way her pulse beat wildly against my thumb as I owned her mouth.

It was painful how badly I wanted to consume her.

The way her chest started to rise and fall in quick succession brought me a sick sense of satisfaction. I affected her as much as she affected me. And fuck, did I love knowing that.

"Let's get one thing clear," I rasped. "While we're doing whatever this is, I won't be sleeping with other women."

What she didn't know was that even if we weren't in this situation, I had no desire to sleep with anyone *except* her. I couldn't get her out of my goddamn head, and I didn't think I was going to be able to stop anytime soon unless I could manage to get a taste. Just...one single taste. That's all I needed.

She took a sharp inhale. "*What?*"

I inched a bit closer, and if either one of us made the slightest movement, our lips *would* brush. Excitement coursed through my body and went straight to my cock. *Jesus*. This was not the time for a boner.

"The last thing we need is another scandal, wouldn't you agree?" I raised an eyebrow. "And I expect the same from you. No sleeping with other men, Kenny. I don't like sharing. You can add that to our little contract."

The background noise from the bar and "Slide" by The Goo Goo Dolls playing from the jukebox were the only sounds filling the otherwise charged silence between us. My eyes raked over her freckled cheeks. Even under the shitty bar lighting, I could count them. The way her skin glowed had me wanting to lick her for some godforsaken reason. I was dying to savor her and find out if she tasted as sweet as she looked. Though I knew better than that. If anything, I knew she'd taste like sweet venom. The worst part? I would have enjoyed every single painful second of it.

"Sorry to break this to you, pretty boy, but I have needs." Her tone held a condescending bite, and the minty freshness of her mouth hit my senses. "We *all* do."

I casually shrugged. "If you ever need help, you know where to find me."

She lifted one of her perfectly shaped eyebrows. "Forgetting about our rules already?"

I took a step back. The need to put some distance between us was suffocating. If I had stayed even one more second near her lips, I didn't know what I would end up doing.

"What can I say? I'm a rule breaker, Kennedy." My tone took on a deeper octave as I rasped her name, wanting her to know I wasn't fucking around when I pinned her with a look and said, "All I'm saying is if you ever need someone to fulfill your *needs*..." I grazed my tongue over my teeth then smiled. "I volunteer as tribute."

I didn't wait for her to react and turned around, walking away with a triumphant smile etched across my lips. It was a bold move, and it might bite me in the ass later, but the ball was now in her court. And fuck if I wasn't eager to find out how she was going to retaliate.

———

EVEN THOUGH I hadn't played, I took the loss hard.

Or, well, that's what I kept telling myself as I tried to forget how my phone burned a hole in the pocket of my pants with a text message from my father.

It was funny how, even though I didn't play, he managed to make me feel like it was entirely my fault. In his world, I was the only one to blame. The logic was nonexistent, and he chose to forget there were a total of twenty-three players on the roster.

All the years of therapy I worked hard during my rookie years always went out the window every time he reappeared in my life. I hated it. I hated the anger it brought me, too.

It was only a matter of time before he showed up at one of my games. But life had been emotionally draining me since the beginning of the season. I *couldn't* bring myself to answer.

When I made the colossal mistake of reading those messages—because curiosity got the best of me—I kept drinking, hoping to drown the feeling of complete uselessness.

It was suffocating, the way worthlessness took hold of me like a weighted blanket soaked in ice water. It was heavy and impossible to shake off. I was drowning, and no one knew. I couldn't bring myself to speak up, to seek help. It was like part of me wanted to punish myself for what I had done.

With a tired sigh, I threw the keys on the foyer table, took off my shoes, and headed straight to my bedroom.

Kennedy left the bar with Val an hour before they closed. I was going to leave with her, but she insisted I stay and have fun.

The guys and I decided to stay and close the bar with Tim and his daughter, Aly. Though Tim ended up kicking us out when we got too rowdy, and we weren't making his job any easier. At some point, Hayes decided to get on top of the bar and pretend to be playing guitar as "Sweet Child O' Mine" by Guns N' Roses was playing on the jukebox. Only for him to stumble and fall onto the floor like an idiot.

I fell backward onto my bed with a laugh as my surroundings started to spin. I was *definitely* a little too tipsy.

Donovan had to stick us all onto his car and drop us off like an after-school bus. We were all going to get fucked in practice when Coach took one good look at any of us—except for Donovan and Owens. He was a sadistic man who loved to stick us with suicide drills until one of us ended up puking all over the ice.

With a groan, I stood from the bed, started taking my clothes off, and threw them into the laundry basket. As I was about to head to the bathroom for a much-needed shower, a buzzing sound stopped me in the middle of my room.

I turned around and reached for my phone on the nightstand, but tilted my head with a frown when I didn't see any missed calls or notifications. I flicked my eyes to Sush, half-expecting him to be playing with one of the many toys Hayes bought him. But when I found him on the brand-new cat bed, he was curled into a ball, sleeping.

Huh. Weird.

I shrugged it off. All I wanted was a hot shower and sleep to forget about everything.

When I dropped my phone back onto the nightstand to continue with my night routine, that's when I heard it—as clear as a sunny fucking day.

A breathless, throaty moan from the other side of the wall. *From Kennedy's room.*

"Oh, fuck," I murmured to myself as my eyes snapped to the wall our rooms shared. I had a sudden hatred for drywall, and I wished nothing more than to tear down the damn wall with my bare hands so I could get a front row seat of whatever she was doing.

It was a thought that ended up taking a dangerous turn.

My bed was propped against the wall we shared, so I sat on my mattress and leaned forward slightly. There was no mistaking that the buzzing sound was coming from a sex toy. I stared at the wall, both shocked and turned on.

I straightened my back and threaded my fingers through my hair.

Well, this sure was one way to sober the fuck up.

What the fuck was I supposed to do now?

I shouldn't have been listening; that much was obvious. The logical thing to do was to lock myself in the bathroom for a good forty-five minutes and take a long, hot shower to give her some privacy. I should have also brought my noise-canceling headphones and put them on for the rest of the night just to be safe.

That *was* the sensible thing to do.

With a solid plan in motion, I stood from the bed. A groan almost escaped my lips, and I bit my lip until I tasted copper, because...*hell.* The boner I was carrying was painful.

But I was determined to be a gentleman.

Well...that *had* been the plan until every muscle in my body tensed. Until my breathing completely halted and my fucking heart practically beat out of my chest when I heard her moan, *"Henry."*

The sharp inhale I took filled my lungs with so much air, my chest hurt.

Her moan was...breathy, and husky, and so *goddamn* sexy.

Music to my ears. But hearing *my* fucking name attached to those delicious moans? I'd listen to it for hours to no end.

Fuck. I felt like one lucky son of a bitch.

Was I imagining things? Was it a wet dream?

There was no way. Though I couldn't remember the last time I had gotten laid or taken care of myself, so it *was* a possibility.

I pinched my forearm as hard as I could and hissed at the painful sting. *Okay, then.* Not a dream.

Do the sensible thing and walk away, Henry.

But I think we'd already established I wasn't that cool-headed, so what did I do instead?

Oh, yeah. I sat on the bed once again, leaned against the wall, wrapped my hand around my hardened cock, and stroked it once as Kennedy breathed another husky moan.

This was all kinds of fucked up. I wasn't going to be winning any brownie points with the universe.

But *fuuuck.*

The need gripped every bit of my senses and clouded my already dulled mind as pre-cum leaked out of me after *one* single pump. My brain was dizzy with desire, my body buzzing with so much adrenaline, you'd think I was in the middle of a tied game about to hit the perfect shot.

I swiped my thumb across the head of my cock to spread the pre-cum, and a moan got lodged on my throat at how sensitive I already was.

I shouldn't have been doing this. It was a terrible, *horrific* idea.

But with each passing, delicious stroke, I managed to shut down the logical side of my brain. This was one of those things I was going to take to the grave with me because I couldn't stop. Between the sounds of her toy—which, by the way, I envied so fucking much—and her breathy moans, my body was trembling.

I was too far gone, and I was too much of a happy motherfucker to care.

Another moan slipped out of her. This one was louder and needier. I pulled my hand away from my cock and spat then fisted it again and shut my eyes as vivid images started to play inside my wicked head.

Kennedy spread on my bed, with her legs open and giving me the perfect view of her glistening pussy and her toy. In the wild depths of my imagination, the toy was pink—because, of course, it was. I knew her. I wouldn't have expected anything else. I stood in front of her and started giving her directions as my eyes eagerly took in every single one of her movements. She may have been a fire of a woman, but something told me she wouldn't be opposed to being controlled in bed.

But if I were being honest, I'd let her boss me around, too. Either option sounded equally hot.

I wondered if she used toys often.

Did she like to edge herself and draw out her orgasm, or was she a quick-and-done kind of person?

The things I would have done to be privy to that kind of information were too many to count.

I would have loved nothing more than to have her teach me how she liked it. To sit and watch and learn what drove her crazy. I wanted to recreate it and make it a hundred times better for her.

I would have been such a good little student if she'd let me. I would have made it *so* good for her.

Did she like her clit stimulated? Or only penetration? Or maybe both? *Fuck*, I hoped it was both.

With that filthy thought in my mind, more vivid images

flickered through my brain. I was on top of Kennedy, and her knees rested against her chest as I *thoroughly* fucked her. The head of my cock hit her sensitive spot repeatedly, and when her pussy started to grip me like a vise, I made her suck my index and middle fingers and used those same two digits to rub her clit in quick, circular motions until she spasmed and came around me.

The image was so vivid, and I gripped my cock tightly. I wished more than anything for her pussy to be gripping me instead, but I needed to make do with what I had.

A pathetic whimper slipped past my lips, and I bit down hard on my bicep to muffle the moans that threatened to escape.

I was pretty sure this right here—listening to my hot room-mate, the woman I couldn't get out of my head, pleasuring herself with a toy—had gained me a prime spot in hell. But, *fuck*, I was more than happy to pay for my sins.

I only wished I had been brave enough to walk up to her door, kick it down, and get myself a heady taste of her. But even though I was half buzzed with alcohol and lust, I wasn't stupid enough to do something so drastic.

We still had rules.

Any other man would have taken it as a good sign to offer themselves if they accidentally heard *her* moan *their* name. Yet, I couldn't bring myself to.

Sure, I loved pushing her buttons, and tonight I entered a flirtatious game I knew was going to be nothing short of amazing, because a woman like Kennedy loved to fight fire with fire. But it was just that—a fun game. I had no plans of pushing it any further. I was going to respect her wishes, even if it killed me.

The rustle of sheets and a soft click, followed by the sound of the vibrator becoming louder made my body tense and my cock jerk eagerly against the palm of my hand. Her moans became choppier and more frequent.

The sound was the best kind of torture. I'd never been so happy to be suffering.

I continued to jerk myself without an ounce of shame—because, let's be honest, that boat had long sailed. My movements became sloppier and faster as the sounds coming out of her pouty mouth continued to become huskier. Her moans were like a siren's song. I was enthralled. They became my sole focus. My heart kept racing. I was panting so hard, you'd think it was my first time touching myself.

She was close. I could tell by the way her toy kept making quick, pulsating sounds and the way she started moaning, "*Fuck*," repeatedly. I quickened my strokes, because I wanted nothing more than to fall over the edge with her. I was so close already, it wasn't going to take much.

And then—by some miracle of whoever was up there in the sky—Kennedy moaned my name *again*, and that's when I completely lost it.

I was transported to another goddamn planet. Stars danced across my line of vision.

With a low moan of her name, I tensed my abdomen, and hot, sticky cum spilled out of me. I came so hard and fast, it coated my hand and my stomach. My eyes rolled to the back of my head, and my cock jerked at a vivid image of Kennedy licking my fingers and abdomen clean and not wasting a single drop.

Once I came down from my post-orgasm high, I stood from my bed, careful not to make more of a mess, and headed to the bathroom. When I stared at myself in the mirror, I was almost embarrassed at how much of a mess I made.

I grabbed a paper towel and cleaned my hands and stomach then hopped into the shower. The hot water running down my sore and tired muscles made me groan, and I rested my forehead against the cold tiles of the shower.

I'm never doing that again, I told myself in a weak attempt to convince myself it was a one-time moment of weakness.

But when I closed my eyes and remembered the way she moaned my name, I found myself wrapping my hand around my cock once again and stroking myself to more images of all the filthy and delicious things I wanted to do to my fake girlfriend.

FOURTEEN

KENNEDY

LIAR, LIAR. PANTS ON FIRE.

"KENNEDY, WHERE CAN WE SET UP?" one of the photographers who was going to be taking pictures of the learn-how-to-skate lesson asked.

"One of the equipment managers will be rolling a carpet on the ice soon. You can set up then," I said without casting him a glance as I kept staring at my phone for what felt like the longest time in pure confusion and disbelief.

EVELYN

> Hey, K! I haven't heard much from you. How've you been? The girls and I miss you so much. We're going to meet for lunch this upcoming Sunday at 1:00 PM at Lorenzo's and then go dress shopping for the anniversary party. I know this is last minute, but hopefully, you can still make it! We would love to see you. :)

I hadn't heard from her in so long, I honestly thought she didn't want me to go to her party anymore because of the breakup. Yes, we were mutual friends, but since I walked away from Joe, I hadn't heard anything from them.

The doubts started to creep in. I didn't think attending was the best idea.

But another part of me, a much more insecure, pathetic part, the one who craved company and friends, came out in full swing. Because, pity invite or not, I missed her. I missed them all. Even when I tried to pretend my life was normal and I was okay with how lonely I'd been feeling...I knew better. The knowledge lodged in my chest, poking me with its sharp edges like a jagged piece of a broken glass, pressing with every gulp of air I took.

Before I let my nerves get the best of me, I typed a quick text.

ME

Hey, Evelyn. I'm good. I miss you girls, too. And I'll be there. Can't wait!

There. It was too late to back out. Here was to hoping I wasn't going to regret it.

"Hey," a gravelly voice rasped, making me jerk and snap my head up.

In all his six-foot-seven glory, Henry stood in front of me, wearing a pair of black joggers and a black Strikers hoodie emblazoned with his player number. He had a backward hat on, and his skates were tied together by their laces and dangled over one of his muscled shoulders. And, of course, the stupid lopsided grin he always flashed when he was around me was firmly in place as his eyes raked over me slowly.

He looked annoyingly good.

My cheeks instantly heated as I remembered what I had done the previous night. I had been trying to sleep for hours, but the ache between my legs was making it impossible. So, because really, how much worse could my life get? I decided to use one of my favorite toys and touch myself to the thought of my fake boyfriend. And, *oh boy*, was it good. I wondered if he was as good as he was in my imagination.

"You're late," I shot back as I pushed the thoughts of the previous night into a mental box labeled *DON'T EVER DO IT AGAIN, IDIOT*.

He flicked his wrist to check his watch. "I'm fifteen minutes early."

I stuck out my hip, resting a fist against it. "And I told you to be here thirty minutes early. We were supposed to talk before the photographers got here."

He waved his hand in dismissal. "I'll teach the kids how to skate, and they'll take pictures. I think I have it under control."

I raised an eyebrow as a grin spread across my lips. "Interesting. I didn't even know the word *control* was in your vocabulary."

Henry shifted closer to me, and his delicious bergamot scent assaulted my nostrils. I couldn't seem to escape it. Even when I was at his apartment, every corner smelled like him. Like life wanted to give me a constant hefty reminder of the sexy giant I had for a roommate.

"Was that a joke I just heard, baby?" he asked with a hint of amusement in his tone.

"I'm simply stating facts," I retorted dryly. "And for the love of God, don't call me that."

He rolled his lips, scrubbing his face. "Mmm, I could stop, but we both know you don't want me to."

He's got you there.

No, he doesn't, I hissed back at my brain.

Great. I was having conversations with myself now. Just what I needed.

My phone buzzed in my hand, and a sense of dread settled in the pit of my stomach before I even read the text.

EVELYN

Yay! The girls are going to be so excited.

I involuntarily cringed. I didn't know if it was me, but Evelyn sounded almost *too* fake. It was hard to gauge people's intentions with a text, but I knew her. She had never been so polite with me.

Henry shifted closer to me. "Hey, you okay? You look..."

I glared at him. "Please, delight me with your detective skills."

He reared back in surprise. "Okay, wow, yeah. You're irritated today. Why?"

Annoyance flickered through me, because how dare he be right? How could he read me so easily and guess all these random things? But what pissed me off the most was how he could act like normal when the previous night he decided to *volunteer as tribute* to satisfy my needs.

This was why I couldn't stand hockey players. They were so overconfident and full of themselves. The way he dared to walk away and act normal for the rest of the night, like he hadn't casually thrown my world off-kilter with his comment.

The man had balls; I'd give him that much. It wasn't like I had any desire to sleep with anyone, but it was a matter of principle. Acting like he had the right to tell me what to do was an asshole move. Though it wasn't like I had the most active sexual life before, anyway.

Sex between me and Joe had been...okay, I guess. But he always made it seem like a chore rather than a way for us to connect through intimacy, so eventually, I stopped trying.

I hadn't had sex in so long for good reason. I couldn't manage that type of personal connection with anyone. Much less with Henry. *No, thank you.* I saw no appeal to being another number on his endless sexual conquest list.

Liar, liar. Pants on fire. Are we going to pretend you didn't have the most mind-blowing self-inflicted orgasm of your life to the thought of him?

"I'm not mad," I snapped. "Go get ready, the training starts in ten minutes."

"Where are your skates?" he asked.

I frowned. "Why the hell would I need skates?"

"You're always near me during photo ops."

"I'll be right here." I waved my hand around. "In dry, normal walking land, where it's perfectly safe."

He looked at me curiously. "Do you know how to skate?"

I locked my phone and placed it in the back pocket of my jeans. "What kind of question is that?"

He sat and started to untie the laces of his skates. "*Huh*," he murmured to himself then looked at me. "Come to think of it, every family skate event we've had since you started working here, I've never seen you on the ice."

"I plan those events, I'm too busy to skate."

"The family skate event is in January, right?"

God, this man was giving me a headache.

"Yes, and?"

"It's settled, then. We'll skate together then."

"Hard pass."

He clicked his tongue with a shake of his head as he started to lace his skates. His fingers were long and sleek, but he moved swiftly like it was second nature to him. "I can't be with a girl who doesn't know how to skate."

I scoffed. "Good thing we're not together, then."

"*Ah*." His eyes gleamed with mischief. "But we are." He dropped his voice to a conspiratorial whisper. "You know, as fake boyfriend and girlfriend, in case you've forgotten."

I tilted my head. "You're enjoying this a little too much, aren't you?"

"How *dare* you question my intentions?" He leveled me with a feigned innocent look.

I let out a sigh as I rubbed my temples. "Go train the kids, and we'll talk about this later. I don't want to be stuck here all day."

Before I had a moment to react, his hand reached for mine and jerked me forward, sitting me on his lap.

I immediately started to squirm, trying to get away. "What the hell do you think you're doing?"

"The photographers are looking," he whispered.

I tried to turn my head to see where they were, but he gripped my chin tightly. I took a sharp, small inhale when his calloused fingers made contact with my skin. The sudden touch was scorching hot, but I tried my best to focus on the situation at hand.

"Don't look over there, or they'll be suspicious." He chuckled softly, the sound making my skin prickle with goosebumps. Was his laugh always this sexy? "Your acting skills are seriously lacking, Kenny." His intense, stormy blue eyes met mine with glee.

"And you're *too* damn good." My tone held no bite. The proximity was making me feel...*off*. Tense. Like I was suddenly too aware of all my spidey senses.

"Relax your shoulders and lean into me." His tone was surprisingly husky and soft, with an underlying command that made the pit of my stomach feel warm and fuzzy.

"No." I could barely manage to be this close; if I leaned into him, it was going to be game over.

"*Do* it. They're still looking."

I was not equipped for this fake relationship shit. It was too damn stressful.

I took a deep breath, and without a word, I relaxed into

him. Even with all the layers we had on, I could still feel his chiseled body pressed against mine.

"I'm going to kiss your cheek now," he whispered. "Think about all the good press we'll get from this." He wiggled his eyebrows.

"Okay, but make it quick. I don't know how long I can keep pretending. Being so close to you gives me the urge to gag. I swear, I can't control it even if I tried," I managed to say in a dry tone despite the way my heart trashed almost painfully at my ribcage at the possibility of having Henry's lips on my skin.

His mouth found my ear with a gruff chuckle. A shiver ran down my spine, and goosebumps bloomed across my skin like tiny warnings. My thighs clenched, and my clit *throbbed* when his voice, dark and husky, whispered, "Oh, Kenny, you and I both know you have *plenty* of opinions about me, but thinking I'm repulsive isn't one of them." He leaned in, and his lips brushed dangerously close to mine, the contact fleeting and maddeningly soft.

Henry had one true disadvantage, and that was being cocky. He truly believed he had the upper hand, and that's exactly what made this victory all the sweeter.

I grabbed his hat, placed it on the bench, and then ran my pink manicured nails through his hair. It was so *soft*, and black, and shiny. *Stupid, perfect hair.*

His eyes fluttered shut, and he took a shaky inhale when my lips hovered over his. Every bone in my body screamed at me to get as far away as possible. Playing these games was toying with a line I desperately didn't want to cross. But I was too competitive by nature, so my fingers kept threading his hair in a soft, borderline sensual way, and he gripped my waist tightly in silent warning. When I knew I had him exactly where I wanted him, I gracefully stood and grabbed his hat, putting it back with a diabolical smile plastered all over my face.

"You're going to be late." I didn't bother hiding the smug undertone in my otherwise casual voice.

He opened his eyes, quickly finding mine in disbelief. I met his stare with a cross of my arms and a playful wink. The triumph I felt was too satisfying to hide.

He arched a brow, his mouth curving into a knowing smile. "Well played, Jonesy."

I mockingly bowed. "Why, thank you, pretty boy."

———

"THE MEDIA IS GOING to eat this up," Val said, sitting next to me as we stared at the ice rink, where Henry was almost done training the kids.

"Tell me about it," I muttered.

The kids were starstruck when they saw Henry gliding around the ice, waiting for them. He was such a natural with them, too. Very patient and a surprisingly good teacher. He was doing a great job putting up the front of a sweet, kids-friendly hockey player. It was almost as if this was what was natural to him. It didn't look exaggerated or over the top, like his usual *I-don't-give-a-shit* personality—though, I hadn't seen that one in a while, which was a win in itself.

"How's the roommate situation going?" Val asked then quickly shook her head. "Actually, how's the *dating* thing going?"

I shrugged one shoulder. "I've managed not to throttle him. So, good news all around."

"Whenever you want to talk about what's happening there, I'm here for you." She dropped a hand on my thigh and squeezed gently.

A pang of hurt hit me out of nowhere. I wanted nothing more than to talk this out with her. But being open had never been one of my strongest suits. The shell I kept around me was ironclad for many reasons, and it had gotten worse after breaking up with Joe.

I pushed down my feelings. There was no time to dwell on anything. My life was what it was, and I needed to learn how to live with it.

My eyes flicked to her hand when I went to wrap mine around it, and I gasped when I saw the shiny, bright diamond. "Val!"

Her eyes followed my sight. "Oh, yeah. That's what I came here to tell you. He asked me yesterday."

"Why didn't you call me as soon as it happened?" I reproached her as I grabbed her hand to inspect the ring. It was...*big*. I knew my best friend, and she was a simple girl. This diamond screamed the exact opposite.

"I was going to, but his parents were there, so I had to play host and sort of forgot." She forced a laugh.

I cringed. "How was that?"

She sighed. "Honestly? Exhausting."

Val and Charles's mother hadn't always gotten along. And Charles was a certifiable mama's boy.

I hummed in understanding. "Have you told anyone else?"

She shook her head.

I frowned. "Not even Owens?"

"Especially not Owens," she muttered.

It was no secret Owens hated Val's now fiancé. The guy could be a presumptuous asshole sometimes, so I couldn't even blame the grumpy goalie for not liking him.

"Why are you here, then? You should be celebrating with your man!"

"Parker had a photoshoot, and Lucas told me to run it. We finished a few minutes ago."

Lucas was the director of marketing and Valentina's boss. He was just another mediocre man in the world of sports who thought he was hot shit because he had a penis. What else was new?

"Wasn't Lucas supposed to be taking care of that?" I asked.

"You know how it works around here."

I rolled my lips with a clipped nod. It was no secret that Val did half of the things Lucas was supposed to be doing as the marketing director, and he always took all the credit.

"And Charles didn't mind you working today?"

She crossed one leg over the other and gave me a small shrug. "He went out of town for one of his friends' bachelor parties or something like that."

My heart tugged hard in my chest at the tone of her voice. It was soft, and when you spent time around a girl like Valentina, you knew she was usually full of life and energy. There was an underlying sadness to her. One that had become more and more obvious with each passing day. She should have been excited about this engagement, but it was obvious she was withholding some information.

"Anything you want to talk about?" I asked softly.

She shook her head a little too quickly as she stood. "No. I'm fine. I promise. We should hang out on Sunday. Go have brunch or something."

"I wish." I slumped my shoulders. "But I have plans." I kept my words vague, because Val had strong opinions about me hanging out with Evelyn. I knew she meant well, but part of me was still struggling to let go of what little people I had left in my life.

She slumped her shoulders, too. "Aw, okay. Maybe next

time. I gotta go. I'll see you later, babe." She threw me a kiss and strode to the exit.

The coach clapped, trying to catch the kids' attention. "Alright, kids, please thank Anderson for being here, and we'll see you here next weekend. Yeah?"

The kids completely ignored their coach and stood in front of Henry to ask him questions. His eyes sparkled, and his smile was genuine as he answered everyone with patience and kindness.

It was a rare sight. One I liked—*a lot.*

"Your parents are not gonna be happy with me if you guys don't get going, let's go," the coach pressed.

Most of the kids listened and shuffled out of the rink, but one, who couldn't be more than eight years old, lingered in front of Henry. He stared at his hands and fidgeted nervously before glancing up and asking, "Will you be here next weekend?"

Henry crouched to meet the boy's gaze. "I won't, I'm sorry," he said, his tone gentle. "We've got an away game, but I promise I'll be here the week after that." He reached out, clasped the kid's small hand, and curled it into a fist to give him a fist bump. A warm and kind smile spread across his face as he added, "You did great today, buddy. Keep it up, and you'll be faster than Hayes in no time."

The kid's eyes lit up, sparkling with excitement. "You think so?" he asked, his voice breathless with excitement. "He's *really* fast."

Henry chuckled and gently tapped the kid's nose with his finger. "Just keep practicing." With that, the kid laughed and hugged Henry before gliding across the ice to leave.

After a few minutes, Henry skated to where I was and sat next to me, making quick work of taking his skates off. "I can't remember the last time I skated where it didn't involve fucking drills." His laugh was breathless, and his cheeks were a bit pink.

"You looked like you were having fun," I replied with a smile. "I also took some pictures for your socials." I waved my phone in the air.

He smirked, raising an eyebrow. "Admit it, you took those pictures for yourself."

"God, help me," I muttered as I stood in front of him. One of the photographers called my name, and I lifted one finger, signaling them to wait a moment, then looked at Henry. "Nice work today, seriously."

His intense blue-gray eyes met mine in genuine surprise. "I'm sorry, was that a *compliment?*"

"Don't get used to it," I replied dryly.

He grinned. "Are you going soft on me, Jonesy?"

With a roll of my eyes, I turned around and flipped him off without a word.

He barked a laugh. "There's my girl."

My stomach fluttered like a high school girl with a crush at his words. And though I meant the compliment with my whole heart, I needed to remember who he truly was. Or, well, who I *thought* he truly was.

FIFTEEN

HENRY

I APOLOGIZE ON BEHALF OF THE MALE POPULATION.

THERE WAS NOTHING LIKE HOCKEY. I loved every bit of it. Putting on my gear and stepping onto the rink. The sound of the edges of my skates against the ice. The moment where it was just me, my stick, and a puck against the world.

Whether it was a game, practice, or even for fun, hockey was my heaven. My safe space. *My everything*.

Every bone in my body ached after the conditioning drills Coach made us do. Still, when he said we were going to end it with a small area game after the atrocious loss we had against the Dallas Riders, while the guys groaned in pain, my adrenaline spiked with excitement. Any time I found to spend time on the ice, I was fucking grateful for, considering I was still benched. All I looked for was that brief moment when the noise inside my head quieted, when I was at peace.

"Anderson," Hayes shouted as he dodged a check from Morgan and quickly skated toward the center, where it was open. As I glided behind Parker, Hayes passed the puck through Parker's legs before he could react. I took a quick breath, gripped my stick, caught the pass in one smooth motion, and fired a quick snapshot.

That brief window between hitting the puck and waiting for it to meet the mesh was like a drug. Adrenaline ran through me like jet fuel in my veins. It was fast, and hot, and I loved every goddamn moment of it.

The puck slammed into the back of the net, making the mesh jump.

"That's three. We win," I called out, grinning as I skated in backward swizzles. "Maybe I should have played with my left. This was far too easy."

"You cocky motherfucker," Parker mumbled under his breath and slashed my stick with his.

"Good to see you're still a mouthy motherfucker even though you're benched, Anderson," Morgan quipped.

I barked a laugh as I skated to the bench, peeled off one of my gloves then my helmet, and took a seat. The gear felt like it weighed a ton, sweaty hair clung to my forehead and nape of the neck, and I smelled like death, but...*fuck*. If they'd let me, I would have done another round. "You all love me that way."

"We don't," Owens deadpanned, peeling off his helmet.

"Make sure you all rest, we have a long stretch coming soon, and we need to get our shit together if we want to make things happen this year," Coach said gruffly.

"If only I weren't benched," I murmured.

Coach shot me one of his death glares. "What was that?"

Shit. I meant to say that inside my head.

Before I could answer, Hayes chimed in, "He said you look intimidating when you glare at us. In a hot way. But, like, respectfully."

This fucking idiot. Knowing Coach Sloane, Hayes was going to pay for that with a few laps.

The rest of the team chuckled. Except for Owens, who

rolled his eyes. The grumpy motherfucker had been in a mood for a few days, and we still couldn't figure out why.

"Go do ten laps for that smart ass response."

"Worth it," Hayes mumbled through a giggle, stepping back into the ice.

"Make that twenty," Coach barked. "The rest of you are dismissed."

———

AFTER TAKING A SHOWER, I stopped by Kennedy's office to see if she wanted to have lunch. I hadn't seen her that morning at the apartment, so I guessed she had an early start, but when I knocked on her office door, she wasn't there, and the door was locked.

"Come in," Valentina said after I knocked on the door to her office. She looked up and gave me a kind smile. There was always something so peaceful about Valentina. She had the energy and personality to work in marketing. She was a people person, always willing to help and very creative, but she was also extremely nice. Some say *too* nice—and yes, this was me quoting Owens. He thought people took advantage of her too often because of her kindness. "To what do I owe this pleasure?"

I rubbed the back of my neck. "I was wondering if you've seen Kennedy today. I went by her office, but she wasn't there."

"She texted me this morning saying she wasn't coming in because she's not feeling well."

My pulse quickened, and worry settled at the pit of my stomach. I almost bombarded Valentina with a thousand and one questions, but I stopped myself. I didn't know if Kennedy had told her about our *special* arrangement, and I didn't want to be caught in a lie. If I were her real boyfriend, of course, I would have known she was sick and wasn't going to come in.

I cleared my throat. "Oh, right. I'm such an idiot. She told me this morning, I just forgot." My laugh was forced and awkward. "Thanks anyway."

Once I said goodbye and stepped out of her office, I shot Kennedy a quick text.

ME

How come you didn't tell me you were sick?

KENNY

Why would I tell you?

ME

Kenny, Kenny, Kenny… I'm your boyfriend, remember? When I went by Valentina's office to find out where you were, I was like a deer caught in headlights when she told me you were sick.

KENNY

Oops. I'm sorry, I've been in and out all day.

ME

What's wrong?

KENNY

It's lady stuff you don't need to worry yourself with.

ME

I'm a grown man. You can use the word period.

KENNY

Most men gag if you even mention it.

ME

I think you meant to type *boys.

KENNY

Tomayto, tomahto.

ME

Have you eaten anything?

KENNY

I'm not hungry, and I'm too tired to even get
out of bed to get something.

ME

I'll be there in a few with some things.

KENNY

No, thanks. I'm good. This will pass, and I'll
be all new by tomorrow.

Goddamn, this woman was stubborn. Always refusing help. Good thing I was one stubborn motherfucker, too.

———

"KENNY?" I whispered as I knocked on her door softly. "You awake?"

"Yeah. Come in," she croaked.

I opened the door and found Kennedy underneath the comforter. Captain Sushi was curled beside her, peacefully sleeping. That cat was more hers than mine at this point. He was practically her shadow. Anywhere she went, there he was, right behind her.

"You okay?" I asked, leaning against the doorframe and crossing my arms.

Kennedy sat on the bed and leaned against the headboard with a wince. "Been better. I usually don't call out at work when this happens, but today was extremely bad."

"I will never understand why women don't get time off. Periods sound like a nightmare."

She looked exhausted. Her lips were a bit chipped, like she hadn't been hydrating herself, and her eyes were puffy, with dark circles. But man...she was still so *goddamn* beautiful. Her hair was in a messy bun, so her curls were in all sorts of directions, with a few wild strands framing her face. Kennedy had always been stunning, but there was something about seeing this real part. No makeup. No suits. Just the girl with a strong personality and big, beautiful brown eyes.

It was debilitating how perfect she was.

She snorted a laugh, but then her face cringed, and she wrapped her arms around her abdomen, like she was in pain. "And give society another reason to say women deserve to be paid less because of shit like this? No, thanks. I'd rather take my chances." She sighed.

"I'm sure the only people who say stuff like that are ignorant boys."

"You'd be correct."

"I apologize on behalf of the male population."

She laughed again. "Stop making me laugh!"

"Never," I said, softly. "I love your laugh."

Why the fuck did I say that out loud?

Her eyes settled on me with a puzzled expression. My heart stammered against my chest, and it took everything in me not to say something else that was probably going to be equally as pathetic (if not more so).

"I brought you some stuff," I blurted.

"I told you I was fine."

I let out a short laugh. "Good thing I don't listen to stubborn people."

"I'm *not* stubborn." She rolled her eyes as she stood from the bed and headed to the kitchen. I was right behind her, and we almost bumped into each other when she suddenly stopped.

I gripped her waist so she wouldn't fall on her face.

"What's all of this?" Kennedy asked, her tone shaky.

"I brought you some soup, which good thing I did, because I bet you're dehydrated." I started taking everything out of the bags. "I also wasn't sure what kind of treat you like when you're on your period, so I brought a few options. Some chocolates, sour gummies, and even salt and vinegar chips. Oh, and some flowers."

"Flowers?"

My cheeks heated, and I avoided her gaze in embarrassment. I hadn't thought this through when I was at the store. What the hell was I thinking? I wasn't her real boyfriend, so why the fuck was I doing this? She probably thought I was mad weird.

"Yeah," I said, sheepishly. "I know you like sunflowers since I see them in your office all the time, and I thought they would cheer you up."

The silence that fell between us was deafening. I inhaled a shaky breath as I took care of the bags and put some stuff away. I'd also gotten a few things for the cat, like food and some other treats.

Every bit of my body tensed, and my eyes snapped to hers when I heard her sniff. I dropped everything quickly and closed the distance between us in two quick strides, gripping her shoulders. "Hey, hey. What's wrong?"

"It's stupid." She tilted her head and wiped her eyes with her knuckles.

"If you're crying, I'm sure it isn't stupid." I squeezed her shoulders in reassurance. "You can tell me."

Her eyes brimmed with a fresh set of tears. "Uhm, no one has ever gotten me flowers."

Well, that wasn't what I was expecting.

"I'm sorry if it made you uncomfortable, I—"

She shook her head. "No." Her eyes settled on me, they

were bright and, *fuck*, I was instantly enthralled. "Thank you, Henry."

A tear escaped her, and I brushed it away with my thumb softly. "Any time, Kenny."

She picked up the flowers and smelled them, letting out a wistful sigh. And though she tried her damndest to keep her smile in check, she failed.

My chest puffed with pride.

Damn. I fucking did that. I made Kennedy Jones feel good. I'd be lying if I didn't admit I was dying to do it again.

SIXTEEN

KENNEDY

MY FAKE BOYFRIEND WAS
UNFORTUNATELY SO VERY HOT.

AFTER THE LONGEST week of my life, I stood in front of a restaurant on my only day off to attend a lunch I wasn't even sure I was welcome to.

My fingers fidgeted with the corners of my pink floral pull-sleeve dress as if the movement would somehow ease my sudden nerves. I chewed my bottom lip as my eyes flicked to the restaurant doors. The steady pulse of my heart became more erratic in my ears with every painful second. Dread settled at the pit of my stomach, and my throat felt like I had swallowed a pound of sand.

I shook my head and gave myself an inner pep talk.

You can do this. You've hung out with them before. They're your friends. Stop overthinking so much.

The dread was there to stay, but still, with a deep breath, I strode inside the restaurant.

I hated this. I hated knowing I'd grown scared of everything and everyone around me, and I especially hated having to act every second of every day.

I wished things were different. I didn't want to get back

with Joe—that was the last thing I would do—but maybe I shouldn't have secluded myself so much. I should have reached out to Evelyn and the rest of my friends and not disappeared off the face of the Earth. Maybe I had brought this to myself.

"Hey, girl!" Evelyn's high-pitched voice greeted me. She enveloped me in a hug, her nauseating floral scent flooding my senses.

"Evelyn, hey—" The words got lodged in my throat when my eyes landed on the table.

Everyone was there. As in, every single one of my friends *and* their husbands. As in, Joe *with* Meghan, too.

What the hell were they doing here?

I plastered on a fake smile. "I thought you said it was going to be just us girls."

She shrugged like it was no big deal. "Yeah, we changed plans last minute. The guys wanted to have lunch with us before we went to the boutique. I thought I texted you."

"No, you didn't," I said through gritted teeth.

"It's not like it matters, right? You're not dating anyone," she replied innocently, though I didn't miss the lilt of her fake tone.

This was a trap, and I'd walked right into the lion's den. It should have angered me, but I was just so fucking tired.

"Actually," I cleared my throat, "I am."

Joe snorted a laugh.

I looked over Evelyn's shoulder. "Is there something funny, Joe?"

His eyes met mine, baffled. "Wait, you're serious? You're dating that *jock?*"

My body flared with annoyance with the way he said the word jock with so much disdain and disbelief. The need to defend Henry was almost overwhelming, because fuck if I was going to let anyone talk bad about him. It wasn't fair. He didn't even know him, and just because Henry was a public figure, it didn't give anyone the right to sputter shit out of their mouth about him.

"That *jock* has a name," I snapped.

Evelyn's eyebrows raised in genuine surprise. "So, the rumors are true?"

"*Yup.*" A sigh of relief wanted to escape me at the casual tone of my voice. I managed to say it without cringing, so I guess I was making some progress.

"If he's not doing anything, he's welcome to join us," David commented.

Joe shot him a disbelieving glare. "What?"

"It's Henry fucking Anderson. I've always been a fan of the guy," David said.

Joe leaned back in his chair, and a malicious glint took over his face. "You know what? Yeah. Invite him. If you are dating him, he'll show up, *right?*"

A rush of nerves took hold of my chest, making it hard to breathe. I didn't understand what his end game was. We were both supposed to be moving on. But Joe loved to have the upper hand. And this was no exception.

"Right," I replied with a visible gulp. "But this is his only day off, and I don't want to bother him."

What a pathetic and weak excuse, Kennedy.

"He's such a shitty boyfriend he can't even drop whatever he's doing to come here?" Joe snorted a bitter laugh. "What a catch."

A fresh dose of annoyance surged through my body, and with my jaw tight and squared shoulders, I put on my imaginary big girl panties and texted him.

ME

S.O.S.

PRETTY BOY

What's up?

ME

I would never ask this, but I kind of need you to come to Lorenzo's…like right now. You know, the Italian restaurant? It's right next to your house.

PRETTY BOY

Yeah. I'm familiar with Lorenzo's. But why exactly do you need me there?

ME

Long story short, I was supposed to have lunch with my girlfriends, but turns out all their significant others tagged along and she forgot to tell me.

PRETTY BOY

I'm assuming Ken Doll is there?

ME

Yes.

PRETTY BOY

Say less. On my way, Kenny.

I almost let out a sigh of relief at his response, but I kept myself in check as I took a seat in front of Joe and Meghan. It was just my luck that the only seat available was across from them. "He's on his way."

David rose from his seat. "I'll go tell the hostess to add a chair."

"Perfect!" Evelyn clasped her hands with a smile, but her eyes lacked any sparks. "The more the merrier." She and Joe shared a fleeting glance that made the alarms inside my head blare, making me all shades of uncomfortable.

Was Evelyn part of whatever sick game Joe was playing? Is that why she invited me?

I tried to move past it, because realizing I was more alone than I thought felt like a thousand little needles prickling my body.

"When are you going to pick up your stuff, K?" Joe asked, making a show of draping an arm around Meghan's shoulders.

My eyes followed the movement, and I expected to feel a pang of...something. Annoyance, maybe. Or the same useless feeling I had the first time I saw them together. But when nothing came, I smiled to myself in quiet triumph. "I'll try to drop by later this week."

"With your jock boyfriend?" he mocked.

"Babe," Meghan whispered, pressing a hand on his chest. "Stop."

I shot Meghan a grateful glance, and she pursed her lips awkwardly.

I didn't hold anything against her. She was nice.

Was it pathetic to feel sorry for the girl? Probably. But I couldn't help it. I doubted Joe had a sudden change of heart and started being different.

"I mean, I'm just saying. You sure moved on quickly, didn't you?" he taunted.

I grabbed the menu and pretended to study it intently. Anything was better than sparring with him. He wanted me to engage in a battle I had no business in, nor wanted to be part of.

"And with a jock, no less," he continued.

Or maybe it was worth it, after all.

My eye twitched as I gracefully dropped the menu on the table. My face remained enigmatic, though there was no denying the way my blood ran hot beneath my skin as I tried to keep my anger in check. "Do you think jock is supposed to be an insult?" I asked coolly. "Because it isn't."

He scoffed out a laugh. "Kennedy, come on. You're a smart

girl. Why are you with a hot-headed guy who up until the other day had the reputation of being a manwhore?"

The rest of our friends remained quiet, their eyes flicking like ping-pong balls between us. Their silence spoke volumes. It was clear to me then that no one was on my side. Joe was a charismatic guy, and people had issues standing up to him. It was like they were all blind to his shitty behavior, just like I was.

I had never been so grateful that my foggy glasses had been lifted. Though it didn't make me any less mad knowing how long it took me to get to that point.

"This is not the time or place to have this conversation, Joe. Please, drop it."

"Admit you're not dating him, and I'll gladly drop it. I know you, Kennedy. You wouldn't date a man like him," he remarked casually.

As I opened my mouth to answer, a deep, rich voice beat me to it. "See, Joe, but *that* would be a lie."

At the sound of Henry's voice, my lungs expanded, and I took a breath of relief. Never, in the three years I'd known him, did I think I'd be grateful for him and his impeccable timing. Fake boyfriend or not, he was the only person who was in my corner. The one who kept saving me over and over again. Part of me warmed at the thought of why he was doing it.

Did he care about me? Is this why he was helping me?

I shut down the ridiculous thought quickly. His reputation took a hit, and he needed me. This was a mutual arrangement. He was only holding up his end of the bargain.

I hadn't even laid my eyes on him, and my skin was buzzing with excitement knowing he was near. The closer he got, the more every cell in my body came alive.

His towering presence was strong, and when I looked up, I found his blue irises shining with silent understanding and concern. His eyes did the same thing they had done the last time he came to my rescue—they managed to ground me. But I chalked it up to coincidence. There couldn't be another reason. Because there was no way I was finding peace with the one guy I still believed I couldn't stand. That was a mindfuck in itself, and I was tired of feeling confused.

He took a seat, and his movements were all smooth and confident, like he'd done this hundreds of times. And maybe he had, you know? But I expected him to at least show *some* nerves. We hadn't exactly planned this. We hadn't even gotten a chance to get our story straight—how long we'd been dating, when everything started to shift to a romantic relationship. *Nothing.*

Anxiety clawed at me. This was going to be a disaster.

"Hey," I said awkwardly, fighting the cringe that wanted to break across my face.

He was right. I was such a shitty actress. I couldn't help it.

One of his hands found the nape of my neck. The warmth of skin meeting skin was electric and spread through my body like wildfire. I absentmindedly leaned into his touch—into *him* —like it was instinct.

He leaned forward, and through a barely audible whisper, he said, "Act cool."

My brain struggled to catch up. I was enthralled by *all* of him. The way his freckles danced across his face. His chiseled jaw. The way his slightly crooked nose made him look more human. Like he was capable of having imperfections, even if he still managed to look ridiculously handsome. His bold, masculine scent that was just so *him* was making me hazy, like I had chugged a heady cocktail.

Before I could process what was happening, Henry's lips collided with mine in a soft kiss. My senses dulled, muting every sound around the restaurant. The logical side of me wanted to get away from his grasp and the unexpected softness of his lips as soon as humanly possible. But my *traitorous* body melted into him instead, like every part of me forgot every practical reason to resist. A low groan of approval thrummed deep within his chest as he tightened his grip in a possessive, *this-is-me-claiming-you-in-front-of-everybody* kind of way. His tongue swiped inside my mouth with a quiet, relaxed demand, and if I hadn't been sitting down, my knees would have easily buckled at the way his tongue met mine. My thighs instinctively clenched, and his other hand found my waist, where he gripped softly as he deepened the kiss. By some miracle of God, I managed to hold back the pathetic whimper that was stuck in the back of my throat as his overwhelming presence continued to intoxicate me. Our lips molded perfectly, like they belonged and they wanted to make sure we didn't forget. I couldn't understand why my body was reacting so out of character. So wildly. Fireworks ignited beneath my skin, spark after spark exploding inside my body as his kiss continued to leave a permanent but invisible mark on me. My lips grew numb, and even though the kiss was slow and unhurried, my lungs demanded a gasp of air. But I couldn't stop.

I didn't know where I was anymore. All I knew was I needed—*demanded*—more.

My fingers threaded through his soft strands of hair as my tongue grazed his. He tasted like sour orange with a hint of sweetness; it was addictive. Kissing Henry was like touching a flame. It burned like no other, but *oh, God*, I didn't care. Not one bit.

Someone cleared their throat, and just like that, the moment was broken like a wine glass being smashed against a wall. My body went rigid as I realized where I was. As it reminded me this was all for show. Though the pool that had formed between my legs begged to differ.

Henry was the one who managed to break us apart at the sound. I wished nothing more than to stay frozen in time, wrapped in his arms, because I didn't want to deal with the reality of the situation I was in.

I slowly opened my eyes and found a set of dilated pupils and darker shades of blue. It was a strange contrast to the pleased look he had on his face and the knowing smirk tugging at the corner of his mouth.

"Hi, Kenny baby," he said huskily, his eyes still sparkling with undeniable mirth. Henry wasn't stupid. He *must* have known how much I enjoyed the kiss.

My heart stumbled at the brand-new nickname. I loved it a little too much, though I was determined to deny it.

My face heated, and I was grateful it couldn't show on my cheeks. "Hi," I said breathlessly, still in a haze.

He gave me a chaste kiss this time, followed by a small smile I couldn't help but match.

There was a tightness in my chest I couldn't understand. What was happening? My heart was confused, and my head was all but screaming at me how stupid I was being.

Henry cleared his throat and straightened in his chair, facing the table. "Sorry, guys. But it's hard to resist Kenny when she wears these cute, floral dresses." He leaned back in his chair and casually draped his arm behind me.

Joe's stare was practically leaving fire in its wake, while Meghan stared at him in confusion.

David extended his hand and said, "Nice to meet you, man. I'm David. I'm a huge fan."

Henry leaned slightly forward, meeting David's handshake with a nod and one of his killer smiles. "Always nice to meet a fan."

Henry's arm was still draped behind me, his fingers lazily caressing my forearm. The touch was innocent enough, but I swear I could feel every brush from the top of my head to the tips of my toes. He was a little too good at this fake dating thing; it was borderline terrifying.

"How long have you two been dating?" Evelyn asked.

"Not long. It's fairly recent. About a month and a half, wouldn't you say, baby?" Henry asked me.

I swallowed hard, my throat uncomfortably dry. "Uh, yeah."

"Moving on so quickly, are we?" Joe asked sarcastically.

The audacity of this man was something else. I understood women were held to a different standard when it came to moving on from relationships, but for him to sit there next to his *new* girlfriend and throw such a ridiculous comment was astonishing. *How fucking dare he?*

Double standards and misogyny were, once again, being taken to a whole new level, ladies and gentlemen. *Who didn't see that one coming?*

"What are you talking about? You started dating Meghan after being broken up with Kennedy for like a month," David commented innocently with a frown.

Henry gripped my arm in silent solidarity, and while I appreciated it, it wasn't needed. I was the one who was pretty set in our decision to break up, anyway. Still, a newfound appreciation took residence in my chest, because Henry didn't have to be doing any of this. I was the one who could have lost my career and damaged my reputation if people found out this was fake. But he was *here*. Maybe it wasn't for me, but it didn't matter. I was still grateful.

The server came and took our drink and food orders at the same time, and everyone fell into a comfortable conversation. Henry had a natural charisma and was like a magnet; people gravitated to him. Joe had been nothing but rude, throwing jabs here and there, and Henry had successfully ignored every single one of them.

The girls had been gossiping, but of course, I had nothing to add to the conversation because I couldn't remember the last time we hung out. Meghan was comfortable around them, which explained why the girls hadn't reached out to me. They were buddies with her now, which made sense. I didn't hold anything over them. And doll-looking Meghan, with her perfect blonde hair and green eyes, seemed nice enough.

I was sure that under different circumstances, we could have been friends.

"How is the anniversary party plan going? Are you nervous?" I asked Evelyn.

It was their tenth anniversary, and they had decided to renew their vows, so it was kind of like a wedding, but more for family and close friends. But Evelyn and David lived an extravagant life, so they were doing the whole thing—bridesmaids, a combined bachelor-bachelorette party (which made no sense to me), renewing their vows in a fancy ballroom.

She took a sip of her wine with a nod. "It's been stressful, and my mother-in-law has been a nightmare to deal with." She rolled her eyes. "She was not happy when I decided to add another bridesmaid."

I frowned. "Who?"

She gave Meghan a side hug like they were the best of friends in the world. "Meghan, of course." She sighed. "Originally, I had asked her because after you broke up with Joe, I honestly thought you were going to bail," she commented casually. "But I mean, you're here, so I decided to just add one more."

The remark stung. I didn't understand why I wanted to hold on to these people so badly. They belonged to a part of my life I was no longer part of, and it was becoming more and more clear.

I reared back in surprise. "Evelyn, I would never."

I may have thought about it, sure, but I would have never *gone through* with it. I knew I wasn't the friendliest person most of the time, but I wasn't a bitch either. Much less to someone I'd considered a friend. But I couldn't lie to myself—I found myself becoming skeptical the longer I sat there. The air was still stuffy and uncomfortable, and I didn't know if it was my insecurities or if they really were acting strange around me.

She shrugged. "It was a precaution."

Joe joined the conversation, like the insistent pest he'd become throughout the lunch. "Give her a break, Kennedy. You walked away from a whole-ass engagement. Of course, she was going to think you would bail on this, too."

I gripped my glass of wine, my knuckles practically going white with the force. This crawly feeling settled on my chest and gave me a pressure I hated. I tried to form words, but I came up blank. Because a sadistic part of me believed he was right.

I had my reasons for walking away. *Good* reasons. *Important* reasons.

But this was what he wanted. He wanted to make me feel like shit for putting myself first.

And he was winning.

It had been a long time since I'd felt one foot tall. He made it so easy for me to fall back into a person I couldn't recognize. The one who remained quiet and took every beating, afraid of speaking up and defending herself. A completely different side of me that only came out when he was around.

"Can you please back off?" Henry forced the words out, jaw tight. "You've been going at it since I got here, and God knows what else you've said to her when I wasn't present."

"Anderson's right, man," David chimed in.

"Whose side are you on?" Joe hissed at David. "Stop being such a kiss-ass."

"Why don't we all calm down?" Evelyn said through a forced laugh.

"I'm not saying anything that isn't true. It's what all of you are thinking," Joe commented, folding his arms across his chest.

"This breakup was mutual, Joe," I replied weakly.

I hated this with every fiber of my being. This was a side of me Henry had only witnessed once. But this was my life. I was only a force to be reckoned with at work. Nowhere else. When it came to Joe? I let a lot of shit fly during our relationship. It was the crude reality I lived in. I was still shocked I had managed to gather enough strength to break up with him in the first place.

It was a constant battle. Part of me wanted to fight back, to unleash my fire. Another side of me—the insecure, unlovable part—wanted him to keep attacking me. Wanted to feel the bite of every jab like a cigarette burn.

"Was it?" Joe asked incredulously. "Because if I remember correctly, you're the one who walked out on me."

The fucking audacity.

"I'm not going to disrespect my boyfriend by talking about this, Joe. And you should give Meghan the same respect." I didn't know how I managed to reply, because my head felt like it was underwater. The words were hard to get out. The world around me was moving in slow motion, but fast at the same time—it was making me dizzy.

He knew damn well the lengthy conversation we had after I left the restaurant. A lot of words were said, and not the kind ones. His true colors came out to play, and it only helped solidify my decision to end the engagement. Maybe part of him thought I was going to stay despite every jab and every condescending insult he threw my way that night. After all, I'd fit into the mold Joe wanted me to be in for most of our relationship. He never expected me to get out, so I was sure part of him was surprised.

Uncomfortable silence fell around the table as Joe's eyes met Henry's. "Enjoy it while it lasts. Her career will always be more important than doing her duty as a woman—"

Henry's chair groaned loudly as he stood and pressed the palms of his hands on the table, leaning forward. *God*, he was impossibly tall and easily towered over everyone with his wide, muscled shoulders and chiseled build. His casual, dark-blue button-down shirt made the freckles of his forearms pop and his eyes a beautiful shade of intense blue.

My fake boyfriend was unfortunately so very hot.

"I'm going to stop you right there. I've let a lot of shit fly during this lunch because I understand I'm new to this group dynamic. I'm the outsider. I get it. But I'm not gonna allow you to continue talking about Kenny this way. Duty as a *woman?*" he asked with a scoff, shaking his head in disbelief. "She doesn't owe anyone anything, much less a piece of shit like you." He spat the words out with clear disdain. "The fact you still feel so entitled and comfortable to say something like that says a lot about you."

My eyes met Henry's in shock as I let his words settle me with a newfound confidence. They wrapped around me like a security blanket, calming my racing heart.

I stood and grabbed my purse as my eyes found Evelyn. "I hope you and David have a wonderful vow renewal. I will always be grateful for your friendship, but it's best if I remove myself from this situation." The words tasted vile in my mouth. Here I was, losing more, more, *more*. They were people I didn't even have in the first place, so in the grand scheme of things, it shouldn't have mattered. But I was only human.

I settled my gaze on Joe. "I will be sending movers tomorrow. All I ask is that you give them access to the guest room, where all my boxes are." I turned around and walked away from my so-called friends without giving them another glance.

Every step I took chipped at my beating heart. I needed to be strong to survive, and masking my true feelings had become as easy as breathing at that point, so that's exactly what I did.

Henry caught up to me and placed his hand on my lower back to guide me out of the restaurant. The simple touch made me nervous, but somehow managed to center me at the same time, like some kind of mind game I couldn't bring myself to deal with.

"Walking away once again, shocker," Joe muttered.

Henry's eyes found mine as his nostrils flared in annoyance. He turned around and started walking back to the table with menacing strides.

I gripped his forearm with both of my hands to try to stop him, but it was futile. "Henry, don't," I whispered. "He's *not* worth it," I urged.

His eyes flicked to the table then to me, and he gave me a reassuring nod. "Don't worry. I got this." Then his eyes found Joe, piercing him with so much intensity that Joe cowered in his seat. "I'm going to make one fucking thing clear: leave Kennedy alone, okay? If you so much as look in her direction or talk to her *ever* again, you will be answering to me." He pointed at his chest with a smirk that didn't reach his eyes. "And if you think I won't find out—trust me, I will. And I'll gladly live up to my hot-headed reputation. Do *not* fucking test me." With that, Henry interlaced his fingers with mine and said, "Let's go, Kenny."

I aimlessly followed him, at a loss for words, with a sense of gratitude and confusion following hot on my trail.

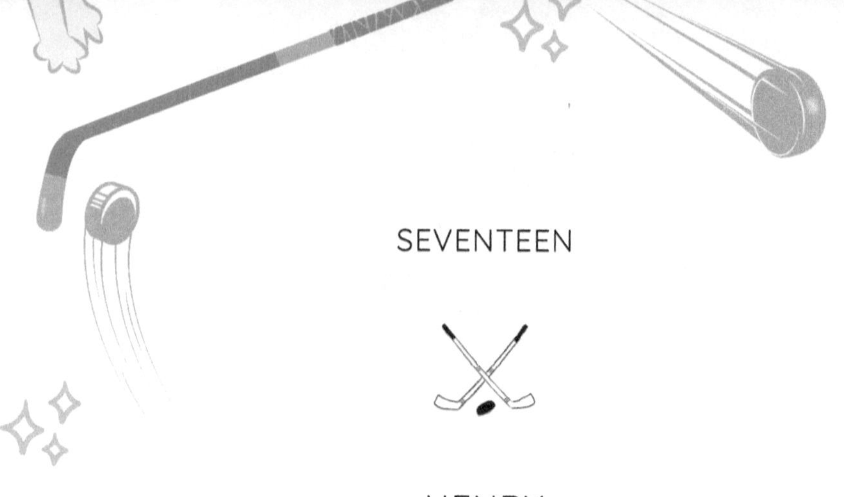

SEVENTEEN

HENRY

I KNEW A PRAISE KINK WHEN I SAW ONE.

THE FUMES from the windy city assaulted my senses as I dragged Kennedy out of the restaurant.

Every feeling imaginable hit me all at once. I was irritated, pissed, *confused* as hell. Mostly, I felt guilty about how I acted. It was shocking how I managed not to grab that piece of shit by the collar of his shirt and punch him. But when Kennedy stopped me, and her voice urged me to take a step back and *think* for once, it calmed me. One look at her was all it took.

Kennedy and I had been making progress, and here I went, fucking it up by threatening her ex-boyfriend.

"Kennedy, I am so—"

She interrupted. "Thank you."

I reared back in surprise. "You're not mad?"

She etched her brows together, which made her look ridiculously cute. "Why would I be mad? He was being a dick."

I let out a humorless laugh as I pinched my index and thumb fingers together. "I was this close to punching him if you hadn't stopped me."

"Thank God you didn't, we don't need another scandal."

She laughed, followed by a sigh. "At least now we know you're capable of listening."

Here I was pissed about what happened back at the restaurant, and she was worried about a *scandal*? The knowledge alone made me irrationally angrier.

"I couldn't give less of a fuck about a scandal," I shot back. "Why did you let him speak to you like that?"

None of these people deserved Kennedy.

Who the fuck was this person standing in front of me? Because she sure as hell wasn't the woman I knew and liked.

Where was her fire?

And why was I so pissed?

There was too much happening; my mind was reeling.

Her body visibly tensed, and she tried to get out of my grip, but I didn't let her.

"Let me go, Henry," she said coldly.

"Not until you answer. What the fuck was that back there?"

She raised her free arm in defeat. "I don't know, *okay*? Joe has always been kind of a douche, but he—"

"Understatement of the century," I deadpanned. "But I'm not talking about his attitude. I'm talking about *you*. If anyone at work dared talk to you like that, you would have brought down hell on them. So why does he get a pass?"

My body trembled with anger. Fuck, I was livid. At her— *for* her. It made me furious the way I witnessed how little she cared about herself and her feelings.

She finally managed to get out of my death grip. "I have to demand respect at work because otherwise, they will all see me as a joke," she shouted with a shake of her head. "And why am I even explaining myself to you right now?!"

She wasn't wrong. She didn't owe me any explanations, but excuse me for being confused as hell at the bait and fucking switch she'd done. The situation was getting out of control with every passing second, and I was eager to get this over with. I loved bantering with Kennedy, but *fighting?* That I loathed with every fiber of my being.

I threaded my fingers through my hair in frustration. "How do we go from you thanking me to arguing? *God*, Kennedy, you're so infuriating!"

Her eyes practically came out of their sockets in disbelief. "*I'm* infuriating? You started it!"

I placed my hands on my hips, letting out a disbelieving laugh. "Forgive me if I'm trying to understand what happened. I was blindsided."

"It's none of your business how I act around people," she snapped.

"I beg to differ," I challenged. "I'm your boyfriend," I said as if that would explain everything. *As if it were true.*

"*Fake* boyfriend," she corrected.

I ate the distance between us and pressed a finger against her mouth as my eyes darted around in panic. "You can't be saying that in public."

She darted her hand to my ribs and pinched me. I let out a pained groan as I took two steps back. *Hell*, the strength this woman had was both terrifying and sexy at the same time.

"*Ouch.* What the fuck was that for?"

"I told you the next time you shushed me, I was going to pinch you." She crossed her arms, a smug smile playing on her lips. "Not so much into masochism anymore, are we?" she asked innocently, batting her long, dark eyelashes.

Silence fell between us as I fought a smile that threatened to break my barriers. I couldn't fathom how Kennedy managed to make me frustrated with her and in awe in a matter of seconds. She was something else.

It was incredible how she managed to breathe life into me.

Every time I was around her, I could be myself. More than anything, when she was around me, I forgot about...*everything*. The pressure of my career. The pressure from my father. The way I self-destructed to keep a sense of control.

Around her, I could be...normal. *And I loved that.*

Not being able to hold back my smile any longer, I widened it as much as I could. She matched the movement, showing her beautiful and bright smile. This woman was perfect, and...*fuck*. The knowledge was so frustrating. All I wanted to do was kiss her again.

Kissing had always been a means to an end for me. Something I did because I knew where it would inevitably end up.

But kissing Kennedy was the closest thing to a religious experience I'd ever had.

Out of all the scenarios I had drawn up inside my head—and believe me when I say there were a lot—that was not how I imagined our first kiss to be. I wished it had happened under different circumstances because I wanted—*needed*—it to happen again. And call me crazy, but I think she wanted it, too. There was no way she hadn't felt how...how *consuming* it was.

"Do you want to go get ice cream?" I blurted.

"Why?"

Because spending time with you is fun even if you frustrate me and confuse the hell out of my fucking feelings.

Because I think I...I like you. Like, really like you.

Because I can't get you out of my head, and I don't think I want to if I'm being fucking honest.

"No point in wasting our perfectly good outfits," I replied in a weak attempt to convince her. "We should enjoy our only day off, too."

She gave me a *you're-so-full-of-shit* look but nodded anyway. "Fine. Lead the way. I guess spending one more hour with you wouldn't be the *worst* thing in the world," she retorted.

And just like that, we fell back into the comfort of what we knew.

———

"MAYBE GOING for ice cream wasn't such a good idea," Kennedy whispered as we strolled into the ice cream shop.

The place practically fell silent as all eyes settled on me. The city of Chicago was always crawling with hockey fans, and it was difficult not to get recognized.

"It's bound to happen. I'm not wearing a disguise," I whispered back. Though I considered it, it defeated the purpose of the *exposure* I told Kennedy we needed.

It was a risk I was willing to take if it meant she would go out with me, even if it was under fake pretenses. I was a desperate man who wanted nothing more than a glimpse of attention from her.

The guys were going to give me so much shit when they figured out what I was doing. I could hardly believe it myself.

"And your massive frame doesn't help either," she commented dryly.

"Massive, huh?" I wiggled my eyebrows.

She hit me in the shoulder with a roll of her eyes. "Stop it."

I fought like hell to keep my grin in check. "What flavor are you getting?"

She pursed her lips, staring at the menu. "I can't decide."

"Then choose two."

She scrunched her nose. "I hate mixing flavors."

"You're weird."

She scoffed. "I'm weird? You probably eat something like fancy toothpaste or fancy grass."

"You mean mint-chocolate chip and matcha?"

"Same thing." She narrowed her eyes. "Your favorite's mint-chocolate chip, isn't it?"

I shrugged as I tried my best to hold back a laugh, because... yeah. That shit was delicious.

When it was our turn, her eyes were still going back and forth between two flavors until she resigned herself with slumped shoulders. "I can't decide, so a small strawberry cheesecake it is."

I nodded and ordered hers and a small rocky road for myself. As they made quick work of serving them, I took my wallet out and paid before she even had the chance to grab her card. This won me one of her sexy-as-hell glares, and I simply winked at her.

When would she ever figure out that paying for things, or doing anything for her in general, was my special kind of drug?

For being the middle of November, it wasn't that cold, so we grabbed our cups and headed to the outdoor seating area the shop had available. Some people were still staring, while others had their phones out and were taking pictures. Kennedy looked a little tense, so I gripped her shoulders in reassurance to ease her tension. Even though she was used to being in front of the camera while at work, I knew firsthand how difficult it could be when people followed your every move while you were only trying to live your life. It was the curse of being a public figure. One I had been carrying for far too long.

"We should play a question game," I said as we took a seat and ate a spoonful of ice cream.

She tilted her head. "Like 20 questions?"

I nodded. "Yeah, but we ask questions to get to know each other a little better. We don't want to look like idiots in front of people."

"If anything, I'll be the only one who will look like an idiot, just like I did back at the restaurant," she mumbled then ate a spoonful of ice cream. She grimaced but still managed to swallow.

"You don't like it?"

She shrugged. "It's fine. The strawberries are too sour for my liking."

Without a word, I exchanged our cups.

"Hey!" She leaned forward to try to grab the cup from my hands. "That's mine."

I brought it close to my chest. "Yeah, but you don't like it. Have mine."

"But that's not the flavor you wanted."

If only she knew I wasn't a huge fan of rocky road—it was the marshmallows, okay? I didn't like them. *Sue me.* The only reason I ordered it in the first place was because it was the second flavor she kept staring at. Better safe than sorry.

I took a bite and fought the grimace that wanted to cross my face. *Damn, that* was *sour.* Instead, I swallowed. "It's good. I like sour things."

"You're such a shit liar." Her laugh was so airy and bubbly, it made my heart flutter.

I frowned. "No, I'm not."

She extended her hand, making a grabbing motion. "Give it back. It isn't fair for you to be stuck with the shitty flavor."

"Oh, and it's fair for you to be stuck with something you don't want?" I retorted.

"Yeah, because it was my choice." She stared at me like I was an idiot.

"My God, Kenny," I huffed a breath, exasperated. "You don't know when to accept nice things from people, do you?"

Her shoulders became visibly tense. "I do, too," she mumbled. It was cute when she challenged me and knew she had no leg to stand on.

"Okay, then be a good girl and eat your ice cream, and I'll eat this one." I wiggled my cup in the air before taking another bite. It wasn't as bad this time around, thank God.

Her eyes widened in shock, her lips softly parting at my words. If I didn't know any better, I'd say she was feeling pretty flustered.

Excitement sparked through my body. I knew a praise kink when I saw one, so I kept that piece of information close to my chest. The knowledge was giving me *many* ideas. My dick ached at the thought of Kennedy splayed on my bed. Playing with her body until I figured out what drove her to the brink of insanity. Rewarding her with mind-numbingly intense orgasms and praises until she begged me to stop.

I slammed the brakes on that thought, because now was so not the time to have a boner when I was trying to get to know more about her. But, fuck, I was dying to take her in any way I could.

Self-control, Henry. Ever heard of that word? my brain mocked.

"You're so annoying." A small huff escaped her lips, but she still grabbed the ice cream cup and started eating it. "Don't go blaming me later."

"I assure you that will not be happening," I replied confidently.

WE FINISHED our ice creams quickly but stayed seated as we talked and asked each other all kinds of questions.

The sour aftertaste still lingered in my mouth, but it was every bit worth it. The look on Kennedy's face while she ate hers gave me intense satisfaction.

She was happy because of *me*.

I got to see her smile because of *me*.

Now *that* was a special kind of drug. Since the last time I'd made her smile, I'd been trying to figure out a way to see it again. Because, as the man who mostly got glares from her, admiring her face light up for a change was like hitting a jackpot.

Kennedy's smiles were rare, but when they happened, all my instincts told me to do was get on my knees and do whatever she desired. It was a dangerous, delicious weapon. Alluring in every way imaginable, and well on its way to becoming my fucking *downfall*.

"How is it having a twin sister?"

"Annoying," I deadpanned.

"Sure, so annoying you go around punching her exes and getting ejected from games," she said dryly.

"*Exactly*." I smirked. "That is why."

"You ever gonna tell me what Holt said?"

"*Nope*." I grinned. "What about you? Do you have any siblings?"

She shook her head. "I'm the Jones's miracle baby."

"Was it hard?" I asked, letting curiosity get the best of me.

She gave me a small shrug. "When I was little, sure. You know how kids are, they always want things they can't have, and I wanted a sister I could play with."

Why did the thought of Kennedy having a lonely childhood tug so deeply at my chest?

And why did I wish I could have gone back in time and done something about it?

The thought was stupid, but the need to fix whatever made her sad was unavoidable. I was aware Kennedy was capable of being fun and playful, and I wanted to pull every laugh and smile she was willing to give me.

Her laugh was a blanket of warmth, and her smile was like the brightest sun after a rainy day.

And I had a lot of those, to be honest. I was always inside my head, working myself to the bones in hopes that one day I would be enough for *someone*, but always falling short. My mind was used to being a jumbled mess, and I did everything in my power to stay away from it—women. *Fighting.*

Nothing worked...until *her.*

To many, she was a woman with an impressive career, but cold and calculating. She was serious and closed off, and it was difficult getting a read on her.

I was one of those people once, too. Until one day, I wasn't.

It was becoming impossible to dwell in the darkness around a woman like Kennedy Jones because, to me, she was sunshine itself.

It was scary, you know? Like jumping into deep waters and not knowing where I would end up. But still, I was ready to jump into the unknown.

And wasn't that pathetic?

"Enough about me." She waved her hand in the air dismissively. "Tell me, why hockey?"

I almost asked why she was trying to deflect, but I thought better of it. Getting on her bad side twice in one day wasn't something I wanted. Not anymore. I craved more of these little moments when she let her walls down low enough, even if it was for a fraction of a second.

Her question threw me for a loop. "What do you mean?"

"There are so many sports you could have chosen, so why hockey?"

The question made me pause and think, which was rarely a good thing. Being too inside my head was a recipe for disaster.

My parents bought me my first pair of skates before I could even walk.

That was the Anderson household way.

My father wanted me to follow in his footsteps, and I was a child who craved his approval. I didn't know better then. When you're a kid, you...*miss* things. Become blind to what the other side of the curtain holds. But the older I got and the more I witnessed, the more I realized how different I wanted to be from him.

Yet, the thought of not playing hockey never crossed my mind, despite knowing this had been something my father instilled in me. The game became my only salvation, and I poured my heart and soul into it for *myself*. If you were to ask my deadbeat of a father, he would say I did it for him. But the truth was, I liked the exhaustion and extreme discipline hockey asked of me because it was better than what waited for me at home. His hockey schedule was demanding until the very end, and the day he got his career-ending injury, he became the monster people warned kids about. And I *needed* the escape, for my goddamn sanity.

Instead of trauma dumping on our first—technically second?—fake date, I said, "I'm Canadian, baby. It's in my blood."

Her brown eyes settled on my face with a scrutinizing expression. "Why are you lying?"

I forced a laugh. "I'm not."

"You do that a lot, you know?"

"What?"

"Deflect."

"When did this become a therapy session?" I joked.

"When you decided to start lying to me," she replied bluntly, leaning back in her chair.

I didn't like this. The way she saw me so openly. It was embarrassing for me, but more than anything? *Terrifying.* Like I was teetering along the lines of something I wasn't ready to face. But as I would come to find out later, Kennedy always pushed me to be my very best and to stay true to myself.

"Okay, if you must know the truth, hockey became sort of an escape." I cleared my throat at the unexpected feeling that wanted to settle in the pit of my stomach. "What about you? Why public relations in sports?"

"You're deflecting again, but I'll let it go." She smirked knowingly then sighed. "I've always loved hockey," she whispered, lost in thought. "But honestly? Ever since I was a little girl, I admired women who weren't afraid to enter a male-dominated field to leave their imprint. It takes a lot of courage. We're often criticized and judged for the same things our male colleagues do, simply because society believes women belong at home." She blew a short breath, shaking her head. "But I want to make a difference and show young girls they can do and be anything they want to be when they grow up."

I nodded, holding on to every word she spoke. This didn't help tame the infatuation I had for her. If anything, it fueled it. The fierce determination in her eyes and the way she shared this information so wholeheartedly, it was attractive.

"Has anyone ever told you how fierce you are?" I asked softly.

She gave me a small smile, avoiding my gaze. "I've been called a lot of things over the years. High-maintenance. Too eager. Too forward. Too loud. But no. Never fierce."

My body all but roared in outrage, but I kept myself in check as I stood from my chair and crouched in front of her. My hands found the warmth of her face, and I caressed her jaw back and forth with my thumb gently. Electricity ran up my arm, like touching her rewired something deep in my bones.

"Then let me be the first," I rasped. It was difficult to breathe with the way my heart stabbed my ribs so painfully. "You're a force to be reckoned with, Kennedy Jones." I smiled when she took a sharp inhale and dropped her gaze. "Talented, fierce, and fearless. Don't let anyone ever make you believe otherwise." My hands found the nape of her neck, and I tilted her face, forcing her to meet my stare. "And if you, for some reason, *ever* forget, I'll be here to remind you. Every fucking day if I have to. Okay?" ·

Her brown eyes swam with an unspoken emotion. Like I somehow managed to tear down the ironclad walls she kept up to keep people out. People had this perception of Kennedy because it's what she allowed them to see. A mask she kept so close to her face it made it impossible to break through. But it had finally cracked, just the tiniest bit, at my words.

I was a determined man on a mission. However long this fake relationship would last, I would make my damndest sure to help her see she didn't have to be like this. She didn't have to hide from me. *Never* me.

I wanted to be her safe space.

It wasn't lost on me I was also living under a lie and keeping people at arm's length. But there was a key difference between us.

It was already too late to save myself. But a woman as wonderful and strong as she was didn't deserve that kind of fate. I had become accustomed to the loneliness life had given me. The suffocating feeling that wrapped its hands around my throat with a vise grip.

Solitude was a dear old friend of mine.

But the emptiness, the anger, the desolation it offered wasn't something I wanted for her.

EIGHTEEN

KENNEDY

IT CAN BE OUR LITTLE SECRET.

THE STRIKERS HAD BEEN PLAYING okay these past two weeks, for the most part. But tonight was one of those nights the team couldn't connect, despite all of their efforts. The team dynamic was alarmingly lacking, and I wondered if it had to do with a certain center who was still being kept off the ice. These guys were like family. They played well because they were like a well-oiled machine, and one of the core members had been stripped from them.

We were almost wrapped up in the media room, where reporters had been throwing question after hard questions at Liam Donovan. Thankfully, he was a level-headed guy and a total media veteran. He knew how to manage. It was one of the many reasons he was captain of the team for the third season in a row. The team trusted him, and the organization did, too.

"Kenny," I heard Val whisper. I looked over my shoulder and found her standing at the door entrance, beckoning me with her fingers.

I glanced at Donovan to make sure he was still good. He was casually talking and making jokes with the reporters, so I turned my attention back to Val and approached her. "What's up?"

"Have you talked to Anderson yet? He probably took the loss hard, huh?" she asked.

I shook my head. "I haven't."

But he had been stuck in my mind for the past hour. I hadn't seen him roaming the halls even though we drove together today. He'd been doing a great job avoiding the media like I'd explicitly told him to.

But I also knew better.

The team had a good streak this week. We had three back-to-back away games and won all of them. But ever since he got benched, he took every loss extremely hard.

My stomach turned sour with worry. I wished there was something I could do. Henry was a typical goofball around people. But when he was away from the public, there were these flickers of moments when he looked...almost sad, defeated.

He needed to get out of his head, and the perfect idea popped into my head. "Let's do an impromptu team dinner at Henry's." It was a Sunday, and they had an early afternoon game, so it wasn't that late, and they didn't have any games for the next two days. It was the perfect opportunity for them to get together.

I stopped to think for a moment.

Was this a good idea?

Was it even my place to do something like this?

I wasn't his real girlfriend, and I wasn't sure if he was going to appreciate it. I only wanted to do something nice for him. He was my roommate, and I'd like to think we were sort of... friends. He would have done the same for me if he had to. He'd proven that much already.

Val's eyes sparkled with excitement. "I'm sure they'll love

that. Look at you, trying to make your man happy." She wiggled her eyebrows.

All I could do was offer her a small smile at her comment. Any day now, I was going to explode and confess everything to her, because I needed someone to talk to about these confusing-as-fuck feelings I'd been experiencing.

"Can you put in an order for that taco place we like and pick it up with Owens? Then I'll go back home with Henry to make sure the apartment is set," I said.

The idea wasn't bad. The guys could use some fun time and maybe spend a relaxing day out of the media frenzy and off the ice to regroup.

More than anything, I knew this was what Henry needed.

No one deserved to be alone with their thoughts, especially when they were the wrong ones. While I thought it was good he was taking responsibility and finally realizing he had fucked up, it didn't sit right with me that he was beating himself up about it.

So...throwing a last-minute dinner party together for my fake boyfriend, who I was beginning to like more than I cared to admit, was exactly what I did.

———

"I'M GONNA CALL IT A NIGHT," Henry said quietly as soon as we entered the apartment.

I gripped his arm to stop him from going into his room. "No. We're not doing this. Throw on some casual clothes and we'll order food or something and watch a movie."

"Kenn—"

"If you accept, I promise we'll go on a fake date when you come back from your away games this week." I raised an eyebrow at him with a cheeky smile. I knew damn well I had him just where I wanted him.

"Wow, so we're *finally* going out?" He crossed his arms with a smirk.

"If you're a good boy and listen, then yes," I replied matter-of-factly.

I did my best to hold back the laughter that wanted to escape me at Henry's flustered face. Was it silly to say he looked so stupidly handsome when he blushed? His cheeks took on this vivid ruby-red color, making his freckles pop. He looked ridiculously sweet.

"Deal."

I snorted a laugh. "I don't understand why you insist on these fake dates so much."

He shrugged. "It's all about the exposure. It'll be good for the media."

"Go change," I said as I strode into the kitchen to start making Sush's dinner—in case you were wondering, I'd given up on his full name. It was a mouthful. Also, this one kind of suited him.

Henry took a few steps closer to me and reached for my arm, gripping it softly. "Oh, and Kennedy?" His voice dropped to a husky whisper. The sound of my name rolling off his lips made my body unexpectedly hot. "Be careful about what you call me next time."

My heart practically skipped at his comment. *Oh, God.* It was just a joke. I hadn't thought about it. And he...he *blushed*. Was he mad? *Oh, this was so awkward.*

"I'm sorry." I stared at him, dumbfounded. "I didn't mean to make you uncomfortable," I said as I tried to mask my embarrassment.

"Oh, don't get it twisted, Kenny baby." His other hand

found my face, and he pressed my chin between his thumb and index finger, tilting my head and forcing me to look at him. The corner of his mouth lifted into a playful smirk. "On the contrary. I liked it a little too much." His dilated pupils dropped to my lips as he licked his own. My eyes shamelessly followed the movement, and my lips started to tingle with the need to close the small gap between us. "If you do it again, I don't know what I'll be capable of. And I don't think you're ready to find out, either." With that, he let go of me and retreated to his bedroom.

I was at a loss for words. My chest heaved and my core tightened almost painfully as his words kept playing in an endless loop. To be completely honest, I enjoyed his confession. I basked in it and let the words glide over me as if they were true.

Because there was no way a man like Henry Anderson was admitting he wanted a stubborn, cold woman with a strong personality like me.

I shook my head and murmured to myself, "Get a hold of yourself, Kennedy." He technically broke the no-flirting rule because that was the type of man he was. Always toeing the line. But I must have had a fever, because I so wished he'd do it again.

I swore my feet felt like they were walking on a cloud, and I didn't know how I managed to get to my room and change. My mind was foggy with the need to be touched or kissed—anything, really—as long as it came from him.

It had been so long since I had been with someone. I wasn't sure if I missed the act itself or the idea of it. I was ashamed to admit this—I faked my fair number of orgasms throughout my relationship with Joe. I know what you're probably thinking—I ignorantly added to society's problem by letting yet another man believe they had an inkling of knowledge about a woman's body. Believe me when I say, I won't be making the same mistake again.

And while I didn't think I was ready to be intimate with someone, the need was still there. Dangling in the front of my mind.

But I had no time to dwell on it, because everyone would be arriving at any moment. I knew, however, that I was going to have to rely on my trusty old vibrator friend while thinking of my hot fake boyfriend, because it was the only thing that easily got me off these days. It was becoming a problem.

As I was finished changing, my phone pinged with a text.

HAYES

Kennyyyyyyyyyyyyyyy.

HAYES

We're in front of your door. I buzzed Val and Owens up so the front office wouldn't call Henry.

HAYES

Open upppppppppp.

I went to get the door, but stopped and turned until I found our fake dating contract placed front and center on the fridge. With the ridiculous piece of paper I was still trying to hold on to—though I was starting to hate it—in a safe place, I opened the door and found Val, Owens, and Hayes carrying a bunch of food trays.

"This is heavy as hell, get out of the way," Val complained.

"I told you I got it, but no, you wanted to prove something," Owens mumbled.

"Shut up, Nico," Val retorted as they all strode into the kitchen and placed the trays on the counters.

"My God, this is a ridiculous amount of food," I said.

Hayes snorted a laugh. "Kenny, we're hockey players. I bet you twenty bucks we will end up ordering pizza or something."

The door of Henry's room opened, and he was staring at his phone with a frown as he read something. His gaze snapped up, and when it landed on all of us, his brows furrowed even deeper. "What's going on?"

"Surprise! Impromptu team dinner." Hayes wiggled his hands in the air.

"We usually do those at Donovan's," Henry commented.

With an easy grin, Hayes threw an arm around me. "It was your girl's idea to throw it here."

Henry's piercing blue gaze landed on mine with a quizzical expression.

My face heated, and I shrugged one shoulder with a small smile. "Wanted to do something special for you guys."

"You going softie on me, Kenny baby?" Henry asked, his voice light, a boyish grin tugging at his lips.

"Never, pretty boy," I quipped, though there was no denying the way my pulse thrummed loudly in my car as my body practically shouted at me, "*Liar.*"

"Where's my child?" Hayes suddenly asked as he shoved his hand into one of his jeans pockets and took a small twinkle star plush out of it.

I held back a laugh at his randomness. I didn't know why it surprised me. Wesley Hayes was the literal definition of a golden retriever. Well, except for the trail of broken hearts he left behind in every city he traveled to. Yeah, it was safe to say Hayes had a reputation. You would never have guessed it based on his sunshine personality and innocent forest-green eyes, but I was almost certain the innocent look he carried was what attracted so many women in the first place.

Though there was no denying a man like him was certainly handsome, he didn't hold a candle to Henry. His beauty was raw and almost *too* overwhelming. The type of beauty that dulled your senses and threw your logical way of thinking out the window, simply by orbiting around you. The type of handsomeness that was impossible to ignore. Believe me when I say this because I had been *trying*—and failing miserably.

"You mean *my* child?" Henry cocked one of his dark eyebrows. "He's probably in the latest cat tower you bought him."

"Say less," Hayes said while striding into what we called Sush's room. "Where are you, Sush? Uncle Wes missed you," he shouted.

With a shake of my head and a laugh, I headed to the pantry in hopes of finding disposable cups and plates. I was sure we had to have some around.

"Need help with anything?" Henry's voice boomed through the small room, causing goosebumps to spread across my body at his smooth tone.

I looked over my shoulder and found him leaning against the door frame with his arms crossed. The simple pose made the muscles of his arms pull the fabric of his hoodie taut, and a throbbing sensation pounded between my legs at the sight alone.

I was losing my damn mind.

"I'm looking for some disposable cups and plates because there's no way ours are going to make it if we use them. I've known you all long enough to know how rowdy you all get," I said.

His deep laugh echoed as he strode closer and reached for something above me. His tall frame enveloped me, and my traitorous thighs clenched involuntarily.

Once he found the items, I expected him to pull away. But when I turned around, he was standing so close, I could visibly count every freckle that dusted across his chiseled face and crooked nose. My fingers itched to trace them, and I curled my hands into hard fists, fighting the ridiculous urge.

"Thank you for doing this," he whispered.

"Like I said, I wanted to do something nice for you guys." I smiled.

He hummed, leaning closer. "For everyone? Or just me?"

I huffed a nervous laugh, the pulse in my neck rising. "Someone sure thinks highly of himself."

"It can be our little secret."

I rolled my eyes, exasperated. "Think what you will." The deflection slipped past my lips easily.

I wasn't willing to accept that, yes, I had done it *just* for him. Because I, Kennedy Jones, was worried about *him*. I didn't want to feel anything toward him. But *oh*, I did. *I so did.*

"You want to know what I think?" he asked. His eyes glinted with something dangerous, a silent challenge I was dying to face head-on. But I knew better than to walk into one of his traps.

"*Nope*," I replied dryly.

"I'll tell you anyway."

The heat rolling off his body was almost tangible. The worst part? My body *craved* more of it. It *burned* me like a sin I wasn't supposed to want. I told myself it didn't affect me. Made myself believe it was my imagination. But the fire crackling beneath my skin told a different story.

The air frizzled with so much tension, I could practically taste it. *And, God, was it delicious.*

He positioned one of his hands on the built-in shelves behind me, successfully caging me in. My eyes became interested in my surroundings as I tried my best not to gawk at him, though there wasn't any point. There was something about the way he wore the simple black hoodie and gray sweatpants that left nothing to the imagination. But what tied it all up into a neat little package with a perfect red bow was the goddamn backward hat. It didn't matter how often he wore those types of outfits, he was still painfully handsome.

His backward hats were becoming my version of torture. All I wanted to do was knock it off his head, run my fingers through his hair, and *kiss* the hell out of him.

The look on his face was almost predatory and hungry. "I think you're starting to like me, but it pains you to admit it."

I fluttered my eyes closed, because his stare, accompanied by those words, was like a shot of aged whiskey. It burned my throat before dropping to the center of my stomach. Then, *oh so slowly*, it spread to the rest of me, making my body burn hot.

"Sorry to break it to you, pretty boy, but I still can't stand you," I replied weakly. My strength to keep lying was quickly crumbling.

What I couldn't stand was the fact that I hadn't forgotten about our kiss. The stupid kiss that felt anything *but* fake.

What I couldn't stand was the fact that he wasn't who I thought he was, and it was putting me in this weird, strange limbo.

What I couldn't stand was the fact that I was starting to like being around him.

"God, Kenny..." He barked a soft laugh. "You are *so* stubborn sometimes. Did you know that?"

"I've been told that multiple times, actually," I replied breezily, though the comment hit an old wound. I could practically hear all the comments I had been hearing throughout my life.

Can you, for once, do as you're told? Why does everything have to be a fight with you? I could hear Joe's words so vividly, as if he were standing right in front of me.

I was being consumed by my own nightmares, by the voices I pretended didn't affect me. I just hadn't expected I would add

Henry's voice to that rotation. He *was* right, that much I knew. I didn't want to be like this. But when you lived your life on edge, always expecting the worst from people, what else was there to do?

"That's okay, though," he replied with a low sigh. "I like you just like this. Stubborn and all."

My eyes found him in silent shock. I didn't know what to say. I was pretty sure I had forgotten how to breathe.

He smirked knowingly. "But can I ask you a question?"

I put myself together long enough to roll my eyes. "If you must."

"When are you going to stop lying to yourself?" His voice dropped to a sensual gravel, and my clit *throbbed* painfully. "Wouldn't it be more fun to give in?"

"What's that supposed to mean?" I asked, even though I knew. I so fucking knew what he was talking about. But denial...Well, you should know by now, denial was practically my best friend.

"You and I both know what I mean," he replied with a smug smile as he took a step back, taking his overwhelming presence and warmth with him. My body shivered, already missing his heat.

He turned around and strode to the door, but before he left, he looked over his shoulder. "Oh, and Kenny?"

I was flustered and at a loss for words, so all I managed to do was look up and breathlessly say, "Yeah?"

"Just so we're clear, that was me flirting."

With that, he walked back out to the party like nothing had happened.

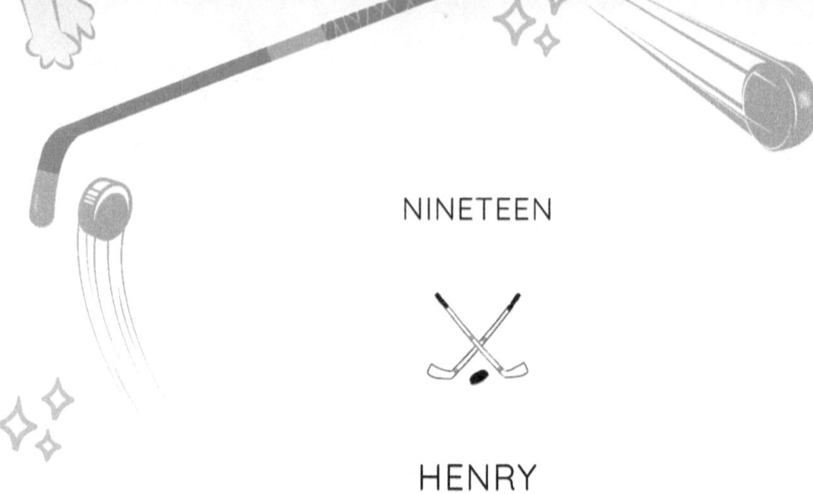

NINETEEN

HENRY

MY FUCKING GOD, I WAS GOING TO THROTTLE MY BEST FRIEND.

"HOW'S IT GOING WITH KENNY?" Hayes asked as he sat on the couch and handed me a beer.

My eyes instinctively looked for her when he asked, and I found her in the kitchen, animatedly talking with Val and Owens. She tilted her head back with a laugh, and my gaze settled on her pretty neck.

I wondered how my hand would look wrapped around it as I fucked her into the very kitchen counter she was leaning against. Vivid images of her thighs wrapped around my shoulders as I feasted on her pussy invaded my mind. I bet she tasted sweet, with just the perfect amount of bitterness to match her personality.

I took a hefty sip of beer, hoping it would settle my dry throat and the painful need spreading through my body.

"We kissed," I mumbled, my eyes still following every single one of her movements. I was a greedy fucker and couldn't keep my eyes off her. How could I? The woman gave the word *beautiful* a whole new meaning.

Hayes's eyes widened in pure shock. "And you're telling

me this now?! When was this? Why did you do it? Did you like it? Do her lips taste as sweet as they look?" His questions came in rapid-fire, barely giving me time to think.

The last one caught my attention, and a rush of jealousy clouded my senses. "Don't you dare ask me something like that ever again. And stay away from Kennedy," I said through a low growl as I slapped the back of his head. "But, if you must know, it was a few weeks back. I ended up spending some time with her friends and *Ken Doll*."

"That's the ex, right?"

I grunted without a word. Every time I thought about that asshole, I wanted to punch a fucking wall.

"And you kissed her to like, what? Stake your claim?"

The question made my head tilt. "I'm not sure what happened before I arrived, but when I got there, I heard him say he was going to drop the topic if she admitted she wasn't dating me. I assumed he was talking about us. It pissed me off, so I kissed her to seal the deal and make them believe it wasn't fake."

"First kiss in front of her ex." Hayes let out a long whistle. "*Ballsy*."

"I was doing my duty as her fake boyfriend," I replied in a weak attempt to convince myself. It didn't work. It was frustrating to know how real and charged that kiss was. And how the tension still lingered between us.

I was trying my best to ignore it and be respectful...until tonight. I may have pushed a bit too far when we were in the pantry, but *fuck*. This wasn't in my head. I knew she felt it, too.

"Get out of here with that shit." He leveled me with a *what the fuck?* look. "You wanted to kiss her and took the opportunity. And I get it. I don't blame you. Kennedy is a beautiful girl. I probably would have done the same thing," he remarked casually with a halfhearted shrug.

I flicked his forehead this time. "What did I just say? *Stop.*"

Hayes barked a laugh so loud, it caught Parker's attention. "Why are you laughing?" he asked, sitting on the coffee table and leaning forward.

"Anderson is in *looooove,*" Hayes crooned playfully, batting his lashes as he fanned his face.

With my quick reflexes, I found one of Hayes's nipples through his shirt and twisted it. We used to do that a lot when we were kids to mess with each other, good to know I hadn't lost my talent of finding his small-as-fuck stupid nubs.

Hayes hissed. "Motherf—"

"Everything okay here, boys?" Kennedy asked as she approached us.

I wrapped an arm around Hayes with a nervous chuckle. "Everything's fine, Kenny baby. Just here talking—"

"About how much he's looking forward to going line dancing at the new bar they're opening next weekend," Hayes interrupted with a malicious grin.

Parker was in the middle of taking a sip of his beer, so when he snorted a laugh, beer came pouring out of his nose. "Shit," he mumbled, though he kept chuckling.

Kennedy frowned. "What?"

"Did I hear someone say line dancing?" Val asked excitedly, joining the conversation. "We should totally go to that new bar when it opens! A college friend of mine is their social media manager, and the place looks so fun."

Owens groaned, "Pecas*, no. That's not fucking happening. We get enough of that when we visit back home."

Val pouted. "Oh, come on, Nico. It would be fun. Like the good old days." She made a show of grabbing her imaginary cowboy hat and placing it on top of Owens's head.

---

* Freckles.

"So fun," Hayes quipped. "Anderson was just talking about it."

My fucking God, I was going to throttle my best friend. That was it. He deserved it. He had a good run. Slept with lots of women and had a good career. I'd be ending his life on a high note.

Kennedy scrunched her freckled nose, and cute lines formed at the top of it. My fingers twitched, itching to trace the lines. "You line dance?"

"Of course, he does. We went all the time when we were freshmen in college," Hayes said.

Kennedy's eyes sparkled with humor. "Is that true, pretty boy?"

I fought the grimace that wanted to take over my face this time. "Yeah, it's true," I said, my shoulders deflating.

Listen, I was an eager, brand-new college student looking to score with some hot college chicks. Unfortunately for me, they happened to always be hanging out at country bars. My college town wasn't big on the college scene. We had to make do with what we had. *Sue me.*

She cocked an eyebrow. "Guess we found the perfect date night for next week."

"Sounds like a plan."

Someone needed to kill me, because I couldn't believe I had agreed to yet another ridiculous plan, all because I was dying to spend more time with Kennedy Jones.

TWENTY

KENNEDY

PREPARE TO BECOME OBSESSED WITH ME.

BARS, believe it or not, had never been my scene.

The thought alone should have been wrong, considering I lived in such a lively city.

When I told Henry we should go to a *country* city bar—God, it even sounded ridiculous to say it out loud—it had been a joke.

Until it wasn't, and somehow, it became more of a group thing than a date night. That made me feel...safer, for some reason. Being in a group setting was the perfect buffer to ignore the strange feelings I was developing for Henry.

It was a busy Friday night, and I had come straight from work with Val since we agreed to meet the guys here. They had a rough game in Seattle the night before, so they needed something to let off some steam.

I was...nervous. My body buzzed with a strange energy I couldn't shake off. I was *excited* to see Henry, and though that newfound information should have scared me, I didn't let it.

It was the bar's official grand opening, so it was lively and loud. The place had a modern feel to it, with a shiny dark wood

front bar and light whiskey barrels that hung over it, acting as lamps. Whiskey paraphernalia filled the sleek space, doused in muted colors of gray and black, save for the neon signs with words like *Howdy* and *Welcome Y'all*, as well as the beer brand signs.

Val interlaced our arms together. "My friends back at Sunset Creek would be appalled by this fancy place." She laughed. "But, hey, I have to make do with what I have. Right?"

"It is very fancy," I conceded.

She took one good look at me and wiggled her eyebrows. "Henry is going to lose his shit when he sees you."

"This is ridiculous. I don't know why we had to dress up."

Everyone around the bar was wearing hats and boots, so maybe it hadn't been a stupid idea after all. Most men were wearing those ridiculous flannel shirts and the typical cheap-looking cowboy hats, and almost every girl was wearing glittery crop tops with either tight jeans or miniskirts and cowboy hats with rhinestones on them.

I stared at my outfit and scrunched my nose. I was severely underdressed in my long-sleeved white V-neck chiffon dress. I mostly owned power suits and sweats, so this was the only thing I had that paired well with my light-pink cowboy boots with hearts scattered all over them. I had used them once for a bachelorette party, and because they were pink, I kept them. Val let me borrow a classic black Western hat with a silver band to complete the look.

"Oh, there they are!" Val exclaimed as she dragged me toward one of the high-top tables.

My shoulders tensed as every woman around the bar was practically shooting daggers at us as we approached the group of athletes.

"Looking good, girls." Hayes grinned.

Owens shot him a glare. "Hey, give them some respect. They're taken."

Hayes shrugged, and before he took a sip of his beer, he replied, "I'm still allowed to respectfully say how hot they look."

"You guys do look good," Parker added.

Owens shot a glare at Parker this time without a word. It almost made me laugh, because Owens was the kind of guy who only knew how to communicate in grunts and glares except when it came to his best friend.

Val hugged him, resting her head against his chest. "My brothers will be so happy to know you still act like an overprotective brother, even though we're literally grown adults. Not even Charles is this protective."

Owens tensed at the mention of Charles but simply grunted and took Val's cowboy hat off, then placed his chin on top of her head and wrapped his arms around her. "Someone has to look after you. You're a danger to society."

The smile etched on my face at the sight of them hurt. I didn't know what was going on with Valentina and Charles; she was still cryptic and didn't want to talk about anything since the engagement. But it was nice knowing she had a man like Owens in her corner. Her childhood best friend protected her fiercely, and I loved that.

"Where's Henry?" I asked.

"Here I am," he rasped behind me.

When I turned around, I didn't expect the sight of him to make me downright *feral*.

My eyes raked over his body eagerly, not knowing where to look first. He wore a white backward hat, and for some reason, I found that a thousand times hotter than any cowboy hat. His jeans were light colored and hugged the muscles of his legs perfectly with a brown leather belt threaded through the loops, paired with a simple white T-shirt that had no business looking so ridiculously hot. And, of course, to tie it all up, plain brown leather cowboy boots.

He stood closer and grabbed my hand to twirl me around. "*Damn.*" Henry whistled with a shake of his head. "You wearing this dress should be illegal, Kenny baby."

My face heated at his words, but I tamed my feelings quickly at the reminder that he was flirting because we were in public. This is what we were supposed to be doing.

I smirked and rested my arms on his shoulders. "You don't look half-bad yourself. Those jeans are really working out for you," I commented casually.

I could sit here and lie and tell you I was flirting because it was my job to play along. But to be completely frank? There were *too many* women looking at him, and it made my blood *boil*. For once in my life, I wanted to be selfish. This was part of the agreement, right? To flirt and act like a lovey-dovey couple in front of the world. *And I planned to take full advantage.*

He cocked an eyebrow and leaned forward. "Are you *flirting* with me?" he asked low enough to keep the conversation between us.

"We're in public, aren't we?" I asked innocently.

I kept trying to make myself believe I was only acting. The truth was, I wanted to spend more time with Henry. He was fun. Around him, all my problems and insecurities were pushed away like they were useless.

I fought what I was feeling with everything I had, but for one night, I was ready to let go of the reins.

———

A FEW ROUNDS of beers later, and I was having a good time.

Hanging out with the guys had become my new norm over the last few months, and I was honestly mad at myself for not doing it sooner. The group was fun, and the guys were respectful. It was like having a bunch of overprotective, funny brothers.

I loved how Hayes and Parker were always like two men on a mission to hook up with whatever girls they had their eyes set on, though we all knew better. They were very handsome men, and no woman in their right mind would refuse them. Donovan even made a quick appearance with his wife, Aurora. We'd never been close, but I'd talk to her from time to time when she attended some of the home games. Morgan usually tagged along, but he couldn't come because he decided to take advantage of the rare time off the team got to visit his parents in the suburbs. Val had been line dancing all night and dragging Owens along every chance she got, while Owens had a glare etched on his face and guarded her from any guy who dared get near her.

Henry and I, well...we fell into some sort of flirting game. His eyes followed my every movement, and though I pretended not to notice, his heated gaze had been lingering on my legs and the perfect cleavage the V-neck of my dress gave me all night.

I basked in the knowledge that little old me managed to get those kinds of glances from him.

His type was no secret. They were usually tall, blonde, and stunning—the type of women who looked like they stepped out of a runway show. I knew I didn't fit the pattern, and the tabloids had no problem pointing it out either.

But I *didn't* care. Fake or not, I reveled in his hungry glances.

I leaned against the front bar as I lifted my beer bottle to catch the bartender's attention to get another round while Henry was in the restroom.

A guy with the shiniest boots I'd ever seen and a fake smile leaned against the bar. "Hey, beautiful. What's a pretty girl like you doing here all alone?"

"Not alone. I'm with some friends." I tilted my head to where Val and Owens were sitting, taking a break from dancing.

He scrubbed his jaw as his eyes raked over my body in a way that made me instantly recoil. He was the type of man I'd been attracted to once—pretty smile, perfectly styled hair underneath the hat, and slim. Exactly like Joe. But I couldn't help but compare him to a certain six-foot-seven athlete. He didn't bring the same energy, nor did the way he was checking me out make me feel the way Henry did every time he stared at me so intensely.

"How about you ditch them and join me?" He leaned closer.

I took a step back. "No, thanks."

"Aw, come on. I promise I'll show you a good time."

Arms I'd come to recognize instantly by the feel of them wrapped around my waist as he pressed my body against his. "She doesn't need you to show her a good time," Henry said gruffly.

The guy craned his neck, and his eyes bulged in shock. "Holy shit, you're Henry Anderson. I'm a huge fan."

"If you're such a huge fan, then stop flirting with my woman," Henry deadpanned.

Dear God, there was no reason why I found the way he said *my woman* so hot, but it did. My back tensed, and my skin shivered under the gruffness of his voice. If any other man had done the same, I'd have been kicking their balls. But with him, I wanted to hear it again.

"She didn't say she had a boyfriend," the guy tried to defend himself.

"I had already said no, though," I fired back with a raise of my brow. "Or are you allergic to the word no?"

The guy had the decency to look embarrassed as he quickly apologized and scurried away without another word.

Henry turned me around and gripped my waist. "You should have waited for me, I could have gotten the drinks."

"I'm perfectly capable of handling myself."

He smirked, the movement making his dimples pop. "Oh, believe me, I know."

I looked at the dance floor over my shoulder then at him. "You still haven't shown me your moves."

An amused laugh escaped him as he grabbed my hand and led me to the dance floor. "How about you show me what you got, Kenny baby?"

"Prepare to become obsessed with me, pretty boy," I said as "Sangria" by Blake Shelton started playing.

One of his hands met my waist, and we swayed together, our boots scuffing against the concrete floor in a perfect rhythm.

His eyebrows shot up in surprise. "You're pretty good."

I gave him a half-shrug. "My grandparents from my mom's side grew up in a small town in Tennessee. They taught me how to dance."

He twirled me once then closed the gap between us. The way his broad chest rested against mine made delicious goosebumps break across my body. "You're full of surprises, Kennedy Jones."

I craned my head, and we were so close, our lips slightly brushed as I replied, "Could say the same about you, Henry Anderson."

His smile was bright, and the corners of his eyes crinkled slightly. I liked his smile and how smitten he looked every time he stared at me, like I was the only thing he was paying attention to. It made me...braver, bolder.

I couldn't fathom what was going through my mind when my eyes flicked to his lips. All I knew was I was drunk on him. I was high on the carelessness of it all.

Without thinking, and through my already stated haze of him, and the perfect night, I gripped the nape of his neck and locked my lips on his in a soft kiss. His body tensed underneath my touch, and his lips remained stilled with shock, but after a beat or two, he gripped my waist tightly with both of his hands and brought me even closer to him. There was not even an inch of gap between us. I was fairly certain that if a piece of paper had been slipped between us, it would have stayed perfectly still.

I tentatively swiped my tongue across his bottom lip, and he heaved a breath as he parted them, his tongue meeting mine with eagerness. My other hand found its way to his shirt and fisted it as I desperately clung to him. I wanted to stay in the moment and keep savoring the way his lips tasted like sour orange mixed with the perfect amount of bitterness from the beer we had been drinking all night.

My body buzzed with need like a fizzling soda. The pressure building in my lower belly was too much. It was debilitating, the way I *wanted* Henry. It was overwhelming, the way I knew I wanted to cross all the lines with him and never look back.

I knew exactly what I wanted when, against his lips, I whispered, "Take me home. *Now.*"

TWENTY-ONE

HENRY

I'D BE HONORED TO BREAK THE RULES WITH YOU.

KENNEDY and I had barely made it over the threshold of the apartment, and she was already bringing our lips together in another intoxicating, deep kiss.

Fuck, there were no words to explain how addicted I was to this woman already. It was insane.

Our kiss grew desperate by the second, and I couldn't get enough.

She nipped my lips, and I groaned against her mouth as I did the same just as eagerly.

She fisted my shirt and brought me closer to her, and I gripped her waist to keep her flushed against my chest. I loved the way my body wrapped around hers. I loved the way we were connected already. How well our energies matched.

"This fucking dress has been torturing me all night," I mumbled against her lips as I gripped her ass and pushed her against the wall.

Her ass was a fucking wet dream. The perfect amount to grab and play with. I was going to—without a doubt—be remembering this moment for the rest of my life.

She moaned against my lips, but I swallowed her sounds with every flick and swipe of my tongue inside her mouth. My hands itched to touch her everywhere, but the little logic I had left made me—painfully so—stop kissing her.

"*Please*, don't stop," she whimpered against my lips.

I heaved a deep breath. "Kenny, wait," I whispered as I took a step back against my will. I was already missing the heat of her body, but I needed to be strong, at least for a minute or two.

Her eyes fluttered open and met my gaze as she frowned.

"Are you—" I stopped myself, debating my next words. This was probably going to be the stupidest thing I was ever going to do, but I had to ask, "Are you sure about this?"

"About what?"

"Breaking the rules."

She took a deep breath as she absentmindedly threaded one of her curls around her index finger. "Are *you*?" she asked instead.

"You already know I'm a rule breaker, Kenny baby." One of my hands rested on my hip as I shot her a lopsided smirk. "The question is, *are you*?" I rasped.

Her chest rose and fell in quick succession as a lingering, charged silence fell between us. My heart thrummed painfully against my chest like a ticking time bomb as I eagerly waited for her response.

"Say the word, and I'll walk away," I said softly. "You're in charge here, Kennedy." I understood her more than she would ever know, and putting her in an uncomfortable situation was the *last* thing I would ever do.

But fuck, I was hoping she would say yes. That she would forget about that stupid contract and have fun with me. I wanted to be the source of her happiness. I wanted her to use me to start *living*.

Her body shifted closer to mine. She reached for my backward hat and plucked it from my head, letting it fall to the floor, then threaded her fingers through my hair. My eyes fluttered, because *fuck*. Her touch was like a shock to my system. It jolted me awake from the inside out.

She stood on her tiptoes and brushed her full lips—which tasted like strawberry and stale beer—against mine, the movement alone making me exhale a shaky breath. "If I'm going to be a rulebreaker, I'd rather do it with you."

A huge sense of relief flowed through my body, and I took a deliberate gulp as I replied, "I'd be honored to break the rules with you."

Not able to hold back any longer, I crashed my lips with hers for the third time that night. This time, it was more explorative, but *just* as explosive. Butterflies took flight in my stomach, and my heart somersaulted in my chest from excitement.

I was one happy man when she said those words. A woman like Kennedy didn't trust easily, and the fact that she was willing to do this? I couldn't believe it. Having her trust was comforting. I wanted to cherish it with everything I had.

She hooked one of her legs around my waist, giving me the perfect access to press my thigh right against her clit. I grabbed a fistful of her curls and tilted her head back, knocking her cowboy hat off in the process. My lips kissed her jaw then the column of her neck, and I sucked the sensitive flesh gently, winning a moan from her. My hands landed on the leg she had hooked around me, and I started to caress it until I gripped part of her outer thigh. I was fucking obsessed with her legs. I couldn't believe I was touching them. She was smooth, soft, and had the perfect amount to grab. I wanted to worship them—*her*.

"Henry, please," Kennedy begged weakly as she started seeking friction against my thigh.

"*Hm*." My lips found her ear, and I nipped her earlobe softly before whispering, "You sound like a fucking dream begging, Kenny baby." Those words won me a breathless moan as she continued to grind on me shamelessly.

I lifted her dress a little, and I almost lost my shit when I pulled back and settled my eyes where we were connected. She was making a mess of my jeans, and the cotton of her white panties clung to her lips with how wet she already was. The sight was out of this fucking world. Damn, how I wished there was nothing between us. But there was something so hot about this, too. Knowing she was so desperate for a release, we couldn't even bother moving from this hallway to one of our rooms. Like we were so hungry for each other, it had to be a *now-or-never* kind of thing.

"Look at you making a mess already." I tsked with a shake of my head as my eyes found her face. And *fuuuuuck*, I was engrossed.

Her lips were softly parted. A droplet of sweat ran from her temple to one of her freckled cheeks, and it took everything in me not to lick it off. My eyes raked downward, and even through the fabric of her dress, I could see how needy her nipples were.

She looked like a goddamn dream, and I was more than happy to stand back and admire everything about her.

"You're doing so good for me, baby. Don't stop," I murmured.

She squirmed, and I couldn't help but smile at how my words affected her. If she only knew all the dirty things I wanted to say and do to her, I was fairly certain she would have run away.

The thought alone scared me, but I pushed the fear to the side, wanting nothing more than to enjoy the moment. I was finally given the opportunity to touch, to kiss, to admire the woman who had been stuck in my head for so long. The last thing I wanted to do was mess it up by getting stuck inside my head.

"More," Kennedy moaned.

I pressed my thigh firmly against her clit and rubbed at the same tempo she was grinding on me. I leaned forward and wrapped my lips around her nipple through the fabric then grazed it with my teeth. This made her hips jolt, and I couldn't hold back the grin that spread across my lips even if I'd tried.

"You like that?" I breathed out the question.

She nodded without a word as her movements faltered when the warmth of my breath prickled the side of her neck.

"Show me how much, then. Grind faster, Kenny. Don't go losing steam on me now," I taunted. Not even while having an intimate moment with this woman was I ever going to stop needling her.

She let out a sharp laugh, but it was quickly drowned by a moan when I wrapped my lips around her nipple again and brushed my thumb in soft circles around the other. Like the good girl she was, her movements started to become faster and harder. Her fingers gripped my shoulders in a death grip, but I couldn't muster one single fuck. I welcomed the pain, because it kept me grounded in the moment.

My lips found hers in another searing kiss. "Fuck, are you going to come on my leg, Kenny?" I exhaled the question in between kisses. "I'll be one happy fucker if you do."

She only managed to moan against my lips, so I took that as a sign to continue. I was determined to find out if I could get her off. I was always up for a challenge, and I had the feeling that witnessing Kennedy come undone before me on my fucking leg was going to be the death of me.

This time, I pushed her dress down, revealing her peaked, brown nipples. I lapped, sucked, and flicked with my tongue, savoring her skin like I was a man in a desert drinking the last drop of water. She was the only answer to this thirst that gripped me like there was no tomorrow.

She pulled my shirt up, and her fingers roamed around the planes of my stomach. The touch was fervent. I couldn't help but tense and whimper, "Please keep touching me." My words were pathetic and desperate against the soft, rich brown skin of her breasts.

One of her hands continued to explore my stomach and my back muscles as the other found my cock, which was throbbing painfully against my jeans. He wanted out, but this moment was all about her. She was my only focus, and my dick needed to get with the program.

She palmed my length through my jeans and gasped. "*Oh.* I don't know how—"

"Hey," I urged softly, my eyes finding hers. "Don't worry. We won't be having sex tonight."

She halted her movements. "Why not?"

I licked my bottom lip then gave her one of my lopsided smiles. "Believe me, there's nothing I'd rather do than fuck you." I rolled one of her nipples between my fingers, pulling a moan from her. I knew then I would never tire of those breathy, husky sounds. "There's nothing more I'd like than to get my fill of your pussy." I husked then dropped a few hot, wet kisses on her neck as I cupped her sex with my hand. Fuck, she was so wet, it was soaking my hand. It took everything in me not to get a taste. "But I've been waiting a long time for this, Kenny baby. I want to take my time with you. I want to know what you love and what drives you crazy." My hand found her throat, and I pressed it softly as my lips hovered over hers. She wrapped her delicate hand around mine and pressed it even more. The way her hooded eyes settled on me made my cock twitch painfully. "And when I finally get to fuck you? I'll make sure you see the stars. That's a promise." I dropped a chaste kiss on her lips.

"Now, I want to see you grind that pussy against my thigh nice and hard. We're not moving from here until you come. Can you do that for me, please?"

She bit her lip and nodded as she started to grind against me again. I was eager to see her come. I wanted her moans. I wanted to feast on her pussy. But all in due fucking time. I was determined to be patient. I was set on taking it slow with her and enjoying any scrap she was willing to give me.

A deep part of me hoped she would give me all of her. But I knew better than to wish for impossible things.

I was so hard I could feel my pre-cum leaking, and she had barely touched me. She didn't need to do much. With the way she eagerly rubbed her pussy against my thigh and the way she moaned and roamed her hands around my body... I was pathetically too far gone.

My forehead rested against hers as I continued to meet her movements, rubbing her clit with my thigh over and over again. Our eyes remained locked on each other's, and the only sounds were her moans and my low grunts. My hands kept playing with her perfect tits. They were small and round, and my hand easily fit around them.

Once her breaths started to become choppier and her movements had no rhyme or reason, I knew she was close. She gripped my length through the fabric of my jeans again and moved her hand up and down. I bit the inside of my cheek to keep my moans in check. But, man, it felt so. Fucking. *Good*.

"Come on my thigh, Kenny. Make a mess. *Now*," I demanded through gritted teeth before I kissed her fiercely.

She moved once, twice more, and her body tensed beneath me as she softly moaned against my lips, "*Henry. Henry. Henry.*"

The way my name came out of her lips like a plea and the way she gripped my cock was all it took for me to tense beneath her touch and chase my orgasm. Stars danced on the corners of my vision as I moaned, *"Fuck, Kenny. Fuck."*

I had never come inside my pants, not even as a horny teenager. Still, this had to be one of the hottest experiences of my life. I'd do it all over again as long as it was with her.

By the time we both came down from our highs, we were still panting. She unhooked her leg from my waist and rested her head against my heaving chest. I dropped a kiss on top of her sweaty curls and inhaled her scent. She smelled like coconut and strawberries, and I engraved the smell into my memory.

I didn't want to forget the simplicity of the moment after one of the best things that had ever happened to me.

"You okay?" I mumbled as I placed my chin on top of her head.

"Yeah," she whispered. "You?"

"Yeah," I croaked.

There was no mistaking the way my throat tightened, or the way my heart felt like a thunderstorm trapped inside my ribcage as it tried to shuffle through all my emotions.

I hadn't even slept with her yet, and my heart fucking knew once wasn't going to be enough.

I was free-falling into the abyss, and what scared me the most was knowing Kennedy wasn't on the same page as me.

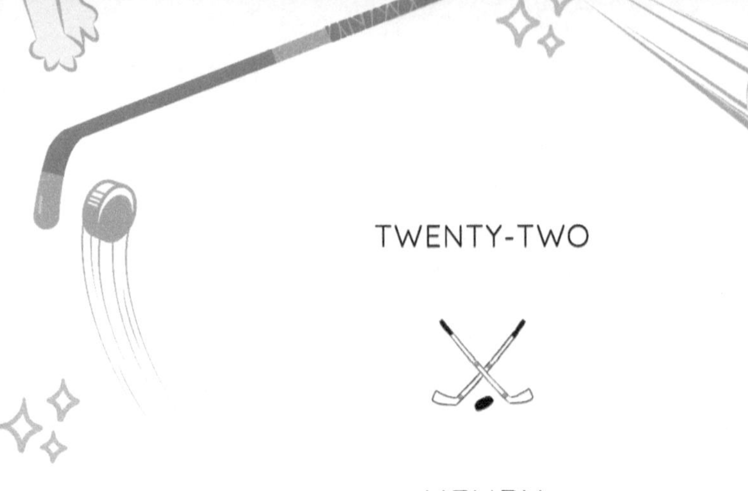

TWENTY-TWO

HENRY

IS CAT DADDY GOING TO SPANK US?

DECEMBER PASSED in the blink of an eye, which was surprising, because I thought being on the bench would have made time move ridiculously slow.

But I kept training—*hard*. It helped me stay out of my head, for the most part. I was also busy every second of every day, and I had Kennedy to thank. Every moment I spent in Chicago, I was either teaching the kids how to skate or doing volunteer work. The press died down significantly, but there were still random articles here and there about our relationship.

It'd been almost two weeks since Kennedy and I had our... *moment*. And I couldn't lie, I wanted a repeat. I was dying to get an *actual* taste of her. To run my hands all over her body and get my fill. I was hungry—and desperate—to make her mine. But between her work schedule and my away games, making time for ourselves was almost impossible.

"Val," Kennedy called out, exasperated. "Wasn't one of the concession managers supposed to bring the popcorn machine and hot chocolate materials? Didn't you schedule that with her?"

Family skate was starting in about an hour, and Kennedy had been running around, stressed out of her mind. Hayes and I tried to help, but one thing you should do when Kennedy was pissed off? Avoid her at all costs. Not that I'd applied the rule to myself. I was like a lost puppy, following her around in case she needed anything.

Val frowned. "I did." She brought her phone out of her white puffer jacket. "Let me text her."

"I'm going to have some very pissed-off kids if those snacks don't magically appear," she murmured, rubbing her temples. Her eyes found mine, and she gave me a confused frown. "What are you still doing here? Aren't the guys playing? Go with them."

"Hell, no. I'm not trying to smell like death before Family Skate starts."

"You play every year," she deadpanned.

I smirked and took a risk by closing the distance between us and wrapping my arms around her waist. I couldn't help it. Touching her had become a necessity. "I know, but I have a hot date this year. I don't want her to think I'm disgusting."

She laughed, her eyes meeting mine with mirth. "Sorry to break it to you, pretty boy, but every time you come home from a game with that bag perched on your shoulders, I think you're disgusting." She scrunched her nose. "You need a new one."

My heart all but leaped out of my chest when she said *home*. It made me happy to know she believed that place was hers as much as it was mine.

I huffed a laugh. "I can't help it."

"Because of your athlete's foot and all?" she asked with a tilt of her head, her tone filled with amusement.

I gasped. "I can't believe you're throwing that at my face!"

"Oh, come on! The joke was *right* there." She laughed. "I had to take the opportunity."

"You do love to humble me."

She casually shrugged one shoulder, giving me one of those smiles I was obsessed with. The one where the corners of her eyes crinkled.

Val approached us. "Uhm, I have bad news."

Kennedy tensed beneath my touch and turned around. "What happened?"

"Matt told her the event got rescheduled, so..." Val cringed.

"No popcorn or hot chocolate for the kids." She tilted her head back with a groan. "Great."

"Why did Matt do that?" Fucking asshole. I knew I hated that guy for a reason. This was one of Kennedy's favorite events, she always went all out to make it special for everybody.

"Because he has a petty vendetta against—"

"That's enough out of you, Val," Kennedy said sternly.

Val clamped her mouth shut and gave me an exasperated look.

I didn't know what the hell was happening, or why Matt decided to do what he did. But what I knew for certain was I'd do anything for Kennedy.

I turned her around and gripped her chin, forcing her to look at me. "Hey, it'll be okay. I will go with the guys to the grocery store and buy bags of popcorn, candy, and everything we can think of. You guys have a microwave in the employees' breakroom, right?"

"Right!" Kennedy exclaimed, her eyes sparkling.

Hell. I'd always liked her brown eyes, but the happiness radiating from them made them even better.

I gave her a soft smile and leaned forward, taking yet another risk by dropping a quick kiss on her plush, soft lips. They tasted like strawberries, and I had to hold myself back and not kiss the fuck out of her in front of her best friend.

What could I say? I liked staking my claim on my fake girlfriend.

"Perfect. Have the equipment manager bring all the tables out and everything. I'll go right now and hopefully, we can have everything ready in time."

Before I could turn around, Kennedy's hand wrapped around my bicep to stop me. Her touch sent a spark through me, igniting every nerve.

My eyes found hers, and she smiled at me so brightly, it made my chest ache like cupid himself had shot me with a fucking arrow right smack in the center of my heart. "Thank you," she whispered.

"Anything for you, Kenny baby."

———

TWENTY MINUTES LATER, we were six hockey players scattered all over the grocery store on an early Sunday afternoon. We divided ourselves into pairs and came up with a strategy.

My goal? To make a certain five-foot-eleven, beautiful, curly-chestnut-haired woman happy.

"How's it going with you and Kennedy?" Donovan asked as he grabbed a few marshmallow bags and dropped them in the cart.

I hadn't exactly been updating any of the guys on what was happening. Not even Hayes. Selfishly, I wanted to keep those moments for myself. More than anything, I knew how risky it would be to divulge information. It wasn't that I didn't trust the guys. I knew they would take the secret to their graves, but there was too much riding on this. The less they knew, the better.

"It's going good. How's Aurora? Is she coming today?" I asked, trying to deflect.

"She said she wasn't feeling well. I tried bringing Isaac with me, but you know how teenagers are. They'd rather hang out with their friends than their old man."

"Dude, you're only thirty-five. Shut up."

Donovan laughed, but we had been teammates for long enough for me to notice it was forced. "Having a kid at a young age doesn't exempt you from being called old when they're in their teens."

"You all right?" I didn't press the Aurora situation any further, nor did I mention the fact we were two and a half months into the season, and we had yet to see her at a home game. She used to go to all of them religiously.

He cleared his throat. "Yeah. I'm just under a lot of stress with the season and all."

A pang of guilt hit me out of nowhere, and I dropped my head with a nod. "That makes sense. I'm sorry."

He gripped my shoulder. "Hey, look at me." When I did, he shook his head. "We're not going to do this. What do I always say?"

"We win as a team, and lose as a team," I mumbled.

He nodded like a proud dad. "Exactly. So get your head out of your ass and keep working on your reputation."

"Kennedy is doing all the heavy work, I'm just showing up where she wants me." I laughed.

"She's damn good at her job."

"That she is," I beamed.

"You like her a lot." He pointed it out like a statement, not a question.

I gripped the back of my neck with a sheepish shrug. "She's cool, I guess."

"You want me to drop the topic, don't you?" He grinned.

"Yes, please."

"Just...be careful, okay?" He pursed his lips in doubt. "I know a lot of people have this perception of Kennedy that she's mean or whatever, but she's a nice girl."

"I know," I whispered.

She was too good for me, but I was too selfish to let her go.

———

"CAN YOU GUYS STOP FUCKING AROUND?" I shouted at Hayes and Parker. They had been getting on my last nerve since we got back from the store.

"*Ohh*, is Cat Daddy getting angry?" Hayes asked, faking a shiver.

"Is Cat Daddy going to *spank* us?" Parker threw an exaggerated wink my way.

"Here I thought you were a sensible man," I mumbled to Parker as I placed the red cups upside down on the table.

"Sensible men can also have fun," Hayes chimed in.

"What the hell do you know about being sensible?" Owens asked dryly.

"I'll have you know, I'm a kind, sensible, and generous man. Tell him why, Anderson."

I scoffed. "Debatable."

He crossed his arms, visibly offended. "Oh, so I guess having your sister as my roommate isn't a generous thing to do at all?"

Morgan was in the middle of pouring the hot chocolate into all the thermoses we bought, but his eyes flicked to mine in shock. "Olivia is moving here?"

I nodded. "Whatever happened with Holt was bad enough that she wants a fresh start. She'll be here probably by next season. If not before."

"Why isn't she moving in with you?" Owens asked.

"I offered to turn Sush's room into another guest room, but you know my sister." I rolled my eyes at the reminder of the lengthy discussion we had about it. "I managed to convince her to live with Hayes for a few months until she gets back on her feet. That way I can keep an eye on her without invading her space, you know?"

Morgan whistled. "Bold move, Anderson."

"Terrible," Owens added.

"Hey!" Hayes frowned. "I've known Olivia since we were like fourteen. We were neighbors when they moved to Oklahoma."

Morgan nodded thoughtfully. "So she can see past your bullshit, got it. That makes more sense."

"Have you forgotten how she and Hayes get whenever they are in a room together?" Parker added. "There's no way Hayes would try anything with her."

Parker wasn't wrong. Being around my best friend and my sister was exhausting. They bickered every second they were around each other. It was always best to walk away.

"Plus, Hayes knows better than to get with my sister."

Parker perked up. "So if Hayes isn't—"

I shot him a withering glare. "I dare you to finish that sentence, Levi James Parker."

"Middle name and everything?" Hayes whistled. "Count your days, dude."

Parker had the decency to look embarrassed as he mumbled, "Sorry."

"That goes for all of you." I looked around the room. "My sister is off fucking limits."

Hayes threw a piece of popcorn in the air and caught it with his mouth. "I don't think you have to worry about that. Olivia would make half of these grown men cry."

I smirked at his comment.

He wasn't wrong. Which was why I was still confused as to why she was leaving New York. Olivia had never been the type to run from her problems. I also knew how much she adored working as an athletic trainer with the Jaguars. But I couldn't lie. I was excited to have her close. I missed her.

I clasped my hands. "Enough about my sister, let's finish this before everyone gets here."

TWENTY-THREE

KENNEDY

I LIKED KISSING MY FAKE BOYFRIEND...A LOT.

I WAS TEMPTED to tell Brad about the shit Matt pulled with one of the most important employee events of the year.

But I didn't.

Because I knew this was exactly what Matt wanted. He was taking every opportunity to make me look bad. I had no idea what I'd done to get on his bad side, but I was so fucking over it. It was obvious he wanted the job as badly as I did, and he was playing dirty tricks to get it. But I was a firm believer in karma. In due time, his was going to arrive.

"Kenny." Henry's voice brought me out of my racing thoughts. He crouched in front of me with a concerned look on his face. "You okay?"

"I need this day to be over. I'm exhausted." The words slipped out of me easily. I almost wanted to laugh at how easy it had become to talk to him.

He reached for one of my curls, wrapping it around one of his fingers and twirling it. It always messed up my hair when he did it, but I didn't have the heart to tell him. I kind of liked it.

"I think you're going to be very happy with what the guys

and I managed to put together." He stood to his full height, interlacing my hand with his. The touch made my body warm and instantly relax.

The plexiglass walls were taken down, and we had gathered all of the couches from our offices to make a comfortable sitting area for the kids with board games and a TV in case they got tired of skating. This event was one of my favorites to plan. It was always this huge, wild day, and the good kind of crazy.

The tables Val and I had found to put the snacks on were covered with tablecloths of the team's colors. An assortment of candies was organized by kind—chocolates, sours, gummies. There were a lot of thermoses with hot chocolate inside, with candy canes and marshmallows of all sorts of colors next to them, as well as a few portable coolers with the Strikers logo filled with all kinds of sodas, juices, and water.

"You did this all in under an hour?" I asked, baffled.

He laughed. "Some of the guys went with me. It kind of works, doesn't it?" His phone pinged with a text, and he quickly glanced at it. "Oh, and I ordered pizza, too. I know we usually have one of the concessions open in case people want to order food, but I assumed that was out of the question with the manager being off and all." He typed a quick text back then looked at me with a smile. "What do you think?"

Breathing was becoming difficult as I took everything in. My stomach fluttered with an army of butterflies, and my chest was tight, but in a good way. Like I had so much happiness inside me, it was hard to contain.

I stood on the tips of my toes and wrapped my arms around his neck in a tight hug. He buried his nose in my hair and inhaled deeply as he placed his arms around my waist, hugging me just as tightly. My heart wanted to take flight at the realization that, once again, Henry Anderson took care of me without an ounce of hesitancy.

I pulled back to meet his eyes. "Thank you."

He offered me a kind smile. "No need to thank me."

My watery eyes made my vision blurry, and I took a step back with a sniff. "This is so stupid, I don't know why I'm crying."

He brushed his thumb across my cheek to wipe off one of my tears. "It's not stupid. You work *really* hard. I don't know why the hell Matt decided to do what he did, but I got you. Always. You say the word, and I'll be there."

"I mean, not always—"

"*Always*, Kenny. I mean it."

I gnawed my bottom lip with a simple nod. Too many emotions were swimming through my head *and* my heart. I didn't know what to make of them anymore.

So...I didn't. Once again, I let go of the uncertainty of it all to live in the moment. I took his act of kindness and locked it in a box I could always go back to and remember.

———

A FEW HOURS LATER, loud music played on the speakers of the rink, and laughter echoed throughout. Everyone was having a good time, and the energy around the arena was good and lively.

Matt showed up at some point with his wife and two kids, and it was hard for him to conceal his shocked face when he found the event was moving smoothly.

That was enough for me to let the situation go. His face alone was worth a million bucks.

The pizzas were a big hit, and some of the older kids were playing board games and playing video games on the TV—I didn't know who had the genius idea to bring their PS5, but I was grateful—while the younger kids were skating their lives away with their endless amount of energy.

I was re-stocking the cups and popcorn bowls when Henry popped up out of nowhere. "Enough work. I have a surprise for you."

"I don't have time for a break," I whined as he gently gripped my shoulders and forced me to sit on one of the benches.

"Sure you do," he countered, waving his hand around. "Everyone is fine. The kids have had way too many snacks, they could use a break from them." He kneeled in front of me and grabbed a box I hadn't noticed was on the floor. "I got you something."

I narrowed my eyes at him and grabbed the square box. When I opened it, my eyes landed on a pair of white, shiny, brand-new figure skates. My heart tugged at my chest with a sense of joy when I noticed the inside of them were pink, and the laces were the same color.

They were fucking perfect, and no one had ever given me such a thoughtful gift.

"What—Why?" A laugh bubbled out of me.

"I told you I wanted to skate with you today. And this is so much better than the rentals, I promise." He quickly took my shoes off and put the skates on. His fingers easily laced them, and in less than five minutes, he was done. "I hope I got the size right. I had to take a peek into one of the shoes you left in the shoe bin at home to figure it out." He chuckled. "Can you stand and try to move your ankles for me?"

I stood and wobbled, but Henry was quick to stand and grip my waist to keep me in place. I tried moving my ankles, but it was hard. "I can't."

He nodded. "That's good. They should feel tight, but not too tight."

I stared at them, loving the way the pink laces gave them the cutest pop of color. "Why are the laces a different color? Don't they usually come in white?"

"I changed them."

"Why?"

His smile was knowing. "Because I know pink is your favorite color."

My bottom lip wobbled as I lifted my gaze to his. The blues of his orbs were a lighter shade, and I couldn't lie—I was mesmerized. "I never told you that," I whispered.

He took a deliberate gulp. "You didn't need to. I notice you, Kenny. I always do."

It wasn't often I was at a loss for words. But there was something about Henry when he gave me these glimpses of sincerity that always got the best of me.

I realized then he was right. There were these little things he did that were easy to miss. I didn't know why he did them. The sadistic part of me was telling me he was only acting. Playing the perfect fake boyfriend role. But my heart was all but pounding in my chest painfully like a string pulled too tight. It was telling me to open my eyes and stop being so naive.

—

"YOU GOT THIS, KENNY!" Hayes shouted.

"Yo, Anderson, let her go, man. She's never going to learn if you don't give her space," Parker said.

"Parker's right, Anderson," Morgan mumbled.

"Let him be! I think it's romantic. It's one of my favorite microtropes," Val commented.

"Microtropes?" Hayes asked.

"Like the one from romance books," Val said.

"You think *everything* is romantic," Owens retorted dryly.

"Sue me for believing in love," Val retorted.

"It's very book boyfriend material," Donovan added.

"When the hell did this become a show? You all need to go mind your business," I shouted over my shoulder.

We had been skating for over an hour. My legs burned, but I was determined to figure it out even if it frustrated me.

Henry chuckled. "You think you're ready to do a lap by yourself?"

"I've *been* ready, but you refuse to let me go," I complained.

"Stop acting like you hate it."

My face heated, because he wasn't wrong. I liked having him near me. He was patient, kind, and *sweet*.

"Whatever," I muttered.

He kept skating backward, his hands never leaving mine. "I think you're starting to like me, and you're mad at yourself because of it," he stated very matter-of-factly.

I hated how easily Henry would call me out on my bullshit. It didn't matter how right he was, I was determined to pretend I didn't like him because it was a safe way to guard my heart.

I shot him the most unimpressed glare I could muster. "And I think you need to stop inflating your ego."

"Accept you like me."

"That's *never* happening."

"Do I need to get another orgasm out of you to accept it?" He wiggled his eyebrows. "All you have to do is ask nicely."

My knees buckled at his words, and I fell forward, but he easily wrapped his arms around my waist without faltering.

"Henry Anderson," I whisper-shouted as I looked around to make sure no one was near us. My pink puffer jacket was suddenly one too many layers, and my face felt hot. "This is a family event. *Behave.*"

His hand reached for a few curls and placed them behind my ear as he laughed ever so casually, like he hadn't just sent my mind reeling. "Fuck, you look pretty when you're flustered."

I straightened and pushed back slightly and quickly placed my hands against the boards, because I didn't trust myself. The last thing I wanted was to fall on my ass. "I am *not* flustered."

"Tell that to your chest. You're breathing pretty hard there." He snickered.

I frantically waved my hand around. "It's all this exercise you got me doing."

He grinned. "Okay, whatever you say, baby."

I crossed my arms. "Glad we're on the same page."

"*Uh-huh.*" His grin was still plastered all over his face as he skated closer to me and rested his hands on the nape of my neck, tilting my head up.

The simple touch made my heart jump a beat. "What are you doing?"

He leaned slightly forward. "Can I kiss you, Kenny?"

My pulse spiked. "Why?"

He swiped his tongue across his bottom lip. "Honestly?"

I licked my own in anticipation and nodded, not able to find the words. His bergamot scent was strong, and it wrapped around all my senses.

His lips brushed against mine as he rasped, "Because I *really* fucking want to."

I let out a shaky, "Okay."

His lips collided with mine with ease, and I relaxed into him. My tongue met his in a lazy, unhurried kiss, but still, every nerve in my body felt like a live wire under his touch. I buzzed with so much energy, it was hard to control.

I didn't know or care if anyone was watching.

I had no excuses in the books, except the truth—I liked kissing my fake boyfriend...*a lot.*

TWENTY-FOUR

KENNEDY

LET'S BREAK THE RULES.

AS SOON AS Henry opened the door and we strode into the apartment, Captain Sushi jumped on the kitchen island with a pissed meow.

"Yeah, yeah," Henry mumbled as he grabbed the treats we kept in one of the kitchen drawers and gave him a piece. "Sorry, bud."

"Do you think he only acts pissed when we're out of the house all day to get treats?"

"Abso-fucking-lutely." Henry scratched Sush's ear. "We're onto you, dude."

The cat simply stared at us as he ate his snack, and once he was done, he jumped off and curled up on the couch.

"What a warm welcome," I shouted so Sush could hear me. "I'll be sure to remember that next time I go to the pet store to buy those organic salmon treats you love so much."

"You spoil him."

I crossed my arms. "There are cat beds that you bought him in every room of this house, even though he literally uses none of them. And you think I'm the one who spoils him?"

He sighed, defeated. "Okay, you may be right."

We both looked at each other and laughed. Once our laughter died, a sudden charged silence fell between us. It was so strong, I could almost taste it. We were toying with the line of no return, but neither one of us was sure of what to do or what the next step was.

I couldn't lie to myself anymore. I wanted *more*. I wanted *him*.

But I was also scared.

This had the word *messy* printed in *bold*, neon letters. Mixing business with pleasure wasn't the best idea—it was *why* I created the contract in the first place.

But I hadn't lied when I told him I wanted to break the rules.

We quietly walked down the hall and stood at our respective doors to retreat to our bedrooms. My eyes found his, and we just stared at each other for a few silent beats. My body buzzed with nervous energy; it was holding me back. It was strange, how the sight of him alone was making my heart quicken.

It freaked me out, to be honest. I couldn't pinpoint when exactly I had started to feel *things* for the guy who, up until the other day, I claimed I couldn't stand.

He leaned against his door and crossed his arms. "Today was really fun."

I rested my head against my door with a nod. "Yeah, it was." I didn't think I had felt so at ease and had so much fun in...*hell*, forever.

He opened his mouth to say something, but stopped himself and simply nodded awkwardly with a smile.

"Night, pretty boy," I whispered.

"Night, Kenny baby," he rasped.

I gave him a small smile and opened the door to my

bedroom. When I shut myself in it with a soft click, I rested my forehead against the sleek white door with a long sigh.

I couldn't shake the disappointment in the pit of my stomach when he didn't reach for me. I was expecting...something. *Anything.* I was terrified of making the first move. I didn't have it in me to do it again.

Haven't you been complaining that you're tired of not living?

I shook my head as I stepped into the shower. My brain was getting too many crazy ideas, and it was clouding my judgment.

Hot water ran down my skin, relaxing my muscles as my head continued in overdrive.

Is it crazy, though? To live and enjoy life? To have causal, fun sex for the hell of it?

When I got out of the shower and slipped into an oversize sweatshirt, I glanced at my door like it was going to give me all the answers I was looking for.

Should I do it? Go up to his door, knock, and be *selfish* for once? If there was anyone I trusted at the time to give me what I was looking for, as crazy as this was to admit, it was Henry.

No, I thought to myself. *That's insane.*

But what if it wasn't? We had already crossed the line. What difference did one more time—*or multiple*—really make?

With my heart lodged in my throat and adrenaline coursing through me, I took three deliberate steps, and with a shaky breath, I grabbed the door handle, opening it.

I was determined to see this through—to be *brave.*

My steps faltered when my eyes landed on Henry standing in front of me in nothing but a pair of black boxer briefs that did *nothing* to hide what I knew damn well he was carrying. My eyes raked over every hard muscle of his forearms, the pronounced veins, the freckles that dusted his pale skin, and his chiseled abdomen. He was tall, broad, and all *man*—it was *overwhelming.*

His broad chest rose and fell quickly, like he was having a difficult time breathing. Which was funny, because my chest was like a drum pounding too hard, too fast, and it made it just as difficult for me to breathe. My eyes settled on his, and they were this darker shade of blue, with flecks of gray that all but screamed how hungry he was for *me.*

If I had to describe how Henry looked, only one word would come to mind—*feral.*

The energy barreling through my body was hot and wild, and impossible to tame. Electricity danced in the space between us, charging the very air we breathed like a live fuse.

My eyes dropped to his lips, and a deep growl bubbled out of Henry's chest as he breathed out, "*Fuck it.*" Then he swiftly threaded his fingers through my curls possessively, searing our lips in a deep, hungry kiss.

I moaned like it was instinct when his lips met mine. He was the only source of air my body demanded. His kisses were explosive, like a collision of stars leaving their hot mark. I *welcomed* the burn. I *wanted* more of it.

We were a mess of hot, wet kisses and heavy breaths as his other hand gripped my waist, and he walked us inside my room and shut the door then turned me around and pushed me against it. He tilted my head to get more access and started to trail kisses from my jaw to my neck and collarbone.

I was fucking *alive* underneath his touch and the way he planted kisses across my skin like I was the only thing he wanted to savor.

It fueled me with reckless confidence, so I pressed my hand to his chest and guided him until the back of his legs hit the bed, forcing him to sit. I straddled him, and his hands gripped my ass while his wild, hooded eyes met mine. My fingers found the hem of my sweatshirt and lifted the fabric without wasting a second.

Henry's eyes landed on my naked chest, and he groaned a low, "*Fuuuuck.*" He was in awe, just staring at me like I was his sole focus.

In my thirty-two years of life, I had never felt truly powerful. Most of my life, I'd moved through with false confidence. But one heated look from him, and I was ready to conquer the whole fucking world. *It terrified me.*

But it didn't matter. The need to be with him was stronger, and it made it easier for me to push all those unwelcome emotions to the side.

I threaded my fingers through his hair and gave it a gentle tug. "What are you waiting for?" I rasped against his lips. "*Fuck me, Henry. Let's break the rules.*"

"*Oh, Kenny.*" His chuckle was dark, gravelly. "I'm going to have so much fun with you."

I moved my hips, pressing my center against his length, and I smirked when he let out a low, pained groan. "Show me what you got, pretty boy."

He swiftly picked me up and splayed me against the soft mattress. His body hovered over mine as his mouth found one of my brown nipples and he swirled his tongue around it, pulling a moan out of me. His calloused hand roamed my ribcage, my abdomen, and my curves like he was committing every inch of me to memory until it landed on my drenched panties.

He met my stare through his eyelashes with a lazy smirk playing on his lips. "Are you wet for me already, Kenny baby?"

"Yes," I replied without an ounce of shame. This was not me. I wasn't the kind of girl who *talked* during sex. But Henry... Well, he made me fearless. "What are you going to do about it?"

He arched a brow. "Is that a challenge?"

"I don't know, is it?" My tone was playful.

His lips traveled with hot kisses from my sternum to my stomach to my hips. I tilted my head back with a moan when he placed a few kisses on my inner thighs. If the way he fucked felt half as good as his lips and hands felt on my body...I didn't know how I was going to survive.

He gripped the hem of my panties as he nipped my inner thigh to get my attention. "Oh, no, no." He clicked his tongue. "You're going to look at me in the eyes while I eat your cunt, Kennedy. I want those pretty brown eyes on me at *all* times."

"*Oh my God*," I moaned breathlessly as my clit throbbed painfully at his words.

What the hell was happening? How was *this* real life?

He took my underwear off in one quick motion then wrapped my legs around his shoulders. "I'm the only one who's going to fuck you senseless." Long, sleek fingers gripped my thighs. His stare was intense and set my body ablaze. "The only name I want you moaning is *mine*," he growled.

I couldn't even form a response, because Henry flattened his tongue against my center and licked it torturously slow. My eyes rolled to the back of my head, and I was transported to another dimension. My body wasn't mine anymore. It was possessed by lust and instantly craved more like an insatiable hunger, ready to devour anything in its path.

"Eyes." *Lick.* "On." *Lick.* "Me." *Lick.*

It took everything in me to open my eyelids and meet his gaze, but when I did, he rewarded me with a twirl of his tongue around my clit. Then he latched his mouth on to me and started sucking and slurping like a thirsty, desperate man. The sounds were downright filthy; it was almost too embarrassing how my core tightened and how wet I became with each suck and erotic sound. But I was so intent on obeying him, my eyes never left his as I propped one of my elbows on the bed then threaded my fingers through his hair.

His tongue continued to circle my clit with precision, and I almost crushed his head with my thighs when he swiped across a sensitive spot. His smile was wicked as he gripped me in a death grip and opened my legs wide. "Keep these legs open for me. I want to lick, suck, and eat *every* fucking inch of you."

All I could do was moan. I was reeling and overstimulated with the way he devoured my pussy, by the feel of his calloused hands on my thighs, and by the heat of his body warming mine.

"Say you understand, Kenny," he commanded.

Who the hell was this man?

With every command he gave me, I was eager to obey. To do whatever he desired. *It was madness.*

"I-I understand," I said through a heaved breath.

"Good girl." *Oh*, the way my pussy clenched at the praise was blistering.

He didn't waste any more time and *consumed* me. He didn't come up for air. He just licked and nipped my outer labia, and kept sucking my clit and swiping his tongue back and forth, then in circles, until I was throbbing painfully against his mouth. One of his fingers slowly entered me, and I clenched around the sudden intrusion. It burned, but it was the good kind of fire—the kind I wanted to lie on and let swallow me whole.

"*Fuck*, you're tight," he rasped against me as he continued to finger me slowly.

I was so close, I couldn't form any coherent thoughts or sentences. When his finger found my sensitive spot, he brushed his middle finger across my clit to pick some of my arousal and slowly entered the second digit. His temple rested against my thigh as he looked at—*no*—admired me. His eyes were hooded and glassy, his face was coated with my arousal, and that just did something to me.

"You're so beautiful," he murmured against my skin.

My pussy clenched around his fingers at his praise. "*Henry.*"

"You look so fucking pretty with my fingers inside your cunt and desperately moaning my name. *God, Kenny.* You're a goddamn dream, baby."

My pussy clenched *again.*

"Does my pretty girl like being praised?" he asked in a husky tone, his smile playful and knowing. I should have guessed Henry was going to read me like an open book in bed, just like he did during our day-to-day interactions.

I nodded with a bite of my lip. I couldn't deny it; every praise he gave me was like his words were fingertips, touching me everywhere at once.

His fingers picked up the pace, sliding out of me faster and harder as his thumb found my clit and started to brush it in circles. "You're doing so good for me. Such a good girl." He dropped a kiss on my hipbone. "That's it. Keep taking my fingers, let's get you nice and stretched for my cock."

"Oh, G—" I stopped myself and choked out, "*Henry, fuck,*" instead. I was so close, my lower belly was tight, and my feet curled as shivers ran down my spine.

"You gonna come for me, Kenny?" He kissed my thigh and shot me one of his panty-melting smiles. "You ready to make a mess on my face and my hand?"

I couldn't handle his dirty words anymore; I was going to detonate any second if he continued. "Henry, I swear to—" My words got lodged in my throat when he curled his fingers and latched his mouth on my clit with a *long,* hard suck.

That's all it took.

The orgasm rippled through me with unavoidable force.

My core tightened, my clit throbbed, and my body felt like a wave crashed violently against me. My legs shook, and I tried to squirm away, but Henry wrapped an arm around me and held me in place as he continued to drink every ounce of me. I chanted his name over and over again as he kept pumping his fingers in and out of me lazily, prolonging my release until I couldn't give him anymore.

My hand reached for his wrist to stop him. "I can't anymore," I whined.

He chuckled as he slipped his fingers out of me then hovered over me. "You did good, baby." His lips met mine in a soft kiss, and I moaned against his mouth at the taste of him and my arousal mixed. "But we're far from over." He dropped a kiss on my shoulder and mumbled, "I'll be right back."

He strode out of my room, and a few moments later, he came back with a condom in his hand.

My heart throbbed wildly in anticipation.

This was it. This was happening. There was no turning back. I was going to be added to the endless sexual conquest list of Henry Anderson.

Surprisingly, I didn't care. I knew what I was signing up for when I was determined to knock on his door. *One unforgettable night.*

After all, I wasn't ready for something serious with anyone, and I couldn't ever see a man like Henry settling down. It was why this made sense.

He took his boxer briefs off, letting his cock bob free. My mouth instantly watered at the sight of it. He made quick work of the condom and rolled it on his length, then, without a word, and with predatory, hungry steps, he closed the distance between us and wrapped his hand around my throat and *owned* my mouth. His kisses were punishing, and every bit intoxicating, like a drug I knew I shouldn't be consuming but wanted more of. They were fierce, like silent promises that he was going to rock my world.

He turned me around and pushed my head against the pillow. I arched my back, and there I was—splayed for him on all fours. I'd never felt so exposed. It was nerve-wracking.

His hand caressed my thighs then my ass as he dropped a kiss on the center of my back. "You look so fucking stunning like this. Ready to take my cock like a good girl," he whispered against my skin.

All I could do was moan at his words, because he was right. I was desperate to feel him inside me. Eager for him to make me feel good.

His thumb brushed my clit in lazy circles, pulling another moan out of me, but the pillows drowned the sounds. "Relax for me."

And so I did. I arched my back even more while relaxing my shoulders and chest against the mattress. The head of his cock pressed against my entrance, and I fisted the bed sheets until my knuckles turned white and the palm of my hands became numb. *It was too much.* He was thick and long, and I was suddenly becoming very aware of how difficult this was going to be.

"Breathe for me, Kenny baby. You got this," Henry murmured as he continued to circle my clit.

The nickname I loved so much rolling off his lips made me relax and breathe out a bit as he slid in a few more inches. And, *oh my God*, was it good.

He dropped another kiss on my back, causing his cock to slide in one more inch. "You're doing so good. That's it. Can you take more?" His voice was tight, like he was holding himself back. *I hated that.*

I wanted to be wholeheartedly absorbed by him and this

moment. I didn't want this moment to be sweet. *I wanted to be fucked.*

I looked over my shoulder. "You said you were going to fuck me senseless. So, go ahead, pretty boy. Show me what you got."

He licked his bottom lip then nipped it to suppress a smile. "I'm trying to be a gentleman here."

"I'm not looking for a gentleman, Henry. I want a man who can *fuck* me," I retorted.

A deep chuckle rumbled from his chest as he shook his head. "Wrong thing to say," he said, his voice thick and gravelly.

Before I could reply with another retort, a loud cry escaped my lips instead when he gripped my hips and, without wasting one more second, filled me to the hilt.

We stilled for a few beats. My heart was in my throat. My core had never felt so tight, and it was hard to breathe with how full I was.

Henry fisted my curls and pressed my back against his chest. Stars danced around the corners of my eyes at how deep he felt in this position. Without a word and a few ragged breaths, he started to *pound* into me. Skin met skin with thrust after animalistic thrust. I fucking loved it. *It was exactly what I was craving.*

"Got nothing to say now?" he asked roughly, the warmth of his breath prickling my skin.

I heaved a laugh. It was hard to speak with how hard and through he was fucking me, but I managed to grit out, "*Harder.*"

"I swear you're going to be the death of me," he growled.

A whimper slipped past my lips when Henry slid out of me. I was already missing the fullness of him and the heat of his skin against mine. He turned me around and laid me on the bed then grabbed a pillow and placed it underneath my lower back.

"What are you—" I didn't get to finish my question, because without missing a beat, he swiped the head of his cock against my center and entered me again. "*Oh,*" I moaned and shut my eyes at the intense sensation. The way my hips were positioned, I could feel him even deeper.

The moment was inexplicable. I was overwhelmed—in a haze of *him.* The way his bergamot, vetiver scent filled my nostrils, his grunts, his words—*everything.*

Henry gripped the back of my head, gently forcing me to stare at where we were connected. "Look at how well you take my cock, Kennedy. *So fucking good,*" he moaned.

I couldn't stop staring, even if I tried. My eyes raked over every inch of him. The tightness of his jaw, the way his eyes were locked on where we were connected, completely enthralled. His sweaty hair clung to his forehead, and he gnawed his bottom lip, trying to hold back his grunts. My clit throbbed, and I reached for it, rubbing it in quick circles as my eyes settled where his cock continued to pump in and out of me with precision.

His eyes tracked the movement. "Greedy girl. You're ready for another orgasm?"

"*Yes.* I'm close," I choked out. Breathing was a difficult task, but I didn't care.

He kept pounding into me harder, rougher, and wilder. And it was like magic, the way Henry fucked me. The way our bodies molded together. It was like a moth to a flame. Explosive. Unstoppable.

I tried to shut my eyes as my orgasm was quickly building, but Henry gripped my cheeks between his fingers and forced me to look at him. It was impossible to describe how feral and uncontrolled he looked. Like he couldn't get enough out of me, of this moment, and he wanted to commit every movement, every touch to memory.

"I want your eyes on me while you come around my cock,

Kennedy. I've been waiting for this moment since the day I met you."

His confession sent a ripple of shock through me.

Had I heard him right? He had been wanting me for that long? *There was no way.*

I kept touching myself harder and faster, and my pussy clenched around him as my climax kept building like a tidal wave surging toward shore.

"Come for me, Kenny. *Please, I need it.*" His plea was all it took to send me over the edge.

As I climaxed, Henry's thrusts became wilder. There was no rhyme or reason for the way he was thrusting in and out of me. It was pure, animalistic need as he continued to hit that spot deep inside of me. He thrusted once, twice more, then rested his forehead against my shoulder as his whole body tensed and his cock swelled inside me.

Every feeling, every moment I'd spent with Henry hit me like a truck. How had this happened? How did I go from disliking him to having the best sex of my goddamn life?

Our breathing was labored and in sync as he slipped out of me, then his body sagged on the mattress next to me.

I sighed in awe. "That was..." There were no words. I was still in a haze.

He laughed, wrapping his arm around me and dropping a kiss to my forehead. "I know. Fucking insane."

TWENTY-FIVE

HENRY

FOR THE RECORD, I MISS YOU, TOO.

MY HEART WAS PAINFULLY TIGHT, and it was hard to breathe.

I was pissed off at the whole fucking world. At Coach Sloane, too. Because why, exactly, was I still benched?

I was doing a *great* job at keeping my head down and minding my business.

But when I approached Coach and asked him if he would consider putting me in to play against the Vancouver Sharks, he simply stared at me with a blank expression and shook his head without a word.

And that was that. End of the conversation.

My head was entering a dark place, and I was desperately trying to hold on to anything to not get drowned by it. Vancouver always brought out the worst in me, and being benched fueled all those feelings with a fresh set of fury and frustration.

Hayes jumped over the boards and sat on the bench next to me with a pained groan as he chewed on his mouthguard. "*Fuck.* That shift was painful."

I gripped my stick in a death grip with a clipped nod. "I know." My eyes remained on the ice, tracking every movement.

We were down 2-1. And everyone on the team was giving it everything they had.

My eyes followed the puck and the left winger of the Sharks, who surged forward and sliced across the ice with precision. He managed to dodge Parker, and his body shifted low to protect the puck. He shot it with a quick flick of his wrist as the center of the Sharks was already breaking past the neutral zone. The center received the pass in one clean motion and kept control as he bolted into the offensive zone.

By some miracle of fucking God, before he could set up for a shot, Morgan arrived at the speed of light. His stick made contact with the puck and nudged off balance. It slid dangerously close to the net, and the right winger of the Sharks swooped in out of nowhere, his stick snapping forward to claim the loose puck.

It was in that moment my heart dropped to my stomach, because I knew it was too late.

Once the right winger of the opposite team gained control of the puck, he fired a wrist shot, and the puck rocketed toward the net before Morgan or Parker could react. Owens dropped into a butterfly stance and reached with his glove, but the puck sailed just past his outstretched hand, high and tight into the top right corner.

The horn blared, a loud, fucking mocking sound, and the whole arena erupted in cheers.

And just like that...we had lost another game.

———

BEING in Vancouver was stressful for many reasons.

But the main one was standing outside the locker rooms, talking and laughing with my coach.

The '90s NHL sweetheart Vincent Anderson—also known as dear old dad.

He looked good for his age, and he maintained his physique well after all these years. He was a god in the eyes of the public, a player who was taken from them too soon after a knee injury that ended his career when he was at his peak.

Coach's eyes landed on me, and he gave me a nod. "I got some press to do, so I'll leave you two to it." He grasped Vincent's shoulder. "It was nice seeing you."

Vincent nodded with a fake smile. The one he did to make everyone believe he was a merry-fucking-happy guy. "Same here."

Once Coach was out of sight, I tightened the grip on my gear bag as I headed toward the exit. I didn't have the patience or energy to deal with him.

I stepped outside, desperate to let the Vancouver chill bite my skin. My body was overheating. I was angry and exhausted.

"Where are you going?" he asked, following me.

I inhaled and exhaled through my nose as calmly as possible. "I'm not in the mood to talk to you."

He gripped my shoulder and turned me around. "Too fucking bad. This is what happens when you don't answer my texts."

"I have nothing to say to you."

He barked a menacing laugh. "So, you go around punching guys and getting benched and think you have nothing to say to me? You owe me an explanation."

I tightened my jaw and shook off his grip. "It's none of your goddamn business, Vincent."

"If you're carrying my last name on the back of your jersey, yeah, it's very much my goddamn business, *son*."

I laughed humorlessly as I slipped a hand in my pocket without a word. There had been many times I've considered changing my last name. To walk away from everything that had to do with the man standing before me. But a small part of me still held on to stupid hope that he would change. I *hated* myself for it. Never told a soul either. It was one of those secrets I knew I would take to the grave.

"When are you getting back on the ice?" he pressed.

My eyes settled on the arena. I refused to look him in the eyes, because if I had, I was fairly certain I was going to punch him.

"Or are you too busy fucking Kennedy Jones?" he mocked.

My eyes settled on him as my nostrils flared. "What did you just say?"

His eyes glinted with malicious intent. *Fuck.* It was a trap, and I fell for it. "Ah, so that got your attention." He shook his head with a laugh. "I can't lie, you got good taste. Guess you got that from me."

My ears rang as adrenaline pumped through me. I invaded his space and gripped the collar of his shirt. I didn't care that we were in public, or that I was probably causing a scene. Anyone who spoke about Kennedy, especially my father, would be on the receiving end of my pent-up anger. "Not another word about her. Do you understand me? Keep her name out of your fucking mouth."

"I'm just a father concerned about who my son is dating." He tilted his head with a knowing smirk. "The last thing I want for you is to get baby trapped like I did."

Anger stabbed the corner of my heart like a poisonous blade, spreading throughout my body at his words.

I balled my free hand into a fist.

The same old story was getting fucking tiresome.

It took *two* people for my mother to get knocked up. And it wasn't like it had been a one-night stand, either. My parents were high school sweethearts.

But leave it to him to place the blame on everyone else because he refused to take responsibility for his actions. It was a bitter realization, knowing he'd never change. It angered me, knowing I should have known better by then.

This was my father to the very core. He was an abuser, physically *and* emotionally. He knew the comment would strike a mark just as bad as if he had punched me. Because, yes. My father wasn't stupid. He may have beaten me when I was a child, when I was weak and still trying to grow my muscles, but he knew better than to try it now. I had the body to stand my ground with him.

A small, sadistic part of me wanted him to try, because I wanted an excuse to unleash everything on him. I was eager for him to punch me. To do *anything,* just so the world could see the real piece of shit he truly was.

The unrelenting anger I felt was because of *him.* My career was up in the air because I always kept thinking about *him.* It always boiled down to *him.*

But I couldn't lie to myself. It would have been hypocritical of me to place the blame on someone else. At the end of the day, I was weak, and that's why he could always reach the only good parts of me and crush them with his cutting words.

Hayes and Donovan stepped outside, and when they saw us, they quickly strode closer to separate us.

Hayes placed his arms around my chest and pulled me back as Donovan did the same with Vincent.

"Anderson, calm down, man," Hayes said as he used his force to hold me back. "What's going on?"

"Yeah, son. *Calm down,*" Vincent taunted.

This motherf—

"That's enough out of you, Mr. Anderson. I think it's time you go home," Donovan said calmly.

A few of my teammates were filtering out of the arena and walking toward the bus that was going to take us to the airport. When Vincent noticed, he concealed his face with a fake smile and a clipped nod.

Before he left, he stood close to me and spoke low enough so no one else could hear him. "Be careful about staining our name again, *boy*. Or I'll make a surprise visit and talk with your little *girlfriend*."

I gritted my teeth without a reply. My chest beat painfully, and my lungs struggled for air. He settled his eyes on me with a knowing look and a smug smile, then nodded and *finally* walked away for good.

"What did he say?" Hayes whispered to me as we got into the bus and sat down.

I shook my head without a word as I leaned my head back on the headrest and shut my eyes.

He was the only one who knew the extent of the issues I had with my father. But I didn't want to talk to anyone about it.

My heart only wanted *one* person.

———

THE FLIGHTS back home were always rough when we lost. The energy was down. No one joked around. Most of my teammates were sleeping, while others were speaking with their partners on their phones.

I stared at my phone with Kennedy's contact page open in contemplation.

Would she even answer if I called? It was past midnight already.

She had texted me saying she was sorry we had lost the game, so there was a chance she was awake.

Does that mean she watched every game?

What was I saying? Of course, she did. I'm sure she had to, just in case. PR responsibilities and all. Though part of me hoped she watched it because of me.

With a deep breath, I put headphones on and hit the video call button before I lost the little bravery I had.

The phone rang twice, and Kennedy croaked, "Hello?"

"Did I wake you up? I'm sorry. Go back to bed."

She centered the camera, letting me get a good look at her. She was devoid of makeup, and her curly hair was braided, allowing me to see her face and how those ridiculously cute freckles popped against her brown skin.

My heart tightened at the sight of her. She was *so fucking stunning*, it physically hurt.

"No. You're fine. I'm on the couch watching TV while Sush is crushing me with his weight." She angled her phone to show me where the cat was curled up, sleeping peacefully. She angled the camera back to her face and rolled her eyes. "You've been giving him way too many treats, by the way. He's fat."

"I want him to like me."

"You can try to buy his love with all the treats you want, but I will still be his favorite human," she quipped.

She wasn't wrong. Those two had become an inseparable duo since she moved in.

I gave her a small smile without a word. My head was starting to clear, and my mood was significantly improving with every moment we spent on the phone.

"So, why did you call me?" She asked.

"Honestly?"

She gave me a knowing smile. "Always."

"I had a rough night, and I wanted to see you and hear your

voice." I let out a long, shaky sigh. I didn't know why I was nervous. "I miss you." The confession had been lodged on my throat for days now. Relief washed through me when I finally said it out loud.

We had been on the road for almost a week, and there wasn't one night I hadn't thought about Kennedy. I was too afraid to call her. I still didn't know where we stood, but something had shifted between us. But I also didn't want to overwhelm her. I mean, she had just come off a three-year engagement, and here I was, eager to get more from her even though I didn't know if she was in the right headspace for it.

Every fucking night, my thumb hovered over her contact, and every night, I went to bed with regret that I hadn't called her. And even though I was a few hours away from seeing her, I couldn't hold back any longer.

Was that pathetic? Maybe. But I was past caring.

"Wanna talk about what's going on with you?" she asked softly.

"Not really," I whispered.

She hummed. "I know I said this already, but I'm sorry about the game. I'll see if I can put in a good word for you with Coach Sloane. You deserve to be back on the ice."

My heart swelled with pride. "You mean that?"

"Yeah." She smiled. "I do."

We fell silent as we stared at each other for a few seconds. My heart wanted to come out of my chest as I looked at her. I was pathetically so far gone for this woman, it wasn't funny. I wanted to hang out with her. I wanted to *actually* date her. Like, *make-her-my-real-girlfriend* type of dating.

"Henry?"

"Yeah, Kenny baby?" I rasped.

Her brown eyes sparkled. "For the record, I miss you, too," she whispered.

You know those moments in rom-com movies? The ones where time stands still when something significant happens? *This* was one of those. Every beat of my heart was loud in my ears, my skin felt like little lights were being turned on, jolting with so much electricity, my body wasn't my own anymore. My brain etched this moment to memory like it was carving it into stone.

Something fearless took hold of me as I blurted, "Would you like to go on a date with me when I get back?" *A real date.* It's what I really wanted to say, but I was too afraid.

She smiled. "Sure. We haven't had one in a minute. I kind of miss those fake dates."

My eyes twitched. A word had never tasted so bitter just from the fucking sound of it. Though it annoyed me, I was determined to play pretend if it meant I got to spend time with her.

TWENTY-SIX

KENNEDY

I LIKE ALL OF YOU, KENNEDY JONES.

WINTER IN CHICAGO wasn't for the weak-hearted. But that didn't stop me from wearing a tight burgundy mini dress with winter black tights and high black boots, even though I knew I had to bundle up with my gray winter coat once we stepped outside.

I had no idea what Henry planned for the evening, but for some reason, I was nervous *and* giddy.

This was stupid. Why was I so excited? This was just another regular old fake date.

I knew having sex with Henry was a really bad fucking idea, because I was feeling all these things I didn't want to face.

Are we forgetting that he called you last night and told you he missed you? Or the fact that you told him you missed him, too?

I strode out of my room and found Henry, his elbows resting on the kitchen island, staring at his phone. *My God*, he looked *good*. He wore a long-sleeved knitted dark-blue sweater that hugged his muscles perfectly, black trousers, and dress shoes.

I cleared my throat, trying to push down the pathetic flop my stomach did at the sight of him.

He looked up, and his intense blue gaze pinned me in place. His eyes were calculating, and there was a heat to them, drinking me in like I was the only thing on the menu he wanted.

It was intoxicating, the way Henry always looked at me. I never wanted him to stop.

"You look..." He took a few deliberate steps toward me, interlaced one of my hands with his, and twirled me around. "*Fucking stunning.*" His gaze lowered to my legs. "Spring cannot come soon enough," he murmured to himself.

I gaped at him. "Are you gawking at my legs?" I learned how to love myself despite the comments I'd gotten over the years about how tall I was, but insecurity took hold of me at the most random of times.

He nodded, still staring at them. "They're one of my favorite things about you."

That was...rather forward. But the compliment filtered through me like a slow pour of honey—thick, and sweet, and every bit addicting.

It shouldn't have been surprising. This *was* Henry Anderson after all. He was an honest and notorious flirt.

"One?" I crossed my arms and kept my grin in check. "As in, there's more that you like?"

He rolled his lips as his eyes found mine. There was a sense of playfulness and mirth he oozed. "What exactly is your question, Kenny baby? I like it when you're direct."

I tilted my head in contemplation. "What else do you like?"

Should I have been entertaining this? Probably not. But I think we'd all learned by now how reckless I was around him.

"Your eyes," he replied without missing a beat.

I arched an eyebrow. "What are you doing?"

He lazily slipped a hand into one of his pockets. "What do you mean?"

"You're acting weird."

"Am I?" His tone held a bit of amusement.

"Stop answering with questions," I groaned.

"Why?"

I rolled my eyes as I strode to the small closet where we kept our coats and grabbed mine. "Forget it."

I was about to put it on, but Henry stopped me and said, "Let me," as he grabbed the coat from my hands and helped me slip into it.

Being so near to him made my heartbeat race. His usual bergamot and vetiver scent hit my nostrils, and I was suddenly dying to stay closer to him just so I could let myself be enveloped in it.

There was something seriously wrong with me.

I EXPECTED Henry to take me to a popular place. Anything public that would have helped get some exposure, so people could take pictures of us and circulate them.

Instead, we were on a winter rooftop bar and restaurant that overlooked the city's busy lights, sitting inside a toasty igloo with a fire pit, some good Italian food, and delicious drinks.

It was quiet, and intimate, but *really* fucking fun.

"You jumped off a fucking roof into a pool?" My drink almost spilled out of my mouth as I tried to keep my laugh in check at the insane college story Henry was telling me. "Are you insane?"

He raised his hands in defense. "I was a bored eighteen-year-old, okay?"

"Thank God for the early draft. Though now I'm

wondering what sort of trouble you would have gotten yourself into if you'd ever finished college."

"Why wonder? We all know my reputation." He winked before he took a sip of his whiskey.

I thinned my lips without a word. There had been so many questions on the tip of my tongue for a while, because the more I got to know Henry, the more I realized the whole "bad boy" center forward reputation was utter bullshit.

But I kept my mouth shut and instead took a sip of my wine and sighed. "This was nice." I waved my hand around. "One of the best fake dates you've taken me on, for sure," I quipped.

Why the fuck do you have to keep saying the word fake? Seriously. We get it, my brain mocked.

I was desperate to keep a sense of normalcy. More than anything, I needed to keep reminding myself this wasn't real.

Henry's jaw ticked, but he took a swig of his whiskey and dropped the glass on the table with a soft clunk. "The night's not over."

"No?" I stared at him, shocked.

He smiled. "I have a surprise. I think you're going to like it."

My heart quivered. This had already been *too* much. I wasn't used to this kind of attention. To be honest, dating Joe consisted of going to work parties. The intimacy of it all, going to a simple dinner just because, or going line dancing for the hell of it, was never a thing. It was like hanging out by ourselves was a task, but I'd been so blind to it, I never realized it.

"This was more than enough, we don't need to do anything else," I said sheepishly.

"This was the bare minimum. If we're going out, I will always make sure we have fun."

My body froze for the slightest moment. He didn't say fake, he didn't mention the media attention or why we were really here. And before I could form a question, he simply stood, grabbed my coat, and helped me put it on without a word. I couldn't speak, even if I tried. So many emotions were lodged in my throat. Both exhilaration and fear rested against my ribcage, making it impossible to breathe, because I wasn't sure if the prospect of this being a real date made me nervous or really happy.

———

IT WAS a little after midnight when a car he had rented for the night dropped us off in front of Millennium Park. It was starting to snow, so flurries dusted our coats, and though it was cold, the park was beautiful and surprisingly quiet. Henry carried a gym bag on his shoulder, and he grabbed my hand like it was the most natural thing in the world as he guided us to an outdoor ice rink. Goosebumps sneaked up my arms at the simple touch. It was always electrifying, like lightning, but there was a comfort behind it now, too.

"Are we breaking in? It's the middle of the night!" I whisper-shouted.

He smirked. "Are you scared, Jonesy?"

"Here I thought we were past that nickname."

"That was rather naive of you," he joked.

I took a seat on one of the benches, and he kneeled in front of me then riffled through the bag until he found my skates.

"Also, no. We're not breaking in. I called in a favor. The rink is all ours for an hour," he said.

I beamed. "Really?"

He nodded as he started putting my skates on. I knew better than to fight by now. It was the little things Henry liked to do the most, like he wanted to be useful. Part of me also liked these little acts of service. In a world where I'd always had to take care of myself because I believed I was too much of a burden, it was a nice change of pace. Being stubborn about it proved to be useless, because if there was one thing Henry knew how to do well, it was be persistent.

I liked that about him, you know? His tenacity. The way he showed the goodness of his heart without even trying. It was why I had been dying to ask him why, exactly, he kept this side of himself hidden. What was he running away from? Why was he hiding?

The man who referred to himself as the *"king of the ice"* and acted like the world owed him something was nowhere to be found. It was like he disappeared with a simple *poof*. So why not show his true personality to the rest of the world?

"I knew you had fun last time, and I thought it'd be cool to do it outside at night. The rink won't be as nice, since it's exposed to the elements and everything, but—"

I interrupted him with a slight squeeze on his forearm. "If I fall on my ass, no one will witness it except for you. This is perfect."

"I won't let you fall. Promise." His eyes sparkled with earnestness. His tone was sincere, like the words carried a double meaning. I wasn't sure where it had come from, but they settled deep in my chest and found their way through the cracks of my heart.

———

I DROPPED onto the couch with a tired sigh. Captain Sushi demanded his daily treat, which Henry so gracefully complied with and even gave him an extra, then he promptly retreated to his favorite cat tower, which was located in my room.

Skating in the middle of the night, while it snowed, was the most unique and fun date I'd ever had. I even managed to let go of the boards at some point without falling onto my ass.

Henry sat next to me, and I rested my head on his shoulder. "Tonight was really fun."

He wrapped an arm around me, and the side hug alone made my heart thump painfully. "Yeah, it was."

The air was thick with a suffocating tension I couldn't explain. Trepidation clawed at my throat like ivy wrapping around stone, slow and tight to the point of hurting. I learned how to be comfortable around Henry and even looked forward to spending time with him. But uncertainty hit me all at once.

Did having sex ruin that for us?

Was it a mistake to break the rules?

A part of me believed it wasn't. We wanted each other, and we acted in pure need. It was as simple as that.

But maybe...maybe we needed to go back to the rules. They were a hefty reminder of what was at stake. This was the real world, and if there was one thing that always messed things up, it was mixing business with pleasure.

My chest tightened at the thought. I didn't want to do it, but what other choice did we have? Whatever tension lingered in the air, I didn't want it to be there any longer. Or worse, I didn't want to lose the weird friendship we had—if you could even call it that.

"Henry," I whispered as I placed my legs beneath me and faced him. "We need to talk about the rules."

He stared at the TV that was playing a random sitcom, refusing to meet my gaze. "What about them?"

"I want to preface, I don't regret what happened." *It's the only thing I've managed to think about,* was what I almost said. But that was beside the point. "I believe we can be adults and admit we had a need we wanted to scratch, so we acted on it."

His laugh was short and held no humor. "Is that what we're calling it? A *scratch?*"

"What else would you call it?" I snapped, then I shut my

eyes with a sigh. This was already not going well. "We had a nice time tonight on our fake date, so why don't we try to move—"

"You and that goddamn word," he growled, his frustration evident.

"What?" I frowned.

Three beats passed, the only sounds filling the silence were the fake laughter from the sitcom and Henry's heaving chest.

His eyes met mine. They were stormy. Wanting. *Needing*.

My core tightened, and the beat of my heart drummed in my throat. Wild and painful.

His hands found the back of my neck, and he collided our lips in a rough kiss. I moaned at the possessive hold he had on me and the way his tongue grazed my bottom lip, *demanding* an entrance I so easily gave him. He tasted malty and smoky, with a hint of the sour orange that was so indistinctively *his*.

I threaded my fingers through his perfectly styled hair and brought him closer to me, desperately trying to tether myself to the moment. My lungs burned from the lack of oxygen, and my lips were numb from how aggressive we were being, like the kiss was meant to be punishing, and we *needed* it to hurt.

Dilated pupils met mine when he stopped the kiss abruptly. "Does this fucking feel *fake* to you, Kennedy?" His breath was ragged, making his chest rise and fall in quick succession. His hand traveled from my neck to the curve of my breast, all the way down to my hip, where he gripped. "Because I don't know about you, but I'm sick and tired of pretending."

My breath hitched. "Henry—"

"*No*," he said, roughly. "Let me finish."

I nodded, giving him a silent go-ahead.

"We tried to play by your rules, but the truth is, everything changed since that night. And I tried to pretend I was fine to go back to how things were, but I can't. Okay? Not anymore."

Time moved painfully slow, and every thump of my heart drowned everything around me. All I could focus on was him. The way his eyes pinned me in place with silent desperation. The way his throat bobbed like this was excruciating. And I supposed it was, considering how my body trembled with bone-deep fear and euphoria all at the same time. God, I wanted him. I *so* wanted him.

Was this it?

Was this the moment when everything would take the turn I hadn't expected, but deep down wished for?

"I like how fearless you are. I like how you're trying to make a difference in the world and show little girls that *anything* is possible." His fingertips traced the freckles on my cheeks. "I like your freckles." He traced my nose. "I like the little lines that form at the top of your nose when you make a funny face."

A wobbly laugh escaped me, but it quickly died when his thumb brushed my bottom lip softly.

"I like the strawberry-flavored lip gloss you wear that makes your lips look fuller." He twirled a piece of my hair around his index finger. "I like your curls." His eyes met mine with a knowing smile. "I'm fucking *obsessed* with your eyes and the intensity of them." Both of his hands cradled my face, forcing me to stare at him as he whispered, "I like all of you, Kennedy Jones. And I'm tired of pretending I don't." His voice was thick and lacked control. Like the words had been caged in his chest for far too long, and they had finally clawed their way out.

A million little fireflies danced across every one of my nerve endings, lighting me from the inside out. Relief washed over me like the tide finally coming home to shore. Another part of me, the one who was constantly scared, the one who pushed everyone away, questioned if this was truly a good thing.

I fiddled with my fingers and nibbled my bottom lip, trying to settle my nerves. "Are...are you sure about this?"

He huffed a laugh. "I haven't been able to get you out of my head since the day you walked through those arena doors three years ago." The way he stared at me was like he was trying to pry my soul open and read me. "But I understand if you want to take things slow."

My heart contracted in my chest. What could I possibly say to that? He read me so easily, without judgment. No one had ever known these parts of me, the insecure parts. And there was something about Henry... It was so easy to be myself. To not be scared.

I took a deep breath, mulling over my words. Did I want to try? Yes. But another part of me, the one I fought every day, was hesitant. I was engaged for three years, and I lost myself in the process. Could I take this sort of risk again? Was it even possible?

He's not asking to marry you, for God's sake. Just take it one day at a time, my brain whispered.

I mean, this was Henry. He was a lot of things, but he *wasn't* Joe. He'd proven that over and over again.

"We can take it slow?" I asked, unsure.

He interlaced our hands together. The warmth of his skin against mine made my heart beat a bit too fast. It was incredible how he managed to be both comforting and thrilling. "Absolutely. We'll keep it casual. Anything you want. But, please, give us a chance, yeah?"

I gave him a soft smile and nodded. Gosh, my heart wanted to explode from excitement and relief. This was good—amazing, even—and I was determined to take it one day at a time.

He let out a huge sigh of relief and draped one of his arms around me. I rested my head on his chest, letting the wild beats of his heart and the scent that had started to smell like home relax me.

"Thank you," I whispered. "For being so patient."

"I never want to hear you thank me for doing the bare mini-mum, Kennedy. Or anyone else, for that matter. This isn't me doing you a favor." He gripped my chin, forcing me to look at him. "This is me seeing you for all you're worth and being more than willing to wait. Even if this doesn't go anywhere, never settle, okay?"

His words hit something deep within me. It was like a huge, heavy rock was being lifted off my shoulders, letting me prop-erly breathe and think for once. Was this how it felt to be seen for who I was? To be accepted with faults and all?

A watery laugh bubbled out of me. "Okay."

"That's my girl," he rasped through a smile.

Without another word, we both stayed on the couch, sharing a blanket and watching silly sitcoms until I couldn't fight the heaviness of my eyes and fell asleep with my head resting on his lap.

TWENTY-SEVEN

HENRY

I LOVED BEING A PART OF SOMETHING GOOD.

MY BODY JOLTED awake at the sound of a phone ringing.

I craned my neck and let out a low groan. Sleeping in a sitting position wasn't one of my brightest ideas, but when Kennedy fell asleep on my lap while we were hanging out in the living room, I didn't have the heart to move her. She looked so peaceful, and I kept staring at her like a pathetic sap for an hour until I dozed off.

My phone was vibrating in my pocket, so when Kennedy got off my lap with a sleepy yawn and a stretch of her arms, I grabbed it.

I frowned at the contact name. It was Lisa, the executive director of the nonprofit I'd founded a few years back.

"Hey, Lisa, what's up?" I croaked, still half-asleep.

"Hey, Henry, just double-checking you'll be coming today for the prepare and serve a meal we've got going today at one of our newest shelters?"

Shit. With how busy I'd been and between all of the away games, it slipped my mind.

I cleared my throat. "Uh, yeah. I'll be there." My eyes

settled on Kennedy as she stood from the couch and headed for the coffee maker. Her curls were a bit messy, but still so goddamn beautiful. Suddenly, an idea popped into my head. "I'll be bringing another person, so make sure we have something for her to do," I said low enough so Kennedy couldn't hear. Then we quickly said goodbye and hung up.

I pursed my lips and threaded my fingers through my hair as I debated on how to bring this up to Kennedy. I'd never shared this part of my life with anyone. Not even my best friend or my family. But if I wanted her to be a part of my life—and I did, more than anything—I needed to be honest. This was a big fucking step for me, and nerves traveled through my body, causing me to break out in shivers.

Kennedy opened a drawer to get a spoon to stir her coffee. She grinned as she grabbed a piece of paper.

"Our contract was in this drawer," she said as she waved it in the air. "I guess it doesn't really matter now, does it?"

I laughed. "Don't throw it away. Put it back on the fridge. It'll be a fun keepsake."

"You want to start collecting memories?" She cocked one of her eyebrows. "Are you going soft on me, pretty boy?"

I rolled my eyes without a word. We both laughed.

I cleared my throat. *Here went nothing.* "Kenny?"

"Yeah?"

"Do you have any plans today? I want to take you somewhere."

"I was going to go into the office for a few hours, but I can skip it. What'd you have in mind?"

I nodded. Fuck, this was happening. There was no going back. "I'll tell you more when we get there. Make sure you wear some clothes you wouldn't mind getting dirty in and comfortable shoes."

She raised an eyebrow. "Well, that's broad."

I smiled. "Be ready in an hour."

———

AS I PARKED in front of the building, I gripped the steering wheel and took a deep, calming breath. Fuck, my heart was beating fast. I'd been fidgeting the whole ride.

"Are you okay?" Kennedy asked.

I cleared my throat. "Yeah, why?"

"You seem tense, and you were quiet the whole ride. What's going on?"

I let out a shaky laugh. "Honestly?"

"You already know the answer to that."

"I'm a little nervous." I let the confession linger between us for a few seconds. "I know you'll probably have a lot of questions when we go in there, and I promise I will answer them later, okay?"

"Now I'm anxious," she said through a nervous laugh. "Where are we?"

"Are you familiar with the Willow House Foundation?"

She stared at me with a frown for a few beats, then recognition filtered across her eyes. "Yeah, they're one of the biggest nonprofit organizations in Illinois for women and children who have experienced DV. I'd been trying to work with them for years, but their waitlist is quite long. They've done some amazing work." Her tone of voice was a bit excited, and I fought the grimace that wanted to cross my face.

There was a reason the foundation wasn't working with the Strikers, and it wasn't because of a waitlist, but I needed to tackle one beast at a time. I didn't think Kennedy was going to be mad, but she wasn't going to be happy with me when she found out I'd been hiding something this big.

I pointed at the building. "This is our newest shelter. We're going to prepare some meals and serve them today."

She narrowed her eyes. "Our?"

Fuck. I hadn't meant to say that.

I leveled her with a look. "What did I say about questions?"

"Fine," she groaned.

I nodded and quickly hopped out of the truck and opened the door for her. "It's going to be a long, tiresome day. Are you sure you want to do this?"

She scoffed and waved her hand dismissively as we strode through the back door, where the kitchen was located. "Have you met me? I love doing things like this."

Lisa, who was practically like a second parental figure to me—she was around the same age as my mother—with her fierce attitude and her blonde hair in a high ponytail, strode to us with a clipboard in hand. "You're late."

"Sorry," I mumbled.

She pursed her lips. "At least you're here. If you stop by the back office, there are some extra shirts for both of you to wear. They're in one of the boxes."

I nodded and tilted my head so Kennedy could follow me. I sifted through the boxes until I found the perfect sizes and handed one to her. She had a camisole underneath her sweater, so she took it off and slipped into the salmon-colored shirt as I changed into mine, too.

"You ready?"

"I have so many questions." She sighed. "But yeah, I'm ready."

THE TIME PASSED IN A BLUR.

I was on prepping duty, because I didn't like being in the front. The marketing team usually took a lot of videos and pictures of the volunteers to post on social media, and for obvious reasons, I always made sure to stay away. When Lisa heard Kennedy tell one of the other volunteers she was talking to that she worked in PR, she had her work in the front, serving food and talking to people.

Lisa had been working as an executive director for *Willow House* since the very beginning, when I was just an ignorant kid with a big dream and didn't know where to begin. She was efficient and knew her job well. Thanks to her, we had one of the best volunteer programs in the Midwest, which allowed us to help a tremendous number of people over the years. We had something good going, because this was something we were both passionate about and we made sure to work with people who were equally as passionate about it. Her eldest daughter and only grandchild were victims of domestic violence, and it pained me to even think about the fact that they didn't make it out alive. This was why I trusted her with everything, because this was just as personal for her as it was for me.

After everything was cleared out and we made sure every woman and child in the building was well-fed, I ordered a bunch of pizzas and wings from a nearby mom-and-pop pizzeria. I was forever grateful for every single volunteer, though the circumstances were fucked, because why the hell was DV such a common thing in the world? I didn't know. But I'd fight against it every day of my goddamn life until my last dying breath, and it was rewarding to know some people felt the same way.

I'd barely seen Kennedy all day. Every time I turned to look for her, she was speaking with a volunteer or with Lisa. I was exhausted and my hands hurt from all the prepping I had done, but man, my heart was full. As it always was, every time I came around to help.

Kennedy took a seat next to me. "Hey, pretty boy."

"Hi, stranger." I smiled. "I feel like I haven't seen you all day."

She laughed. "I'm sorry. I just..." She looked around, her brown eyes shining. "I loved talking to some of the volunteers. If you could hear their stories and how they got here."

I nodded. If only she knew how familiar I was with all of them. Most of them had been with us from the beginning, and some of them even needed help once, and when they finally got back on their feet, they became volunteers to pay it forward. "It's amazing, isn't it?"

"It's incredible how the community comes together and helps women and children in need." Her smile was so bright, and she was radiating so much happiness, I couldn't help but smile, too.

"I know you must have a lot of questions."

She rested her hand on top of mine, squeezing it gently with a nod. "We can talk about that when we get home."

I nodded without a word and took a breath of relief. I was dreading the conversation, because there were so many dark parts of me I still didn't understand, and I was about to lay it all out there for the woman who was becoming one of the most important people in my life in such a short time.

"Thank you for bringing me here, Henry. I loved being a part of something good."

My heart swelled with pride. I knew Kennedy was amazing, and though part of me was worried, I was glad I shared this part of myself.

I just hoped she wouldn't be too mad when I told her the whole story.

TWENTY-EIGHT

KENNEDY

FUNNY HOW LIFE WORKS, ISN'T IT?

"IT'S OPEN," Henry said when I knocked on his bedroom door a few hours after we'd arrived home.

When I opened it, Captain Sushi was next to me, but with his cute, fluffy white paws, he took a few steps and jumped on the bed, settling between Henry's thighs with a low purr.

He scratched Sush's ear while he patted the space next to him. "Come here."

I hopped onto the bed and got underneath the comforter, letting the fluffy cotton warm me up. "I'm exhausted."

"I bet." He laughed. "I'm tired, too. But you had to talk to people all day, I'm sure that took the energy out of you."

I yawned and rested my head against the headboard. "I love talking to people, it fills my energy cup. But standing all day killed my legs for sure."

"Energy cup?"

"Yeah, like, you know how there are certain things that replenish your energy? I imagine it's like a cup. Talking to people replenishes it."

"That's such a weird analogy."

I hit him in the arm. "Shut up," I said with a laugh then craned my neck to look at him. "We've postponed the conversation long enough. Spill the beans, pretty boy."

"I'm not sure what you're talking about," he quipped.

I shifted upright, folding my legs under me as I turned to face him. "Why were we at Willow House today?"

"Volunteering."

"*Henry*," I groaned.

His lips pursed, and he didn't say a word for a few seconds. He tilted his head back and stared at the ceiling, almost like he was lost in thought. "I-uh, honestly, I'm just going to come out and say it, because there is no easy way to approach this subject," he said, then he inhaled a quick breath and blurted, "I founded Willow House."

I reared back in shock. That was certainly the last thing I was expecting, so a million questions were running through my head. I didn't know where to start.

"I'm sorry, but did you just say you're the *founder* of one of the biggest nonprofit organizations in the Midwest?" I gaped at him in disbelief.

He nodded as he avoided my gaze. "Kennedy, what I'm about to tell you..." He scrubbed his face and sighed. "Please don't tell anyone, yeah?" His voice took on a vulnerability I had never heard from him. He was usually all confidence and cockiness, maybe even a little silly at times, but this side of him was... new. My heart was all too aware, because it tightened in my chest with hope. Was this it? Was he *finally* letting me in?

I gripped his hand and squeezed it gently. "You can trust me," I said softly. "I would never. You know that." I mean, we shared a secret that could destroy us—one that could get him in trouble, too. The thought alone brought some fierce protection out of me. Whatever he was about to tell me, I was going to keep close to my chest for the rest of my life.

"When I got drafted, I was an eighteen-year-old kid with a whole lot more money than I knew what to do with. When my agent casually mentioned that most players tended to invest or give to charity, an idea popped into my head." His Adam's apple bopped. "My childhood wasn't easy, and my mother had to, uh, escape a dangerous situation, you know?" he murmured. His words were tight, like it took everything in him to keep his emotions in check.

He didn't give me the details, but I was already putting the pieces together on my own, and my heart felt like it was lodged in my throat at the newfound information.

"I saw my mom struggle for years. She worked multiple jobs to make the transition as easy as possible for me and Olivia. She sacrificed herself to keep me in hockey, which was the only thing that brought a sense of normalcy during those uncertain times. She did everything she could to make us happy and to get us away from him." His voice cracked, and it was like there was an invisible string connecting us, because my heart broke then, too. "Did you know that one out of every three women has experienced DV in their lifetime? Did you also know that one in every four children has been exposed to this horrible thing, too?" He shook his head and straightened up. This woke Sush up, and he moved to his cat bed, where he peacefully curled up to continue sleeping. "I felt so fucking powerless when I was a kid, and when I finally had the money to do something good with it, I went for it."

It was a lot of information to process, and I wanted to be sensitive to the heaviness of the conversation and treat it with care. "Henry, if you don't want to continue telling me this story, you don't have to."

His eyes met mine, and they shone with so much heaviness and unspoken emotions. "No. I want to," he rasped.

And so he did.

He told me everything his family endured after Vincent Anderson had his career-ending injury. The beatings, the screaming, the constant berating. Tears welled in my eyes after he shared details on how bad it had gotten and what gave Henry's mom the courage to pick up her things and her two kids and...leave. Start all over again.

If I ever had the opportunity to meet Henry's mom, all I wanted to do was give her a big hug. Because that was a brave thing to do. She was a superwoman, and I hoped nothing but happiness and peace for her.

Henry was brave in a way, too. So fierce, and kind, and willing to make the world a better place. As he kept talking, this whole new light shone above him, and it was like I was finally seeing him for who he truly was. He was showing me the rawest parts of himself, and I couldn't help but admire how much bravery it took for him to be so honest and show me his emotional scars.

I couldn't breathe properly, because there was this desperate need I had to be near him. To somehow show him he could lean on me. That I was someone he could depend on. Without thinking, I straddled him and gave him a fierce hug. He rested his head against my chest, and we stayed quiet for a few minutes. His breaths were heavy, and the way he wrapped his arms around my waist was like he was doing everything in his power to anchor himself. The proximity alone had my heart wanting to leap out of my chest, and my body buzzed with energy, but I didn't dare move. There was something so comforting about the moment, like our silence said more than words ever could. I *admired* this man. I'd found a new respect for him, and I wanted to protect him with everything I had.

He sniffled, his eyes rimmed red and shining as they met mine. "That's why I created Willow House."

I nodded as my fingers brushed the soft strands of his hair.

"There are not enough words in the world I can use to properly express how angry I am that you experienced something so horrible." My thumb caressed his jaw. "What you're doing to help people is something you should be proud of. Why don't you share this with your friends? Your family? The *world*? They'd be so proud, and they would love to help, too. You know this."

He shook his head. "I stay anonymous for a reason. And it's why we make volunteers sign NDAs so the word doesn't get out. I don't want the spotlight, the bad things I've done in my career, to overshadow the great place Willow House is, because you know how the media works. It's not a risk I'm willing to take. We do many great things already without my name being attached to it."

I nodded in understanding, but there was a question nagging at me. The air was thick with tension, but honesty was important to me. "So why do you act the way you do in front of the media? It's clear to me that's not who you are."

His laugh was short and bitter. "That is a whole other topic I'm not sure you're ready to hear."

I cradled his face in the palms of my hands, forcing him to look at me. He was so...goddamn beautiful, but his eyes looked so sad, and lost, it broke my heart into a million pieces. "There's nothing you can say that can scare me off. I promise."

He let out a long sigh, relaxing his shoulders. "I've always struggled with my anger, but I didn't want to be like my father and take it out on the people I care about. So fighting on the ice, putting it all out there, seemed like the best way to cope at the time." He cringed, pursing his lips to the side. "I was young and stupid, and that bad boy persona stuck with me, so I rolled with it until it became the norm. A mask I could easily slip into when shit got too real or when people wanted to see that part of me. When I got traded to the Strikers, I vowed to take a step away from it, because it was—*is*—a toxic coping mechanism. But then Holt happened and..." His fingertips started to brush my legs, ever so softly. "Well, you know the rest. And I promise you, Kenny, when you handed me my ass in that locker room the night I got ejected, I was ready to take responsibility for everything." His eyes shifted, darkening into a stormy blue. "But my father has this fucked-up cosmic timing, and he texted me before the interview, and the pent-up anger I've tried to work through for years came rushing back tenfold. It was like I was a useless twelve-year-old boy all over again." He let out a hollow laugh, the kind that held more pain than amusement. "It sounds like a lame excuse, I know. But it's something I couldn't control. I wish my father had no power over me, but in a way, he still does, and I beat myself up about it every single day."

Wow. I was breathless; *speechless.* Words were hard to form, so all I managed to say was, "I'm sorry."

His eyes met mine with confusion.

"I always thought you were this cocky, hot-headed hockey player for no reason. I was quick to judge you without knowing the whole story, and for that, I'm sorry."

"You have nothing to be sorry about. You saw what I wanted to show you, but now..." His voice lowered to a whisper. "Things have changed."

"Yeah?" I croaked. My body lit up from the inside out with hope. Because I wished, with all my heart, he was talking about us.

I didn't know how or when it happened, but somehow I went from not being able to stand being near him to searching for him the moment we were in the same room, like there was this gravitational pull that pushed us together.

Funny how life works, isn't it? It's fickle. One day, you're not even thinking about that person, and the next, you can't remember what it felt like before they made you feel everything.

He nodded. "I want to be honest with you. I'm far from perfect, but I am trying every fucking day of my life to be better. Just be patient with me, okay?"

I rested the palm of my hand on his jaw, caressing it with my thumb back and forth ever so lightly. "I think you've been doing a pretty good job."

He shot me a half-smile. "It's all because of you."

I let out a disbelieving laugh. "*Me?*"

His intense blue-gray eyes met mine, and they were earnest and shone so brightly when he said, "There's this sunshine you radiate that makes my rainy days better. I don't know how you do it, but please"—his voice cracked, barely more than a whisper—"don't ever stop."

My eyes welled with involuntary tears, and my heart tightened like I'd just been handed something fragile and terrifying, but beautiful.

I'm... I'm his sunshine?

I'd never been anyone's source of goodness. I'd never been anyone's light. For most of my life, people only wanted me on their terms, and I became compliant with it. Became a doll they could rebuild to their liking, over and over again. Afraid that if I didn't allow it, they would never stay. That they would always leave me.

When I thought back about how much I let people walk all over me, I got angry. It was a stupid, useless thing to do. Because with Henry, I'd only been myself. Unapologetically and without doubt. He *saw* me. Better yet, he *appreciated* me despite all of my flaws.

"I don't know what to say." My voice was tight, and it hurt to talk due to the lump that was lodged in my throat.

"You don't need to say anything."

"I promise every word you told me will stay between us," I said, wanting to make sure he understood he could wholeheartedly trust me.

"I trust you."

I let out a wistful sigh. "Good." I patted his face playfully. "I'm going to go, you have morning skate tomorrow, and you need to rest."

He gripped my thighs, keeping me in place. "Can you stay? Please. I just—"

I interrupted him. "Absolutely."

He didn't need to explain anything. He needed the company, and honestly? I was hoping he'd ask.

His smile was so blinding, it made my heart leap with excitement. Knowing I was his source of happiness should have been terrifying, but instead, it just felt...right. Meant to be.

He stretched out on the bed, and I nestled against him, my head on his chest. His arm wrapped around me as our legs instinctively tangled together. My hand rested against his abdomen, where I started to draw intricate patterns, wanting to feel every part of his skin.

He buried his nose in my hair and took a deep breath, letting out a long, wistful sigh. My breathing slowed, my eyes growing heavy after such a long, exhausting day. And just as sleep pulled me under, I swore I heard Henry whisper, "Thank you for being the safest place I've ever known."

TWENTY-NINE

KENNEDY

I AM A HOCKEY ROMANCE CONNOISSEUR.

"THIS IS A STUPID IDEA," I mumbled to Val as the Uber dropped us off in front of Tim's.

"Just because the guy is still benched doesn't mean he won't lose his shit when he sees you in his jersey."

"It's cliché," I said dryly, though knowing that I had Henry's last name and number etched on my back made me a little *too* happy.

She pointed a finger at me with a wink. "*Exactly*. And that's why it's perfect. Prepare to have the best sex of your life."

"For a girl who has never dated a hockey player, you sure know a lot about this stuff."

"I may have never dated a hockey player, but I am a hockey romance *connoisseur*. I've read enough books to know you'll thank me soon enough."

I rolled my eyes with a laugh as we strode into the bar, the beats of "The Reason" by Hoobastank welcoming us.

The guys played against the Nashville Devils and won, 3-1, so of course, they were at Tim's celebrating. Truth be told, I was starting to love coming to this place. It was a great way to unwind after a crazy day. My workdays had become longer, now that the gala was approaching. Matt had been surprisingly quiet and hadn't tried anything since the Family Skate fiasco. However, I wasn't willing to risk it, so I attended every meeting and ensured I was involved in every single decision. It was driving us both insane, sure, but what other option did I have? I was *not* gonna let the man pull another one over me.

My eyes found Henry, and he was animatedly talking with Parker and Hayes. My heart all but stopped beating when I took him in. I hadn't seen him in almost a week and...*hell*. I couldn't deny it even if I tried. I missed my big, tall, cocky athlete.

We'd been casually dating for a month or so. The deeper we got into the season, the more he traveled, and the busier I got, too. Normally, I would have traveled with the team, but this season, Brad kept me and Matt around for more administrative and managerial tasks. I think this was his way of testing us and giving us enough workload to see who could take over once he retired.

I stood behind Henry and tapped his shoulder. He turned around, and when his eyes found mine, his demeanor changed from normal to *ecstatic*. His smile was wide and bright, and his blue-gray eyes were a lighter shade and sparkled as they drank me in.

And just like that, I was an instant puddle.

I wrapped my arms around his shoulders to hug him. "Hi, pretty boy," I whispered.

"Hi, Kenny baby," he whispered back then dropped a kiss on top of my head and hugged me tighter.

His whole presence these past few months had started to become soothing for me. But his hugs? They were like coming home. Comforting and warm.

"Get a room," Hayes groaned.

"You guys make me sick," Parker added, faking a gag.

Henry took a step back and gave them a glare without a word. His gaze settled back on me, and the corner of his eyes crinkled in the way I liked when he smiled at me again.

"Turn around, Kenny. Show your boy what you got on today," Val snickered as she took a seat next to Owens. The grumpy goalie looked instantly relaxed as he sagged his shoulders, almost like he was relieved, and draped an arm behind her chair.

"You're a pain in my ass, Valentina," I groaned.

He narrowed his eyes as he stared at my jersey. "Is that what I think it is?"

With a knowing grin on my face, I turned around and looked over my shoulder. "*Yup.*"

My core tightened when Henry's pupils dilated. "*Oh, fuck,*" he murmured under his breath.

I turned to face him with a playful wink. "Your number kind of looks good on me, doesn't it?"

With a deep chuckle, he closed the distance between us. "Yeah, it does. But it's gonna look a lot better on the floor of our apartment tonight." His voice was gravelly and thick, low enough to keep the conversation between us.

The way he so casually said *our* apartment made my heart tug.

"Is that a promise?" I asked sultrily.

"It's a guarantee, baby." With that, he leaned forward and met my lips with an unhurried, torturous kiss.

I couldn't help but whimper, a sound he gracefully swallowed as his tongue coaxed my mouth to open in a playful taunt. His kisses were like velvet and fire. Soft at first, but searing underneath. It was addictive.

He broke the kiss and, without glancing at the group, he

interlaced my fingers with his and walked us to the exit as he said, "I'll see you guys later."

"That's my boy!" Hayes shouted with a clap.

"*Nice.*" Parker nodded, visibly impressed.

"Both of you, *behave,*" Morgan chastised Hayes and Parker.

"Be safe, kids!" Donovan shouted.

They were *all* idiots. But they were quickly becoming my friends, and I had a newfound appreciation for this group. The loneliness that tried to grip me and stay was less intense as more time passed by, and I had all of them to thank. *I had Henry to thank.*

I giggled. "We're leaving? But I just got here."

"There's no way I can stand in this bar one more second without ripping your clothes off and fucking you," Henry replied simply. Unapologetically. It made my skin scorching hot.

I looked over my shoulder and shouted at Val, "Thank you!" because I knew I was about to be one lucky girl.

She barked a laugh. "I knew it!"

The February Chicago winter hit my cheeks the second we stepped outside, but the cold vanished the moment Henry turned me around, pressed me against the wall, and crashed his lips into mine in a kiss that was all heat and desperation. His body pressed against mine, and I moaned and fisted his shirt to bring him even closer, wanting nothing more than to be swallowed by all of him.

"We should probably not do this here," he groaned painfully. "But, fuck, baby. *I need you.*" His tone was husky, with a hint of urgency. It spurred me to action. My hands fumbled while I tried to find the keys in his pockets. Once I did, I unlocked the truck and got in the back seat.

He placed his forearm on the roof of the truck and leaned forward. "What are you doing?"

"What does it look like?" I gnawed my bottom lip and kicked my shoes off then started playing with the waistband of my leggings, slowly bringing them down.

His eyes sparkled with heat. "Who are you, and what did you do with my girl?"

The way *my girl* rolled off his lips made my thighs clench. Leave it to Henry to make me discover that I had, *in fact*, a praise kink.

"Get in, pretty boy."

A low growl erupted from deep within his chest as he got in and shut the door. My leggings were halfway down, but he got them off in one swift motion then dropped me in his lap like I weighed nothing more than a feather and *devoured* my mouth. His tongue eagerly met mine, and we were a mess of desperate kisses and heavy breathing as I rolled my hips against his length. *God, he was big.*

"*Henry,*" I moaned.

"What do you want, Kenny? Let's hear it." His tongue flicked the side of my neck before he sucked the soft flesh. The feel of his lips against my skin made me buzz with need.

"I want your cock." Lust consumed me like rapid fire. It was suffocating how much I needed him.

I kneeled on the seat and made quick work of his jeans and boxers, bringing them down low enough to give me access to his thick and throbbing cock. The sight of it made my mouth water, so I leaned forward and stroked it once. When pre-cum leaked out of it, I darted my tongue out and lapped it up. It was sweet and salty, and I rolled my eyes in pleasure and moaned at the taste of him.

He groaned, "I can't hold back anymore. I need to be inside you."

I faked a gasp. "Henry Anderson, are you *begging?*"

Hooded eyes met mine. He licked his bottom lip, leaving a

trace of moisture that made them look more enticing. "Yes. And I'll gladly beg for the rest of my life if it means I get to feel your tight pretty pussy around my cock."

The ache between my legs intensified at his words. Henry was a grade-A dirty talker, and that somehow made me braver. I liked it—*a lot.*

"Condom?" I asked.

He found his wallet and grabbed the foil packet. Once the latex was rolled on, I sat on his lap, moved my panties to the side, and brushed the head of his cock against my folds back and forth.

Henry's breath hitched as his shaft throbbed in my hand.

I smirked. "Someone's eager."

His hands fisted the sides of my jersey. "How can I not be? You look like a fucking dream with my jersey on." He softly grabbed a fistful of my curls, bringing my ear to his mouth. The warmth of his breath prickled my skin as he roughly whispered, "Stop fucking teasing me, Kennedy. Put it in."

I hummed. "Beg a little and I will."

His laugh echoed. "You are such a brat."

I rolled my hips, letting the head of his cock slide in an inch, but quickly took it out. "You said you'd gladly beg, right? Let's hear it, then."

This won me a pained groan. "*Kennedy, please.*"

Oh, God. It was hot to hear this hulk of a man beg. I wanted more. "You can do better, pretty boy."

He gritted his teeth, trying to hold himself back. His neck was strained, and a droplet of sweat ran down the side of his forehead. "I promise to be a good boy and do anything you want. *Fuck.* Anything, okay? Just, fucking *please*"—his voice cracked—"*Put. It. In.*"

"Such a good boy, begging for me," I rasped against his lips and sank onto his cock in one fell swoop. We both moaned,

"*Yes,*" at the same time. I then gasped, all the air leaving my lungs with how full I was.

I couldn't move. I couldn't breathe. All I could do was shut my eyes and kiss him like he was the only thing anchoring me to real life.

Henry wrapped his arms around my hips and lifted me slightly then started pumping in and out of me at the perfect rhythm, like he knew exactly what I needed. All I could do was rest my forehead on his shoulder and moan. The position allowed the head of his cock to hit my G-spot, and I was already so fucking close.

There wasn't much space for us, but it was the least of my concerns. This was what I needed. To be fucked, and wanted, and touched by him. To have his touch and kisses on my body at all times.

"*Fuck,* your pussy is tight. You're close already, aren't you?" He gritted out.

My forehead met his with a nod. I couldn't form words. I was in a haze of *him.* The way he smelled like husk, with a hint of sourness and sweetness at the same time. The way his lips brushed against mine as we both kept moaning. The way our chests heaved in sync like we were one.

My fingers found my clit, and I started to circle it, desperately chasing my climax. Henry dropped kisses on my neck, and every single one of them was like a newfound wave of electricity. It was maddening how he made me feel. It was like disconnecting from the world, and my body was only aware of him and everything he did.

With a few more deep thrusts, my core tightened, and the orgasm rushed through me like a rollercoaster drop. I cried out Henry's name, and he gripped my waist tighter and continued to pound into me. It was rough. Animalistic. And so goddamn addicting. My pussy tightened again, and somehow, another orgasm—stronger than the first—hit me out of nowhere. My throat was sore, so my moans were breathless, barely audible.

"Fuck, fuck, *fuck*," Henry chanted over and over again as he kept slamming into me.

He was so close, and through my haze after those two mind-blowing orgasms, I wrapped my hand around his throat as best as I could and brushed my lips against his before kissing him and tightening my grip. He moaned against my mouth, and with three shaky, languid thrusts, he swelled and throbbed inside me as his climax took over him.

Once the post-orgasm high started to wear off, we stared at each other and laughed.

"Why is sex always so fucking explosive with you?" I asked in awe, still breathless.

He gave me a chaste kiss and moved some of my sweaty curls off my face. "I don't know. But what I *do* know is that we're going home to do *that* a few more times."

THIRTY

HENRY

WHO KNEW YOU WERE AN
ACTS OF SERVICE KIND OF GUY?

LIKE ANY OTHER regular man on earth, I enjoyed sex.

But sex *with* Kennedy? *Mind-fucking-blowing.*

It was stupid to believe that one time was going to be enough. What the fuck was I thinking? And even if you took sex out of the equation, there was an undeniable chemistry between us.

I loved hanging out with her. I loved making her smile. I loved how she was unapologetically herself around me.

It was pathetic how much I wanted her to be mine. How deep in I already was, even though I promised her I was going to take it slow. It was killing me not to ask her where this was going, what she'd been thinking. We'd been casually dating— though the media still believed otherwise—and all I wanted to do was get on my knees and beg her to be my actual girlfriend. I'd never been a patient man, but for her? I could stand still, even if it killed me, as long as she gave us the chance we deserved.

"How come Sush isn't all up in our faces demanding treats?" Kennedy asked with a worried frown.

I laughed. "Hayes picked him up this afternoon, claiming he wanted time with his nephew."

"He needs a pet. He's kind of lonely, isn't he?"

I shrugged. "Olivia is moving with him in a few months, and she has a golden retriever. He'll be plenty entertained and hopefully will stop sniffing around Sush."

Kennedy hopped on the kitchen island with a smirk. "Look at you, embracing being a cat daddy and all."

I settled between her legs with a grunt. "He needs to back off. Sush is ours."

"Well, he's yours."

I shook my head. "*Nope*. I meant what I said."

She rested her arms on my shoulders as her lips pursed to keep her grin in check. "Does that make me a cat mommy, then?"

I smiled. "I like the sound of that."

Her laugh was airy, like golden sunlight, and I basked in the sound of it, letting the warmth seep into my bones.

I settled my nose in the crook of her neck and inhaled then dropped a few kisses as my hands caressed her thighs. The need I had for her clouded me like a heavy fog. It didn't matter I had just taken her in the backseat of my truck, my cock was already throbbing, ready to go.

"I love your legs," I rasped against her soft brown skin, my hands trailing to the waistband of her leggings. She lifted her hips slightly, giving me the space to slide them off completely.

Her body shivered with a low whimper, and I trailed kisses down as I lifted her jersey then took one of her nipples in my mouth through the lacey fabric of her bra. "I love your tits, too. They're perfect. *You're* perfect." I grabbed the other and squeezed as I continued to twirl my tongue around the other.

"Careful, pretty boy. You sound obsessed with me," she said through a grin.

A low laugh rumbled deep in my chest as I continued south, kissing her abdomen. But my heart? It stammered painfully at her words.

I was completely and wholeheartedly obsessed with Kennedy Jones, and I was too fucking scared to admit it. Terrified that if I had, she would have walked away from me for good. What we had going on was lighthearted, fun. *Just not enough.* But I knew this was all she could handle, and there was nothing I could do except...wait. Wait for her to *see* me. *All of me.*

My lips landed on her hip bone with a soft kiss, and I held back a pathetic, needy groan at the sight of her panties that clung to her lips with how wet she already was. My cock all but screamed at me to let him out, but I pushed the thought away. I wanted to take my time. To feast and let myself drown in her.

It had been a long fucking week, and even though my father's threats still lingered in the back of my head, especially since he strangely went AWOL after we had that fight last month, Kennedy was the center of my universe. All my problems and struggles went away when she was near.

"Fuck, you're *drenched.*" I lazily swiped my knuckles against her damp underwear, winning a soft whimper from her. "Lie back for me, Kenny. I told you I'd be a good boy and give you anything you wanted. And you want me to eat your pretty cunt, don't you, baby?"

"Henry, I swear, your dirty talk is insane," she said through a soft laugh as she got comfortable.

I couldn't help but smirk. If only she knew I'd never really been a talker. Sure, I knew how to satisfy women, and they always left my bed happy. But it had always been about the release. With Kennedy, though...everything was heightened. Different.

She lifted her hips slightly, and I slowly slid her underwear off then placed the lacy fabric into my pocket.

She propped her elbows on the counter. "What do you think you're doing?"

I shrugged. "Getting a souvenir for when I'm on the road."

"You're depraved, pretty boy."

"And you love every filthy second of it, Kenny baby."

I kneeled in front of her, spread her long, delicious legs wide, and dived in. My tongue found her clit and twirled it, followed by a long and relaxed suck. She trembled and tried to close her legs, but I gripped her thighs and kept them in place as I continued to lick, twirl, and suck every inch of her. Tartness with a hint of sweetness coated my tongue, and I was dizzied by it.

"Your cunt tastes fucking delicious," I groaned against her pussy then flattened my tongue against it and licked it whole.

"Then be a good boy and keep eating your dessert," she replied huskily. Unashamed and unapologetically.

My cock twitched at her words. *Fuck, that was hot.* I didn't know Kennedy was capable of being this bold in bed. The more time we spent together, the more she came out of her shell, and I was like an excited dog, eager for more.

Don't get me wrong, I loved to be dominant, but when Kennedy called me a good boy? When she stood her ground and ordered me around? I was *eager* to obey. If she ever decided to take the reins completely, I'd let her. I'd let her do anything she wanted.

I kept my mouth on her, savoring everything her pussy had to offer, and she threaded her fingers through my hair and tugged it when I found a particularly sensitive spot. I kept the pace, determined to only make her come with my mouth. With a few sucks and slurps, then some quick flicks with my tongue around her clit, her legs shook with a loud cry of my name. Her climax coated my tongue, and I kept licking it off, not wanting to waste a single drop. I enjoyed eating pussy as much as the next guy, but this...this was different. It possessed me with a hunger that was impossible to satisfy.

"Henry, stop. I can't anymore." Kennedy tugged my hair and pushed my head back. "I'm too sensitive."

I took a breath, followed by a grin. "I'm not done with you yet. I'm dying to fuck you against that window while you have my jersey on."

She started at the floor-to-ceiling living room windows then at me. Her eyes were heated and a delicious, darker shade of brown. "That sounds..."

"Hot? *Oh, yeah.*" I stood to my full height. "But first, on your knees, Kennedy. Time to pay for the little stunt you did in the car."

She hopped out of the counter. Her fingertips found the hem of my shirt, and she got rid of it. Her manicured nails trailed feather-light touches across my chest and abdomen. It burned like a low fuse sparking beneath my skin, and I craved more of it.

"You're acting as if you hated it. But let's be real for a sec here..." She dropped to her knees and made quick work of my jeans and boxers. My cock was so painfully hard, I was already leaking some pre-cum. She gripped my length and licked it off with a torturously slow lick. I groaned. "If I told you to crawl, you would. Wouldn't you, pretty boy?" Her tongue darted and licked the full side of my length. "I think you like obeying." She stared at me with those big, angelic eyes of hers, but her smile was wicked, like a devil in disguise. Without an ounce of shame or breaking eye contact, she opened her mouth wide and flattened her tongue, taking me as deep as she could. The head of my cock hit the back of her throat, and she gagged, but even then, her eye contact remained steady.

My brain short-circuited. I was a fucking goner, and all I could do was whimper and moan, *"Kenny, fuck."* The way her hot, wet mouth felt against me was like dipping into pure, molten bliss and every bit sinful.

Kennedy's head bobbed as she continued to take me. Saliva ran down the sides of her mouth, and her eyes watered, but my girl was no quitter. She gripped what was left of my length with her hands and moved them in sync with her head. Every time she bobbed her head back, she twirled her tongue around the head of my cock, and every time she went in deep, her teeth slowly grazed my length. The sensations were inexplicable and every bit explosive.

I sank my fingers into her curls, loving the way they filled my hand. We always fit perfectly, Kennedy and I, like two puzzle pieces who were never meant to be apart.

The thought made my chest swell with excitement and relief.

My balls tingled, so I tightened my core and gritted my teeth to hold myself back. But Kennedy's mouth was *out* of this world. She wouldn't let up. She just kept sucking, and slurping, and making those gagging sounds like she couldn't get enough. Her thighs clenched, and she started writhing, her pussy seeking some friction.

"Does sucking my cock make you wet?" I asked huskily. "You're desperate to come again, aren't you, greedy girl?"

She hummed against my length with a nod, and the vibration was like electricity swimming through my body. It was too powerful, so I fisted her hair tighter and took my cock out of her mouth. My hands gripped her hips, and I picked her up, wrapping her legs around my waist in one swift motion as I kissed her desperately. Hungrily. Kissing her was like feeding a side of me that had been hungry for most of my life, and Kennedy was the only recipe capable of taming the relentless want.

I somehow managed to find one of the windows and pushed her against it. My cock pressed against her wet, slick cunt. My whole body trembled with eagerness to fill her to the tilt. "Fuck, wait. The condom." I was ready to let her go, but she clung to me like a koala.

"I..." She sighed, mulling over her words. "I took a test after, you know, the breakup, and I was clear. And I'm on birth control."

My eyes met hers in shock. Was she suggesting...? *Fuck.* I hoped she was.

"Only if you want to, Henry. I don't want to pressure you into anything," she continued softly.

"I got tested at the beginning of the season, and it was clear, too. I've never done it without one." I gulped, trying to hide my excitement. "Are you sure?"

She nodded. "I trust you."

Those three little words coming from the woman who I knew didn't trust easily were like a heavy weight pressed against my chest. Something I knew I'd treasure for the rest of my life, even if it was the last thing I did.

I was already in deep when it came to her, but something had shifted in this moment. Like she was finally leaning in, too. Maybe it was wishful thinking, but it made me believe we were moving forward...*together*.

Hope took flight in my chest like there was no tomorrow. All I could do was collide our mouths together, wishing my kisses were clear. Wishing they conveyed how determined I was to make this thing between us work. Even if I was afraid, because even though all these feelings I had been sifting through were very much real, there were dark parts of me who believed I wasn't capable of having something good. Not with a woman as perfect as Kennedy.

Don't dwell on it now. Stay in the fucking moment.

With my forehead resting against hers, I lifted her slightly and bottomed out inside her slowly. Our breaths hitched in sync. My body stiffened, and I shut my eyes and bit the inside of my cheek until I tasted copper.

Take a fucking deep breath. Don't go embarrassing yourself now.

"*Henry,*" Kennedy moaned as her hands caressed the muscles of my back, my forearms. Her touch was pure fire, like a brand searing into my skin. Like my body was hers to leave a mark, and she knew it. "*Move.* Do something, *please.*"

"Give me a sec, baby." My voice was strained and lacked control. "I'm trying not to embarrass myself here."

She huffed a laugh and stared at me with those bright fucking eyes, and that was all it took for me to settle into the moment. Once I had a handle on my emotions and my dick, I started pumping slowly, unhurried. It was...surreal. Her pussy was warm, and perfect and tight. My gaze landed on where we connected, and I was ready to lose it all over again with the way her juices coated me.

"Look at that pretty cunt, taking my cock like it's desperate for my cum." I bit my lip to hold back the pathetic groan that wanted to escape me. Only a woman like Kennedy could make me want to be vocal and loud; it was almost too embarrassing.

Her pussy clenched at my words. "I *am* desperate for it. Please, keep fucking me nice and hard." Every word she spoke was breathless, with an undeniable, raw need.

With a satisfying deep growl, I slid out of her. Her feet met the ground, and I turned her around. Then I bent her over and pushed her chest and face against the window. My gaze landed on her jersey, and something possessive came over me. I moved her hair to the side to take a good look at the way she wore the number eighteen and my last name so easily.

Thousands of people around the world wore it every day,

but this...this was a moment I was going to remember for the rest of my days.

I gripped her hips and slid inside in one languid stroke, admiring how her pussy clenched around me like a vise. I continued to thrust lazily, wanting to prolong the moment. She met every single one of my thrusts with gasps and moans. Those sweet symphonies were like little droplets of heaven for my ears.

Fucking her with my jersey on unlocked a fantasy I didn't know I had, but I couldn't take it anymore. I needed her naked. I wanted to touch every inch of her skin. So I fisted her jersey and took it off then unclasped her bra and pushed her tits against the window as my hands caressed her hips, her back, enjoying the soft feel of her.

I leaned forward and nipped her ear as I continued a delicious, steady pace. "You look like a dream bent over for me, letting me fuck you against this window. What would you do if people could watch, huh?"

Thankfully, the windows were tinted from the outside, and the only light that was turned on in the apartment was the one underneath our kitchen cabinets. But there was no denying the way her breath hitched, followed by a loud moan as her pussy gripped me tight at my words.

Interesting.

I let out a knowing chuckle. "You'd like that? For people to watch as I fuck this tight, pretty hole?"

"God, *yes*," she moaned.

"Too bad I'm a selfish man, and I don't share what's fucking mine." I didn't care how unhinged I sounded. I didn't give a fuck we hadn't talked about exclusivity. I was a madman consumed by this intoxicating goddess.

She balled her hand in a fist and hit the window. "*Henry, fuck.*"

"What, baby?"

"That had no business sounding so hot," she replied through a breathless laugh.

Her comment pulled a genuine smile out of me. I loved how open and unapologetic she was. I was sure it was what made sex between us so good.

Feeling bold and wrapping myself in the moment, my thumb found her clit, and I circled a few times to get my digit nice and wet. Then I moved my finger and slowly prodded her puckered hole.

She let out a hiss followed by a low, "*Oh*."

"Has anyone ever taken you here, Kenny?" I rasped.

She shook her head without a word.

"*Hmm*." My voice was deep and gruff. "I'd love to be the first one day," I said as I continued to stimulate her tight hole. "Would you like that?"

"Yes," she moaned, but then followed it with, "only if you let me play with yours, too."

Fucking hell.

It was in this moment I decided I was going to marry this woman one day. Even if I had to speak it into existence and manifest the fuck out of it.

"Sounds like a plan to me." I inserted my thumb deeper as my thrusts continued to become more frantic.

Those words alone spurred me into action. I was an open guy in bed, willing to try anything. The sound of it was... Well, let's just say there was another fantasy unlocked.

"Harder, please," she begged.

And so I obeyed. I pounded into her deep and thoroughly as I kept playing with her ass. She looked like a dream, and I had to shut my eyes and order myself not to come.

She was close; I could tell. So I took my finger out of her tight hole and flushed her back against my chest, wrapping my hand around her throat. My thrusts became faster and sloppier with the new position, and I loved the way I could get even deeper. Her hand found the back of my head, and she fisted my hair, while her other hand wrapped around mine and tightened my hold around her neck.

"I'm close," she cried out.

"Give it to me, Kenny baby. Come for me and I'll reward you by filling you up. Can you do that for me, please?" My tone was commanding and urgent all at the same time.

She was so, so fucking close. I was eager to feel her come around me. My free hand found her clit, and I pinched it ever so slightly, and just like that, she detonated. Her pussy spasmed around me, and I fought the dizziness that wanted to take hold of me with how tight she felt. Every part of my body stiffened, my lower back tingled, and with two more thrusts, my orgasm hit me with undeniable force. I shuddered as my cock twitched inside her. A low groan escaped my lips at the feel of her pussy milking every single drop out of me.

We were a mess of sweat and heavy breaths. Kennedy rested her forehead against the window, and I rested mine against her back.

After a few seconds, I slid out of her slowly and murmured, "Bend over, baby." She obeyed, and the sight of her, with her ass on the air, her back arched while her pussy was painted with my seed got my dick wanting to go another round. A bit of it was coming out of her, and something indescribably posses- sive came over me when I picked it up and pushed it all back in. "You look so fucking pretty full of my cum." I continued to lazily pump my fingers in and out of her.

She let out a low whimper. "What are you doing?"

"Making sure it stays where it belongs, Kenny baby."

She stared at me over her shoulder. "Do you have a breeding kink?" Her tone was amused.

I blinked once, at a loss for words for a moment. "*Shit.*" I laughed as I slid my fingers out of her. "I think I do."

"You *think* you do?" She giggled as she turned around.

"Never too late to unlock a new kink, as long as it's with you." I winked.

She shook her head, and before she could reply, I picked her up, pulling another giggle out of her, and cradled her in my arms as I walked us to my shower.

Once we got in, I took the head of the shower and wet her hair. Then I grabbed the brand-new shampoo, put a little bit in my hands, and lathered it.

"What's that?" she asked through a yawn.

"Shampoo. I'm going to wash your hair."

She sniffed then turned around with a frown. "That smells like my shampoo."

"It is."

"How did you—"

I leveled her with a look as I started to massage the coconutty, tropical shampoo into her scalp. "When are you gonna learn I pay attention to everything that has to do with you?"

She let out a contented groan, sagging her shoulders in relief. "I don't know if I should be creeped out or flattered."

I half-shrugged with a smile. "I like to be observant."

Her eyes met mine. They looked tired, but her face beamed with contentment. "Who knew you were an acts of service kind of guy?"

"Glad to be of service," I joked, but my laugh was forced.

My heart stammered as I wondered if she would ever find out I only wanted to be whatever she needed. She'd always been a strong, fiercely independent woman. So, how exactly could I take care of someone like that? I wasn't sure, but these little things were the perfect steps in the right direction.

Kennedy deserved the quiet kind of love. The kind whispered between light touches and soft kisses. She deserved slow mornings tangled in sheets, with forehead kisses that could say more than words ever could. She deserved someone who noticed when she was overwhelmed and was willing to step in and help before she even had to ask for it.

But Kennedy also deserved the loud kind of love. The kind where they'd go to her favorite store with her and do a mile-long line at the coffee shop to get her favorite drink while she browsed the aisles. The kind who saw her for who she was and reminded her to keep fighting for her dreams when she felt like giving up. She deserved someone who remembered her favorite color was pink, and that she liked to eat her lunch with a diet soda. The kind of person who'd feed her because she always forgot to eat when she was too busy. She deserved the kind of person who would defend her until the end of time.

She deserved the kind of love that made her feel seen. One that was both a safe place for her to be and a force that would do just about anything to see her shine.

I rinsed her shampoo and put on the conditioner as she instructed, and as it settled in her hair for a few minutes, we continued showering in silence. She dropped a few kisses on my pecs and my abdomen. Every time, without fail, they made me shiver. I dropped kisses on her cheek, her lips, her forehead. I traced her freckles with my fingertips, following them like they were a roadmap to her. Admiring the way the droplets of water glided against her beautiful skin. Loving the way she stared at me with this bright fucking smile that debilitated me in the best possible way.

We rinsed her conditioner and stepped out of the shower. I took my time to dry her and then myself, then grabbed one of my sweaters so she could put it on. She went to her room to grab the rest of her hair products, and when she came back, she was going to step into my bathroom again to do the rest of her hair routine, but I stopped her and sat her on my bed.

"I got it. Just teach me how," I said.

She nodded as she tucked her legs underneath her, and I got comfortable behind her and followed her instructions, sectioning her hair, applying some sort of cream that also smelled like a tropical sunny day, and brushing her curls with a detangling brush.

Right then, in the simplicity of the moment, in the quiet of the night where we enjoyed each other's company without trying to fill the silence with small talk, I knew I was hopelessly and endlessly in love with her. It wasn't the fleeting kind of love, either. No. It was the kind that lasted. She was my comfort, my place to land, and the warmth I'd been missing almost my whole life.

And I wanted—*needed*—to keep it. Keep *her*.

THIRTY-ONE

KENNEDY

AM I ENOUGH?

"I LOVE MY JOB. I totally, completely love my fucking job," I murmured the latest mantra I'd come up with every time I had to deal with the aftermath of Matt fucking Smith.

For our annual gala event, we always had a minimum of four charitable organizations to raise money for. This year, I wanted to add one more since we had raised so much money in the last three years, it made sense to scale the event even more. I wanted to prove to Brad I could handle the workload, but I also genuinely admired the work *FirstGen*—the organization I was trying to bring on board—was doing. Their mission centered on supporting BIPOC college students who were the first in their families to attend college, giving them the mentorship and opportunities they deserved.

The first time I met with the executive director, everything went smoothly, and she was excited to potentially work with us. That was until she dropped by our offices to speak with me and our charitable foundation manager about some logistics. I was pulled into a last-minute photo-op with Parker. I loved the fact that he was such a charismatic man and everyone loved him (and wanted to work with him), but the guy sure kept us busy. I tried to reschedule her, but she was already in the building and read the email too late.

Somehow, Matt was the one who ended up meeting with her, and just like that, the next day, I received a vague email from her saying that even though she loved meeting me and thought my heart was in the right place, she didn't believe the Strikers organization values aligned with theirs, so they wouldn't proceed. There were less than two weeks left until this event. At this point, I wasn't going to be able to research and find the right charitable organization in time. All the work I did went down the drain, and to say I was pissed was putting it mildly.

There was a moment when I considered asking Henry about *Willow House*, but I stopped myself. He made it clear he wasn't ready for it. And I understood why. I supported and respected his decision. Hopefully, one day, he would be able to. I'm sure he'd love to at some point.

I was on my way to Brad's office with my pulse practically trying to claw its way out of my throat. I could handle Matt being passive-aggressive with me and throwing his stupid and outdated sexists insults. But when his attitude started to affect the work I cared about—and to an extent, affecting the organization's image—that was where I drew a hard fucking line. I was so close to ignoring this and looking the other way like I'd done hundreds of times, because I was terrified Brad was going to think I wasn't going to be able to handle a managerial role if I couldn't even smooth things over with a coworker. And maybe I couldn't, you know? Perhaps this was the universe's way of telling me to let go of the idea of becoming a director.

With a shaky deep breath, I knocked on Brad's door and stepped in once he gave me the go-ahead.

"Do you have a few minutes to talk?" I managed to keep my

voice steady, though every nerve in my body felt like it was humming.

Brad gave me a quick nod with a smile. He'd always been a kind and patient man and knew how to handle every crisis that came across his desk. He was the sort of person who was born to be in PR. Always steady, but ready to pounce and be quick on his feet to solve any problems.

"I want to preface, I am in no way complaining or trying to throw anyone under the bus. You know my work ethic, and I'm not one to ever be involved in issues—" I was speaking as fast as I possibly could so I wouldn't lose my nerves, but Brad interrupted me.

"I know how you work." He shut his planner and placed the pen he was holding on top of it. "If you're here, it must be serious."

I thinned my lips with a silent nod as I took a seat in the blue velvet chair.

He leaned back in his chair, arms crossed, the leather creaking beneath him. "What's going on?"

I hesitated to speak. There was a moment when I considered only telling him about what happened with *FirstGen*. It would've been easier, safer. But another part of me, the one that was tired of shrinking, wanted to be brave; to be honest. To stop letting men who weren't worth a penny talk down to me like they were kings when all they ruled was their own inflated egos.

So I told him everything. What happened with *FirstGen*. Every passive-aggressive comment Matt threw my way for three whole years. What he pulled for Family Skate, and how, without the guys' help, it wouldn't have been a success.

"I tried to get details as to what happened in that meeting, but she was extremely vague." I circled back to the situation at hand.

"I'm familiar with her. We went to college together. I'm going to give her a call and find out what happened," Brad said. "Thank you for telling me."

"I know it's my fault." My breath hitched as I tried to find the courage to continue speaking without my voice breaking down. "I should have sent one of the interns to Parker's photo-op, but you know this sponsor is *very* specific—"

"You don't need to give me any excuses. I know, Kennedy." His eyes settled on me with a tilt of his head. "But, may I ask, why didn't you bring the other things to my attention? Three years is a long time to stay quiet."

I straightened in my seat, crossing one leg over the other. "With all due respect, Brad, I believe you've worked long enough in this industry to know how difficult it is for women to make it. The prejudice, the looks, and the comments are always there. All I have been trying to do since I stepped into this building is prove myself and let my work ethic speak for me. I didn't want to be pitied or get special treatment, so I decided to stay quiet."

He shook his head. "It wouldn't have been special treatment or pity, Kennedy. It would have been my duty as your boss to take care of a person who has been harassing you. You know how we work in this organization. We have zero tolerance for bullshit. I think having one of our best players benched for most of the season has proved that."

Shame crept up on me, settling in my stomach like a heavy stone. He was right. The truth was, I let my pride get in the way. I let my *I-can-deal-with-everything-myself* attitude ignore the red flags and take shit I wasn't supposed to be taking in the first place.

"I'm sorry," was all I could manage to say.

"I understand where you were coming from. I will look into

everything and we'll meet again, hopefully soon. Thank you for bringing this up."

I stood from the chair with a nod.

"You've been doing great work this season. With Anderson's reputation, the gala. You've done a lot you should be proud of. Don't let something like this set you back."

Pride filled my chest. This, coming from the man who taught me everything I knew about public relations—because having a degree was one thing, but hands-on experience was a completely different ball game—meant everything.

"Thank you," I replied with a genuine smile before I turned around and stepped out of his office. Once I shut his door, I let out the biggest sigh of relief, letting go of the fear and anxiety once and for all.

It was stupid for me to let Matt continue to get away with this. I knew then I had ignorantly fueled one of the core problems of the sports industry. The longer women stayed quiet when they were being harassed by men who owed them nothing, the longer those men would get away with it. This angered me like no other. Three years was a long time, and I could only imagine how many other women he had done this to, but they also remained quiet because they were terrified, just like me.

Was part of me still terrified? *Absolutely.* With every step I took in my career, I always wondered about many things.

Was this the right move?

Am I enough?

How can I be perfect?

Am I too much?

How much harder do I need to work to prove I deserve a spot?

Do I even deserve a spot in this cut-throat industry in the first place?

So many questions remained unanswered, but all I could do was hold my head high and keep putting in the work—for myself, and for every woman who would eventually take the same scary step.

THIRTY-TWO

KENNEDY

PLEASE, YOU LIKE ME JUST LIKE THIS.

LATER THAT WEEK, when Valentina dropped by my office mid-morning and said she was going to go bother the guys to get some marketing content done and asked me if I wanted to go with her, I quickly said yes. I desperately needed the break, plus watching a bunch of hockey players visibly groan when Val stepped into the barn with her phone in one hand and the ring light in the other was too funny to miss. They all loved to huff and puff every chance they got, but they knew they didn't have an option. For one, Coach Sloane would rip them a new one if they didn't participate—since it was part of their contracts and all. But worst-case scenario? Owens was there to get them in line, because when it came to his best friend, he didn't play.

When we arrived, the guys were doing some suicide drills while Coach kept barking orders. The guys looked miserable.

"I wonder who's at fault for this? Probably Parker," Val whispered through a giggle.

"Are you *crazy*? I bet you twenty bucks it was Hayes's fault," I murmured back, trying to contain my laughter.

That was the thing about suicide drills—if they were doing them after such a long practice, it was either because they'd lost a game the day prior, or one of the guys said something to piss off Coach Sloane. And, well, we'd won 4-2 against the Florida Bay Kings the previous night.

As soon as Coach blew the whistle to end the practice, a few of the guys collapsed onto the ice like exhausted starfish while Parker skated straight up to Hayes and smacked him with his stick. "Fuck you for that."

Val groaned while sagging her shoulders. "I don't have my purse with me."

"Drinks are on you tonight, then." I chuckled.

"Damn you, Wesley Hayes," Valentina murmured to herself.

I let out a quick laugh, but before I could say anything, Henry and Owens stepped into the tunnel.

Henry took off his helmet and tucked it under his arm, while his stick hung loosely in his hand. His cheeks were flushed, making the freckles across his face stand out, and damp strands of hair clung to his forehead. "This is a nice surprise," he said, slightly out of breath.

"And you've just been baited," I said, grinning smugly.

He frowned, then his eyes landed on Val, who was already setting up the ring light and phone. A groan escaped him. "Fuck, no. I'm not doing this shit."

When he tried to make a quick escape, Owens gripped him by the back of his practice jersey. "You're going to do whatever Val tells you to do. Got it?"

"It's fine if you don't want to, Anderson. I don't need the whole team," Val said with a kind smile.

"*Nope*. He doesn't get an option. None of them do. I'll go get the other guys," Owens said then leveled Henry with a look.

"You better obey every single fucking instruction she gives you."

Henry shot me an exasperated look, and it took everything in me to keep my laughter in check. He then sighed as he sagged his shoulders. *"Fine."*

Even though all the guys were exhausted, Owens, with his grumpy and *do-not-fuck-with-me* attitude, got all the guys in line to play a quick game of Would You Rather. Valentina, the sweet girl she was, even managed to get the assistant coaches to participate, since none of us were brave enough to ask Coach Sloane to be a part of it.

A quick thirty minutes later, Val was done and on her way to edit and post the video on our socials. I wanted to wait for Henry as he showered and changed, so I stayed in the tunnels while I worked on my phone, sending some emails to our catering company for the gala. I had locked down the menu a while ago, but I wanted to make sure we had more than one vegetarian option just in case. Every detail mattered. For many, it was a simple gala. For the guys, it was just another activity they were forced to attend as part of their contract. But for me? It was everything. Not only did working with amazing charities helped us as an organization to show how much we cared about the community we were part of, but this was also the last opportunity I had to prove I *could* do this job.

I was too distracted, skimming through a few other emails to notice what was happening around me. Suddenly, a hand gripped my forearm, too tightly for comfort. My head snapped up, and Matt was there. Standing way too close with his jaw tense.

"Can I help you with something?" I bit out my response, trying to get out of his grip.

He tightened his hold on me as his eyes flashed with annoyance. "Care to tell me why I have a meeting with Brad and HR tomorrow?"

Wow. That was quick.

"Isn't this a conversation you should be having with Brad?"

"Do not play stupid games with me, *girl*." He gritted out.

I gaped at him and scoffed in disbelief. "Get your hand off me, and I have a name, in case you've forgotten."

"Not until you tell me what the hell you told him."

"I suggest you take your hand off her, *right the fuck now*, Matt," a low, gravelly voice snapped from behind me. I didn't even have to turn around, because I could recognize that voice anywhere.

Matt's eyes snapped up, sharp and narrowed. "Back off, Anderson. This doesn't concern you."

The warmth of Henry's body felt stronger with each purposeful step he took. Without a word, he ripped Matt's hand off my forearm. "Do you have some sort of death wish?"

Matt took a sharp gulp, eyes going wide as Henry continued to close the distance. His height alone made Matt look like he was shrinking. "She owes me an expla—"

"She doesn't owe you shit," Henry snapped, his eyes never leaving Matt's. "Anthony will be hearing about this. I'll make sure of it. Don't ever put your hands on Kennedy, or any other woman for that matter, *ever* again."

My adrenaline kept my body on high alert, getting ready to step in. I wanted to trust Henry was going to make the right decision and walk away from the situation. But now that I knew better, and how triggering the scene must have been for him, I worried. The last thing he needed was to get in trouble for someone who wasn't worth it.

Matt let out a deep breath and took a few steps back. "Whatever. My career is probably fucking ruined already because your girlfriend couldn't keep her mouth shut."

Henry's nostrils flared, and he balled his right hand in a fist, but before he could react or say anything, I stepped in front of him, cradled his face between my hands, and forced him to look at me. "Don't. He's not worth it. Okay? Just focus on me, please. Ignore him." I looked over my shoulder. "Whatever they want to talk to you about, it's your problem now, Matt. Not mine. Leave us the hell alone." I grabbed Henry's hand and walked us to the nearest exit.

I pushed through door, letting the late March breeze, paired with the bright-blue sky and sunny day, welcome us.

"What the hell was that about?" Henry asked.

"It's nothing. I already dealt with it."

Henry's chest rose and fell with heavy breaths as his eyes flicked to the exit door then back to mine. "I didn't know you were even dealing with something in the first place. Has he been bothering you?"

I reached for his forearm and squeezed it gently. "It's a long story. One I will be more than happy to tell you when you can promise me you won't lose your shit."

He sighed heavily, pressing his thumb and middle finger to his forehead, the other hand planted on his hip. "Okay. Fine. But maybe when we're home and far away from that piece of shit."

I shot him a soft smile. "Sounds good to me."

"I'm sorry I took so long. He wouldn't have been able to find you if I hadn't been stopped by Coach to talk."

I perked up. "What did he say?"

He finally put me out of my misery by smiling. My favorite smile, too. The kind I knew was real because his eyes lit up and the corners crinkled just enough to give him away. "He's putting me back in. I'll be playing this weekend against Vancouver."

I quite literally jumped up and down—which was no easy

feat in four-inch heels—then wrapped my arms around him. "I'm so fucking happy right now."

His laugh was loud and carefree. He gripped my waist and met my gaze. "It's all thanks to you. Thanks for keeping me in line this season, Kenny baby."

I shook my head. "You've done amazing despite being benched for most of the season. I know it was hard, but hey, at least you get to play the day we'll find out if we clinch a playoff spot or not. So, you know, no pressure."

He smirked. "Have you met us? We got this in the bag."

"I forget how humble you are," I said sarcastically.

"Please, you like me just like this."

I think I love you just like this, was my first thought.

It hit me out of nowhere, right in the chest, like a sudden lightning strike that left me a little breathless. My mind didn't want to accept it. It tried to trick me into believing it was too soon. Maybe it was, you know? But I was also at a point in my life where I was *truly* happy. This was Henry, the guy who'd seen me at my lowest. The guy who saw me for who I was and embraced all of me without question.

While the knowledge was easy to accept, I wasn't ready to tell him. I still needed to take things slow, just in case. Because I owed it to myself to protect my heart.

So instead, I smiled and gave him a chaste kiss before replying, "It's kind of annoying how right you are."

THIRTY-THREE

HENRY

WE'RE SO BACK, SONS OF BITCHES!

THE WAY ADRENALINE kicked and rushed through my veins as over 23,000 fans filled the United Center and cheered for us as our intro song, "Thunderstruck" by AC/DC, boomed through the arena was an indescribable feeling. Knowing how important this night was and how close we were to the playoffs should have been nerve-wracking. But *this* was where I thrived the most. Every play we made was crucial. The pressure intensified the deeper we got into the season, but we were a well-oiled machine. Not only that, but every single one of us was thirsty for another chance after coming so close last season. We knew we had the talent to go all the way to the finals; it was just a matter of putting in all the hard work.

The second the puck dropped, the noise vanished. Not literally. I could still hear the fans slamming the plexiglass, chanting my name like I'd never left. But in my head? Dead silence. Only the scrape of my skates against the ice, the thrum of my heartbeat slamming against my ribs, and the *whoosh* of adrenaline reverberating through my veins.

It was like time never passed. Like the fight that put my

career on the line and got me benched like a goddamn rookie never happened. But I had a lot to prove tonight. I needed to prove to Coach I was the same quality player as ever. I needed to prove to my teammates I was someone they could count on. I desperately needed to prove to Kennedy I was the kind of man she could be proud of, and that without her, I didn't think I'd ever see the ice again. The way I played needed to speak for itself, so I could show everyone I was capable of keeping a cool head, even when the angry monster was trying to rear its ugly head. I couldn't let it control me. I had too much to lose.

The puck bounced wildly off the faceoff, and I lunged, cutting off Vancouver's center and stealing it clean. My body shifted automatically, remembering every movement and all the hours I'd put into this sport. I weaved my way between the defenses as my eyes scanned and calculated every possible outcome. Hayes and Donovan were with me, and it felt so goddamn right and meant to be to play next to my best friends once again. But even then, I barely saw them. All my attention was locked on the net.

For a split second, I hesitated. Not because I was scared, but because there was this fire burning inside of me. I was excited and ready to reclaim my spot in this team for good. After so long being benched, I was ready to put it all out there and show the world why I was the right player for this team and this position.

I could hear my teammates trying to get my attention, and the way the crowd screamed in anticipation. Every sound fueled the fire I couldn't tame, the same fire that'd kept me going even at my lowest.

With my eyes still on the net, I fired. Low glove side.

There was a second where everything moved in slow motion, where my focus tunneled in, heart pounding, breath caught somewhere between hope and exhilaration. Then everything came roaring back in a flash when the puck snapped past the goalie and slammed into the back of the net.

The red light flashed as the horn blared, and the arena erupted in a roar.

I glided across the ice with a smile so bright, my cheeks hurt. Hayes, Donovan, Parker, and Morgan crashed into me as they tapped their gloves against my helmet and slapped their sticks against my back.

I couldn't help but laugh when Hayes yelled, "We're so back, sons of bitches!"

My eyes scanned the crowd, and I inhaled a deep breath as I took everything in, trying to savor the moment and commit it to memory. My heart nearly skipped a beat when my eyes landed on the first row, just to the left of our bench. Every fan was slamming the glass, trying to get my attention, but there she was. Tall, chestnut hair curled and tumbling over her shoulders, wearing my jersey, with her hands tucked under her chin, gazing at me like I was the only person in the arena. Her eyes shimmered with tears, and her smile, *God, that fucking smile*. It filled my chest with something tender and fierce all at once.

I skated closer, the crowd erupting around me, but I tuned it all out. Not because I was trying to be a dick, but because Kennedy was all I could ever see. She was the golden hour, and I never wanted it to end.

I tugged off one of my gloves, not caring if a ref was going to whistle me for it, and pressed my bare palm to the glass.

My eyes locked on hers as I mouthed, *Hi, Kenny baby*.

Her smile was shy, and she raised her hand to meet mine on the other side of the plexiglass. Her lips moved just enough for me to catch the words. *Hi, pretty boy*.

Fuck. I was a goner for this woman. Completely. I loved her so much, it was starting to spill out of me in ways I couldn't control anymore.

———

EVERY PART of my body ached, and I could barely breathe after the horn blared, signaling the end of the game.

We won against the Vancouver Sharks, 5–4. It was a grueling game. At one point, I was sure we were headed for overtime, but during our last shift change, I stepped onto the ice just as Vancouver was scrambling through their own line change. I took off like the speed of light, and Parker swiftly fired the puck my way, and on instinct, I wound up and blasted a slap shot straight past their goalie.

I looked for Kennedy before going into the tunnel, but I couldn't find her, so I walked in with Donovan and Morgan toward the locker room. The whole place was a zoo, and it buzzed with so much energy, it was infectious.

When I stepped into the locker room, I barely had time to process the cheers before a wave of cold splashed over me. Hayes dumped an entire cooler of blue Gatorade on my head, and the room erupted in laughter and shouting as helmets banged against the lockers.

"That's the price of glory, baby!" Hayes shouted, cackling as the ice-cold Gatorade soaked my back.

I laughed as I shook the liquid from my hair and grinned like an idiot. The sweat mixed with the stickiness was awful, but I didn't care. We gave it all out on the ice, and we clinched a playoff spot, so I was happy to be the sacrificial victim. I'd take a thousand Gatorade showers if it meant I'd get to play this game with the people I considered family and bring us one step closer to the Cup.

"Not bad for a welcome party, huh?" Donovan chuckled as he gave my back a solid pat.

"I should have known better than to believe you guys weren't going to pull some shit like this."

Hayes draped an arm over my shoulder. "The night's not fucking over, Anderson."

"Oh, hell no," I groaned. "I am *not* going to Tim's."

All I wanted to do was take a nice, hot shower, find Kennedy, and do *another* kind of celebration with her.

"Hell yeah, you are. It's tradition. You sure you want to break something so sacred after today?"

I scrubbed my face. "Shit, no. You're right. But I'll stay an hour, tops."

"When did you become such a grandpa?" Hayes whined.

"Since knowing what's waiting for him at home, I'm sure." Parker snickered.

"Watch it," I warned. But he wasn't wrong. I was eager to spend every waking moment with my girl if they'd let me, like one sappy motherfucker. I also missed Captain Sushi, but that was a secret I was going to take to the grave with me. I'd been traveling so much, I was lucky if I got to spend time with him a day or two out of the week.

"Alright." Coach clapped his hands as he stepped into the room. Everyone quickly settled down and faced him. "I know we're excited to have Anderson back, and it was a great come-back for him, but this is not the time to be fucking around. We managed to win tonight, yes, but it was a struggle. Things that could make us or break us. This is not the time to be distracted. You all get the next two days off for the gala, but after that, you know how grilling this is going to be. It's going to be hard as fuck, but I believe in every single one of you."

"Yes, Coach," we all said in unison.

He nodded. "Great job tonight, guys. Keep it up, and for the love of God, *get some rest.*"

"Sure you don't want to join us tonight at Tim's, Coach?" Hayes asked.

"Absolutely not."

We all chuckled. Hayes always tried to get him to come out with us, and without fail, Coach Sloane always turned down his invitation.

"If we win the Cup, you *have* to go with us," Donovan said.

Coach crossed his arms and narrowed his eyes. After a few beats, he gave us a quick nod. "Bet. If we win, I'll go celebrate with you all."

We all broke into applause while Hayes and Parker added to the chaos, whistling sharply with their fingers and shouting, "*Fuck, yeah!*"

I was still part of the team and participated in every practice and locker room talk during the months I was benched, but there was something that made this moment so much better. Like I was finally back home, where I always belonged.

THIRTY-FOUR

KENNEDY

GOOD THING I'M NOT IN THE BUSINESS OF PLEASING MEN WHO THREATEN ME.

WE'D WON THE GAME, and while the guys went out to celebrate, I decided to come back home, get in some comfortable clothes, and work on the last details of the gala while hanging out with Captain Sushi in Henry's bed.

It'd become my new norm. I couldn't remember the last time I slept or hung out in my own room. There was something comforting about being in his bed, where Henry's familiar scent lingered. It was like being at peace and at home.

I took one last look at the number of people who had RSVP'd. Almost double the attendees we had the previous year —which was exciting—but it also served as a fresh reminder of the opportunities we'd be missing since *FirstGen* decided to drop out of the charity event. Through no fault of their own, of course. I just wish Brad had been able to convince them to stay.

My chest tightened at the thought. While Brad didn't blame me and assured me time and time again the job I did was still great, I still doubted my ability to lead. To manage. I blamed myself, even if just a little. I should have known better and kept a closer eye on Matt. I should have scheduled all

meetings outside of HQ. There were so many things I could have done differently.

A knock on the door pulled me out of my spiraling thoughts. Sush's ears perked up at the sound, but when I reached down to pet his head, he went right back to batting around his favorite plush toy. Another knock followed a few seconds later, more insistent this time. I grabbed my favorite pink cardigan, slipping it on as I made my way to the hallway. The moment I opened the door, my pulse spiked.

"You must be Kennedy." The gruffness of his voice caught me off guard, because it was similar to Henry's but not quite the same. It was hard not to notice the similarities between Vincent Anderson and his son. Their builds were nearly identical, and his hair had the same soft texture and dark color as Henry's, though his was streaked with gray. His eyes were blue, but they lacked the familiar warmth I'd come to love from Henry's.

"May I help you?" Feigning ignorance was the safest bet. I put on the professional mask and hoped to God I wasn't going to crack.

"I'm Vincent Anderson, Henry's—"

"I know who you are," I replied coldly, but as professionally as I could.

He smirked while his eyes roamed my body in a way that made me recoil. "I bet you do."

It took everything in me to keep my scoff in check. "How did you get past security?"

"Well, my name *does* carry some weight."

Figured as much.

"Are you not going to let me in?" he asked.

I gripped the frame door and opened it wider. Maybe if I obliged him, he'd leave faster. "Of course, come on in. Would you like something to drink?" I asked as I strode into the kitchen, opened the fridge, and grabbed a water for myself. I wasn't even thirsty. I only needed to keep my hands busy.

"No, thank you. This will be quick."

I turned around as I opened the water and took a sip, hoping to ease some of my nerves. "Henry's not here."

"I know. I came here to see you." He leaned forward, resting his elbows on one of the barstools. "I'm not one to beat around the bush, so tell me. How much is my son paying you?"

I took a step back, like I'd been slapped in the face. "*Excuse me?*"

He clasped his hands with a laugh, but the sound was calculated. It held no humor. "How much is my son paying you to date him? To clean up his reputation. There must be some sort of arrangement here, because you're not the typical woman he goes for."

A few months ago, the comment would have slashed me. There was no denying the evil glint in his eyes. He was fishing. Looking for a way to hurt me. But I knew better. Henry showed me time and time again how much he appreciated me with every little thing he did. While his father certainly wasn't wrong, and Henry used to cycle through different kinds of women in the past, that was then.

"I'm not quite sure what you're implying, but I think you should choose your next words carefully," I replied as evenly tempered as I could.

He chuckled, and the way he met my eyes made my body tremble slightly with unknown fear. But I quickly shoved it down. Men like him feasted on fear and insecurity.

"I looked into you," he said, straightening as his hands gripped the leather of the bar stool with casual authority. "Kennedy Jones. Thirty-two years old. Only child. Graduated top of your class at USC. Their PR program's no joke, so that was a nice surprise. You've been working for the Strikers for about three years now."

I opened my mouth to speak, but he didn't give me the chance.

"You were engaged for a while. Called it off a few months before the wedding. Left you in a fair amount of debt, calling it off so late. What a shame, truly." He let out a low whistle as he straightened to his full height and stepped closer, crowding my space, trying to intimidate me.

My pulse spiked, and I could feel my face pale. *How the hell did he know that?*

His grin was diabolical, calculated. "You look stunned. Can't say I blame you. But this is what I do. If someone's trying to get close to the Anderson name, I make sure I know who they are."

I crossed my arms and balled my hands in a fist, letting my nails bite at the flesh of my palms. I was entering anger territory and holding on by a single thread. "To be honest with you, Mr. Anderson, I couldn't care less what Henry's last name is."

He clicked his tongue with a quick nod. "You should. Not every woman can carry the last name gracefully. Henry's mother certainly couldn't."

Oh, this motherfucker.

I bit the inside of my cheek until pain shot through me. There was so much I wanted to say. But I couldn't destroy the trust I'd built with Henry. Not over a man like the one who stood in front of me.

"Nothing to say? *Interesting.*" His voice was laced with a quiet malice that clung to every word. "I'll keep talking, then, and you listen, okay?"

I furrowed my brows, stunned by how casually he kept sputtering shit out of his mouth like he didn't give a damn about anything. Like the world revolved solely around him.

"You're going to break up with my son," he continued, and this time he slowly stepped toward the other side of the kitchen island until we both faced each other, right in front of the fridge. "In exchange, I'll pay off your debt. I'll even put in a good word with the team's owner about that director position you've been eyeing. He and I go way back. I can cash in the favor at any moment." He shrugged like it was nothing. "You could go far with me in your corner, Kennedy. *Real* far."

My blood ran cold. Anger curled in my stomach like a fist, and my chest tightened to the point of pain. Every breath I took was harder than the last. This man acted like humans were transactions. And right now, I was another deal to him. A woman with debt and ambition. A problem with a price tag. This was my first time meeting him, and he already spoke to me like he had me all figured out.

There were no words to explain the fury that ran through my veins like liquid fire. It burned my insides. Suffocated me. Who the fuck did he think he was? Was he delusional enough to think I'd turn against the man I *loved* for money?

Yeah. *Loved.* I loved Henry with everything I had. He didn't know it, but that didn't change the fact that it was the truest thing I'd ever felt.

I smoothed my expression, forced my shoulders to relax, and met his gaze with a stare as steady as ice. "You can memorize all these facts about me, but don't get it twisted. This doesn't mean that you *know* me." A humorless laugh bubbled out of me. "It's funny you think you can buy me."

He clenched his jaw and glanced toward the fridge. I saw it then—a flicker of annoyance, maybe even surprise.

Good. I hoped it pisses you off, I thought.

His gaze lingered on the fridge, a slight frown tugging at his features—then a low, menacing chuckle slipped from his throat. "You don't want to make an enemy out of me, Kennedy," he said smugly, reaching behind me to grab something from the fridge. When he pulled back, my blood ran cold. He held up a single sheet of paper, casually pinched between his fingers like it was nothing. "I wonder what the organization would think if they knew about this?"

My stomach twisted, nausea rising in my throat the second I recognized it. It wasn't just any piece of paper. It was *the* contract.

This is not the time to freak out, Kennedy. Get. It. Together.

I lifted my chin and took a steady breath, trying to calm the pain in my chest. I casually reached for the piece of paper. To my surprise, he let me grab it. "Good thing I'm not in the business of pleasing men who threaten me." Every word I spoke was cold. Strong. Filled with venom. God, I hated this man. For everything he'd put Henry through. For him, striding into *our* home and thinking he could get away with anything.

He grazed his teeth with his tongue, keeping his smug smile in check. "You have until the day after the gala to decide what you want to do. Break up with him, and everyone comes out unscathed. Go against me, and I will tell the organization the discovery I made today. I will make it seem like you took advantage of his kindness, and your career will be over. His will be over, too. They'll drop him. I will make sure of it. Is this what you want? For everything you've both worked for to go up in flames? Are you willing to ruin his career?"

"Why are you doing this?" My question came out breathless. I couldn't understand it. Why was he trying to make his son so miserable? Hadn't he done enough damage already? How could someone be so *evil*?

Before he could answer, the sound of keys rattling and the door opening made me jump.

"Kenny?" When Henry came into view, his eyes landed on me first. They were soft and welcoming, but when his gaze flicked to his father, he stopped dead in his tracks. His jaw ticked. "What the hell are you doing here?"

Mr. Anderson took a casual step back, his expression morphing into a fake smile. "We were having a little chat," he said. "Getting to know each other better."

"No, I mean, what are you doing here in Chicago? In *our* fucking apartment?" Henry asked through gritted teeth as he took a few steps closer.

"I heard through the grapevine that tonight was your come-back. Against our home team, no less, so I came to watch. I dropped by to say hello, but you weren't here, so I asked Kennedy if I could wait."

Henry narrowed his eyes with a scoff. "Okay, so...you already said hello. You can leave now."

A few seconds of uncomfortable silence fell between us. Then Mr. Anderson met my stare. They held a silent warning that was hard to ignore. "It was lovely to meet you, Kennedy."

"Likewise," I forced out.

Mr. Anderson took a few deliberate steps until he stood in front of Henry. "Let's hope this wasn't a happy accident and you're actually able to lead the team to a win this season. You've been on this team long enough, it's time you make a statement with our last name once and for all."

"*Aaand* there it is," Henry muttered to himself. "Is that all?"

"I'm here for a few more days. We should go have dinner. My treat," Mr. Anderson said casually.

My God, this man was the textbook definition of a psychopath. The way he so easily went from a full-on villain to this was genuinely concerning.

Henry shook his head with a bitter laugh. "No, thanks."

Mr. Anderson nodded, and as he walked toward the exit,

he turned around and walked backward, shooting me a wink that sent shivers down my spine—and not the good kind.

As soon as the door closed, Henry was all over me. He cradled my cheeks between his calloused hands as he scanned my whole face with a concerned frown. "You okay?"

No. I desperately needed my inhaler, but I didn't want to do it in front of Henry. I didn't want to remind him how far from perfect I was.

I couldn't answer right away. But after a few silent beats, I cleared my throat and managed to give him a simple smile. "Yeah."

"Why didn't you call me?"

"I was about to, he'd only been here for a few minutes."

"Did he say anything to you?"

"No," I blurted. "We were just talking about the season. You know how retired hockey players are. That's the only small talk they can handle." I forced a laugh.

Was lying to him a mistake? Most likely. But how exactly was I supposed to say, *"Yeah, so, your dad threatened me to make me break up with you. But hey, welcome home and congrats on making the playoffs!"*

It was Henry's first night back, and I refused to let his father taint it. He'd already done enough damage. I would figure something out. I'd taken care of myself my whole life, and I could do it again.

This isn't about just you anymore, my brain all but screamed. *You have Henry to think about. A relationship to take into consideration. This doesn't only affect you.*

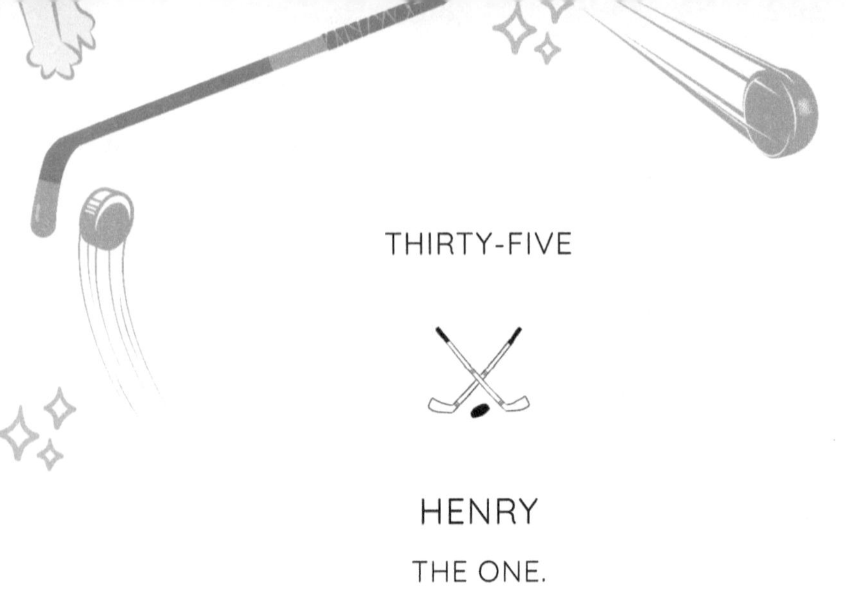

THIRTY-FIVE

HENRY

THE ONE.

"YOU'RE GOING to be the death of me," I said, almost breathless, when Kennedy stepped out of her room in a sleeveless light-pink dress, with a slit high enough to make my pulse spike and my cock twitch against my tuxedo pants.

"Is it too much?" she asked, eyes flicking down to the slit, a hint of worry in her tone.

"I'm obsessed with your fucking legs," I said without hesitation. "If it were up to me, I'd ask you to wear a mini dress so I can admire them all night long." I chuckled then leaned in and pressed a kiss to her lips, doing my best to hold back a groan at the familiar taste of her strawberry lip gloss. My hand slid down to her exposed thigh, fingers gliding over soft skin as I slowly traced up and down. "You look so goddamn beautiful, baby."

She looped her arms around my shoulders, her smile small and a little bashful. Her eyes darted away for half a second, like she was flustered. The sight pulled a genuine smile out of me. "Thanks." She scrunched her nose in the way I loved so much

when her gaze settled on my bow tie. "I can't believe you're wearing a pink bow tie."

I grinned. "And it matches your dress perfectly. Weird, right?"

Her eyes did a full, dramatic roll. "Yeah. *Soooo* weird," she drawled. "It's not like I *totally* missed Valentina holding up bow ties to my dress the day we picked them up."

"I told her to be subtle."

"Subtle is not Valentina García's MO," she deadpanned.

"It's the thought that counts," I quipped.

"Yeah," she whispered. "Thank you for always thinking of everything." Her eyes shone brightly.

I brushed her cheek with my thumb, giving her a pointed look. "What did I say about thanking me for the bare minimum?"

"For you, *everything* is the bare minimum."

I winked. "Glad you're catching up."

"You're an idiot."

"You like me just like this, though."

She pursed her lips while she straightened my bow tie. "Yeah, I do."

I chuckled as I leaned in and brushed my lips against her neck, slow and deliberate. "We can be a little late, right?"

She let out a low whimper. "I wish, but we only have fifteen minutes."

Before she could react, I grabbed her by the waist, and she squealed as I hoisted her onto the island.

"Challenge accepted," I murmured with a knowing smirk as I dropped to my knees, my eyes traveling slowly upward, admiring every bit of exposed skin and how the dress fit so perfectly against her body.

"*Henry...*" She tried to sound firm, but the heat in her eyes and the way her breath hitched gave her away.

"I only want a little taste," I rasped as I unhurriedly opened her legs and scrunched her dress up a little. When I found her completely bare, I groaned. "Why aren't you wearing anything?"

She gave me a nonchalant shrug. "Didn't feel like it."

I gripped her thighs and licked her outer labia, followed by a light suck. "You little brat." My chuckle was barely audible. "You wanted me to find you like this, didn't you? All bare, with this pretty little clit swollen and begging for my attention."

She tried to close her legs to seek some friction as she let out a breathy moan, but I tightened my grip. Without breaking eye contact, I latched my mouth around her clit, licking and sucking like the desperate fool I was. I already knew Kennedy's ins and outs. What tickled her body, what drove her wild, and what brought her to the brink of an orgasm.

I gripped and caressed one of her legs while I slid two fingers inside her and continued between sucking her clit and twirling my tongue around it. "Come on my tongue, Kenny. I want to be able to taste you for the rest of the night." My fingers found the spot that made her moan turn into a small cry. "Because when we get home, I'm going to rip this dress off you and fuck this tight, pretty cunt. Maybe even play with your ass a little." Her pussy clenched around my fingers, and I couldn't help the playful smirk that tugged at my lips. "Yeah, that's what I thought. My girl wants to be used tonight like a little whore, doesn't she?" I didn't give her a chance to give me a retort. I started to finger her at a steady but fast rhythm. When her moans became more desperate and she started chanting my name in that little high-pitched tone I liked, I ran my tongue up and down her center, then sucked her clit one more time, letting her orgasm completely detonate against my tongue. She gripped the back of my head and kept me in place as she continued to ride her climax, and I drank every single ounce she was willing to give me.

When her post-orgasm high wore off, I stood to my full height, helped her down from the counter, and gently adjusted her dress back into place, smoothing the fabric and making sure she looked perfect.

"Would you look at that?" I said with a wink. "We still have eight minutes to spare."

"We didn't even take care of you!" she exclaimed as we stepped out of our empty apartment.

Captain Sushi was being babysat by Donovan's kid tonight. We knew it was going to be a long day, and since we'd be home late, neither of us wanted him stuck alone for hours. That damn cat had grown on me more than I ever expected. I couldn't imagine life without him now. I almost got him a tuxedo and brought him with us to the gala, but I didn't want to freak him out with the crowd and noise.

"Oh, don't you worry." I gave her ass a playful squeeze and pressed a quick, teasing kiss to her mouth. "The night's still young."

I WAS at a loss for words the moment I stepped into the venue. Everything screamed *Strikers*, but in a polished and sophisticated way.

The *Strikers Unite* yearly gala had been a tradition for decades, but in recent years, they'd been scaling it up, carefully curating each event to support different charities, always making sure they aligned with the values the organization believed in and wanted to represent.

One day—when I was brave enough—I wanted *Willow House* to be part of something like this. I knew it could do so much good. I just couldn't. Not yet. I was still terrified, so I protected them with everything I had. Maybe I went a little overboard sometimes, but we'd helped so many people, I didn't want to take any unnecessary risks. Because who knew what could happen if people found out I was behind it all? The internet had been ruthless to me over the years, and it would kill me if it affected *Willow House* in any way.

"I'll see you in a bit. I gotta talk to a few sponsors," Kennedy said, dropping a kiss on my cheek.

Before she could completely turn around, I gripped her hand and brought her close to me. "Save me a dance?" I asked as I played with one of her curls.

She smiled with a soft nod. I matched her smile before colliding our lips in a kiss. I couldn't get enough of her, of her presence, her intoxicating lips. Everything.

After a few seconds, she lightly pushed me. "Okay, now I *really* gotta go."

I let out a wistful sigh as she walked away from me. I strode to the open bar, where I ordered a diet soda. This was technically our last night to have fun while working for a good cause, but my mind was already in the next game. I couldn't mess anything up. We had two months left to survive. This was when it mattered, more than ever.

"Why are you late?" Olivia, my twin sister, asked as a greeting.

"Knowing lover boy, he was probably getting it on with his girl." Hayes snickered as he swirled his scotch and took a sip.

"You're disgusting, Wes," Olivia deadpanned.

"Hello to you, too, dear sister. I'm not late." I made a show of checking my watch. "I'm actually a whole minute early."

She rolled her eyes but leaned in for a side hug. "Why'd you have this idiot pick me up from the airport? Do I not matter to you?" she groaned dramatically.

"I was busy. And you're the one who insisted on coming to the gala at the last minute."

"I would have rather taken an Uber if I had known."

"I was basically your personal airport concierge. Except I charge nothing and have better hair," Hayes said with a cock of his brow.

"See what you had me dealing with all day?" Olivia muttered with a weary shake of her head.

"Sounds to me like someone's being ungrateful, Livvie," Hayes sing-songed. "Be careful, or you'll have to find a new place to live when you move here. And spoiler alert, you *don't* want it to be your brother's place. Unless you're into listening to him fuck like a caffeinated rabbit."

God, these two were fucking exhausting; it was making me dizzy. They'd been acting like this since we were kids, so you'd think I'd be used to it by now. But...*nope.*

"Who are you calling Livvie? Because it sure as hell isn't me," she snapped, crossing her arms. "I'm done with this conversation. Walk away from me before I smack your head."

"You know I like my women feisty, *Livvie*. Be careful," Hayes quipped.

"Watch it," I warned. I knew he was joking, but still.

She shot Hayes a glare without a word then looked at me. "Where's Kennedy? I want to meet her."

"You've already met her." Multiple times, actually. My sister was an athletic trainer for the New York Jaguars, and they'd crossed paths when Kennedy traveled there with us.

"Yeah, but I need you to reintroduce her as your *girlfriend*." She stared at me like I was an idiot.

I looked around the room and found her speaking with Brad and Anthony. "Maybe later, she's busy."

"Fine, I'll—" Olivia didn't finish her thought. Her face paled, and her shoulders trembled lightly. With a confused frown, I looked over my shoulder. When my eyes landed on our father, I cursed under my breath.

Olivia went into a full no-contact relationship with our father when she graduated from college. He was gracious enough to pay for it, but paying for my sister's tuition came with terms. He was eager to control her. It was a constant war between them.

She had big plans—med school, a career in sports medicine. But the pressure eventually caught up to her, and after earning her bachelor's, she cut him off for good. I offered to help, begged her to let me pay for her MD, whatever she needed.

Because here's the thing my sister—and our mom—never quite understood: I *wanted* to take care of them. After so many years of being useless, not knowing how to protect the two most important women in my life, I wanted to make it right.

But Olivia could be stubborn. I was almost shocked she even let our father pay for her undergraduate degree. When I asked her why, she just shrugged and said, "He should pay for my emotional damage."

I know what you're probably thinking, but what can I say? My sister's humor always turned a little dark when it came to her trauma.

"Did you know he was going to be here?" she asked, barely above a whisper, her voice threaded with something between fear and dread.

I shook my head. "I mean...he showed up at my apartment the other day—"

"I can't be here," Olivia murmured, more to herself than to me. Her hands trembled slightly, and her voice wavered.

"We can go back to my place and forget about this night," I offered quickly, already stepping forward.

Before I could reach her, Hayes slipped off his suit jacket and gently draped it over Olivia's shaking shoulders.

"I got her," he said, firm and soft all at once. "This is a big night for Kennedy, you should stay here. I'll take care of this."

"No, I'm sure Kennedy will unders—"

"Wes can take me. I'm staying at his place anyway. It's fine." Olivia met my eyes. They were swimming with something uncertain. A type of pain I wanted to pull out of her and carry myself. "*I'm fine*," she said, though we both knew she wasn't.

Hayes wrapped an arm around her shoulders, pulling her close to his chest as they walked toward the back exit, taking the long way so my father wouldn't see them. They bickered like an old married couple, but when it mattered the most, I knew Hayes would be there for my sister in a heartbeat. I wholeheartedly trusted him.

I took a deep breath, trying to calm the rage that was quickly bubbling out of me. Without a thought, only all-consuming anger, I strode to him with menacing steps. "Why are you here?

His gaze lingered around the venue, like he was looking for someone. "Where's your sister? I was told she was going to be attending."

"She wants nothing to do with you."

"I'm her father."

"She hasn't spoken to you in seven years for a fucking reason," I snapped, taking a step closer until he was forced to meet my eyes. "I have been stupid enough to keep you in my life, God only knows why, because we both know you don't deserve it, but you stay away from Olivia. Do you understand?"

"How's that anger management issue going, son?" His question was laced with sarcasm.

My chest felt like it weighed a thousand pounds. He was trying to get under my skin. That's all he wanted out of me. To show me I was just like him. But fuck him, if he thought I was going to let him trick me into something so shitty. I *wasn't* like him. It was something I had slowly learned how to come to terms with. Yes, I had my moments when I had to work through my anger, but I would continue to fight against my demons every fucking day to find better ways to deal with them. "Better than you, that's for sure."

"It's only a matter of time," he replied with a bored tilt.

"Why are you here?"

"Like I said—"

"*No*," I hissed. "Why are you really in Chicago? Why did you go to my apartment the other day?" He went to speak, but I raised my hand to stop him. "Don't tell me it was because you wanted to see me, because we both know that's bullshit. You wanted to see Kennedy alone for a reason. *Why?*" The way blood pumped through my veins, I could hear the palpitations as clear as day in my ear, almost too painfully.

"Can we not do this here?" he asked through gritted teeth.

My hand shook as I rubbed it against my mouth. He was right. In other instances, I wouldn't have given a single fuck, but I wasn't about to ruin Kennedy's night. She'd worked so hard. I looked over my shoulder to make sure she was distracted. My eyes found her, and she was animatedly speaking with a few season-ticket holders and Donovan, so I waltzed out of the venue, with my father hot on my trail.

"I'm trying to rectify your mistake," he said as soon as we stepped outside.

"*My mistake?*" I let out a disbelieving laugh as I turned around. "This is *my* career. And I have already paid for *said* mistake. For the better part of the season, actually."

He shook his head adamantly. "I'm talking about Kennedy." He took a few steps closer to me. "She *will* destroy your career. You need to remain focused. The last thing you need is to lock yourself down to one woman. It will *distract* you."

"I am a thirty-year-old man who's at the prime of his career. I'm not some eighteen-year-old rookie who just started. And frankly, my love life has *nothing* to do with the legacy I've been slowly building." I pointed a finger at him. "And *you* have no say in my life either. When are you going to get that?"

It was like he wasn't even listening. Because that's who my father was. Self-centered. Careless.

"You're going to regret it. Just like I did." His eyes held unspoken fury.

Fuck, I was frustrated. I'd reached my boiling point.

"*Stop trying to blame everything on Mom!*" I roared. My throat was scratchy and painful, but I couldn't hold back any longer. "She did everything she could to support your fucking career. And what did you do to repay her? *Cheat* on her. Then, when your career ended, you decided to damage your fucking family all because of your own inflated ego!"

"Lower your voice—"

"*No*," I growled. Fuck, I'd never been so frustrated. "I would love nothing more than for the world to find out who you truly are. The kind of monster they adore."

"You pull that stupid stunt, and I will tell the organization about the little contract you and Kennedy have." My eyes widened, and his mouth curled into a cruel smile. "Oh, *yeah*. I saw it. I know everything."

"You know *nothing*," I barely managed to spit out.

My stomach tightened, and my heart was thrashing against my ribcage painfully.

No *one* knew. No one had a clue how irrevocably, helplessly in love I was with Kennedy. How loving Kennedy wasn't a choice—it just *happened*. It took over everything. What started as pretend turned into the most real thing I'd ever felt.

She crept into every part of me until there was no part of my life untouched by her. She wasn't just the best thing that ever happened to me. No.

She was it.

The one.

"You're probably right. But that's the thing about being a man with influence," he remarked casually. "All I need is to make one phone call, and your precious Kennedy will be on every tabloid for things she didn't even do."

My nostrils flared. "If you touch her—if you even *breathe* in her direction—so help me God, I will go to the media and tell them everything."

I'd get my mother and sister's permission first, of course. But I knew them. They supported me through it all. And we were aware of how long this charade had been going on for. I'd taken the higher road my whole goddamn life, and for what? For him to believe he held some sort of power over me?

His eyes darkened. "Your career will be over if you do that. Half—if not all—of your endorsements will drop you if you go forward with your little sob story. No one will believe you. *I will make sure of it.*"

"I don't fucking care," I shouted. "At least I won't be the coward hiding behind a fake image anymore."

"Don't be stupid," he snarled, jabbing a finger at my chest. "Everything you have, you have *because of me.*"

I stepped forward until there was barely an inch between us. I remembered in this moment how small he used to make me feel. How part of me always believed I was never going to have the opportunity to stand against the monster that hid behind the shadows.

"*No.* Everything I have, I built in *spite* of you." My eyes met his, without an ounce of fear or shame. All I felt was bravery. It was cathartic, the way I stood my ground. "I'm done trying to make this work. Believing that if I kept you around, at least you'd let me live my life. Believing that maybe you'd change one day. But you don't have one good bone in your body, and you think the world owes you everything, but this is not *how it works*. I'm done."

Speaking my truth was like finally being able to breathe properly for the first time. Like my head had been underwater my whole life, and I'd finally come up for air.

"Break up with her, or her career is fucking over. I will bury her in the *goddamn* ground. Do you hear me, boy?!"

I should have known better than to believe he wasn't going to try to have the last word. "And I'm telling you, if you do that, I will ruin *your* reputation."

"It's my word against yours. Who do you think has more influence?" His laugh was manic. "If you care about her, let her go and focus on making yourself worthy of the Anderson name."

I couldn't handle being around him any longer. Without a word, I started walking to get away from him. From everything. I needed time to think. What angered me the most was that he *was* right. My father had too much influence. It was a risk to go against him.

Only one question remained... Was that going to stop me from protecting the woman I loved with every fiber of my being?

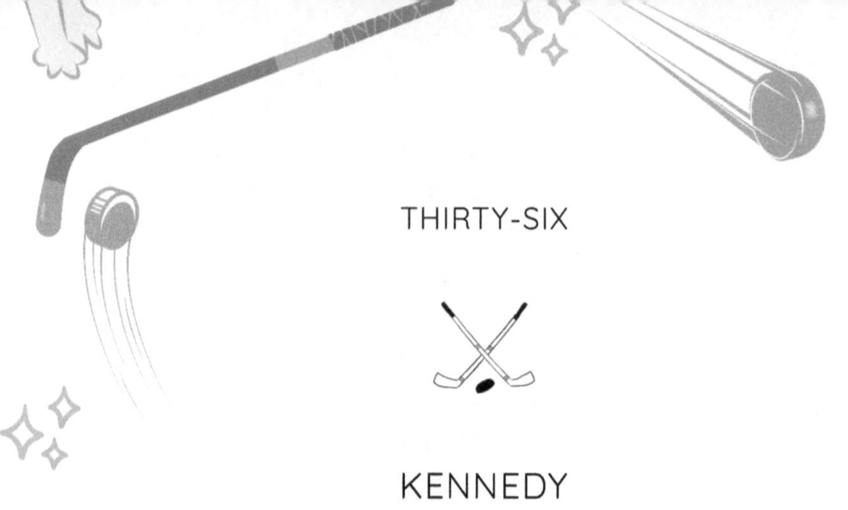

THIRTY-SIX

KENNEDY

HENRY ANDERSON—
ALWAYS THE PROTECTOR.

MY FEET WERE KILLING ME, and my throat was sore from how much I had talked, but none of it mattered. The event had been a success.

Everyone had gone home, and I hadn't seen Henry since we parted ways for me to make my rounds. But when I found out his father was in attendance—a last-minute addition no one told me about—I understood why he was nowhere to be found. I didn't blame him.

It was a bittersweet moment, standing in the middle of the empty venue. My heart was full, and tears welled in my eyes as I took a deep breath, my gaze landing on the Strikers logo centered on the stage. The venue crew was already tearing it down—packing up lights, folding chairs, peeling back the illusion. With every piece that disappeared, something in my chest cracked a little more.

It felt like the end of something I wasn't ready to let go of. A symbolic gut punch—my hopes and dreams being dismantled right in front of me. This was all I wanted. Just one more day of

normalcy. One more day to pretend my career was still going somewhere with this organization. Because tomorrow morning, when I strolled into Anthony's office and told him everything, I'd be walking straight into the end of it all.

"Kenny."

I quickly dried my tears and turned around, finding Henry standing a few feet away from me. His bow tie was untied, hanging around his neck. His hair was disheveled, and his eyes were a little bit red. It cracked my heart.

"I'm sorry I disappeared," he began to apologize, but I shook my head.

"You don't have to explain yourself. I saw your father. Trust me, I would have done the same." My laugh was small, wobbly. It took every ounce of energy out of me.

He took a few steps closer. "We need to talk."

A heavy silence fell between us. Anxiety slithered up my spine and curled around my chest, squeezing until each breath felt like a battle. I didn't say a word, because part of me knew. This was it. This was the moment I had to come clean.

"What did my father say to you?" His question was barely audible.

"I don't know what you're talking about." I flinched. It was instinct to be dismissive. Old habits die hard, or whatever.

"*Kennedy*," he warned. His eyes met mine in a desperate plea. It gutted me. I didn't want to be the source of his pain. "Please, don't lie to me. We're better than that."

I took a deep breath, trying to steady the tremble in my voice, trying to will the truth back down my throat. But it clawed its way up anyway, bitter and heavy. "He knew everything about me and tried to pay me off to break up with you. I said no, of course, but then...he saw the contract." I tilted my head up to keep the tears at bay. "And he put me in an impossible position." My voice cracked. I was so angry at myself. I was so adamant about having that stupid contract, thinking it was going to keep everything professional between us. As if Henry and I hadn't already been falling for each other little by little. As if a flimsy piece of paper with some dumb written rules and signatures was going to stop me from falling in love with the man who stood in front of me. The man who saw every part of me.

He stayed quiet, just looking at me, giving me the silent go-ahead to continue.

I shook my head with a deep sigh of defeat. "Your father is not a kind man. He's out to ruin both of our careers. Which is why I'm telling Anthony it was all my idea."

"But that's a lie—"

"I don't care if it's a lie. I got you into this mess." I let out a short, humorless laugh, the kind that came from somewhere deep and exhausted. "You think I don't know you were thinking of me when you came up with this idea?" I looked at him, my chest aching. "You forget I know you now. I know how selfless and kind you are. I know you'd be willing to risk every-thing for the people you care about. And don't tell me you did this because you cared about your reputation, because we both know it isn't true."

The silence was so thick and deafening, it was suffocating me. Burning my lungs as I held my breath, bracing for impact.

His sigh was heavy. Resigned. "At the beginning, maybe, yeah. But eventually, I wanted to take advantage of it, too," he said, taking two steps closer. "You can't take the whole blame. This is not how it works."

I took two steps back. I couldn't let him touch me—I couldn't even meet his eyes, because if I did, I'd break. I'd cave. "I'm not going to make you choose between me and your career. You've worked so hard, you've—"

"And you haven't?" he snapped, his voice louder now, raw with frustration as he raked both hands through his hair. "*Jesus, Kennedy.*"

The room echoed with his words, but it was otherwise empty. No staff. No background noise. Just us, standing in the middle of a night that was supposed to be a milestone in my career. Now it felt like the undoing of everything.

He took a step toward me, his jaw clenched. "What about *you*? Everything you've done to get here? If you think I'm going to stand here and let you throw that away for *me*, then you don't know me at all."

"This is an impossible situation your father put me in. He can ruin both of us. Don't you get that? And I'd rather go down for it." My throat bobbed, and it felt like I was gulping thick pieces of broken glass. I wanted him to understand me, but even if he didn't, it wasn't going to stop me. This was probably the most selfless thing I'd ever done for someone. But it was the right thing to do. When you love someone with every piece of your soul, when that person shows you there's more to you than you ever thought possible, it's easy to let go of the things that, in the grand scheme, didn't matter.

I could build a career somewhere else. That wasn't the problem. But what Henry and I had—that was one in a million. I felt it in my gut. I felt it in my bones. It took being in a long relationship, planning a whole wedding with a man I thought I loved, and breaking my own heart to finally understand what real love was really like. The universe, God—whatever force was out there—put me through those experiences for a reason. To shape me. To prepare me. Because something better, something truer, was waiting for me on the other side.

And now that I had it, I wasn't going to let it go. Not without a fight.

"Then maybe we give him what he wants," he whispered.

My heart sank. It was like the ground dropped from beneath me. Everything around me blurred. The chandelier above us, the fading murmur of voices in the hall, even the way Henry was looking at me. It all disappeared beneath the sting of those words. Tears stung my eyes so fast I didn't have time to stop them. My lungs tightened like they'd forgotten how to work.

"What?" My voice trembled, barely audible over the rush in my ears.

"I'm not going to let you sacrifice your career for me." There was a crack in his composure, a flicker of guilt in his eyes that told me this wasn't what he wanted. Like he was convincing himself it was the only way.

Henry Anderson—always the protector. Always trying to be fucking noble.

"You don't get to decide what I do with *my*"—I jabbed a finger against my chest—"life. I'm not a problem for you to fix. I am an adult capable of making my own decisions."

"It's just for the meantime," he replied weakly.

"*No.*"

"Kennedy," his voice cracked. "Please. I am only trying to help."

"And you think breaking up is the solution?" My voice rose, brittle and sharp as glass. My chest was heaving now, the anger mixing with the inevitable heartbreak in a way that made it hard to breathe.

He flinched but didn't look away. "I think it'll keep you safe."

"*Safe?*" I let out a breathless, humorless laugh. "*God, Henry.* You don't get it. Do you?"

"Get what, Kennedy? That my father is insane? Believe me, I understand—"

"That I would do anything for you, because I love you, you idiot!" The words tumbled out of me, raw and furious and terrified all at once. I shook my head as my shoulders sagged. "I love you so much it makes me selfish. It makes me willing to give up everything just so you don't have to suffer anymore at the hands of *him*."

Everything happened in a blur. In the next second, he moved. Three long strides, and he was in front of me. His hands cradled my face with a kind of desperation that stole the breath right from my chest, and before I could even blink, his mouth was on mine in a fierce kiss. It wasn't gentle or careful. His lips moved against mine like it was the only way he knew how to say all the things he couldn't voice. The kiss was every bit consuming, like he'd lost the last shred of self-control and decided that if we were going to burn, we'd do it together—tongue, teeth, heartbreak, and all.

When he pulled back, I gasped for air. My brain was dizzy. My body hummed with euphoria. Every nerve ending sparked beneath his touch, overwhelmed by his presence.

His forehead came to rest against mine, and his breath was sharp before he whispered, voice rough, "I love you so damn much it fucking terrifies me. Which is why we're going to figure something out—*together*." His eyes searched mine, glimmering with quiet desperation and fierce determination. "You don't have to carry the weight of the world on your shoulders anymore, because I'm here, okay? I'm fucking here, and I'm not going anywhere. I'm sorry I even suggested it."

Tears ran down my cheeks, but he wiped them with his thumbs, holding me like I was something precious. "I understand why you had that reaction. Trust me, I do. But we can't let him break us apart. I can find another job with another team. Honestly, it doesn't even have to be sports. I'll be *okay*."

He shook his head adamantly then leaned in and pressed his lips to my forehead. His arms wrapped around me—tight, fierce, protective. The kind of hug that felt like a promise. "We'll figure it out," he murmured against my hair. "But you're not taking the fall for this. Not alone. Not ever."

THIRTY-SEVEN

HENRY

DID YOU SERIOUSLY ROMANCE-BOOK-FAKE-DATE ME?

I DIDN'T THINK either of us got one lick of sleep last night.

We talked...a lot. We weighed every possible scenario, played out the worst-case outcomes like a bad movie on repeat. But no matter how we tried to slice it, we always came back to the same conclusion.

We needed to come clean.

There was no other way around it. Logically speaking, my father didn't have hard evidence. All he saw was a single piece of paper with our signatures and a few vague rules. So what? It wasn't like the media had access to it. Not unless someone handed it to them, and after the big scare we had, even though I refused to throw it away, because it will always carry the reminder of how we started, I made sure to put it in a safe place.

"Are you sure about this?" It was the first question she asked when I opened the passenger door and helped her out of the truck. We were parked in the employees' parking lot at HQ, ready to face the music.

I nodded. "It's the right thing to do."

"We're both idiots for thinking this wasn't going to blow in our faces," she muttered.

I squeezed her hand and brought it to my lips, pressing a soft kiss to her knuckles. "I don't regret it one bit. It led me to you."

Her eyes softened for a moment, but she let out a low laugh. "You have to accept it was kind of crazy, though."

"You can blame the guys for that," I quipped.

She patted my arm playfully. "Stop trying to pin your crazy ideas on them!"

"It's the truth." I chuckled. "When I proposed the idea to you, all I wanted to do was help. But..." My cheeks heated. I couldn't believe I was confessing something so stupid. Like we were in goddamn high school.

She narrowed her eyes and crossed her arms, giving me the silent go-ahead to continue.

"Donovan may or may not have asked Aurora for advice since she loves to read romance books, and they may or may not have come up with the idea for me to take you to all these fake dates and spend time with you so you could see the real me or whatever," I mumbled. Saying it too loud felt ridiculous and pathetic.

She gaped at me. "Did you seriously *romance-book-fake-date* me? Like—like I'm the unsuspecting heroine and you're the broody love interest with a secret plan to win me over?"

I scratched the back of my neck, trying not to laugh. "I mean...when you put it like that, it sounds worse."

"*Oh my God,*" she said, half laughing, half horrified. "And the whole team?"

"Hayes was the master planner," I muttered under my breath. "There was a group chat."

Her mouth dropped open again. "*A group chat?!*" she

groaned into her hands. "I cannot believe I fell for something so cliché."

"But a good one, right?" I wiggled my brows. "Slow burn, fake dating, forced proximity—"

She raised an eyebrow. "Are you a reader now or what?"

I scrubbed my face, where some stubble was already growing. "I didn't read any books, but I could probably get into it. Sounds fun as fuck. I could learn a thing or two, make things interesting." I wiggled my eyebrows.

She rolled her eyes without a word. I dropped a kiss on her cheek with a laugh, and she pushed me playfully as we strode into the building.

Once we were right outside the conference room, I stopped and gently tugged Kennedy back toward me. Sometimes things could be fun and games, but now, everything was on the line. We didn't know what was going to happen. There was so much up in the air; the uncertainty of it all was terrifying.

"Whatever happens in there," I said, brushing her hair behind her ear, "we face it together. Okay?"

She smiled, just barely, with a silent nod.

I took a deep breath then knocked twice before opening the door.

Anthony was already inside, seated at the head of the small conference table. Coach Sloane was sitting to his right, arms crossed over his chest, with his face serious as always.

"Morning," Anthony said as we stepped inside. "You said you needed to talk to us?"

I nodded, motioning for Kennedy to sit before I did. My palms were already sweating. "There's something we need to be upfront about before someone else has a chance to twist the narrative."

I caught Kennedy's eye. She gave me the tiniest nod.

Anthony and Coach stared at us expectantly.

Here goes nothing.

"The relationship between us...didn't start as a real one," I admitted, my face cringing. The words felt heavy against my mouth. I was struggling. "When the whole article dropped, the pictures were taken out of context, but the PR backlash Kennedy was going to receive wasn't fair when it wasn't even her fault. We both did what we thought was best at the time for both of us."

Kennedy gripped my hand in reassurance as we both held our heads high. There it was. We laid everything on the table. There were no takebacks. Just pure honesty.

Coach leaned back slowly, tilting his head with that unreadable expression that always made me sweat during lineup reviews. Anthony just stared with a blank expression. Both were completely silent.

My stomach was in knots. I could practically hear my heartbeat pounding in my ears.

Fuck. This was the part where everything came crashing down, wasn't it?

This was it for us. As soon as the playoffs were over, I was going to be dropped. And good luck to me finding another team. Who the hell would want a player dumb enough to fake a relationship and risk PR hell?

And Kennedy? She'd lose everything. Her job, her reputation. It was unfair. She didn't deserve that.

Panic clawed its way up my throat. I actually thought I was going to throw up right in the middle of the conference room table.

After a long, agonizing beat, Coach glanced at Anthony, then back at us, and chuckled. The man who barely laughed *actually* chuckled. This was worse than I ever imagined.

Anthony let out a long sigh. "Yeah, we were wondering when you were going to come clean."

Kennedy and I blinked. "What?" we said in unison.

"Come on," Coach said, gesturing between us. "You two weren't exactly subtle." He looked at Anthony. "Remember when they met with us? Kennedy practically jumped out of her skin when Anderson kissed her hand." He shook his head. "And when we grilled Anderson with questions, he jumped to her defense." Coach's eyes settled on me. "That's when I knew that even though it was obvious you got together to put the rumors to rest, it was going to become real at some point."

Anthony nodded then added, "We've been watching this little soap opera unfold for months. Quite entertaining."

"I'm surprised he made a move so quickly. He's been pining for Kennedy for so long," Coach said. "I thought for sure he wasn't going to do anything until at least next season."

Anthony clicked his tongue. "*Nah*, I was rooting for him since the beginning."

Unbelievable.

I gaped at them. "Why are you both talking like I'm not in the room?"

Kennedy chuckled but didn't say a word.

They both laughed, which made my shoulders relax and share a laugh with them, too.

"But why now?" Coach asked, his tone turning serious underneath the amusement. "What made you decide to finally tell us the truth?"

I swallowed hard. This part was harder to explain.

"My father," I said. "He's a difficult man, to say the least. He showed up at our place and threatened her. Told her to break up with me or he'd tank her career—and mine."

Anthony scoffed. "*Wow.*"

"He found out about our past arrangement and tried to use it against us," I continued. "Tried to pit us against each other. I just didn't want to keep secrets from you guys, not when it could blow back on the organization. I'm sorry."

"And just so we're clear, this isn't fake anymore," Kennedy added. "But we both know this was unprofessional and risky. As a PR professional, I should have known better, and for that, I am sorry. We're willing to accept any punishment you all see fit."

Anthony was quiet for a second before leaning forward, resting his arms on the table. "Let me make something very clear. Even if your father brought this to our attention, it wouldn't change a damn thing. You two are part of this organization. You're practically family."

Coach nodded. "Do we like the way you both went about it? No. It could've exploded in all our faces if the media ever sniffed it out."

"And even though I'm sure coming forward was scary, you guys did the right thing, even if it meant risking it all. That counts for something," Anthony said.

"You're not getting benched," Coach added. It was like he was reading my mind, because that was the one question I had on the tip of my tongue. "The focus will stay on your performance, Anderson. You've earned that. We can all accept that you had a rocky time in the beginning, but you earned your spot back fair and square. The relationship had no play in it."

Anthony nodded and leaned back in his chair. "We'll spin this the way we need to if it ever comes to it."

Relief swelled in my chest so fast it made me dizzy.

"Thank you," Kennedy said beside me, her voice trembling slightly.

Anthony smiled faintly. "Don't thank me yet. We still have to get ahead of this. Brad will probably want to draft a statement just in case."

Coach shook his head. "I played with Vincent for years.

He's a prideful man, and his reputation is important to him. I don't think he'll go to the media with this information. Especially since he has no evidence, right?"

We both nodded as I replied, "Right."

I suspected as much. My father wasn't going to taint the Anderson reputation. He wasn't that stupid. But Kennedy was still fair game.

"He will try to come after Kennedy. I wouldn't be surprised if he's meeting with Marcus as we speak," Anthony murmured.

His comment didn't shock me. Marcus—Striker's team owner—and my father go way back. And that...was not good news.

"What does that mean for me?" Kennedy asked. "And don't sugarcoat it. If I need to step down from my job and this organization, I will. I care about this place so much, and I don't want to see it damaged because of all of this."

Anthony held Kennedy's stare for a few beats. "Your work for this team hasn't gone unnoticed. I hope you know that."

"With all due respect, Anthony, that doesn't answer my question," Kennedy said. Her voice was steady, but the grip she had on my hand was vise-like. I was so damn proud of her. She was so strong, even when everything felt like it was hanging by a thread.

Anthony leaned back slightly, lips tugging into a faint smirk. "This is what I like about you. Always so honest. So direct." He let out a short breath. "Brad's going to be pissed I ruined the surprise, but...he already submitted the name of the person he's recommending to take over the PR department when he retires."

Kennedy's eyes bulged, her lips parting like she wasn't sure if she had misheard him.

"It's you, Kennedy," Anthony said, his tone gentle now.

"Brad said you were the only one with the grit, heart, and vision to lead that department the way it deserves."

I watched her eyes widen, watched her try to process it all. Damn, I was so goddamn proud of her. I could only imagine how overwhelmed she must have felt.

Kennedy blinked, stunned silent for a moment. "But...even after everything? Maybe you should think about it—"

Anthony cut her off with a shake of his head. "You've built something here, and we want to see what you do next. The last thing we would do is punish you for falling in love."

Her eyes welled, but she held it together with a single, shaky breath. "I didn't expect this."

Anthony's smile was soft. Kind. "And he also wanted to be the one to tell you that after launching an internal investigation into Matt Smith, some things came to light. He was officially terminated this morning."

"So fast?" she asked. "I only brought up my concerns less than two weeks ago."

"You'd be surprised how many people came forward and made this investigation a slam dunk. And while I cannot go into details since it's sensitive information, on behalf of the management team, I want to say I'm sorry for not noticing what was happening."

Kennedy took a deep, shaky breath. "Thank you."

Anthony nodded without a word.

"So, what do we do now about our situation?" I asked.

Anthony sighed, rubbing the back of his neck. "We stay ahead of your father. I will meet with Marcus and talk to him. We won't let anything happen. This team stands by its people."

Coach nodded. "And you're one of us, Kennedy. You both are. Always have been. We're not going to let anything happen to you."

KENNEDY

YOU THINK EVERYTHING IS ROMANTIC.

TEAM DINNER WAS BECOMING one of my favorite activities.

We still didn't have a set schedule, especially since the guys were still deep into the playoffs, so we kept putting everything together at the last minute every time they had a home game, but still, every damn time, I loved it.

Tonight, we were at Donovan's house. After we had some lasagna—sponsored by Aurora, who was an amazing cook—I was sitting on the patio with the girls while the guys were inside. Some were watching a game tape, others were playing video games.

It was weird, in the best kind of way. Because a few months ago, I never would've imagined this. At the start of the season, I'd felt so untethered—like someone had knocked the wind out of me and I was still trying to figure out how to breathe again. I'd lost people I thought were my friends, people I trusted, and suddenly I was left standing alone.

But then Henry happened. And this team, too. Slowly—so slowly I didn't even realize it was happening—these people gave me something I'd been aching for and never thought possible. A family. The kind of friendships I'd see in movies or read about in books. The kind that felt like home. A place where I finally belonged.

"I cannot believe he told you," Aurora said through fits of giggles after I finished telling them all about the fake dating fiasco.

"My brother is a literal idiot," Olivia groaned. "Scratch that. The real idiot is Wes. He loves to do dumb shit like this."

"I think it's romantic," Valentina piped wistfully. "I'm still mad you didn't tell me, though."

"You think *everything* is romantic," I deadpanned, setting my eyes on Val. "And we both know if I told you, you were probably going to run off to Hayes and help him scheme something."

Valentina grinned. "Damn, woman, you know me too well."

"Did he also tell you I said they were all idiots and that it wasn't going to work?" Aurora asked.

I laughed. "He did—*well*, I read the texts. I asked him so many questions, he ended up resigning by handing me the phone and telling me to have fun." I shook my head, still in disbelief. "It was a whole ridiculous scheme."

"It may have been ridiculous, but look at where it got you. It worked the same way the jersey thing did," Val commented before taking a sip of her wine.

My cheeks felt hot to the touch when I rested them against the palms of my hands at the reminder.

"Hi, ladies," Henry said as he stepped out with Hayes, the door clicking shut behind them. His eyes immediately found mine, and a warm smile tugged at his lips. He dropped into the seat beside me, pressing a kiss to the side of my head. "Why do you look so flustered?"

"Oh, you know," Valentina said with zero shame, "just reminding her about the night she wore your jersey. The amazing sex and all."

A smirk curled in his mouth. "That *was* a pretty epic night."

"Um, hello?" Olivia waved in the air. "In case you've forgotten, your sister is here and very much within earshot of this horrifying conversation."

"Oh, come on, Livvie," Hayes said, sliding into the seat beside her. "Don't act like you've never gotten freaky."

"You're disgusting." Olivia gagged. "Zero manners."

"And you have zero sense of fun," Hayes shot back, grinning.

Olivia rolled her eyes. "You know, if you talked less, you'd be more tolerable."

Hayes leaned back, casually draping an arm on the back of her chair. "And if you smiled more, you'd be almost charming."

"Is this how it usually is between them?" I whispered the question to Henry as those two continued to bicker in the background. It was like watching an intense tennis match.

He let out a tired sigh. "Pretty much."

Olivia gaped at Hayes. "And if you—"

"Okay." Henry clasped his hands. "If I don't shut this down now, neither of you will ever shut up."

"Noooo," Val whined. "I was having fun."

"Watching these two banter is more entertaining than the enemies-to-lovers book that's waiting for me in my room," Aurora said.

"It's not bantering if I'm only pointing out how annoying he is."

"Oh, like you're—"

"*Guys*," Henry warned. "Enough."

"Whatever," they both muttered.

I dropped a quick kiss on Henry's cheek before getting up to pour myself a glass of wine. As I filled it, the sound of footsteps against the concrete caught my attention.

I turned just as Olivia stepped into view. "Hey, want a glass of wine?" I offered.

She shook her head. "If I drink one more glass, I'll end up bickering with Wes all night, and I'm already wiped from today's flight."

I took a sip and leaned back against the wall. "When are you officially moving?"

"As soon as the season's over. *Finally*," she groaned.

"I'm excited to have you work with us," I said honestly. I loved hanging out with Olivia. She was sharp, and had a no-bullshit attitude I admired. Which made sense, considering she was an athletic trainer. She had to be tough if she wanted these players to take her seriously.

"I'm excited, too," she beamed.

"Even if it means living with Hayes?" I asked, a knowing grin tugging at my lips.

"Surprisingly, yes." Olivia's gaze drifted toward the pool, her expression softening. "I want out of New York. Desperately," she murmured.

I reached out and gave her arm a gentle squeeze. She still hadn't opened up to any of us—not even her brother—about what really happened with Holt or what made her pack up her life and walk away. She'd been saying it was because she wanted to be closer to family, but Henry wasn't convinced.

"You know you can still come live with us, right?" I said. "I moved into Henry's room—well, our room—already."

She wrinkled her nose. "I love my brother, but I don't want to live in an apartment where he's constantly..." Her voice trailed off, and I lifted a brow. "You know," she added, waving her hand vaguely.

I pretended to think. "I believe Hayes called it 'fucking like a caffeinated rabbit,'" I said while doing air quotes.

She faked a shiver. "Oh God, not you, too."

We both shared a laugh without a word.

The door to the back patio opened, and Owens's head popped out. "I've had enough socialization to last me a lifetime. You ready to go, Pecas*?"

"Yeah." She gulped the rest of her wine, and when she stood, she wobbled a little. "*Whoops*. I think I overdid it with the wine tonight."

Owens stepped outside and was next to her in an instant, holding her by the waist. "I got you."

Val padded his cheek. "You're always so nice to me, Nico."

I swore I saw Owens's cheek blush. "Let's get you home before you start talking too much," was the last thing I heard him say as they went back into the house to get their things and head out.

"We should head out, too," Henry said as he approached me and Olivia. "Big game tomorrow."

I couldn't help but smile as a spike of excitement shot through me. The guys had given their blood, sweat, and tears during the playoffs, and now they were battling it out against the Florida Bay Kings in the finals. Tomorrow could be *the* night we—they—brought the Cup home. And I couldn't be more excited about it.

---

* Freckles.

THIRTY-NINE

HENRY

HOW DID I GET SO LUCKY?

THE UNITED CENTER WAS VIBRATING.

That was the only way I could describe it. Every inch of the arena pulsed, like the building itself had a heartbeat synced to the crowd's.

I didn't think I'd ever been so nervous. Not even chewing my mouthguard helped calm my nerves.

My heart was practically skating laps in my chest, but my eyes stayed locked on the game as I watched and calculated every move. The ice was a blur of motion. The air crackled with every shot on goal. And the sound... *Christ*, the sound was deafening. It swallowed everything whole, from the scratch of blades to the refs' whistles, until all I could feel was noise in my bones.

The score was 2–2. Third period. Game 6. Barely any time left on the clock.

If we won tonight, it was over. We'd clinch the Cup right here, in front of our home crowd. We were so close, I could practically taste it.

I gripped my stick like my life depended on it as I saw Morgan bark an order to Parker and they both skated back on the ice after a change.

My eyes quickly flicked to the clock then to the ice. The Bay Kings were pushing hard. One bad bounce and we were looking at overtime.

And we couldn't fucking afford that.

I jumped over the boards in sync with Donovan and Hayes, our skates slicing into the ice. Morgan read the moment perfectly, backing off the pressure just enough to receive a pass from Parker, who had just stopped a big play near our goal.

Morgan absorbed the puck on his shin pad, barely flinching, then corralled it and sent a laser up the boards to where Parker was skating toward, who caught it clean and wasted zero time snapping it forward.

Donovan easily caught it and had already taken off to the right wing, skating past the neutral zone like he had a rocket strapped to his back. Hayes peeled wide left to draw coverage with him. I cut through the center ice, skating full throttle.

Every bone in my body burned. I was exhausted, but I kept my strides long and purposeful. Donovan looked up, and as soon as he spotted me, he sent the puck my way. It flew across the ice and hit my stick with a crisp *clack*.

The world around me slowed.

I could feel it in my bones. This was *it*. This was the shot that was going to seal our fate.

When my lungs expanded in an exhale, I went for it.

And as I released my breath, I saw everything play out in slow motion.

The goalie dropped and reached with his quick reflexes, but the puck was faster. Officially putting the scoreboard 3–2.

My knees nearly buckled as the horn blasted and the arena

exploded in cheers, to the point where it felt like the place was going to crumble at any minute.

The rest of the team jumped the boards, and sticks and gloves went flying into the air as everyone was jumping and screaming around me. I was in shock. I couldn't move. I couldn't breathe.

Hayes jumped and hugged me. "We fucking did it! We're champions, baby!" he screamed from the top of his lungs.

Holy...fuck.

We did it.

We actually did it.

I hugged Hayes back with a loud laugh, but like an invisible string had pulled me, I turned, searching for Kennedy.

The second our eyes met, I yanked off my helmet and tossed it somewhere across the ice. She was already running, and a moment after the next, she was in the air. I caught her effortlessly, her legs wrapping tight around my waist as I gripped her thighs.

My heart had never been so full.

She buried her face into my shoulder as confetti rained in bursts of blue, white, and silver around us.

I found the nape of her neck, gently pulling her back so I could see her.

Her brown eyes shimmered, brimming with happy tears. "You did it, pretty boy." She grinned.

"We all did it, Kenny baby." I leaned in, pressing my forehead against hers, and whispered, "I love you so much. I love you, I love you. I *fucking* love you."

Her smile turned soft as she swept my sweaty hair off my forehead. "I love you, too," she whispered.

The way she looked at me like I'd hung the goddamn moon... It felt right. It felt like fate. It felt like every version of me had always been waiting for her to look at me *just* like that.

———

IN TRUE STRIKERS FASHION—SINCE we were creatures of habit and all—the celebration moved from the rink to Tim's. We shut the place down, with only players, family, and front office staff in attendance. The Cup sat in the center of the bar like a holy relic, gleaming under dim lights as we all stared at it in collective awe.

The night was chaotic in the best way.

At some point, Parker set up karaoke and started singing all his favorite songs. But then, when he started singing "My tears ricochet" by Taylor Swift (his go-to song every time he was completely wasted), Valentina cut him off, declaring it too much of a downer for the night and swapped in a playlist packed with 2000s throwbacks. We screamed the lyrics with half-lost voices and danced with our sore bodies, but it had been so much fun.

When the bar finally closed, the energy was still too buzzed to call it a night. So a few of us headed to my place to keep the party going on the rooftop of my apartment.

"Aaaand that's game," Olivia announced triumphantly as the last ping-pong ball dropped into a red cup. She slapped Kennedy's hand with a grin.

Hayes groaned, plucking the ball out of the cup before downing the beer in defeat.

"How the hell are you so good at this?" Donovan asked, genuinely baffled.

Olivia shrugged like it was nothing. "Had my wild days back in college."

I shot her a look. "I don't need to hear about my little sister playing beer pong at some frat house."

"We're twins," she deadpanned.

"I was born two minutes before you."

"Oh my God," she shrieked. "Not this again! Is this why I moved to Chicago? For you to *torture* me?"

"Welcome home, little sister." I grinned, lifting my cup in salute before taking a sip.

"Leave her alone, Anderson," Kennedy said, feigning sternness.

I arched a brow. "What, you're both going to gang up on me now?"

"*Duh.* Girls gotta stick together, bro," Olivia quipped without missing a beat.

I couldn't wipe the grin off my face. We'd won the fucking Cup, and I still barely believed it. But another part of it was everything else. Anthony had pulled Kennedy and me aside at Tim's to tell us my father had tried to throw her under the bus with Marcus, but he shut him down. Things got heated, and security escorted my father out of Strikers HQ.

My father tried to reach me tonight, but when I saw his contact pop up on my phone, I finally bit the bullet and blocked his number.

It was hard to cut him off without fixing anything first, but sometimes in life, things didn't get resolved. Sometimes you had to choose distance and call it survival. It was what I needed to do to start healing, to let go of the resentment I'd been dragging around for years. Having Kennedy in my corner made that possible. She didn't push. She just stood with me every step of the way. Always patient. Always kind.

And though I wasn't ready to tell anyone about *Willow House*, tonight was the first step in the right direction—a step toward the life I *actually* wanted. I was even going back to therapy. I made my first appointment last week, and I was really looking forward to it. Excitement bubbled inside of me, knowing that little by little, I was going to gain control of my life again.

I looked around and took everything in with a deep breath. Everyone was playing around, being loud and messy. Completely unfiltered and still riding the high of the win.

And yet...it felt like home. Found family in every sense of the word.

"I have a surprise for you," Kennedy said as she grabbed my hand and took us downstairs to our apartment.

When we stepped inside, she turned to me with a mischievous glint in her eye. "Stay right here," she ordered before darting into her room.

"Your wish is my command," I answered.

After a few minutes, she yelled, "Close your eyes!"

"Why?" I called out.

"Just do it!" she groaned.

Laughing, I gave in. "Fine." I shut my eyes and crossed my arms.

Her footsteps padded across the sleek floors until she stood right in front of me. "Okay, open them."

I blinked my eyes open, finding Sush on Kennedy's arm.

Captain Sushi stared up at me with all the enthusiasm of a brick wall, but I couldn't even focus on his expression. He was wearing a custom Strikers jersey. My last name stretched proudly across the back, with the number eighteen stitched in bold silver thread.

I stared, speechless. "You put our cat in a jersey."

"I did," she said, grinning. "And I have absolutely no regrets."

She handed me our furry child like it was the most normal thing in the world, and I couldn't help the disbelieving laugh that slipped from my chest. I cradled the cat in one arm and pulled her in with the other, holding both of them close.

"You're insane," I murmured into her hair.

"Don't lie to yourself. You love it."

I smiled, pressing my lips to her temple. "You're damn right I do."

Captain Sushi meowed like he was over it, so I set him down. He rubbed against our legs before waddling over to his usual spot on the couch, where he flopped dramatically with a tired sigh.

Kennedy and I stood facing each other, her smile soft, her eyes glowing. I slipped my fingers to the back of her neck, letting them rest there as I studied her.

"How did I get so lucky?" I asked quietly.

She gave me a look that turned my insides to melted honey. "I ask myself the same thing every day."

My thumb caressed her neck as I leaned forward, my lips meeting hers in a kiss. It was slow and soft, like we had all the time in the world. I threaded my fingers through her curls, and she let out a low whimper, which I eagerly swallowed as I deepened the kiss.

"This is the life," I murmured against her lips. "The team. Our pet-child"—we both chuckled—"and you. *Always* you." I pulled back just enough to look at her. "I feel like a winner."

She snorted. "Well, yeah. You are."

I shook my head, my thumb brushing her jaw. "No. What I mean is, I became a winner the moment you decided to give me a chance, the moment when you chose to love every part of me. Since that day...I've had everything. Winning the game was just a bonus."

Her eyes softened. "I could say the same, you know?" She draped her arms around my shoulders. "Thank you for loving every part of me when I thought nobody ever could," she finished quietly.

My heart contracted in my chest at her words.

"Loving every part of you it's the easiest thing I've ever

done," I whispered, staring into the most beautiful eyes I'd ever seen, like it was the simplest truth I'd ever spoken.

Without a word, she let out a wistful sigh and leaned in to kiss me again.

And that was when I knew—I had it all, right here, with the woman of my dreams.

THANK YOU!

If you enjoyed reading *False Play*, consider leaving a review on Amazon. Reviews are like tips for authors, and it helps spread the word to other lovely readers like you!

Would you like to be the first to know what I'm working on, get some amazing book recs, and much more? Then join my newsletter, The Romance Sidelines News! PS. I always share extra, exclusive teasers over there. ;)

OTHER BOOKS BY YINN QUIRÓS

WINDY CITY BILLIONAIRES SERIES

BROKEN PIECES

BROKEN DEAL

ACKNOWLEDGMENTS

Can you all believe this is my third book?

Scratch that.

Can you believe this is the start of a SIX-book hockey series?! Because I still can't.

Henry and Kennedy came to me in the middle of writing my debut series—*Windy City Billionaires*. They were so loud in my head, I actually had to pause writing the *final* book in that series (and if any OG readers who've been waiting on that book for what feels like forever are reading this: I'm so sorry, but I hope this one makes the wait worth it?! Hehe). That's how badly they wanted their story told.

And wow—what a *rollercoaster* this one was.

But if I've learned anything in this wild and wonderful career of mine, it's that the rollercoaster never really stops. You'd think I'd feel less nervous with each book, but it's kind of the opposite? I just never want to let any of you down. Ever.

Also...this book was a whole new adventure for me!

I've always been a fan of sports—I've played and/or been a part of a bunch over the years: volleyball, soccer, even varsity cheerleading (and yes, whoever says cheer isn't a sport can go argue with the wall, because it *absolutely* is). But hockey? I didn't really get into it until I moved to the U.S., and ever since, I've been in a *full-blown* rabbit hole. I love the adrenaline it gives me. I love watching every second of it.

Anywaaaaaaaay...enough rambling.

As always, I want to start by thanking you—the reader. Thank you for picking up this book. I hope you loved it as much as I loved writing it. Thank you for always giving my stories a chance. I hope you stick around, because I've got *so* much more coming your way.

Anthony— Thank you for always being my ride or die, and for being my biggest inspiration. Just the other day, I caught myself wondering: why do all my fictional guys show their love through little acts of service? It's because of you. Because you're always there for me, doing all the little things that make my life better and easier. I love you.

Andrea & Karian— Mis nenas! Thank you for always being there for me and listen to all the ideas I have. You both are my biggest supporters and I couldn't have done this without both of you.

Ginger— Thank you for talking me off the ledge every time I spiral into "*I want to quit! Please, let me quit!*" mode. You keep me sane. I still can't believe we're still doing this for a living, but it's whatever (lol), right?

Elle— My twin! Girl, thank you for *everything*—our talks, your jokes. You also keep me sane.

Bruna & Layla— I don't think I'll ever get over how stunning this cover turned out. Bruna, you brought these characters to life, and I can't wait to see what else we dream up together. Layla, you gave this cover its soul, and for that, I'm beyond grateful. I'm so excited I get to work with you both for the rest of this series.

Andrea— I've said it before, and I'll say it a million more times: I'm so lucky to have you as my editor. You're a rockstar, and I'm so excited for what's ahead. Thank you for helping me get to the finish line and for believing in me even when I didn't.

Ramona— Thank you for all your hard work. I truly couldn't have asked for a better proofreader.

Love Notes PR and ARC team— Thank you for supporting me and for helping make this release the best it could possibly be. I couldn't have done it without you.

Until the next time!

Xo,

Author Yinn Quirós

ABOUT THE AUTHOR

Yinn Quirós is an indie romance author who loves writing epic love stories with laugh-out-loud banter, men who yearn like it physically hurts them, and plenty of spice. She loves all things sports (especially F1 and hockey), romance, and music.

When she's not writing, you can find her watching games or races, walking around the windy city with her rescued puppy, or listening to music and curating playlists for all the stories that live rent-free inside her head. You can find Yinn on all socials under **@yinnquirosauthor**.